USA TODAY Bestselle... for her stories everyw... watcher. She has pub... in several subgenres c... writing, Lucy likes to re... She's an unashamed book geek, but loves movies and the theatre too. She adores her family and truly enjoys hearing from her readers! Visit her website at: http://lucymonroe.com

Abby Green spent her teens reading Mills & Boon romances. She then spent many years working in the Film and TV industry as an Assistant Director. One day while standing outside an actor's trailer in the rain, she thought: *there has to be more than this.* So she sent off a partial to Mills & Boon. After many rewrites, they accepted her first book and an author was born. She lives in Dublin, Ireland and you can find out more here: www.abby-green.com

Sabrina Philips first discovered Mills & Boon one Saturday afternoon at her first job in a charity shop. Sorting through a stack of books, she came across a cover which featured a glamorous heroine and a tall, dark hero. She started reading under the counter that instant and has never looked back! Sabrina now creates infuriatingly sexy heroes of her own, which she defies both her heroines and her readers – to resist! Visit Sabrina's website: www.sabrinaphilips.com

The Mistresses

COLLECTION

Mistresses:
His Unexpected
Heir

LUCY MONROE

ABBY GREEN

SABRINA PHILIPS

MILLS & BOON

Mistresses: His Unexpected Heir © 2020 Harlequin Books S.A.

Valentino's Love-Child © 2009 Lucy Monroe
Mistress to the Merciless Millionaire © 2009 Abby Green
Prince of Montéz, Pregnant Mistress © 2009 Sabrina Philips

ISBN: 978-0-263-28100-2

MIX
Paper from
responsible sources
FSC® C007454
www.fsc.org

This book is produced from independently certified FSC™ paper
to ensure responsible forest management.

For more information visit: www.harpercollins.co.uk/green

Printed and bound in Spain
by CPI, Barcelona

VALENTINO'S
LOVE-CHILD

LUCY MONROE

CHAPTER ONE

VALENTINO GRISAFI brushed a silky auburn curl away from where it blocked his view of his sleeping mistress's face.

Mistress. An old-fashioned word for a very modern woman. Faith Williams would not appreciate the label. Were he to be foolish enough to use it within her hearing, she would no doubt let him know it too. His *carina americana* was no wilting flower.

Pretty American. Now, that suited her. But if he should let on he thought of her like a mistress? *Ai-yi-yi.*

Eyes the blue of a peacock feather would snap with temper while she lectured him on how inappropriate the term was. And he supposed she would have a point. He did not pay her bills. He did not buy her clothes. No matter how many hours they spent together here, she did not live in his Marsala apartment. She did not rely on him for anything but his company.

So, not his mistress. But not his girlfriend, either. Long-term commitment and love had no place between them. Theirs was a purely physical relationship, the duration and depth of which was dictated purely by convenience. Mostly his. Not that Faith had nothing to say in the matter.

She could walk away as easily as he and had no more incentive to make time in her schedule for him than vice versa. Luckily for them both, the relationship— such that it was—worked for each of them.

Perhaps they were friends also and he did not regret it, but that had come after. After he had discovered the way her sweet, curvaceous body responded to the slightest touch of his. After kisses that melted his brain and her resistance. After he had learned how much pleasure he could find basking in her generous sensuality, once unleashed.

The sex between them was phenomenal.

Which was no doubt why he could already feel the loss of the coming weeks.

Tracing her perfect oval features he leaned close to her ear. "*Carina,* you must wake."

Her nose wrinkled and the luscious bow of her mouth twisted into a moue of denial, her exotically colored eyes remaining stubbornly closed. Her recently sated body not moving so much as a centimeter from its usual post-coital curled position.

"Come, *bella mia.* Waken."

"If you'd come to my apartment, I could stay in bed sleeping while you had to get dressed and leave," she grumbled into the pillow.

"Most nights, I leave as well, *carina.* You know this." He liked to have breakfast with Giosue. His eight-year-old son was the light of Valentino's life. "Besides, I am not waking you up to go. We need to talk."

Faith's eyelids fluttered, but her mouth did not slip from its downward arch.

"You are adorable like this, you know?"

That had her sitting up and staring at him with grumpy startlement, the tangerine, supersilky, Egyptian cotton sheet she'd insisted he use on his bed clutched to her chest. "Sane people do not find cranky attractive, Tino."

Biting back a smile, he shrugged. "What can I say? I am different. Or perhaps it is you. I do not recall finding any of my other *amantes* so cute when they were irritable."

He did not like using the word *lover,* but knew better than to refer to her as the equally ill-fitting title of *mistress.* And she had already cut him off at the knees for referring to her once as a bed partner. She said if he wanted to use such a clinical term, he should consider getting an anatomically accurate blow-up doll.

Why these thoughts were plaguing him tonight, he did not know. Defining her place in his life was not something he spent time doing, nor was he overly fond of labels. So why so preoccupied with them tonight?

"I have no interest in hearing about your past conquests Signor Grisafi." Now she really looked out of sorts, her eyes starting to flash with temper.

"I apologize. But you know I was hardly an untried boy when we met." He had already loved and lost a wife, not to mention the women who had warmed his cold bed after.

He and Faith had been together for a year, longer than he had been with any other woman since the death of his beloved Renata. But that hardly altered his past.

"Neither of us were virgins, but it's bad form to discuss past relationships while in bed with your current lover."

"You are so worried about following protocols, too," he mocked.

He had never known someone less concerned with appearance and social niceties. His *carina americana* was the quintessential free spirit.

A small smile teased her lips at that. "Maybe not, but this is one social norm I'm one hundred percent behind."

"Duly noted."

"Good." She curled up to him, snuggling against his chest, her hand resting casually on his upper thigh and causing no small reaction in his nether regions. "You said you didn't wake me up to send me on my way?"

"No. We need to talk."

She cocked her head to one side. "What about?"

He couldn't help himself. He leaned down and kissed the tip of her straight nose. "You really are adorable when you first wake up."

"I thought it was when I was grumpy."

"Have you ever woken up *not* irritable?"

"I have a perfectly sunny disposition in the morning. Not that you would know that little fact as we've never spent a full night together, but you'll have to take my word on it. It's only when I have to wake up after being sated so gorgeously with your body that I complain."

It was an old argument. She had never taken his refusal to spend the entire night together with full grace. She understood his desire to be home for breakfast with his son, but not his insistence on leaving their shared bed after at most a short nap after their lovemaking.

Her continued pressing the point frustrated him and that leaked out into his voice when he said, "Be that as it may, there is something I have been meaning to tell you."

She stiffened and pulled away, her blue-green gaze reflecting an instant emotional wariness. "What?"

"It is nothing bad. Well, not too bad. It is simply that my parents are going on a trip. They wish to visit friends in Naples."

"Oh, really? I didn't know."

"Naturally, I did not tell you."

"And?"

"And I cannot leave Giosue at night when he does not have his grandparents there to watch over him." Never mind the staff that lived on site at their vineyard, Vigne di Grisafi, much less the housekeeper that had her own room in the house. It was not the same.

"I understand." He could tell from her expression that she really did. "How long will your parents be gone?"

"Two weeks only."

"I won't see you at all?"

"It is unlikely."

She looked like she wanted to say something, but in the end she simply nodded.

"I will miss you," he found himself admitting. Then he scowled. He hadn't wanted to say that. "This." He brushed his hand down her body. "I will miss *this*."

"I heard you the first time, tough guy. You can't take it back now. You may as well admit you like my company as much as me in your bed."

He bore her back to the bed, his mouth hovering above hers. "Maybe almost as much. And speaking of sex. I will have to do without you for two weeks, I think we should take advantage of our time together."

"Have I ever said no to you?" she asked with a husky laugh.

"No and tonight is no time to start."

Faith woke surrounded by warmth and the scent of the man she loved.

Her eyes flew open and a grin split her face. It hadn't been a dream. After making love into the wee hours of the morning, Tino had asked her to spend the night. For the first time ever.

Okay, maybe not asked…more like informed her that she was staying, but it was the same result. She was in his arms, in his bed—the morning after they'd made love.

And it was glorious.

Every bit as delicious a feeling as she had thought it would be.

"Are you awake?" his deep voice rumbled above her.

She lifted her head from its resting place on his hair-covered chest and turned the full wattage of her smile on him. "What does it look like?"

"It looks like you were telling me the truth when you said you had a sunny disposition in the morning. Maybe I will have to start calling you *solare*."

Sunlight? Her heart squeezed. "Tay used to call me Sunshine."

"A past boyfriend?" Tino asked on a growl, the morning whiskers on his face giving him a sexily fierce aspect. "You are right, discussing past *amores* while in bed with your current one is definitely bad taste."

She laughed, not in the least offended. "He was my husband, not a past boyfriend," she said as she scooted out of the bed, intent on making coffee.

"You were married?"

"Yes." Weird that after almost a full year together, she was telling him about having been married before for the first time. But then, that was the nature of their re-lationship. She and Tino focused on the present when they were together.

She'd learned more about him—and a tragic past similar to her own—from his mother than she'd ever learned from him. Strangely enough, where Tino showed no interest in Faith's art, his mother was a fan. They'd met at one of Faith's showings in Palermo. In spite of the generation difference in their ages, the two women had hit it off immediately and both had been thrilled to discover they lived so close to one another. Vigne di Grisafi was a mere twenty-minute drive from Faith's small apartment in Pizzolato.

Not that she'd ever been there as Tino's guest. She'd been seeing Tino for two months before she realized the Valentino Agata mentioned so frequently was Tino, the man Faith spent her nights making love with. At first, she'd found it disconcerting, but she'd soon adjusted. She hadn't told Agata about the fact she was dating Tino though.

He'd been careful to keep their relationship discreet and she felt it was his prerogative to determine when his family would be told about her.

In another almost unreal twist of fate, Faith was his son Giosue's teacher, too. She taught an art class for primary school children in Marsala once a week. She may have lost her one chance at motherhood, but she still adored kids, and this was her way of spending time with them. Giosue was an absolute doll and she more than understood Tino's desire to be there for him. She applauded it.

"Divorced?" Tino asked, his brown eyes intent on her and apparently not done with the topic of Tay.

"Widowed." She didn't elaborate, knowing Tino wouldn't want the details. He never wanted the details. Not about her personal history.

He said he liked to concentrate on the here and now. Since that was her own personal motto, she didn't balk at the fact he showed no interest in her life before Sicily.

She had to admit, though, that he didn't show much interest in her life here, either.

He knew she was an artist, but she wasn't sure he knew she was a successful one or that she was a clay sculptor. He knew she lived in Pizzolato, a small town a few minutes south of Marsala, but she doubted he knew exactly where her apartment was. In the entire year they'd been together, they had made love in one place only—his apartment.

Not his home, because he didn't live there. He said he kept it for business purposes, but she thought he meant the business of getting sex without falling under the watchful eye of his mother. Tino had been very careful to keep their lives completely separate.

At first, she hadn't minded. She'd been no more interested in a deep emotional connection than he had been. He'd promised her sex and that was all he'd given her.

Only, at some point along the way, she'd realized, she couldn't help giving him love.

Even so, she'd been content to keep their relationship on a shallow level. Or at least convinced herself to be. She'd lost everyone she'd ever loved and had no doubt that one day she would lose him, too. That didn't mean she hadn't loved spending the whole night together—she had. But as for the rest of it, the less entwined in her life he was, the better for her it would be when that time came.

At least, that was how she had thought. She wasn't so sure anymore.

"So, that is all you have to say on the matter?"

She pushed the start button on the coffeemaker and turned to face Tino. "What?"

He'd pulled on a pair of boxers, leaving most of his

tall, chiseled body on mouthwatering display. "Your husband died."

Were they still on that? "Yes."

"How?"

"A car accident."

"When?"

"Six years ago."

He ran his fingers through his morning tousled dark hair. "You never told me."

"Did you want me to?"

"I would think that sometime in a year you would have thought to mention that you were a widow." He came into the kitchen and leaned against the counter near her.

"Why?"

"It is an important piece of information about you."

"About my past."

He frowned at her.

"You prefer to focus on today, not yesterday. You've said so many times, Tino. What's going on?"

"Maybe I'm just curious about the woman I've been bedding for a year."

"Almost a year."

"Do not banter semantics with me."

"I'm glad you're curious."

"I..." For the first time in memory, her lover, the über-cool Valentino Grisafi, looked lost for words.

"Don't worry about it, Tino. It's not a bad thing."

"No, no, of course not. We are friends as well as lovers, *si?*"

"Yes." And she was more relieved than she could say that he saw it that way, too.

"Good. Good." He was silent a second. "Do I get breakfast to go with my coffee?"

"I think that can be arranged."

He got a borderline horrified look on his face. "You do know how to cook, don't you?"

She laughed, truly tickled. "We aren't all filthy rich vintners, Tino. Some of us can't afford a housekeeper or to eat out every meal—thus, knowing how to cook is essential. But I don't mind telling you, I'm pretty good at it as well."

"I'll reserve judgment."

She laughed and launched herself at him to tickle the big man into submission, or at least a lot of laughter before he subdued her wandering fingers.

Faith finished the third form of a pregnant woman she had done in as many days. She hadn't done women *enceinte* since the loss of her baby in the accident that had killed Taylish and any chance Faith would ever have at a family.

Or so she had believed.

Her clay-spattered hand pressed over her still-flat stomach, a sense of awe and wonder infusing her. It had taken her four years and fertility counseling for her to become viably pregnant the first time.

Her first actual pregnancy had occurred a mere two months after she married Taylish at the age of eighteen. They'd been ecstatic when the home pregnancy test showed positive, only to be cast into a pit of despair short weeks later when the ectopic pregnancy had come close to killing her. And of course, there had been no hope of saving the baby with a tubal pregnancy.

Her near death had not stopped her and Tay from trying again. They both wanted children with a deep desperation only those who had no family could appreciate. After a year of trying with no results they'd sought medical help. Tests had revealed that she'd been left with only one working ovary in the aftermath of her ectopic pregnancy.

The fertility specialist she and Tay had sought out had informed them that the single working ovary significantly decreased their chances at getting pregnant. However, she gave them a regime to follow that would hopefully result in conception. It had been grueling and resulted in an already passionless sex life turning flat-out clinical.

But it had worked. When the test strip had turned blue, she'd felt as if it was the greatest blessing of her life. This time she'd felt as if it was a full-on miracle.

Tino was careful to use condoms every time. The number of chances they'd taken by waiting to put the condom on until after some play, and the single time one had broken (Tino had changed where he bought his condoms after that), could be counted on one hand. With fingers left over. However, one of those times of delayed sheathing had occurred a couple of months ago.

With only one working ovary, her menstrual cycles were on an erratic two-month schedule. She hadn't paid any attention when her sporadic period was later than even normal. It wasn't the first time. Pregnancy had never even crossed her mind. Not when her breasts had grown excessively tender. She'd put it up to PMS. Not when the smell of bacon made her nauseous. She wasn't a huge meat eater, anyway.

Not when she got tired in the afternoons. After all, most Sicilian businesses were closed for a couple of hours midday so people could rest. Maybe she was just taking on the habits of her adopted home. She hadn't even clued in she might be pregnant when she burst out crying over a broken glass one morning when she'd been preparing a heavier breakfast than usual. She'd been craving eggs.

The shoe hadn't even dropped when she made her fourth trip to the bathroom before lunchtime one day. She'd made an appointment to see her doctor to test for a suspected bladder infection, only to be stunned with the news she was carrying Tino's child.

She pressed against her hard tummy with a reverent hand. All the symptoms of pregnancy now carried special significance for her. She, a woman who'd had every chance at family she'd ever had ripped from her by death, was expecting. It was almost impossible to believe she'd been so blind to the possibility. With her fertility problems, Faith had assumed there wasn't even a remote chance she could or would ever get pregnant again.

Yet, according to the test her doctor had run, she was. *She was.*

Oh, man.

She hugged herself while looking down at the faceless pregnant figure she'd been working on. The incredible awe and joy she felt at the prospect of having a baby—Tino's baby—could be seen in every line of the figure whose arms were raised above her head in an unmistakable gesture of celebration. Faith turned to look at the first woman she'd done after finding out she was pregnant.

That figure showed the fear that laced her joy. This woman had a face, and her expression was one of trepidation. Her hand rested protectively on her slightly protruding stomach. Faith had done the woman as a native African. Clinging to one side of her traditional dress was another small child, not so thin it was starving, but clearly at risk. The two figures were standing on a base that had been created to look like dry grass.

It was a moving statue, bringing tears to her own eyes. Which wasn't exactly something new. The one place Faith allowed herself to express her inner pain, the feelings of aloneness that she accepted but had never quite learned to live with, was her art. While some pieces were filled with joy and peace, others evoked the kind of emotion few people liked to talk about.

Despite that—or maybe because of it—her art sold well, commanding a high price for each piece. Or at least each one she allowed to leave her workshop. The pregnant woman she'd done yesterday wasn't going anywhere but back into a lump of clay. It was too jumbled a piece. No single emotional connotation strong enough to override the others.

Some work was like that. She accepted it as the cost of her process. She'd spent the entire day on that statue, but not late into the night like she had on the first one. Part of it was probably the fact that Tino had called her.

He rarely called her, except to set up assignations. Even when he traveled out of country and was gone for a week or more, she did not hear from him. But he had called yesterday. For no other reason she could discern other than to talk. Weird.

Really, really.

But good. Any loosening of his strictly sex relationship rule was a blessing. Especially now.

But still. Odd.

She wasn't sure when she was going to tell him about the baby. She had no doubts she would do so, but wanted to time it right. There was always a chance of miscarriage in the first trimester, and with her track record she wasn't going to dismiss that very real possibility. She'd lost every chance she'd had for a family up to now, it was hard to believe that this time would work out any differently.

She could still hope, though.

That didn't mean she was going to share news of the baby before she was sure her pregnancy was viable. She had an appointment with the hospital later in the week. Further tests would determine whether the pregnancy was uteral rather than ectopic. Though her original fertility specialist had told her the chances of having another tubal pregnancy were so slim as to be almost nonexistent, Faith wasn't taking any chances.

And she wasn't telling Tino anything until she was sure.

CHAPTER TWO

THE day before her appointment at the hospital was Faith's day to teach art to the primary schoolers. She'd fallen into the job by accident. Sort of. Faith had told Agata Grisafi how much she loved children and spending time with them, but of course her career did not lend itself to doing so. The older woman had spoken to the principal of her grandson's school and discovered he would be thrilled to have a successful artist come in and teach classes one day a week to his students.

That's how it had begun and how Faith had ended up knowing her lover's mother and son longer than she'd known him. Some people might say Providence had lent a hand, and Faith thought maybe, just maybe they might be right.

Giosue, Tino's darling eight-year-old son, was in the second group she taught for the day.

He was his normal sweet self, shyly asking her opinion of the drawing he had done of Marsala's city hall. They were doing a project combining their writing skills and art to give a picture of their city as eight- and nine-year-olds saw it.

"That's beautiful, Gio."

"Thank you, *signora.*"

She moved on to the next child, helping the little girl pick a color for the fish she wanted to draw in the sea so close to Marsala.

It was at the end of class, after all the other children had left, that Giosue came to her desk. "Signora Guglielmo?"

The children called her by the Italian equivalent of William rather than Williams because it was easier for them and she didn't mind a bit.

"Yes, sweetheart?"

He grinned at the endearment, his cheeks pinkening a little, but so obviously pleased that she made a note to use it again. Sparingly.

No matter how special the place in her heart Tino's son had, she would not draw attention to it. To do so would embarrass Giosue, most likely infuriate Tino and compromise Faith's position with the school.

"I would like to invite you to join my family for dinner tonight," he said formally. It was clear he'd practiced the phrase, as well.

"Does your father know you are inviting me to dinner?" she asked, seriously concerned by this turn of events.

"Yes, *signora.* He would be very pleased if you came."

Shock slammed through her. "Did he say that?"

"Oh, yes." Giosue gave her another of his shy smiles. "He is very pleased I like you so well."

Hope bubbled through her like an effervescent spring. Perhaps the black cloud over her life was finally dissipating. Was it possible she had a chance at a real family once again—one that would not be taken away from her? The hope scared her so much it hurt. "I would be honored to join you for dinner."

"Thank you, *signora.*" Giosue handed her a folded

sheet of paper. "My father made you directions for coming, in case you need them."

She took the paper. "Thank you, I appreciate that."

She'd been there a few times for lunch with Agata, though the older woman preferred to meet in Pizzolato because she loved visiting Faith's studio. She said she basked in the privilege of seeing the artist's work before it was finished.

"It was my idea to make the map. I helped Papa with it."

That was her cue to open it and marvel over the drawing, which had obviously been done by a child's hand. The detailed written instructions were in Tino's distinctive slashing scrawl, however.

"You did a wonderful job, Gio. I particularly like the grapevines with grapes on them you drew to show me what to expect to see."

"They are ripening on the vines now. Nonno said they will be ready to harvest when he gets back from Naples maybe."

"If your grandfather says it, than I am sure he is right."

"He is a master winemaker," Giosue said proudly.

"Yes. Do you help with the harvest?"

"Some. Nonno takes me into the fields with him. Papa does not work the fields, but that is okay. Nonno says so."

"Your father's gift is for the business side of things, I think."

"Nonno says Papa is very good at making money," Giosue replied artlessly.

Faith laughed. "I'm sure he is."

"He can support a family. Nonna says so."

"I'm sure he can." Was Giosue matchmaking? Faith held in the smile that wanted to break over her features.

She did not want to hurt Giosue by making him think she was laughing at him.

"She thinks he should marry again. She is his mama, he has to listen to her, I think."

It was really hard to bite back the laugh at that, but she did not think Tino would share his son's view on this particular subject. "What do you think, Gio?"

"I think I would like a mother who is not so far away in Heaven."

She couldn't help it. She reached out and touched him. Just a small pat on the shoulder, but she wanted to hug him to her. "I understand, Gio. I really do."

He cocked his head to one side. "You never talk about family."

"I don't have any." Her hand slid down to her stomach. She hadn't. Before. But now, maybe she did.

"You have no mama, either?"

"No. I prayed for one, but it was not God's will." She shrugged.

"Do you think I will have another mother?"

"I hope so, Gio."

"Me, too, but only if I could love her."

Smart boy. "I'm sure your father wouldn't marry a woman you couldn't love as a mama, too."

"She would have to love me also." Giosue looked at her through his lashes, worrying his lower lip with his teeth.

Sweet little boy. "You are very lovable, that would not be a problem, I'm sure."

The next group of children came rushing into the room along with Giosue's teacher, who was apparently looking for her missing lamb.

"I will see you tonight?" he asked as crossed the room to join his teacher at the door.

"Yes."

He was grinning as he exited the room.

So, Tino's son *was* matchmaking. With her. And seemingly, he had Tino's tacit approval. Unbelievable. The prospect terrified her as much as it thrilled her. Had she suffered enough? Was she done being alone?

Somehow, she couldn't quite picture it.

If nothing else, Tino was allowing her into another aspect of his life. The most important one to him. That was so huge, she could barely wrap her mind around it.

The fact that he was doing so without knowing about the baby boggled her mind even more.

He might not love her, but she had a different place in his life than any woman had since the death of his wife six years ago.

Faith concentrated on the strains of classical music filling her Mini. At least, she tried to. She was extremely nervous about this dinner. She shouldn't be. Over the past year, they'd discovered that she and Tino were compatible in and out of bed. She and Giosue got along great in the classroom as well. It should all be good.

Only, telling herself that didn't make the butterflies playing techno music in her stomach go away. This was the two of them together. Tino *and* Giosue. The three of them really.

How they interacted would dictate a big chunk of her future; she was sure of it. Tino had to be testing the waters and, as absolutely inconceivable as she found that, it sort of fit in with his odd behavior lately.

He'd called her again today. She'd missed the call and when she'd tried to return it he'd been in a meeting. His message had simply said he'd been thinking of her.

Seriously strange.

If he'd said he'd been thinking of sex with her, she wouldn't have been surprised at all. The man had the libido of an eighteen-year-old. Sex was a really important part of his life. Important enough that he pursued it even though he had said he never wanted to remarry or get serious with a woman.

But he hadn't said he was missing the sex. He'd said he was missing *her*. Well, they would be together again soon enough. And then they would see what they would see.

Her phone rang, playing his distinctive ring tone. She never answered when she was driving, so she forced herself to ignore it. Besides, she was almost to Grisafi Vineyard. He could say whatever he wanted when she got there. Most likely, he was calling to see where she was.

But she wasn't late.

Well, not much, anyway. Maybe ten minutes. He had to be used to her sketchy time-keeping skills by now. It was one of the reasons that she loved living in Sicily. Tino was very un-Sicilian in his perfect punctuality and rigid schedule keeping. She'd teased him about it more than once.

He'd told her he had no choice, doing business on an international scale. She suspected it was in his nature and that was that.

She couldn't see Tino changing for the convenience of others, not even when it came to making money.

She turned down the long drive that led to Casa di Fede. Faith House. She'd thought it was neat the house shared her name when she'd first come to visit Agata. Later, when she realized Tino lived here, she'd seen it as an indication they were meant to be together. Even if it was temporary.

Thinking about the coincidence sent another bubble of hope fizzing through her. Maybe it meant something more than what she'd thought. He and his family were wrapped around her life, and she was threaded through his, in ways neither had anticipated or even wanted at first.

She pulled up in front of the sprawling farm house. It had been in the family for six generations and been built onto almost that number of times until it had two master suites, one in its own wing with two additional bedrooms. There were four more bedrooms in the rest of the house, a formal salon, a family entertainment room that opened onto the lanai beside the oversize two-tiered pool and spa area, a huge kitchen, a library and two offices.

One was Tino's, and the smaller, less-organized one was his father's. Agata used the library as her office when she was working on her charity work. She had her own sitting room off the master suite, as well.

Faith had learned all of this on her previous visits with the older woman. What she hadn't known was how overwhelming she would find the familiar home now that she was here to share dinner with Tino and his son. She sat in her car, staring at the proof of generations of Grisafis living in the same area. Proof of Tino's roots and his wealth. Proof that he already had what she had most craved her whole life.

A family.

The prospect that he might be willing to share all that with her was almost more than she could take. Terrifying didn't begin to describe it. Because even if Valentino Grisafi wanted her in his life, she of all people knew there was no guarantee she could keep him. No more than she'd kept the father she never knew, or her mother, or the first family that said they would adopt her, or Taylish…or her unborn son, Kaden.

Dwelling on the pain of the past had never helped her before; she knew it wasn't about to start now. She needed to let the past go and hope for the future, or her own fears were going to destroy her chance at happiness.

With that resolved, she opened her car door. Her phone trilled Tino's ringtone again as she stepped out of the car.

She flipped it open. "Wow, I know you're impatient, but this is borderline obsessive, Tino. I'm here already."

"I merely wished to—"

She rang the bell and he stopped talking.

"It is the doorbell. I must let you go."

Shaking her head at that, she shrugged and disconnected the call.

He opened the door and then stood there staring at her as if she was an apparition—of not particularly friendly aspect. In truth, he looked absolutely horrified.

"Faith!"

"The last time I looked, yes."

"What are you doing here?" He shook his head. "It does not matter. You need to leave. Now."

"What? Why?"

"This is my fault." He rubbed his hand over his face. "I can see where my phone calls may have given you the wrong impression."

"That you might be impatient to see me?"

"Yes, I am. I was. But not here. Not now."

"Tino, you aren't making any sense."

"This is not a good time, Faith. I need you to leave now."

"Won't Gio be disappointed?"

"Gio…why would you ask about my son? Look, it doesn't matter, we have a dinner guest coming."

She rolled her eyes. "Yes, I know. I'm here."

"This is no time for jokes, *carina*."

"Tino, you're starting to worry me." Really. Definitely. Positive that Giosue would not lie and say his father had approved inviting her for dinner, she was flummoxed. Besides, hadn't Tino helped his son make the map? What was going on? "Tino—"

"Signora!" An excited little boy voice broke into the bizarre conversation. "You are here!"

Giosue rushed past his father to throw his arms around Faith in a hug. She returned the embrace with a smile, loving the naturally affectionate nature of most of the Sicilians she had met.

Tino stood there looking at them in abject horror.

Giosue stepped back, self-consciously straightening his button-up shirt. He'd dressed up for the dinner in an outfit close to the uniform he wore to school of obviously higher quality and minus the tie. He looked like a miniature version of his father, who was wearing custom-tailored brown slacks with a champagne colored dress shirt—untucked, the top button undone.

The clothes were absolutely yummy on the father and adorable on the son.

Faith was glad she'd taken the time to change from the clothing she wore to teach in. Her dress was made from yellow silk batiked by a fellow artist with strands of peacock blue, sunset orange and even a metallic dye with a gold cast. Faith had fallen in love with the silk when she'd seen it at an artists' fair and had to buy it. She'd had it made into a dress of simple design with spaghetti straps that highlighted her curves and made her feel deliciously feminine. A new addition to her wardrobe, Tino had not yet seen it.

Regardless of his other reactions to her arrival, that certain gleam she knew so well in her lover's eyes said he approved her choice.

Unaware of the strange overtones to the adults' conversation, Gio took her hand and held it. "Papa, this is Signora Guglielmo." Then the boy smiled up at her with pure innocence. "*Signora,* this is my papa, Signor Valentino Grisafi."

"Your papa and I have met," Faith said, when Tino remained silent and frozen like a statue. An appalled statue.

"You have?" Gio looked confused, maybe even a little hurt. "Papa told me he did not know you. Nonna told him he would like you though."

"I did not realize that Signora Guglielmo was the woman *I* know as Faith Williams." He looked at her accusingly, as if it was her fault.

"You are friends?" Giosue asked.

Faith waited to hear what her lover would say to that.

Tino looked from her to his son, his expression impossible to read. "*Si.* We are friends."

Giosue's face broke out into a grin and he giggled. "You didn't know? Truly?"

"Truly."

"That is a good joke, isn't it, Papa?"

"A good joke indeed," Tino agreed, sounding anything but amused.

Faith wasn't feeling too lighthearted, either. Tino hadn't approved inviting *her* for dinner. He hadn't written those directions out with *her* in mind to use them. He'd had no intention of inviting her into an aspect of his life he had heretofore kept separate from her. In fact, he was clearly dismayed and not at all happy by this evening's turn of events.

He'd approved inviting *his son's teacher*. Another woman. A woman who Tino would have been told by his son and mother was single, near him in age and attractive (or so Agata said every time she lamented Faith's unwed state). If the fact that Giosue had been matchmaking was obvious to Faith, it had to have been just as apparent to his father. Add to that the little detail that Agata had patently put her two cents in, and Faith was painting a picture in her mind that held no gratification for her.

Tino had approved inviting to dinner a woman his son and mother were obviously hoping he would find more than a little interesting.

All of the little pipe dreams Faith had been building since spending the night for the first time at Tino's flat, crashed and burned.

But she wasn't a wimp. Far from it. She'd taken a lot more that life had to dish out without giving up. She was here now. And she had important motivation to make this evening work in spite of her lover's negative reaction to her appearance.

Perhaps if Tino saw how good they could be together around his family, he'd rethink the parameters on their relationship. Then telling him about the baby wouldn't be so hard.

And maybe the Peruvian rain forest would freeze over in a freak weather anomaly tonight, too.

Okay, that kind of negative thinking wasn't going to do her any good. She had to think positive. No matter what, she wasn't about to beg off dinner. That would hurt Giosue, and Faith didn't let children down. Ever.

She'd experienced that particular phenomenon too many times herself to inflict it on the young people in her life.

She gave both males her best winning smile and asked, "May I come in now, or were you planning to have dinner on the front porch?"

Giosue laughed and dragged her over the threshold, forcing his father to move out of the way or get knocked into. "We're eating outside, but in back, silly *signora*."

"And did you cook, Gio?"

"I helped. Ask Papa."

She looked back over her shoulder at the silent man following their progress through the house.

"Indeed he did. He is a favorite with our housekeeper."

"It's easy to understand why. Gio's a little charmer."

"Signora!" Gio exclaimed in the long-suffering tone only an eight-year-old boy could affect so perfectly.

"Do not tell me it embarrasses you to discover your favorite teacher also holds you in high regard," his father teased him.

The boy shrugged, blushing, but said nothing. Faith's heart melted a little more toward him. He would make such a wonderful stepson and big brother. But she was getting ahead of herself. By light-years.

"So, what are we having for dinner?" she asked.

Especially after realizing Tino had not intended to invite her to dinner. That he had, in fact, been wholly ignorant of her relationship with his son and mother.

"Wait until you see. I got to stuff the manicotti. The filling is yummy."

Giosue was right, the manicotti was delicious. As was everything else, and the company wasn't bad, either. Tino started off a little stiff, but being around his son relaxed him. As hard as he so plainly tried to keep things between himself and Faith distant, his usual behavior got the better of him. He touched her when he talked to her, nothing overtly sexual. Just the normal affectionate-Sicilian-nature style, but it felt good—right.

Gio asked tons of questions about her art, questions there wasn't time for during class. Several times she caught Tino looking surprised by her answers. But then, he knew almost nothing about that part of her life. For the first time that really bothered her. Her art made up the biggest part of her life and he was sadly ignorant of it.

That realization, more than anything else, put the nature of their relationship into perspective. While his behavior lately might indicate it was changing, theirs was still primarily a sexually based connection.

"You are asking so many questions, *amorino,* I am beginning to think you wish to grow up to be an artist."

"Oh, no, Papa, I want to be a winemaker like Nonno."

"Not a businessman and vintner like your papa?" Faith asked.

"He will have to have another son to do that. I want to get my hands dirty," Giosue said with absolute certainty.

Rather than take offense, Tino laughed aloud. "He sounds just like my father." He shook his head, the amusement still glittering in his eyes. "However, there will be no brothers, or sisters either. Perhaps Calogero will finally marry and have children, but if not—when I get too old to do my job, we will have to hire a business manager."

"You will never be too old, Papa."

Tino just smiled and ruffled his son's hair. "You know there is nothing to stop you from making art a hobby while you follow in your grandfather's footsteps. Isn't that right, Faith?"

She was still reeling from the dead-on surety in

Tino's tone when he said there would be no sisters or brothers for Giosue, but she managed to nod and smile at the expectant little boy.

CHAPTER THREE

Tino rejoined Faith on the terrace after tucking his son into bed.

Gio had wheedled, pleaded and distracted every time Faith had started making noises about going home. When it was finally time for *him* to go to bed, he had even gone so far as to ask to have her come in and say good-night to him before going to sleep.

She'd done so without the slightest hesitation, kissing Gio's head before wishing him a good sleep and pleasant dreams and then leaving the room. Tino found it disconcerting that she was so relaxed, not to mention good, with his son. Their friendship was of longstanding duration, and he wasn't sure how he felt about that. Except uncomfortable.

He didn't like feeling unsettled. It made him irritable.

And it wasn't at all cute, like his lover when she was woken to go home after an evening of lovemaking.

Faith stood on the edge of the stone terrace, looking out over the vineyard. The green, leafy vines looked black in the moonlight, but she glowed. The cool illumination of the night sky reflected off her porcelain features, lending her a disturbing, ethereal beauty. She looked like an angelic specter that could be snatched to the other realms in the blink of an eye.

It was not a thought he wanted to entertain. Not after that very thing had happened to Maura through her death. The one challenge to their life together that he could not fight.

He was frowning when he laid his hand on Faith's shoulder. "He is on his way to dreamland."

"He's so incredibly sweet. You are a very blessed man, Valentino Grisafi." She turned to face him.

"I know it." He sighed. "But there are times he puts me in an inconvenient situation."

"Like when he invites your current lover to dinner?"

"Yes."

She winced. "You could have said no."

"So could you."

"I thought you wanted me here."

"*I* thought he had invited his teacher from school."

"I am his teacher," she chided. "His art teacher, anyway."

"Why did you never mention this to me?" It seemed almost contrived to him.

"How could you *not* know? I mean, I'm aware you are supremely uninterested in my life outside our time together, but I've mentioned teaching art to primary schoolers in Marsala."

"I thought you did it to support your art *hobby*. My mother told me Gio's teacher was a highly successful artist who donated her time." Realizing how wrong he'd been made him feel like fool.

Another unpleasant and infrequent experience. Grisafi men did not make a habit of ignorance or stupid behavior. His pride stung at the knowledge he was guilty of both. Knowing more about Faith would have saved him the current situation.

"And in your eyes I could not be that woman?" Faith asked in that tone all men knew was very dangerous.

The one that said a husband would be sleeping on the sofa for the foreseeable future. Faith was not his wife, but he didn't want to be cut off from her body, nevertheless. Nor did he wish to offend her in any case.

"In my eyes, that woman, Signora Guglielmo, was Sicilian—and you are not."

"No, I'm not. Is that a problem for you, Tino?"

Where had that question come from? He was no ethnic supremacist. "Patently not. We have been lovers for a year now, Faith."

"Almost a year."

"Near enough."

"I suppose, but I'm trying to understand why my being a Sicilian art teacher would make me an appropriate dinner companion for you and your son, but being your expatriot American lover does not."

"It will not work."

"What?"

"Attempting to use Giosue to insinuate yourself into my life more deeply than I wish you to go."

Hurt sparked in her peacock eyes, and then anger. "Don't be paranoid, not to mention criminally conceited. One, I would never use a child—in any way. Two, I knew your son before I met you. What would you have had me do? Start ignoring him in class once you and I had become lovers?"

"Of course not." He sighed. What a tangle. "But you could have discouraged outright friendship."

"We were already friends. It would never occur to me

to hurt a child with rejection that way. I won't do it now, either, Tino, not even for you."

"That is not what I meant."

"Then what *did* you mean?"

He swore. He wasn't sure, and that was as disturbing as any other revelation from this night. He fell back on what he considered the topic at hand. "Let's not make this more complicated than we need to. You know I do not allow the women I sleep with into my personal life. It would be too messy."

Cocking her head to one side, she gave him a look filled with disbelief. "You don't consider what we do together as personal?"

"You are nit-picking semantics here, Faith. You know what I am meaning here. Why are you being willfully obtuse? You knew the limitations of our relationship from the very beginning." She was not normally so argumentative, and why she had to start being so now was a mystery to him.

Certainly she had strong opinions, but they were not, as a rule, in opposition to his.

"Maybe I'm no longer happy with them." She watched him as if gauging his reaction to that bombshell.

Alarm bells for a five-alarm fire went off in his head. Her words filled him with pure panic—not an emotion he was used to feeling and not one he had predisposed reactions for. "Faith, you must understand something. I have no plans to remarry. Ever."

"I know, but—"

Those three little words sent a shard of apprehension right through him. She could not keep thinking in this manner. "If I did remarry, it would be to a traditional Sicilian woman—like Giosue's mother."

Some Sicilian men married American women, but it was rare. Even rarer still, almost to the point of nonexistent, were Sicilian men who continued to live on the island after marrying them.

Regardless, *were* he to remarry, he felt compelled to provide a female influence as like Giosue's real mother as possible. He owed it to Maura.

Being honest with himself would require he acknowledge that his reasons were not limited to cultural gaps and the obligation he felt to his dead wife, but had as much to do with a promise to keep. Only one woman put his promise to Maura at risk, his promise not to replace his wife, who had died too young in his heart.

And that woman was a smart, sexy American.

Faith crossed her arms, as if protecting herself from a blow. "Is that why you didn't nip your son's obvious attempt at matchmaking in the bud? Because you believed the woman he was trying to fix you up with was Sicilian?"

"Yes." He could not lie, though the temptation was there.

This time Faith didn't just wince, she flinched as if struck. "I see."

"I don't think you do." Needing her understanding—her acceptance—he cupped her face with both hands. "My son is the most important person in my life, I would do anything for him."

"Even remarry."

"If I believed that was what he truly needed for happiness, yes." But not to a woman who would expect access to more than his body and bank account. Not to a woman who already threatened his memories of Maura and his promise to her.

Not Faith.

"Do you?"

Again wishing he could lie, he dropped his hands. "I did not, but after tonight, I am not so sure. He loves his grandmother, but he glowed under your affection in a way that he does not with his nonna."

"He's very special to me."

"If he is so special, why did you not tell me he was your student?"

"You already asked that and the simple truth is that I thought you knew. I assumed he and, well, your mother, talked about me. We are friends. I suppose that's going to send you into another tizzy of paranoia, but please remember, she and I were friends before I even met Gio."

"You and...and...my *mother?*"

"Yes."

Tonight had been one unreal revelation after another. "You did not tell me this."

"I thought you knew," she repeated, sounding exasperated. She turned away from him. "Perhaps Agata and I are not as close as I assumed."

The sad tone in Faith's voice did something strange to Tino's heart. He did not like it. At all. He was used to her being happy most of the time—sometimes cranky but never sad. It did not fit her.

"She did talk about you, but I did not realize it was *you* she was talking about." His mother had mentioned Gio's teacher on occasion. Not often, though, and he too wondered if the two women shared as close a friendship as Faith believed.

His mother was a true patron of the arts. She had many acquaintances in the artistic community. He could easily see her warm nature and natural graciousness being mistaken for friendship. But the only artist she mentioned often was TK.

For a while, Tino had been worried his mother had developed a *tendre* for the male artist. However, when he had mentioned his concern to his father, Rosso Grisafi had laughed until tears came to his eyes. Tino had drawn the conclusion that clearly there was nothing to worry about.

"That's hardly my fault, Tino."

"I did not say it was."

"You implied it by asking why I didn't tell you."

What was it with her tonight and this taking apart everything that he said? "You are apparently very close to both my mother and my son and yet you never once mentioned seeing or talking to them."

"You always discourage me from discussing your family, Tino."

It was true, but for some reason, the reminder bothered him. Probably because everything was leaving him feeling disconcerted tonight. "I did not think they had a place in our combined life."

"We don't have a combined life, do we, Tino?" She was looking at him again and he almost wished she wasn't.

There was such defeat and sadness in her eyes.

"I do not understand what has changed between us?"

"Nothing. Nothing at all has changed between us."

"Then why are you sad?"

"Perhaps because I thought it had."

Why had she believed this?

"You were under the impression I wanted you to come for dinner tonight," he said, understanding beginning to dawn. Clearly she had liked the idea. Learning differently had hurt her. Even though he had not meant for this to happen, he had to take some responsibility for the outcome.

She nodded, silent, her lovely red hair swaying against her shoulders. He had the wholly inappropriate—considering the gravity of their discussion—urge to run his fingers through the familiar silky strands. Worse, he knew he did not want to stop there.

Focus, he must focus.

"It is not good for Giosue to be exposed to my lovers."

"I understand you think that."

"It is the truth."

She said nothing.

He could not leave it there. The compulsion to explain—to make her understand—was too great. "When our relationship ends, he will be disappointed. Already he has expectations that cannot be fulfilled."

"I'm his friend."

"He wants you to be his mother."

"And you don't."

"No." It was a knee-jerk response, the result of ingrained beliefs since his wife's death.

Shocking to realize he wasn't sure he meant it. With that came grief—a sense of loss that made no sense and was something he was not even remotely willing to dwell on.

"Because I'm not Sicilian."

"Because our relationship is not a love affair." But was that true?

How could it be anything else when he *could not* love her? He had promised Maura that he would love her always. Her sudden death had not negated that pledge.

"I thought we were friends, too."

"We are friends." Friendship he could do—was necessary even.

"But not sweethearts."

His heart twinged, making his tone come out more cynical than he meant it to. "What an old-fashioned term."

She shrugged. "It's one Tay used to use." She said the dead man's name with a wistfulness that he did not like.

"I gather he was an unusual man."

"Yes. He was. One of the best, maybe even the best man I ever knew."

"But he is *gone*."

"Yes, just as Gio's mother is gone."

"Maura will never be gone from my heart."

"No, she won't, but are you so sure your heart has no room for anyone else?"

"That is not a discussion you and I should be having." It was one he frankly could not handle.

A Sicilian man should be able to handle anything. Even the death of his wife and raising his child without a mother. But most definitely any conversation with his current mistress. The fact that he could not shamed him.

"Because we agreed that sex and friendship was enough?" she asked in a voice husky with emotion.

"Yes."

"And if it isn't any longer...*for either of us?*"

That could not be true. He would not allow it to be. "Do not presume to speak for me."

"Fine. What if I am only speaking for myself?"

"Then we would need to talk about whether what we have is still working." It was not a discussion he wanted to have. He was far from ready to let her go.

She nodded and turned from him. "I think it's time I was going." She was hurting, for all that she tried to hide it.

"No." He hated the melancholy in her voice.

He hated the sense that somehow it was his fault. He hated thinking of going to bed alone after spending the whole evening in her company. Even worse, he hated feeling as if he might lose her and *really* hated how much that bothered him.

Perhaps he could erase her sorrow while easing his own fears. He was a big proponent of the win-win business proposition. It was even better when applied to personal relationships.

Before she could take more than a couple of steps, he reached out and caught her shoulder.

"Tino, don't."

"You do not mean that, *carina*." He drew her back toward his body. He could not imagine doing the opposite—pushing her away.

Yet he knew he could not hold on to her forever. One day she would tire of life in Sicily—so different from her home—and would return to America. Isn't that what all American women did eventually?

Faith was currently the only single American woman he knew who was making a go of actually living permanently in Sicily. For all its charm, Marsala was a far cry from New York or London.

That only meant they should not waste the time they did have. "We are good together. Do not allow tonight to change that."

"I need more, Tino."

"Then I will give you more." He was very good at that.

"I'm not talking about sex."

He turned her to face him and lowered his head so his lips hovered above hers. "Let's not talk at all."

Then he kissed her. He would show her that they

were too right together to dismiss their relationship because it wasn't packaged in orange blossoms and meters of white tulle.

She fought her own response. He could feel the tension in her, knew she wanted to resist, but though she might want to, she was as much a slave to their mutual attraction as he. Her body knew where it belonged. In his arms.

But her brain was too active and she tore her lips from his. "No, Tino."

"Do not say no. Say rather, 'Make love to me, Tino.' This is what I wish to hear."

"We're supposed to be exclusive."

"We are."

"You were willing to have a blind date with another woman, Tino." She wrenched herself from his arms. "I cannot be okay with that."

"It was not a date."

She glared at him, but it was the light of betrayal in her eyes that cut him to the quick. "As good as."

"I did not consider it a date."

"But you knew your son and mother were match-making."

"I had no intention of being matched."

"But that's changed. You said so. You said you would do anything for Gio, even give him a second mother—*if she's Sicilian*." The tone Faith spoke the last words with said how little she thought of his stance on the matter.

"I said I was considering it, not that I had decided to date other women. You are all the woman I want right now."

"And tomorrow?"

"And tomorrow."

"So, when does my sell-by date come into effect? Next week? Next month? Next year."

He wanted to grab her and hold on tight, but he laid gentle hands on her shoulders instead. "You do not have a sell-by date. Our relationship is not cut-and-dried like that."

"I won't be with you if you're going to date other women," she repeated stubbornly.

"I would not ask you to."

"What does that mean, Tino?"

"It means you can trust me to be faithful while we are together. Just as I trust you."

Her eyes glistened suspiciously, sending shards of pain spiking through his gut. He did not want to see her cry. He kissed her, just once, oh so carefully, trying to put the tenderness and commitment—as limited as it might be—that he felt into the caress.

"Let me make love to you." He was pleading and he did not care.

They needed each other tonight, not empty beds where regrets and memories would haunt the hours that should be for sleep. Or making love.

"No more blind dates."

"It wasn't—"

But she shushed him with a finger to his lips. "It was. Or would have been. Don't do it again."

"You have my word." Then, because he could not help himself; because he needed it more than breathing or thinking or anything else, he once again kissed her.

He poured his passion and his fear out in that kiss, molding their lips together in a primordial dance.

At first she did not respond. She did not try to push

him away, but she did not pull him closer, either. It was the only time in their relationship she had not fallen headfirst into passion with him.

She was still thinking.

He would fix that. Increasing the intensity of their kiss, he stormed her mouth, refusing to allow their mutual desire to remain a prisoner to circumstances that would not…could not…change. Bit by bit her instincts took over.

And once her brain caught up to her body, she melted into him, ending her resistance and giving him access to the interior of her mouth at the same time. She tasted like the coffee laced heavily with rich cream and sweet sugar she had drunk after dinner. It was a flavor he had come to associate only with her.

He drank his own coffee black unless he wanted an erection tenting his slacks—something that was more than inconvenient during his business day, but could be downright embarrassing. This, what they had, was beyond good. It was fantastic, and she *would* not end it. He could not let her.

Tonight, he would remind her how well he knew her body, what he alone could do to it, how much pleasure *he* could give her. Her husband had not elicited those sensations in her, or she would not have acted so shocked by each new one when Tino and Faith had first begun their affair.

She had been almost virginal, many of her reactions belying the existence of previous lovers, much less a husband.

He refused to dwell on the sense of alarm he felt realizing the extent of his ignorance about her life. She'd been his son's art teacher since before they met a year ago, and she had known his mother even longer. Yet Tino had been totally unaware of those facts. As unknowing as he had been about the reality of Faith's widowhood.

How had her husband died? She'd loved him, thought he was a *special* man.

A primal need to erase memories of the other male from her drove Tino to deepen the kiss even further.

Faith made a soft sound against his lips. He loved kissing her. Had from the very first. She was more responsive to his lips claiming hers than any woman he had ever known. And she was far from shyly submissive. She gave as good as she got, with a passion that turned him inside out.

Damn. He wanted her.

But not out here where someone might see what should be entirely private between two people. The temptation to once again make her his, right here under the stars, was strong however. He fought it, sweeping her up into his arms and carrying her inside.

He went directly to his room, no thought of taking Faith anywhere else even entering his mind. This was *his* bedroom. *His* bed. And for now at least, she was his woman.

The huge four-poster with wooden canopy had been used by his family for generations. Though the mattress and box springs were new—a pillow-top with extra coils imported from America on his younger brother's recommendation. It had been a good piece of advice, for more than one reason.

Not only was it incredibly comfortable, but giving up the mattress and even the bed linens he had shared with his wife had been instrumental in Tino finally being able to sleep in his own suite once again.

Pulling back the coverlet, he then laid Faith onto the bed.

She looked around the room, her expression going from curious to surprised. "This is your room."

He locked the door and returned to the bed, unbuttoning his shirt as he went. "Where else would I take you?"

"I don't know." She licked her lips, her focus on his chest as he peeled the shirt from his body. "You're such an incredibly sexy man, you know?"

"You have mentioned believing so before."

She laughed, the sound husky and warm. "I meant it then and I mean it now. I love looking at you."

"I thought it was men who were supposed to be the visual sex."

"Maybe." She shrugged, kicking her sandals off. "Maybe if all women had such yummy eye candy to look at, we'd be considered the visual sex, too."

"So, I am eye candy?"

She licked her lips as if tasting something really sweet and nodded.

His sex jolted at memories of what it felt like to be partaken of by that delectable little tongue. "I think you are a minx."

"You think?"

"I know."

She gave him a saucy wink and stretched her body, putting her curves on sensual display.

He shook his head but knew he had no hope of clearing it. He'd been here before with this woman, so filled with desire that everything else was just a gray fog around them. He unzipped his slacks, hissing as the parting fabric made way for his steel-hard manhood.

This woman affected him like no other.

"I love it when you make that sound."

"You are the only one who has ever heard it." With his admission, he stripped off the remainder of his clothes—the need to deflect automatic.

"Really?" she asked, nevertheless.

"Yes." He joined her on the bed, on all fours above her. "I want you naked."

She brushed her hand down his flank. "I like naked."

He could no more suppress the growl her touch evoked than he could the need to return it. He brought their mouths together again as he reached down and caressed her through the silk of her dress. All evening he had wanted to do this, to feel the curves he knew intimately through the thin fabric. Regardless of how surreal the night had been, his desire for her was as strong as always, building with each minute he was in her company.

She moaned into the kiss, arching into his touch, begging silently for more.

And more was what he was an expert at giving her. He would remind her of that. Show her that each time could be better than the last.

He continued the strokes along her breasts, the dip of her waist and bow of her hips. Over and over again, he touched the places on her body that he knew drove her wild.

Her hands were busy, too, skimming along his heated skin, kneading his chest, but best of all was when she grabbed him—her fingers digging into his shoulders with white-knuckle intensity. When she got to this point—where she could no longer concentrate on pleasuring him—he knew she was past thought. Past control.

Exactly where he wanted her to be.

CHAPTER FOUR

IT WAS time to take her clothes off. He did, using the opportunity to tease and tantalize her further. But revealing her peaches-and-cream body was a double-edged sword. The light smattering of freckles over her shoulders and upper breasts were his downfall. She had none on her face, so the cinnamon dots felt secret—private—for him alone. A special knowledge shared just between them. He was tempted to count them—with kisses—every time he got her disrobed.

This time was no different.

The allure of her body for him never diminished.

He traced the light dots on her skin. "You are so beautiful."

"You've got an unnatural affection for my freckles." It might be a full sentence, but the way she said it, breathless with pauses between words, told him that she was no more in possession of her faculties than she had been a moment before.

"You think?" he asked against her silken skin, tasting the brown sugar dots that his mind told him could not be sweet but his tongue told him they were. But then, everything about her was sweet.

Dangerously so.

Her only answer was a moan as his lips trailed the natural path to one pebbled nipple. She shuddered beneath him, her body translating her every feeling with sexy clarity. She loved nipple play and he loved tasting and touching the turgid buds.

He delicately licked the very tip, then circled the peak with his tongue, moving slowly to lave her aureole despite the need riding him hard enough to make him ache. He refused to rush this. He had something to prove to her.

He kept at it until even the act of huffing a warm breath over her sensitized skin made her tremble and whimper. Then he moved to minister in the same way to its twin.

"What are you doing? Tormenting me?" she cried out as he sucked her nipple gently into his mouth.

He lifted his head and met peacock blue eyes glazed with pleasure. "I am giving you more."

"I don't want more. I want you in me." Then she bit her lip as if realizing what she'd said.

"Trust me, this—" he carefully slid two fingers into her superbly lubricated, swollen channel "—this is where I wish to be also, but only when I have given you *more*." He thrust with his fingers, hitting that interior bundle of nerves some women referred to as their G-spot.

She cried out, the sound adding to his own arousal, making it harder to wait, but he would.

Tonight would be spectacular.

He continued to massage her as he leaned down and once again claimed her mouth as his. Her return kisses were desperate and filled with the feminine fire he found so irresistible.

Her walls clenched around his fingers as he moved

them in and out, stimulating her G-spot with each slow stroke. She undulated, her body straining toward him and moving with those tiny, involuntary jerks that enhanced her pleasure.

He could feel her need to climax rolling off her in palpable waves of sexual energy. Her little whimpers against his lips were an inarticulate form of begging he'd become addicted to their first time together.

His Faith did not play mind games or try to hide her physical needs or desires. She expressed them in a dozen different ways, all of which turned him on. Sex with this woman was volcanically hot, but it was also honest. She amazed and delighted him.

Now it was his turn.

He brushed her clitoris with his thumb, just a light movement back and forth…back and forth, but that was all she needed. Launching upward with her pelvis, she convulsed around his fingers. Her sharp little teeth bit into his lower lip as she made a keening sound in her throat, telling him without words that this was exactly what he wanted it to be.

More.

He kissed her through the orgasm, helping her to come down, but not too far. He was not done with her yet. Not nearly.

When her breathing was less ragged, he gently lifted her legs so they draped over his forearms and he used the position to spread her thighs until she was completely open to his gaze. Her entire body was still flushed from her climax, a beautiful rose red that he could not wait to spear with his own throbbing and as yet unsatisfied flesh. Diamond hard, her nipples poked straight up, pleading for his touch. A soft sheen of perspiration coated her upper chest, attesting to the level of pleasure she had already received.

He started to speak and had to clear his throat.

She smiled at him and the words came out in a masculine growl he wasn't in any way ashamed of. "You are so incredibly beautiful like this."

"Sated from your lovemaking?"

"You are not sated." He tipped his pelvis, brushing her entrance with the tip of his penis, eliciting a second keening sound from her. He smiled. "You still need me."

Something flashed in her eyes, something he could not quite read but that looked a lot like vulnerability. "Yes."

"I need you as well."

"I know." But the words came out sounding bleak.

He did not like it. There was no place for melancholy in their bed.

"You are not my mistress." He didn't know why he said it, but he felt compelled.

Her eyes widened. "What?"

"You are not my mistress. You are *amore mio* and my friend."

"Yes." The smile she gave him was still tinged with sadness, but a glimmer of hope shone in her gaze.

Why it should matter to him that it was there, that he would even desire such a thing, considering what it implied from her earlier words, he did not know. But illogical as it might be, he was glad.

"I am going to give you more now, *carina*. Are you ready for me?"

She nodded, her breath coming out in little pants, but her body did not tense in his hold. She trusted him completely. Amazing. Although she had climaxed, her body was ready for *more*. Ready for *him*.

He pressed forward, allowing the head of his granite-hard penis to brush her opening again, but did not go in, teasing them both. Her lips curved in a familiar smile as she seemed to simply melt against the bed, waiting on him with a sexy expectation he adored. It said she knew he would take care of her wants.

He thrust his hips, allowing his length to slide along her slick folds. It felt so good—so perfect—he groaned, the sound reverberating deep in his chest. With her, he was primal man. "You are so wet."

"You are so earthy, Tino. No one would expect it." Using her lower back muscles, she lifted herself and increased the stimulation, showing the uninhibited aspect of her own nature.

"Only you get to see this side of me." That had to count for something.

"I better be the only one, mister."

He laughed softly as he allowed his thickened member to enter her. "You are like hot silk. I feel like I am going to lose my mind every time I enter you."

"I lost mine a long time ago." She pressed her head back into the pillow, her eyelids going half-mast.

He smiled and shook his head as he moved forward with rocking motions that made it possible for her to take his entire length. He was long and thick, and that had overwhelmed more than one lover. His and Maura's intimacy had been loving and passionate, but nothing like what it was like with Faith.

Maura had never been as comfortable exposing her desire, which was to be expected as she had been raised in the very sheltered environment of a traditional Sicilian household. But he adored that element of Faith's lovemaking. The way his current lover not only *could* take his full length, but *craved* it was something a man like him could and would never take for granted.

He could not help rejoicing in the amount of belief in him that Faith expressed every time they came together.

"You never flinch from me." The wonder that laced his voice embarrassed him a little, but like so many things with this woman—was an uncontrollable response.

In so many ways she was dangerous to him, but he continued to play Russian Roulette with his emotions—risking the promises he had made to his dead wife. His brain told him he should get out before he got in too deep, but everything inside him rebelled at the idea.

"Why would I?" Her brows wrinkled in genuine confusion. "We are a perfect fit."

Perfect only because she relaxed so well for him—for she was tight. Oh, so damn tight. *"So, perfect."*

"Mmmm…" She licked her lips. "You're big, but it's *good,* Tino."

"It is better than good."

"Yessss…" she hissed as he finally sheathed himself to the hilt in her fantastic heat.

He tucked her legs around his hips. "I need to kiss you."

"Please, Tino." She was straining toward him even as he brought their mouths together.

Nothing had ever felt so good.

The part of his brain where guilt resided rejected that thought even as he set a steady, slow rhythm. Kissing, their bodies moved together in a motion filled with tenderness he did not want to examine.

He could feel her desire building as was his. He refused to go over, no matter how much his body clamored for the ultimate release. He was determined to bring her to another shattering peak. Her second climax would be more intense than the first.

It would be *more*.

Of its own volition, his pelvis swiveled on each downward thrust, as if his body had been trained to pleasure this woman exactly as she needed. Pavlov's response. Her pleasure gave him intense satisfaction and pleasure, therefore he did all that he could to bring out every little gasp, each sweet moan, every tightening of her muscles, each shudder she could not control.

Suddenly they were both coming together, his own orgasm taking him over before he could even hope to stop it.

But he did not want to as she contracted around him, her peak lasting seconds that turned into minutes while his body vibrated with matching sensation until his muscles felt like they would collapse.

Their mouths separated, allowing each of them to take in gasps of air and he collapsed, managing only to deflect part of his weight to the side, but maintaining skin contact. From past experience, he knew she preferred that. Thank the Holy Mother because he could not have moved if he tried.

"Thank you."

"No, *cara,* thank you."

She made another sound, but he knew she would slide into sleep soon. People said men fell asleep after sex, but he rarely did. His little American lover, however, experienced orgasm as some kind of somnolence button. He did not mind. He looked forward to these moments when he could cuddle her without having to put up his macho facade.

But tonight he did something he never did. Or at least had not until their last time together in his apartment in Marsala. He let his body relax in preparation for sleep.

Although Giosue woke early, Valentino always woke even earlier. He was not worried about being caught with her. Besides, there just seemed to be something so cold about kicking her out of his bed after such an intense experience. It had been getting harder and harder to do so lately, anyway.

He was going to have to get a handle on this softening of his relationship rules, but not tonight. He wanted to sleep, for just a little while, holding Faith.

Gio would never know and therefore could not be hurt by it. He would no doubt sleep even later than he normally did on a Saturday morning. Valentino had allowed his son to stay up later than usual because of their guest.

Their *guest*.

His lover.

He mentally shook his head at that. He would never have guessed that she was so ingrained in the life of his family. He still was not sure how he felt about that, but he wasn't going to dwell on it tonight. Tomorrow was soon enough to try to figure out how the woman who had shared his bed for almost a year was such an enigma to him.

Just as it would be soon enough to reinstate his necessary rules for the women who shared his bed. Or perhaps he should reconsider those rules for Faith. At least a little.

After all, she was more than a mere bed partner.

She was his friend.

A friend he apparently knew less about than any of

his business rivals. And he trusted her enough to share an intimate side of his life.

For the second time ever, Faith woke in the arms of her lover.

Tino had allowed her to *sleep in his bed? In his family home?*

Maybe he really had given her *more* last night.

Or had that move been an unconscious one? It didn't really matter if he had considered it, or acted on instinct—it had to mean something.

Just as his promise not to go searching for that perfect Sicilian paragon right away meant something. Gio was Tino's heart, but the dedicated father had still reaffirmed his commitment not to date other women while he and Faith were together.

She'd thought her heart was being ripped right out of her chest when he said he thought Gio might need a new mother, but that mother could not be Faith. She'd been angry and hurt and scared and a lot of other emotions that confused her because she couldn't be sure if they were genuine or induced by the pregnancy hormones rampaging through her body.

The two pregnancies she'd had before had sparked serious inner upheavals as well. She and Tay would have argued constantly if he hadn't taken her hormone-driven insecurities in his stride. Would Tino have the same patience? Did she want him to? There had been instances when Tay's tolerance had felt more patronizing than understanding.

Right now she felt she was out of control when it came to her feelings and she didn't enjoy the experience. There had been times the night before she'd been sorely tempted to sock Tino good and hard, but then the pendulum that was her emotions had swung to needing the reassurance that sex provided.

She didn't think Tino was any surer of his feelings than she was. Because in the same conversation he'd spoken of getting Gio a Sicilian mother, he'd also spoken of not wanting to end things with Faith. He knew she wouldn't be any man's mistress.

Early in their acquaintance, she'd made sure he was aware of how she felt about those kinds of double standards.

Their intimacy last night had been awesome, she couldn't deny it. She'd felt more connected to Tino than ever before. He'd been so intent on giving her pleasure, but more than that, he'd given her something of himself. It was in the way he'd moved inside her, with an undisputable tenderness that brought tears to her eyes just before they'd found the ultimate pleasure *together.*

As much as she hated to, she forced herself to slide from his embrace. Even if she thought Tino could handle it, she did not want to be caught in his bed by anyone in his household, but especially by Gio. She loved the little boy too much to spring such a relationship on him without some sort of leading up to it.

He might be playing matchmaker, but that didn't mean he was ready for the reality of his father having a lover, a woman who had taken his mother's place in the huge four-poster bed. She still could not believe they had made love in his bedroom. That not only had he initiated the lovemaking, but *he* had *carried* her in here.

She took a quick shower in his en suite, halting midstep on the way out by the sight of the statue on his dresser. It was of a faceless woman, her arms outstretched to a man holding a baby boy. The man was faceless and so was the baby, but she knew it was male.

How could she not? She'd done the statue. The original, complete with perfect replicas of her own face and that of Taylish holding a little boy whose features were an amalgam of both of them resided in her studio at home.

"My mother bought it for me."

That didn't surprise Faith. Nor did the fact that Tino was awake. He slept too lightly not to have woken to the shower running. "Do you like it?"

"Very much. It reminds me of when Maura was alive."

"Oh." Of course…there was nothing in this statue to show the deep sorrow that etched her face in the original.

"It is as if she has her arms open, welcoming Gio and myself into them."

"Or as if she's letting you go." That's what she'd titled the first one she'd done, but when she created another faceless rendition, she'd simply called it *Family*.

"Is that wishful thinking?" Tino asked, an edge to his voice.

She turned to face him. "What do you mean?"

"Are you hoping my wife has finally let me go so that I might claim someone new in her place?" There was nothing to give away what he was thinking in his face.

It didn't matter. The only course open to her—especially now—was honesty. "If I say yes?"

"I will remind you that if I ever do remarry it will be to a Sicilian woman, someone who can give Gio that little part of his mother at the very least." Pain flashed in his eyes, quickly followed by guilt and then both were gone, leaving only the stoic expression behind.

Promise not to date others notwithstanding, she could really have done without that reminder. The knowledge he was still so adamant about not marrying her hurt. Badly. And she was absolutely certain that pain was not a hormones-gone-wild-induced emotion.

"Why did you let me sleep here last night?" she had to ask as she fought against showing the pain his words had caused.

"I fell asleep."

"You never just fall asleep."

"There is a first time for everything."

So it had been subconscious. She'd wondered and now she knew. He didn't know why he'd brought her to his bed in his family home. And honestly? That didn't matter right now. What did matter was that he regretted it. That much was obvious. Anything else he might be feeling was hidden behind the enigmatic mask he wore.

And she should not be surprised.

She was the first woman to share that bed since the death of his wife. As hard as his regret was for her to bear, the situation was equally difficult for him. Only in a different way.

She'd had her own moments of letting go in the years since Taylish and their unborn son had died. She knew how wrenching they could be. Regardless of her own feelings right now, she could not ignore the pain twisting inside Tino. It was not in her nature to do so, but beyond that—she loved him.

She caressed the statue. It was a beautiful piece. One of her favorites. The one in her studio expressed and brought a measure of peace for an emotional agony she had been unable to give voice to. No one had been there to hear.

She would be there for Tino now, if he wanted her to be. "Tino—"

"I won't be able to see you again until my parents return." The words were clipped, hard.

"I understand." She really did.

He stood there, silent, as if he expected her to say something else.

"It's all right, Tino." She gave one last lingering glance at the statue and then began dressing.

He flinched, as if those were not the words he wanted or expected to hear. "I *will* see you then?"

She paused in the act of slipping on her sandals. "Of course."

"Good." He nodded, looking at a loss. So different from the typical Tino—business tycoon and suave but distant lover.

When she was done dressing she stopped in front of him and leaned up to kiss his cheek. "It really is going to be all right." Letting go was a necessary part of grief.

The fact that Tino was doing so, even if only on a subconscious level, gave her hope.

"No doubt."

"It isn't easy for any of us."

"What do you mean?" he asked, edgy again. Or still. He hadn't relaxed since she came out of the bathroom.

"Letting go."

"I have nothing to let go of."

She didn't argue. There would be no point. And it would only make him more determined to prove himself right. He had enough to overcome in moving forward, without adding another dose of his stubborn will to the mix.

"I'll see you when your parents return from Naples."

* * *

Valentino swore and slammed his hand down beside the statue Faith had admired. His wife letting him go? He did not think so.

Maura would be in his heart forever. He had promised.

The memory was as visceral today as it had been an hour after it happened.

His beautiful young wife had started off not feeling well that morning. He'd had the temerity to hope it meant she was pregnant again.

But that had not been the case.

Ignorant of the tragedy to come, he'd flown out of country for a business meeting in Greece with hope in his heart of increasing his family. He remembered that while his wife's body betrayed her and she slipped further away from him, he had spent the day smiling more than usual, feeling on top of the world. And then his world had come crashing down.

His meeting had been a success, opening the doors for the major expansion of the Grisafi family interests. He would exchange that success and all that had come later for one more lucid day with the mother of his son.

Valentino's mother had called him just before he boarded the jet for home. Papa had taken Maura to the hospital because she had passed out walking up the stairs. By the time Valentino had reached the hospital, his wife was in a coma.

Petrified for the first time in his life, sweating through his expensive shirt, he'd rushed into the room. Maura had been so damn pale and completely motionless. He'd taken her lifeless hand, his heart ceasing at its coolness. He had begged her to wake up, to speak to him, to squeeze his hand—anything.

But nothing. Not then. Not later. No fluttering eyelids. No half-formed words. No goodbyes. Absolutely nothing.

The only sounds had come from him—his desperate pleas and constant talking until his voice was no more than a horse whisper in hopes of sparking a connection to her shut-down brain—and from the machines hooked up to her. Machines and medications that had been unsuccessful at saving her life.

Her first discernable diabetic attack had been her last. Nothing the doctors did brought her blood sugars under control and she died without coming out of the coma.

He'd spent every minute with her, but it had done no good. And when she'd gone into cardiac arrest, the doctors had called security to force him from the room. He'd been in another country when she fell into the coma and out in the hall when she let go of life.

The doctors said her reaction to the disease was extremely rare. But not rare enough, was it? His wife, the mother of his child was dead and nothing would ever change that.

He would never forget the rage, the grief and the utter helplessness he felt holding his small son in his arms as they said goodbye to her. He had promised then, standing over her grave, holding their sobbing son who just wanted his mama. Valentino had promised he would never stop loving her, that he would never replace her in his heart.

Valentino Grisafi had never broken a promise and he wasn't about to start now.

This thing with Faith had to get back on track, or it had to end.

There simply was no other option. No matter what he might want or think he needed.

CHAPTER FIVE

TRUE to his word, Faith did not see Tino again while Agata and Rocco were in Naples. There were no more phone calls, either.

She didn't expect there to be.

Tino wasn't going to accept the change in their relationship gracefully. If he accepted it at all. She had to believe he would though.

Especially after allowing him to make love to her that night. Not that she'd had a lot of choice. Once he set his course on seduction, she was a goner. She loved him. *Needed him*. While that truth scared her to death, she didn't try to deny it. Self-deception was not something she indulged in. She'd accepted the physical intimacy because it substituted for the emotional connection she craved after learning she carried his baby. And sometimes, when he made love to her, she actually felt loved by him—if only for that short while.

It was that simple. And that complicated.

But maybe it was on the way to something better... something truly *more*.

He had initiated the shift in their relationship in the first place. Initially, sleeping all night with her in his apartment in Marsala, and then making love to her in his family home. That reality mitigated her fears for their future, although it did not completely rid her of them.

He might not want to admit it, but he was already thinking about her in broader terms than simply his "current convenient partner." They'd been exclusive from the very beginning—something they had both insisted on. Add that to how well she fit with his family and their friendship and they had a strong basis for a lasting relationship. The fact that she loved him would only make it easier to raise a family with him.

Even if he never came to love her as he'd loved Maura, it would be enough to be his wife and mother of his children. She had never expected to have this much claim to family again. She certainly did not expect it all.

Not after everything she had lost.

Besides, she'd never loved Taylish like she loved Tino, but *he'd* been happy in their marriage. Content to have her loving commitment if not her passion.

There were times she knew he had wanted more, but he'd never regretted their marriage. Only leaving it in death. He'd told her so, just before breathing his last.

But she didn't want to remember that day. It belonged in her past—along with the two families she'd lost. The only real families she'd ever had. Until now.

Her current hopes and dreams were reflected in the series of joy-filled family centric sculptures she did over the next week.

Agata called her when the older couple returned from the continent. Faith did not tell her about having dinner with Tino and Giosue, leaving that bit of information for them to reveal. She also avoided having Agata come to her studio the following week. She did not want Tino's mother to see the revealing pieces of art before Faith had a chance to tell him of his impending fatherhood.

Every day that went by and she did not hear from him, she missed him more. She wanted to share the miracle of her pregnancy with him, but it was important to give him space. He had to come to terms on his own with the new parameters of their relationship.

However, when the silence between them stretched a week beyond his parents' return, she called him. Only to discover he'd had to fly to New York to meet with his brother and a potential client. She tried his cell phone, but the call went straight to voice mail. After that had happened a couple of times, once very late in the evening, she figured out he was avoiding her with diligence.

It bothered her, feeling a lot like rejection. She clung to the knowledge that if he wanted to break it off with her, he would do so definitively. He would not simply begin avoiding her like an adolescent. No, he was just struggling with the changes between them more than she'd anticipated.

It made her nervous about how he might react to the news of her pregnancy. Thankfully, he was as Sicilian as a man could get. Some might think that meant unreconstructed male, but she knew that for Tino that translated into an all-out love for family and children especially. He might not be thrilled about her new role in his life, but he would be happy about the baby. Being the traditional Sicilian that he was, it would never occur to him to seek a relationship with the child that excluded her.

Thank goodness.

His desire to marry a Sicilian woman if he ever did

remarry worried her a little, but he would just have to buck up and deal with it like a grown-up. It wasn't as if he objected to her personally. He liked her as much outside the bedroom as in it. She was sure of it. Even at his apartment they did not spend all their time in bed together.

And when they were in bed, they didn't only have sex. They talked. Not about anything personal, but about politics, faith, what they thought of the latest news, his business—the types of things you didn't talk about with a bare acquaintance.

He might know much about her art career, but he knew her stance on environmentalism, government deficits, latch-key children and his desire to dominate his own corner of the upscale wine market.

Right now, though, he had to adjust to the fact that she was a part of his family's life and a bigger part of his than he had intended when they first got together.

In the meantime, she agreed to join Agata for lunch at the Vineyard.

A day earlier than he had told his family to expect him, Valentino pulled his car into his spot in the newer multicar garage he'd had built to the side of the house when he married Maura. So she could keep her car parked inside for her comfort. She'd teased him about spoiling her, but it had been so easy to do. His dead wife had been a very sweet woman.

Much like Faith.

He sighed at the thought, frustrated with himself.

The trip to New York had been longer than he wanted or expected, though it had one side benefit. It had made it easier to distance himself from Faith. Though forwarding her calls directly to voice mail had taken a larger measure of self-control than he would have expected. Much larger.

Which only went to show that he had to become serious about getting their relationship back on track.

Or he would have to let her go, and that was not something he wanted to do.

The craving he felt to hear her voice filled him with anger at himself along with a sense of helplessness he refused to give in to. He had been fighting the urge to sleep all night with her since the beginning. Never before had he been tempted not to be home in the morning for his son to wake up to because of a woman. He'd known giving in would come with a cost, but he had not expected it to be his sanity.

It had felt right taking her to his bed in the family home. Too right. Now he questioned his intelligence in doing so. For that insanely stupid choice had come at an emotional cost, as well, one he had no right to pay.

If he were a truly honorable man, he would let her go completely. He'd told himself so over and over again while in New York. What did it say for his inner strength that he could not do it?

Certainly it was nothing to be proud of.

Physically distancing himself from her was not the same as regrouped emotions, he had learned. His need to see her grew with each day even as he fought it. He might have won, but he hungered for not only the sound of her voice, but the shiver of her laughter and the feel of her skin. He was like a drug addict shaking for his next fix.

It would be a couple of days at least before he could go to her, too. Agonizing days if those in New York were anything to go by. But Gio had missed his papa and had to be Valentino's first consideration.

Of course, if he left when his son was sleeping, Gio would be missing nothing.

The thought derailed from its already shaky tracks as he recognized the melodious laughter mingled with his mother's voice coming from the terrace. He stood frozen, uncharacteristically unsure of what to do. No doubts about what he *wanted* to do. He wanted to see Faith. But what *should* he do?

His decision was taken from him by his mother's voice. "Valentino, *figlio mio,* is that you?"

"*Si,* Mama. It is me."

"Come out here."

He had no choice but to obey. He might be thirty years old, but a Sicilian man knew better than to dismiss a direct command from his mother. It would hurt her and cause her distress. Hurting those he loved was something he avoided at all costs. Even when it was his peace of mind at stake, like now.

Walking out onto the terrace, he found not only his mother and Faith, but his father and Giosue as well.

His son jumped up from where he'd been dangling his feet in the water beside Faith and came running full tilt at Valentino. "Papa, Papa…you are home!"

"*Si,* I am home and glad to be here." He swung his son high into his arms and hugged the wiggling, eight-year-old body to his.

"I missed you, Papa. *Zio* Calogero should not call you to New York."

"Sometimes it is necessary, *cucciola.* You know this."

His son ducked his head. "Papa! Do not call me that. It is a name for little boys, but I am big. I am eight!"

"Ah, but a man's son is always his little one," Rocco Grisafi said as he came and hugged both Valentino and

Giosue. "Welcome home, *piccolo,*" his father said, emphasizing his point with a humorous glint in eyes the same color as Valentino's.

It had been decades since his father had last called him that and Valentino laughed.

Giosue giggled. "Papa is bigger than you Nonno, how can he be your little one?"

Valentino's father, who was in fact a head shorter than he, winked at his grandson. "It is not about size, it is about age, and I will always be older, no?"

"That's right," Valentino agreed. "And I will always be older than you," he said as he tickled his swimsuit-clad son.

Giosue screeched with laughter and squirmed down, running to the pool and jumping in, his head immediately coming up out of the water. "You can't get me now, Papa."

"You think I cannot?"

"I know it. Nonna would be mad if you got your business clothes wet."

That made everyone laugh, including Faith, drawing Valentino's attention like a bee to a rose. *Damn, damn, damn.* She was beautiful, wearing a bright green top and matching pair of Capri pants she had rolled up above her knees so she could dangle her feet in the water of the pool. Her gorgeous red hair fell loose around her shoulders and her sandals were nowhere to be seen.

Even his mother's hug and greeting got only a portion of his attention as the rest of him strained toward the woman he wanted to take into his arms and kiss the daylights out of.

"So, I hear from my grandson that you and my dear friend are well acquainted already," his mother said, finally garnering his whole focus.

Well versed in how his mother's mind worked, he immediately went hyperalert to any nuance and ultracautious in his own reactions. She was on a kick to get him married and fathering more grandbabies for her. His argument that it was time for Calogero to do his duty by the family was met with deaf ears.

His mother wanted more grandchildren from Valentino. Full stop. Period.

And now she'd discovered he was friends with Faith.

He had to be very careful here. If his mother even got a hint of the intimate nature of his relationship with Faith, Agata Grisafi would have her oldest son married off before he could get a word in edgewise. "We'd met before, yes."

"You'd met? I am sure your son said you were friends," his mother chided with a gleam in her eyes, confirming Valentino's worst fears.

He simply shrugged, confirming nothing. Denying nothing. Sometimes that was the only way to deal with his mother and her machinations. Deflection wasn't a bad tactic, either, when he could get away with it.

He'd long ago acknowledged he never wanted to face his mother across a boardroom table. She made his toughest clients and strongest competition look like amateurs.

"More interesting to me is your friendship with her," he said. "You rarely mention Faith."

"You are joking me, my son. I talk about my dear friend TK all of the time."

"Yes, but what has that to do with Faith?"

His mother's eyes widened and she flicked a glance to the woman in question. Faith was not looking at them, but her shoulders were stiff with unmistakable tension. This grilling had to be causing her stress as well.

"You are *not* good friends, are you?" his mother asked, in a tone that said she no longer had any doubts about the superficial nature of their relationship.

Relieved, but unsure what had convinced her, he simply said, "We know each other."

"Not very well."

He shrugged again, but had a strong urge to deny what felt like an accusation. Though the words had been spoken in his mother's normal voice, his own emotions convicted him.

Mama shrugged, looking smug, her expression that of a woman who knew what he did not. "Faith Williams is TK."

"Your artist friend?" he asked in genuine shock. "I thought he was a man!"

"No, she is very much a female, as you can see." The laughter lacing his mother's voice did not faze him.

The memory of Faith saying maybe the woman in the statue on his dresser was letting go did. *She* was the artist of that particular piece of art. When she'd made the comment, she could have been hinting, but more likely she was exposing the true inspiration behind the figure.

Which meant what? That she had a son? "You did not tell me you had a child," he said to her.

She stood up and faced him. "If you will recall, the *father* is holding the child," she said, proving once again that their thoughts traveled similar paths.

"What is that supposed to signify?"

"Figure it out for yourself, Tino. Or better yet, ask your mother. Agata understands far more than you do and knows me much better."

He couldn't believe she was being so argumentative in front of his family. His mother was bound to realize there was more between them than a casual friendship if Faith kept this up. Hell, if he had to explain what they were talking about, things would get dicey. The statue was in his bedroom, after all. How could he explain Faith—his not so good friend—seeing it?

"It's not important," he said, in an attempt to put sand on the fire of his mother's curiosity.

"No, I don't suppose it is." Faith turned to his mother and gave her a strained smile. "It's time for me to be going."

"But I thought you would stay for dinner."

"Yes, do not let my arrival change your plans." He wanted to see Faith, even if it meant being judicious under the watchful eye of his family.

He knew it was not the smartest attitude to take. He was supposed to be cooling down their relationship, but seeing her brought into sharp relief just how hard that had been over the past weeks. How much he had *missed* her.

"I feel the need to create." She hugged his mother. "You know how it is for me when I have a fit of inspiration. You are not offended, are you?"

"Will you let me see the results of this inspiration?" Agata asked. "I am still waiting to see the pieces you made while Rocco and I were in Naples."

Faith's hand dropped to her stomach, like she was nervous. "I'll let you see them all eventually. You know that."

"You promise? I know how you artists are. Especially you. If you think a piece is not up to standards, you will pound it back into clay."

That strained smile crossed Faith's beautiful features again. "I can't promise to keep something I hate, but you should be used to that by now."

His mother gave a long-suffering sigh, but she hugged Faith warmly. "I am. You cannot blame me for trying, though. You have spoiled me, allowing me access to your work before you do others."

Faith's laugh was even more strained than her smile. "You are my friend." Even though he was wet from the pool, she hugged Giosue goodbye, as well. "I will see you next week in school."

Her leave-taking of his father was the usual kisses on both cheeks. But she simply nodded at Tino before turning to go. Though it fit in with the facade of casual friendship he had tried to create, he felt the slight like a blow to his midsection.

He understood being careful in front of his parents, but this went beyond that. Had it been deliberate? Or was she simply doing her part to allay suspicion? Unfortunately, he could not ask her, nor could he request a more warm goodbye without looking suspect himself. They would have to talk about how to act in front of his family, as it was clear that was going to be an issue in the future. He was only surprised it had taken so long for the matter to arise, now that he knew how close she was to his mother and son.

That was secondary as he watched Faith walk away, and he had to fight everything in himself not to go after her.

"And you worried your mother was developing a *tendre* for TK," his father said with a big, amused laugh.

"Never say so!" His mother shook her head. "Sometimes, my son, you are singularly obtuse."

"But he is good at business," Giosue piped in, as if trying to stand up for his deficient father and not knowing exactly what to say.

Apparently everyone else in his family knew Faith's life more intimately than he did.

He was determined to rectify that ignorance. Starting now. "Mama, what did she mean by saying that the father was holding the baby in my statue?"

It was one of the reasons he loved the piece so much. It showed the father having a tender moment with his child as well as his wife.

His mother's pause before answering gave him time to realize what a monumentally stupid question that had been to ask. He had just gotten through admonishing himself regarding this very topic and here he was drawing attention to it.

No doubt about it. Faith Williams messed up his equilibrium and made mush of his usually superior brain function.

There was nothing wrong with the way his mother's brain was working, however. "Do you mean the statue that I bought you? The one that you keep on the bureau in your *bedroom,* Valentino?" she asked delicately like a cat licking at cream.

"Yes, that is the one," he said with as much insouciance as he could muster under his mother's gimlet stare.

He offered no explanation and, surprisingly enough, she did not demand he do so. He could read the speculation in her eyes as easily as a first-year primer.

She looked down at her hands as if examining her manicure, which was incidentally perfect as usual, before looking back at him. "I'm not sure that is something she would care for me to share with you."

He wasn't about to be deterred after the huge gaffe he'd committed to get the information. "Mama," he said with exasperation. "She told me to ask you."

"*Si,* well, I suppose. You know she lost her husband to a car accident six years ago?"

"I know she is a widow, yes."

"She lost her child in the same accident."

"How horrible." It had nearly destroyed him to lose Maura; if he had lost Giosue as well, he did not know how he would have stood it.

"Just so." Mama reached out and hugged her wet grandson to her. "She sells her artwork under TK as a tribute to them. Her husband's name was Taylish and her son would have been named Kaden."

"Would have been?"

"She was pregnant. And from what she said, that was something of a minor miracle. Her life has not been an easy one. She was left an orphan by her mother's death years earlier. She never knew her father—or even who he was, I believe."

"Life has enough pain to make joy all the sweeter," his father said with the same pragmatism he spoke the well-used Sicilian proverb, *cu' avi 'nna bona vigna avi pani, vinu e linga.*

He who owns a good vineyard has bread, wine and wood.

The Sicilian people were a practical lot. The fatalism of their cultural thinking reflected in the fact that Sicilian vernacular had no future tense. Just past and present.

Regardless of his pragmatic heritage, Valentino found it almost debilitatingly painful to discover that his happy-go-lucky Faith had such a sorrow-filled past. Her optimistic nature was one of the things he found most attractive about her. She made him feel good just being around.

To discover that her attitude was in spite of past agonies, not because she had never had any, was so startling as to leave him speechless.

"I think Signora Guglielmo wanted to be a mama very much," Giosue said. "She loves all the children at school, even the bratty ones."

His son's observation made Valentino chuckle even as it made him sad for the woman who had to find an outlet for her nurturing nature with other people's children.

He remembered her once telling him that she believed she was not meant to have a family. He had assumed that meant she thought she was not cut out to be a mother. He had not minded knowing that at all, as it assured him she would not expect marriage and children someday down the road. Now he saw a far more disturbing meaning behind the words.

When Faith had said she wanted more from him, she truly had meant *more*. She wanted what she had thought she could not have. A family.

And the only way he could give it to her was to break a promise that for him was sacred.

It was not an option.

But neither was letting her go so she could find that with someone else.

CHAPTER SIX

FAITH drove like an automaton toward Pizzolato. *They'd met? They knew each other?*

Each word Tino had used to answer his mother's innocent questions had driven into her heart with the precision of an assassin's dagger. And the wounds were still raw and bleeding. As they would be for a very long time.

How could he dismiss her as if she meant *nothing* to him?

But she had the answer to that, an answer she wanted to ignore, to pretend no knowledge of for the sake of her lacerated heart. She only wished she could do it—that she could lie to herself as easily as she had deluded herself into believing things were changing between them.

He could dismiss her as someone of no importance in his life because that was exactly what she was. She was his *convenient sex partner.* Nothing more. Friends? When it was convenient for him to think so, but that clearly did not extend to times with his family.

They'd met. The words reverberated through her mind over and over again. A two-word refrain with the power to torture her emotions as effectively as a rack and bullwhip.

She did not know why he had slept with her that night in Marsala. She had no clue why he had taken her to his bed in his family home, but she knew why he hadn't called her for two weeks and had ignored her calls to him.

Perhaps he regretted that intimacy and was even hoping to end their association.

The pain that thought brought her doubled her over, and she had to pull to the side of the road. Tears came then.

She never cried, but right now she could not stop.

She sobbed, the sounds coming from her mouth like those of a wounded animal, and she had no way of stopping them, of pulling her cheerful covering around her and marching on with a smile on her face. Not now.

She had thought maybe it was her turn for happiness. Maybe this baby heralded a new time in her life, one where she did not lose everyone who she loved.

But she could see already that was not true.

She had lost Tino, or was on the verge of doing so.

Her body racked with sobs, she ached with a physical pain no one was there to assuage.

What if Tino's rejection was merely a harbinger of things to come?

What if she lost this baby, too? She could not stand it.

The first trimester was a risky one, even though her doctor had confirmed her pregnancy was viable and not ectopic. The prospect of miscarriage was a dark, scary shadow over her mind.

Falling apart at the seams like this could not be helping, but she didn't know if she had the strength to rein the tears in. How was she supposed to buck up under this new loss?

The pain did not diminish, but eventually the tears did and she was able to drive home.

She had not lied when she told Agata she felt the need to create, but the piece she did that night was not one she wanted to share with anyone. Especially not a woman as kind as Tino's mother.

Faith could not make herself destroy it, though.

Once again it embodied pain she had been unable to share with anyone else.

It was another pregnant figure, but this woman was starving, her skin stretched taut over bones etched in sharp relief in the clay. Her clothes were worn and clung to the tiny bump that indicated her pregnancy in hopeless poverty. Her hair whipped around her face, raindrops mixed with tears on the visage of a mother-to-be almost certain not to make it another month, much less carry her baby to term.

The figure reflected the emotional starvation that had plagued Faith for so long. She'd tried to feed it like a beggar would her empty belly in the streets. Teaching children art, sharing their lives. Her friendship with Agata. Her intimacy with Tino, but all of it was as precarious as the statue woman's hold on life.

Faith had no one to absolutely call her own and feared that somehow the baby she carried would be lost to her as well.

She could not let that happen.

Valentino called Faith the next day. He'd tried calling the night before several times, after Gio had gone to bed, but she had not answered. He'd hoped to see her, but she had been ignoring the phone.

It was the first time she had done so during their association. He had not liked it one bit and had resolved not to avoid her calls in the future.

This time however, she answered on the third ring, just when he thought it was going to go to voice mail again.

"Hello, Tino."

"Carina."

"Do you need something?"

"No 'How was your trip?' or anything?"

"If you had wanted to tell me about your trip, you would have called while you were away...or answered my calls to you."

Ouch. "I apologize for not doing so. I was busy." Which was the truth, just not the whole truth.

"Too busy for a thirty-second hello? I don't think so."

"I should have called," he admitted.

"It doesn't matter."

"If it offended you, it does." Of course it had offended her.

He would not have cared with any of the other bed partners he had had since Maura's death, but this was Faith. And he cared.

"I guess you didn't have time for phone sex and saw no reason to speak to me otherwise," she said in a loaded tone.

He had already apologized. What more did she want? "Now you are being foolish." They had never engaged in phone sex, though the thought was somewhat intriguing.

"I seem to make a habit of that with you."

"Not that I have noticed."

"Really?" She sighed, the sound coming across the phone line crystal clear. "You must be blind."

Something was going on here. Something bad. Perhaps he owed her more than a verbal apology for avoiding her as he had done. It was imperative they meet. "Can we get together tonight?"

"For sex only or dinner first?"

What the hell? "Is it your monthly?"

She was usually disconcertingly frank about that particular time of month and did not suffer from a big dose of PMS, but there was a first time for everything. Right?

She gasped. There was a few seconds of dead air between them. Then she said, "No, Tino. I can guarantee you it is not that time of month."

Rather than apologize for his error yet again, he said, "It sounds like we would benefit from talking, Faith. Let's meet for dinner."

"Where?"

He named a restaurant and she agreed without her usual enthusiastic approval.

"Would you rather go somewhere else?" he asked.

"No."

"All right, then. Montibello's it is."

She was early, waiting at the table when he arrived. She looked beautiful as usual, but gave a dim facsimile of her normal smile of welcome.

He leaned down and kissed her cheek. "Did you have a good day?"

Looking away, she shrugged.

This was so not like her he really began to worry. Was she ill? Or returning to the States? His stomach plummeted at the thought. "Anything you want to talk about?"

"Not particularly."

Right. He was not buying that, but obviously she was hesitant. Maybe they could ease into whatever was making her behave so strangely by talking about other things. "There is something I think we should discuss."

"Fine." The word came out clipped and infused with attitude.

Okay, then. Reverse was not a gear he used often in his professional or personal life, so he went forward with the original plan. "We need to come up with a strategy for how we behave around my family."

"You really think that's going to become a problem?" she asked in a mocking tone he'd never heard from her. "We've been sleeping together for months and have only been around them together twice in all that time. The first instance would not have occurred if you had known I was your son's teacher, and the second could have been avoided if I had known you were due to return a day earlier than expected."

"Nevertheless, the occasions did happen and I feel we should develop a strategy for dealing with similar ones when they happen again."

"I think you handled it already, Tino. Your family is under the impression we are something between bare acquaintances and casual friends." Her hands clenched tightly in her lap as she spoke.

He wanted to reach out and hold them, but that would be pushing the boundaries of what he considered safe public displays. Both for his sake and hers. He did not hide the fact that they saw each other, but he did not make it easy for others to guess at their relationship, either.

Marsala was a big enough city that he could take her to dinner at restaurants where he was unlikely to run into his business associates. Even less probable was the possibility of being seen by family. However, there were still some small-town ideals in Marsala, and Faith, as a single woman, could not afford to have her reputation tarnished if she wanted to continue teaching art at the elementary school.

"Did my saying that bother you?" Surely she understood the implications if he had reacted differently.

"Does it matter? Our relationship, such that it is, has never been about what I was comfortable with." Her eyes were filled with a hurt anger that shocked him.

"That is not true. You were no more interested in a long-term committed relationship than I was when we first met."

"Things change."

"Some things cannot." He wished that was not the case, but it was. "We do not have to lose what we do have because it cannot be *more*."

"You spent two weeks ignoring me, Tino."

"I was out of country."

It was a lame excuse and her expression said she knew it. "You forwarded my calls to voice mail."

"I needed a breathing space. I had some things to work out," he admitted. "But I have apologized. I will do so again if that will improve things for you."

She flicked her hand as if dismissing his offer. "Did you work out your *problems?*"

"I believe so."

"And it included treating me like a nonentity in your life in front of your family?" she asked with a definite edge to her voice.

"If I had not, my mother would have gotten wind of our relationship. She knows me too well."

At that moment, Faith's eyes reflected pure sorrow. "And that would have been a catastrophe?"

"Yes." He hated giving the confirmation when she looked so unhappy about the truth, but he had no choice.

"It would not be appropriate to have my mistress visiting with my family."

"I am not your mistress."

"True, but were I to try to explain the distinction to Mama, she would have us married faster than the speed of light. She likes you, Faith, and she wants more grandchildren from her oldest son."

"And the thought of marriage to me is a complete anathema to you?"

No, it was not, but that was a large part of the problem. "I do not wish to marry anyone."

"But you would do so."

"If I was absolutely convinced that was what was best for Giosue." Only, he would not marry a woman he could love, a woman who could undermine his honor.

Faith nodded and stood.

"Where are you going? We have not even ordered."

"I'm not hungry, Tino."

He stood as well. "Then we will leave."

"No."

"What do you mean?" Panic made his words come out hard and clipped.

"It's over. I don't want to see you anymore." Tears washed into her peacock-blue eyes.

For a moment they sparkled like grieving sapphires, but she blinked the moisture away along with any semblance of emotion from her face.

He could not believe the words coming out of her mouth, much less the way she seemed to be able to turn off her feelings. It was as if a stranger, not the woman he had been making love to for almost a year, stood across from him. "Because I needed some space and neglected to call you for two weeks?"

"No, though honestly? That would be enough for most women."

"You are not most women."

"No, I've been a very convenient sexual outlet, but that's over, Tino. The well is dried up." A slight hitch in her voice was the only indication she felt anything at all at saying these words.

"What the blazes are you talking about?" The well? What bloody well?

She talked like he'd been using her this past year, but there relationship had been mutual.

"You wanted me just as I wanted you."

She shrugged. *Shrugged,* damn it. Just as if this conversation wasn't of utmost importance.

"Along with agreeing that this thing between us wasn't some serious emotional connection, we also agreed that if it stopped working for either of us, we were completely free to walk away. No harm. No foul. I'm walking." Her voice was even and calm, free of her usual passion and any feeling—either positive or negative.

"How can you go from wanting more to wanting nothing?" he asked, dazed by this turn of events.

"You aren't going to give me more, and nothing is a better option than settling for what we had."

"There was no settling. You wanted me as much as I wanted you," he said again, as if repeating it might make her get the concept.

"Things change."

He cursed loudly, using a word in the Sicilian vernacular rarely heard in polite company.

"You promised."

"What did I promise?"

"To let me walk away without a big scene."

Damn it all to hell. He had, but he had never expected her to want to walk away. "What about my mother?"

"What about her? She's my friend."

"And my son?"

"He is my student."

"You do not intend to ditch either of them?"

"No."

"Only me."

"It's necessary."

"For who?"

"For me."

"Why?"

"What difference does it make? You won't give me more and I can't accept less any longer. The whys don't matter."

"I don't believe that."

"Not my problem."

"I did not know you had this hard side to you."

"I wasn't aware you could be so clingy."

Affronted at the very implication, he ground out, "I am *not* clingy."

"I'm glad to hear it. Goodbye, Tino. I'm sure I'll be seeing you around."

"Wait, Faith…"

But she was gone and the maître d' was apologizing and offering to move their table, asking what they had done to offend. Valentino had no answers for the man. He had no answers for himself.

In a near catatonic state of shock, Faith stood beside her car outside the restaurant. The coldness she had felt toward Tino at the table had permeated her body until she felt incapable of movement.

She had broken up with him.

Really, truly. Not a joke. Not with tears, or hopes he would try to talk her out of it, but with a gut-deep certainty the relationship they had, such as it was, was over.

She hadn't gone to the restaurant with the intention of breaking up. Had she?

She knew her pregnancy hormones had her emotions on a see-saw and she'd been trying to ride them out. She laughed soundlessly, her heart aching. A see-saw? More like an emotional roller coaster of death-defying height, speed and terrifying twists and turns.

She didn't just teeter from one feeling to the next, she swooped without warning.

It hadn't been easy the two weeks he had avoided her calls, but it had been even worse since Tino had denied their friendship to his mother. Faith had realized that what she believed was affection had only been the result of lust on his part. He wanted sex and she gave it to him. Only, she couldn't do that anymore.

She wouldn't risk the baby.

The doctor had said normal sexual activity wouldn't jeopardize her pregnancy, but then he didn't know her past, how easily she lost the people who meant the most to her. She'd known she would have to put Tino off from being physically intimate for at least another few weeks, but she hadn't realized that somewhere deep inside that had meant breaking things off with him completely.

It had all crystallized when he said he wouldn't marry her—at any cost. Once he knew about the baby, that attitude would change, but the underlying reasons for it wouldn't. She knew that. Just as she knew that a marriage made for reasons of duty and responsibility was the last kind she wanted.

It was one thing to marry someone knowing you loved them and they only liked you and found deep satisfaction in your body. But to marry someone you knew did *not* want to marry you and did in fact see something so wrong about you that they would marry someone else over you, that was something else entirely.

She wasn't sure she could do it.

But could she take the baby from Sicily, from its family and raise it alone, knowing it could have a better life in its father's home country? She didn't know. Thankfully, that decision did not have to be made right this second.

She forced her frozen limbs to move, and slid into her car, turning on the ignition.

She drove toward her home while those questions and more plagued her. Plagued by a question she told herself did not need an immediate answer. Her mind refused to let it go, the only eye in the storm of her emotion being that she had no intention of revealing her pregnancy until she was through the more-dangerous first trimester.

At that point she would have to have answers.

Though she normally saw the older woman at least once a week, Faith managed to avoid showing Agata the pregnancy statuary. Faith promised Tino's mother she would be the first to see all the pieces for the new show she was putting together for a New York gallery. Faith had sent pictures of the pieces she'd been doing to a gallery owner on Park Avenue who loved TK's work. The woman had called Faith, practically swooning with delight at the prospect of doing a show for the fertility pieces.

Like her emotions, Faith's work swung between hope

and despair, touching on every emotion in between. It was the most powerful stuff she'd done since the car accident that had stolen her little family. As much pain as some of the pieces caused her, she was proud of them all.

An art teacher had once told Faith's class that pain was a great source of inspiration, as was joy, but that either without the other left an artist's work lacking in some way. Faith was living proof both agony and ecstasy could reside side by side in a person's heart. And she had no doubt her work was all the better for it, even if her heart wasn't.

Tino tried calling Faith several times, but his calls were sent straight to voice mail every time. He left messages but they were ignored. He sent her text messages that received no reply either.

He could not believe his affair with Faith was over.

He wouldn't believe it.

She wasn't acting like herself, and he was going to find out why. And fix it, damn it.

Morning sickness was just that for Faith, with the nausea dissipating by noon. While that did not impact her ability to work much, it did make it more difficult on the days she taught. She'd considered canceling her classes for the first trimester, or withdrawing all together. She doubted they would want an unwed pregnant woman teaching art to their children; it was a traditional village. However, she saw little Gio only on the days she taught and she could not make herself give up those visits, brief though they were.

She loved the little boy. A lot. She hadn't realized how much she had come to see him as something more than a pupil, something like family—until she broke things off with his father and contemplated not seeing the precious boy again. She simply could not do it.

He was as sweet as ever, showing he had no idea she was now persona non grata in his papa's life. He hung back after class to talk to her and she enjoyed that. Today, though, he was fidgeting.

"Is something the matter, sweetheart?"

He grinned. "I like it when you call me that. It's like a mama would do, you know?"

Suppressing the stab of pain at his words, she reached out and brushed his hair back from his face. "I'm glad. Now, tell me if something is wrong."

"Nonna said I could invite you for dinner."

"That is very kind of her."

"Only, Papa said you probably wouldn't come."

"He did?"

Gio looked at her with pleading eyes only a heart of stone could ignore. "Why won't you come again? I thought you and Papa were friends."

"I didn't say I wouldn't come."

"So, you will?" Giosue asked, his little-boy face transforming with the light of hope.

"When does your *nonna* want me to come?"

"She said this Friday would be good."

"It just so happens I am free this Friday."

Gio grinned with delight and gave her a spontaneous hug that went straight to her heart.

Perhaps it was foolish to agree, but she couldn't stand to see the hurt of disappointment come into Giosue's eyes. Besides, Faith had told Tino that she had no intention of giving up her friendship with his mother and son. And she'd meant it.

Being pregnant with Giosue's sibling and Agata's grandchild only made those two relationships more important. Tino wasn't going away and she needed to work on her ability to be around him and remain unaffected. The dinner invitation was an opportunity to do just that.

Her unborn baby deserved to know his or her family and Faith would not allow her own feelings to stand in the way of that.

Besides there was a tiny part of her that wanted to show Tino he was wrong and that she could handle being around him just fine.

Just a small part. Really.

CHAPTER SEVEN

LESS CERTAIN OF HER ABILITY to withstand Tino's company unscathed than she had been in the safety of her art classroom, Faith rang the doorbell of the big villa.

The door opened almost immediately, making her heart skip a beat. However, it was only Giosue on the other side.

Relief flooded her, making her smile genuine. "Good evening, Gio."

"Bueno sera, signora."

She handed him a small gift.

"What is this?" he asked, his voice tinged with anticipation mixed with confusion.

"It is traditional to give one's dinner host a gift. I forgot yours when you invited me before, so I've brought it tonight along with one for your grandmother."

"Because this time she invited you?"

"Exactly."

Gio looked at the present and then up at her, his eyes shining. "Wow. Can I open it now?"

She nodded.

He ripped the package apart with the enthusiasm usually reserved for the young and sucked in a breath as he saw what was inside. They were leather gardening gloves made to fit a child's hands.

"I didn't know if you already had a pair…"

"I do, but they are made of cloth and not nearly so nice. Come, I want to show Nonno."

She smiled, glad her gift had gone over so well, and followed Gio to the lanai, Agata's favorite place to entertain. When they arrived, she saw both Agata and Rocco, but no Tino.

Relieved at what she was sure would be only a temporary respite, Faith watched Gio run to his grandfather to show him the new gloves.

Agata smiled in welcome and hugged Faith, kissing both her cheeks. "It is good to see you."

"Come, Mama, you speak as if it had been weeks rather than a few days since the last time you saw your friend." There was an edge to Tino's voice that Faith could not miss.

She wondered if Agata noticed, but the older woman seemed to be oblivious.

Shaking her head at her son, who had just arrived, she said, "Faith is a dear friend I would see every day if I could. She is good for Gio too."

"Save your matchmaking attempts for someone susceptible, Mama. I do not believe Faith likes me at all."

Oh, he was in fine form tonight. Faith refused to rise to the bait and show her chagrin at his words.

"Nonsense. You're my son, what is not to like?" Agata demanded.

Faith could make a list, but she forebore doing so for Agata's sake. See? She could handle this. She *would* handle this.

Her desire to strangle Tino for his leading comment

morphed to unwilling concern as she saw how haggard he looked. Oh, he was his usual gorgeous self, but there was a certain cast to his skin and lines around his eyes that were not usually there—all of it bespeaking a bone-deep exhaustion.

"You look tired," she blurted out.

"*Si,* this one has been working too many hours. Like a man possessed, he returns to his office after our little Gio goes to sleep and works into the early hours before returning home."

"I told you, I have some things going on that require extra attention right now."

Agata frowned. "You say that to your father and maybe he will believe you. Men! But I am your mother and you are behaving much the same as you did after Maura's death. I do not understand it."

"There is nothing to understand. I am not grieving, I am working." He said it with so much force, Faith couldn't help believing.

Agata did not look so convinced. But then, she was a mother and tended to see the softer side of her child, even if such a side did not exist.

"Is the new venture going well?"

"Yes." Tino's voice was clipped and the look he threw his mother was filled with frustration. "Regardless of what my family thinks, I am damn good at my job."

Rocco had joined them and was shaking his head. "Of course we know you are a success. How could you be anything else? You are my son, no? And I am the greatest vintner in Sicily. Why should you not be a businessman of equal talent? You are a Grisafi."

Faith was tempted to laugh, but knew Rocco would

not take it well. He was serious. Of course. But Faith had no problem seeing where Tino got his arrogance from.

"He is that," Agata said with asperity. "Which means that in this home, he is my son, not some bigshot businessman. And you are my husband, not the maker of the best wines in the country."

"Yes, of course." Rocco did not look the least cowed, but sounded more than willing to be compliant.

Agata shook her head. "Men!"

It was a word she said often over the next few hours, with the same slightly exasperated and amused tone. Faith was gratified that despite the stress of being around Tino, she found the evening highly entertaining and surprisingly comfortable.

So long as she avoided direct contact with her former lover, that is. It wasn't easy in such a small group.

And Tino wasn't helping. He had to know she found being around him difficult, but he engaged her in conversation, and she barely avoided sitting beside him at dinner. In that, Gio was her unwitting accomplice.

However, once dinner had been eaten, it was clear that Gio and Agata both intended to see that Faith and Tino spend as much time together as possible.

Right now she was being given a tour of the vineyard, ostensibly by Rocco. Only, the old man and Gio often moved ahead, or lingered behind, leaving her alone with Tino for brief spurts of time.

"You never answered my mother's question," Tino said during one of those moments.

"I don't know what you mean."

"She asked what there was about me not to like."

"She's biased. She's your mother."

"*Si,* but that's not the point."

"And what is the point?"

"That you never answered her question."

"She didn't seem bothered by that." The older woman had not brought it up again.

"Perhaps not, but I am."

"That's too bad. I'm not here to visit with you, Tino."

"My family will be disappointed. They are matchmaking."

"In vain."

"Yes, but won't you tell me why?"

He was insane. He was the one who refused to consider marriage. Ultimately, wasn't that a far more effective deterrent to his family's attempts at matchmaking than her supposed dislike of him?

"You're arrogant."

"I am a Grisafi."

"So, it comes with the territory?"

"Definitely."

She rolled her eyes.

"What else?"

"I never said I didn't like you, Tino." And she couldn't do so now in honesty. He'd hurt her, but she did like him. She loved the callous lout, but yes, she liked him, too. Just not some of his attitudes.

"You said you never wanted to see me again."

"I said our affair was over."

"And yet here you are."

"Visiting your family, Tino. Not you!"

"You could have arranged to come a different night."

"Why should I?"

He laughed, the sound too sexy for her peace of mind. And highly annoying. "Ah, proving me wrong,

Faith? Making sure that I know I don't matter enough for you to avoid dinner in my home?"

"I told you I wouldn't give up my friendship with your mother or son."

"You wanted to see me, or you would not have come tonight." He brushed her cheek with his hand. "Admit it."

She jumped back from the gentle touch that felt like a brand. "If I hadn't come, your parents would have suspected something was wrong between us. I would think *you* would have realized that and tried to avoid it. You could have made arrangements to be gone tonight without causing suspicion."

"I had no desire to do so." He shrugged, looking scarily determined.

"I don't see why."

"You have refused to answer my calls for the past week."

"That should have given you a message."

"It did. Something is wrong and I want to know what."

"I told you."

"You want more or nothing at all."

"Yes."

"I cannot give you marriage, Faith."

"You would be surprised at what you are capable of giving in the right circumstances, Tino." Why she said it, she didn't know.

The need to challenge him?

"What circumstances would those be?"

She shook her head, absolutely not going there right now. "Just leave it alone."

"I cannot."

"You have to."

"I know about your lost husband and child. I am sorry.

If I could take that old pain away, I would. But I cannot fill the gap they left in your life. That is not in my power."

Did he really believe that? And here she'd thought he was smart. "You have your own past tragedies to deal with," was all she said.

He did not get a chance to answer because they caught up with Gio and Rocco. Faith was given a fascinating description of what happened to the grapes once they were picked. She found it difficult to focus on, however with Tino a brooding presence beside her.

They were once again on their own as Gio and his grandfather had hurried back to the house much too quickly for Faith to keep up in her high-heeled sandals. "How did you find out about Taylish and Kaden?" she asked, posing the question to Tino she could not get out of her mind.

"My mother."

Stunned, Faith stopped walking altogether. She could not imagine Agata sharing Faith's confidences without a prompting to do so. Not even in the effort to matchmake. "You asked her?"

"Yes." Tino stood only a couple of feet away, but the moonlight was not strong enough to illuminate the expression in his eyes.

She could feel its intensity though.

"Wasn't that dangerous?"

"In what way?"

She rolled her eyes, though she doubted he could see it. "Don't play dumb. It showed a more-than-passing interest in me."

Something he'd said he didn't want his mother to get wind of.

"It was worse than that, even," he said, sounding

rueful, but not particularly bothered. "I allowed it to slip that we had discussed the statue in my bedroom."

Did he have any idea what he was revealing of his inner thoughts? Tino—Mr. Certainty, the man who never changed his mind and always knew best—was acting as if he did not know his own mind. Acting in direct opposition to his stated purpose. Maybe he had a deeper insight into the long-term effect of his words than she did.

She shook her head. "You're kidding."

"Sometimes my curiosity gets the better of me." He did not shrug, but the negligent movement was there in his voice.

"I guess," she said with emphasis. "I don't see your mother making a list of wedding guests as you feared."

"She is matchmaking, but being surprisingly low-key about it."

"And that doesn't bother you?"

"That she is matchmaking?"

"Yes." What the heck did he think she meant?

"So long as she maintains subtlety and does not make it into a family argument of dramatic proportions, no."

Maybe she understood his insouciance better now. "In other words, as long as it's easy for you to avoid the outcome she is looking for."

"You could put it that way."

"I just did."

"Si."

"Don't play with me, Tino."

He closed the distance between them but did not touch her. "I am not playing. I want you back."

"As your mistress."

"And my friend."

"That's not what you told your mother."

"I explained that."

"And I found your explanation lacking."

"Faith—"

Lucky for her, because she really didn't want to get into this right now—or ever really—Giosue came running up. "You two are too slow. Nonna said we could swim if you wanted, *signora*."

Faith moved toward Gio, putting distance between herself and his father once again. "Actually, I think it is time I returned home."

There was that look, the disappointment Faith hated to see, but Gio did not attempt to cajole her. He simply nodded and looked down at the ground.

And it was more effective than any type of whining might have been.

She grabbed his hand and said, "Maybe just a short swim. All right?"

He looked up at her, eyes shining. "Really, *signora?*"

"Yes."

"We can play water ball. *Zio* Calogero sent me a new net."

Faith had seen the basketball net attached to the side of the pool on a short pole. "That sounds like fun."

"Yes, it does." Tino took Gio's other hand. "Your papa will join you as well. Provided I am invited?"

"Of course, Papa." Gio's voice rang with joy.

And why shouldn't it? This was exactly what her favorite pupil wanted—the three of them together. Faith had wanted it, too, but she couldn't fight a ghost.

Tension filled her as she contemplated the next thirty minutes. She hadn't counted on Tino joining them in the pool, but she would have to deal with it. She wasn't about to renege on her promise to Gio. Though, for the first time in her life she was seriously tempted to back out on a commitment she'd made to a child.

Fifteen minutes later she was desperate enough to do so.

Tino had been teasing her, touching her under the guise of the game. A caress down her arm. A hand cupped over her hip. An arm around her waist, ostensibly to stop her from going under. But the final straw was when he brushed his lips over the sensitive spot behind her ear and whispered that he wanted her.

She shoved herself away from him and climbed out of the pool in the space of a couple seconds.

"*Signora,* where are you going?"

"It is time for me to leave." She tried to keep the frustration and anger she felt from her voice. It was not Gio's fault his father was a fiend.

"But why?" The little boy's eyes widened with confusion. "We were having fun."

"*Si.* I thought we were having a great deal of fun," Tino said with a purr.

"Really?" she asked—this time making no effort to hide her displeasure. "I'll leave it to you to explain to your son why I need to leave, then."

It was Tino's turn to look confused and he was the mirror image of his son in that moment, only older. Would their child take after him or her? What was she thinking about? This was not the time to consider whether the baby in her womb would resemble its father. Not when she wanted to bean the man.

Without another word, she spun on her heel and stormed to the cabana where she changed back into her clothes. A shower would have to wait until she got home.

She left moments later after hugging Agata and a hastily dried Gio. Rocco had gone to check on something in the wine cellars.

Her goodbye to Tino was perfunctory and verbal only.

Valentino stood outside Faith's apartment in Pizzolato, uncharacteristically hesitant to knock. The evening before had been an exercise in frustration for him. Every time he got a step closer to Faith, she took two backward. And he did not understand why.

He'd used their time in the pool to remind her of what they were both missing. Valentino was sure it had been working, too. Faith's breath had shortened, her nipples growing hard under her one-piece swimsuit. Heaven above knew he'd been hard enough to drill through cement. But then she had pushed away from him with the clear intent to reject and climbed from the pool, saying she had to go. She didn't back down, either, not even when Gio looked heartbroken.

She'd left him there to explain her precipitous departure to his upset son.

What the hell was going on with her?

It was not like her to be so unfeeling. But the look she'd given him could have stripped paint.

It had been weeks since they made love in his family home, but it was not merely her body he craved. He missed her. Like an ache in his gut that no medication could take away. Which was why he was here right now, ready to make it right.

Whatever *it* was.

He gave the closed door a glare. What was he? A wimp? He did not think so. Not Valentino Grisafi.

He knocked on the door. Loudly.

His mother had told him that Faith got caught up in her work and didn't hear the door lots of times. That she worked whenever the mood struck her, the hour of the day not a deterrent no matter how late or early. She'd said a lot more about Faith.

Add this knowledge to everything she'd told him previously about TK, and Valentino had a completely new picture of his lover, an image that convicted him about how little he'd known before. Not that it should have mattered, but with Faith it did. Their relationship would be a year old in two more weeks, and he didn't want to spend the anniversary of their first date grieving her loss.

Taking a deep breath, he knocked again.

"Coming," came from inside.

A few seconds later the door swung open. "Agata, I wasn't expect—"

"My mother is at a fundraising meeting for Giosue's school, I believe."

Faith looked at him with something like resignation and sighed. "Yes. That's what I thought she was doing."

"Are you going to invite me in?"

"Will you go away if I don't?"

"No."

"Why do you want to come in? You've never stepped foot in my building, much less my apartment. I didn't think you even knew where I lived."

He hadn't. He'd had to ask his mother, but Faith didn't need to know that. "I want to see where you work."

She grimaced, but stepped back. He followed her into the apartment. It wasn't huge, but it wasn't small, either. She'd converted the main living area, which opened to a glassed-in balcony, into her studio. The half-glass ceiling bathed the room in the glow of natural light, and he could easily see why she'd picked this location to work.

Although the area was clearly a working studio, she had created a conversation area in one corner with a love seat and two chairs around a low table decorated with traditional Sicilian tiles.

He settled into one of the chairs after declining a drink. "Is my mother the only person who visits you here?"

"No, a couple of the teachers from the school have been by, as well, but since the school day is not yet over…" She let her explanation trail off.

"What about other artists?" He was trying to get a picture of her life, but it was still pretty fuzzy and that bothered him.

She gave a half shrug. "I'm a private person."

"You always came off as friendly and outgoing to me."

She wiped at a spot of clay on her hand with the rag she held as she took the seat farthest from his. "Yes, well, maybe I should say that TK is a private person. I have some friends in the artistic community, but none of them live close enough to drop in during the middle of the day."

He considered this and what she had said about other teachers coming over sometimes, which he read to mean rarely. "You're a very solitary person, aren't you?"

She shook her head, not in negation, but as if she couldn't think what to say. "Why are you here, Tino?"

After last night she could ask that?

"I miss you." There. The bald-faced truth.

"I don't see why you should." She stiffened, drawing herself up into a ramrod sitting posture. "You still have your hand."

Shock struck him like a bolt of lightning, making it hard to breathe for just a second. "That is crude, and implies our relationship is nothing but mechanical sex."

"We no longer have a relationship."

He did not accept that, but to say so would violate their initial agreement. He decided to change the subject instead.

"Are those the pieces my mother is salivating to see?" he asked, referring to several cloth-covered shapes around the room.

"Yes. I told her she could see them when they are finished."

Sharp curiosity filled him. "She likes to see your work in progress." *He* wanted to see Faith's work.

"Not this time."

"Why not?"

"I don't want her to see them before they are cast and glazed."

"You are using the clay as models?"

"For some. There will be a numbered series cast before I break the mold for several, but some will be fired as is and be one-of-a-kind pieces."

"I know very little about your process." Even less than he knew about her.

"True." She didn't look inclined to elaborate.

But didn't most people enjoy rhapsodizing about their passions? From the way her work took over her home, he assumed her art was Faith's biggest passion. "Perhaps you would care to change that now?"

"I don't think so."

Her negative response stunned him. Though why it should, in the face of the way she'd been behaving, he didn't know. He kept expecting her to go back to acting the way she had until a few short weeks ago. "You don't feel like talking about your work?"

"I don't feel like talking to you."

"Don't be like that, *carina*." He didn't want to examine the way that made him feel, but it was not good. "We are friends."

"That's not what you told your mother."

Must she keep harping on that one moment in time, an answer to his mother's questioning he was past regretting and into mentally banging his head against a wall? "I was protecting myself, I admit it. But I was trying to protect us too, Faith. What would you have had me tell her?"

"The truth?"

"That we are lovers?" He did not think so.

She glared, her eyes snapping with anger and something akin to disgust. "That wouldn't be true, though, would it?"

"We are lovers, perhaps on hiatus, but still together."

"You are delusional. We are not and never were lovers."

"*Now* who is being delusional?"

She stood up, her hands fisted at her sides. "You have to give more than sex to be considered someone's lover. We were *sex partners*. Now we are past acquaintances."

"That is not true. We have more than sex between us." After all, that "more" had cost him the sleep of several nights.

"Oh, really?"

"Yes, *our friendship*."

"Again, let me refer you to that afternoon by the pool at your family home. You told your mother we were not friends."

"I made a mistake." There, he had said it. "I am sorry," he gritted.

"That was really hard for you, wasn't it?"

He just looked at her.

"Admitting you were wrong isn't your thing."

"It doesn't happen very often."

"Being wrong or admitting it?" she asked with dark amusement.

"Both."

"I don't suppose it does."

He too stood, taking her by the arms and standing close. "Let me back in, Faith. I need you." Those last three words were said even less frequently than an apology by him.

Tears filled her eyes. "I can't, Tino."

"Why not?"

She just shook her head.

"Tell me what is wrong. Let me make it right." He felt like he was drowning, but that wasn't right. He did not want this thing between them to end, but if it did, it shouldn't be *this* wrenching.

"You can't make it right."

"I can try."

"Can you love *me?* Can you make me your wife?"

Something inside him shattered. "No."

"Then you can't fix it."

CHAPTER EIGHT

FAITH spent the next few days in a borderline state where the numbness of loss fought the tendrils of hope each day her pregnancy continued. She missed Tino. She wanted him—both emotionally and physically. She craved his touch, but not in a sexual way, and he didn't want her to give him anything else. She wanted to be held, cuddled and comforted as her body went through the changes pregnancy brought. She wanted someone to talk to in the evenings when she found herself too tired to create but too restless to sleep.

She had not realized how much his presence in her life staved off the loneliness, until he was gone. She found herself in a pathetic state of anticipation every time she spoke to Agata, hoping the Sicilian woman would drop news about her oldest son.

Faith's morning sickness had gotten worse the past few days, but she was more adamant than ever she would not give up her job teaching. She'd lost Tino. She didn't think she could stand to lose her only contact with his son, as well. When had the little boy become so important to her? She didn't know, but she could not deny that the love she felt for the child growing inside her was in equal intensity for the emotion she felt toward her former lover's son.

One evening, almost a week after Tino had left her apartment, she got a phone call from Agata.

"*Ciao, bella.* How are you?"

"Fine."

"You were not home today."

"No, I went shopping in Marsala." She'd needed to get out. To be around other people. There were moments when she felt she was going mad from loneliness.

"I stopped by hoping to have lunch."

"Oh," Faith said with genuine regret. "I'm so sorry I missed you."

"Yes, well, I would only have begged you to show me your work."

Faith laughed. "Soon." She knew just how she was going to announce her pregnancy to her dear friend, but not until the risky first trimester was past.

How she was going to tell Agata that the baby was Tino's was less clear however.

"I would like that." There was an emotional note in Agata's tone that surprised Faith, but maybe it shouldn't have.

She'd never known another human being as connected to her art as the older woman. Not even Taylish had understood the emotion behind the pieces the way Agata did.

"So, how about lunch tomorrow?" Agata asked.

"That would be lovely."

They rang off and Faith turned to face her empty apartment, wondering if her newfound evening nausea would allow her to eat an evening meal.

* * *

Valentino's mother took the seat beside where he watched his son frolic in the pool with his papa.

The worried expression on her face concerned Valentino. He knew she had planned to call Faith. "Mama, what is the matter?"

His mother twisted her hands in an uncharacteristic display of nerves but did not answer.

"Mama."

She looked up as if just realizing he was sitting there. "Oh, did you say something, son?"

"I asked if there was anything the matter."

"Nothing bad. Well, there may well be ramifications, but I'm in a quandary and do not know what to do."

"About what?" he asked with some impatience. Was this about Faith?

His mother sighed heavily. "I did something I should not have."

"What?"

"I do not think I should say."

Valentino waited patiently. He knew his mother. She would not have said anything if she did not want to confess to someone. Apparently, he was that someone. And if it was related to Faith in any way, he was glad.

Not that he should be pining over the woman who dumped him like yesterday's garbage. She'd thrown down her ultimatum and he had refused terms. She'd been unwilling to negotiate—that should be the end of it.

Still, he waited with uncomfortable anticipation for his mother to speak.

She sighed again. Fidgeted some more and then sighed a third time. "I have a key to Faith's apartment."

"Ah." But he didn't feel nearly as insouciant as he sounded. His mother had a key to his lover's apartment, but he did not. Nor did Faith have a key to his apartment in Marsala. Why not? Why was it that his mother had spent more time in Faith's studio than he had?

They were friends. They did not limit their time together to sex. So, why had he never seen any of her works in progress? Why had he not known she was the highly successful sculptor TK?

"I stopped by today. Unannounced."

"I see." Though he didn't.

"I let myself in, you know, thinking she might be back soon." Mama shuddered. "I did a terrible thing."

"You are not the criminal type. I doubt what you did was *terrible*."

"But it *was,* my son. I wanted so badly to see Faith's newest work."

"You peeked."

"Yes, and that is bad enough—but in looking at her work, I revealed a secret she is clearly not ready to share."

"A secret?" What kind of secret? Had Faith been making clay tiles of the fifty states because she missed her homeland? What?

"*Si*. A secret. I have betrayed my friend."

"Mama, whatever it is, I am sure it will be fine. Faith loves you. She will forgive you." If only Faith was as tolerant of her lover.

"But a woman has the right to determine the timing of when she will share such news with others. I have, what is that saying your brother uses—oh, yes—I have stolen her thunder. I cannot pretend not to know when she tells me, for that would be a lie. I cannot lie to my friend." She grimaced. "I did tell her I still wanted to see her work and I do. I stopped looking after the first one because I knew. I knew what it meant."

Valentino ground his teeth and tried not to glare at his mother with impatience. "What *what* meant?"

"The statue. It is so clear to see. You could not miss it," she said, as if trying to convince Valentino.

"I am sure you are right. What was the statue of?" he asked without being able to help himself.

"It is just that I am so worried. If it means what I think, and I'm sure it does—and there is no father in sight. Things are going to get difficult for my friend."

"What does a priest have to do with Faith?"

"A priest? Who said anything about a priest? Faith is Lutheran. They have pastors, I believe."

"Mama, I don't understand. You said 'father.'"

"Yes, the father of her child."

"Child? Faith has no children. Her unborn baby died in the accident with her husband."

"The baby inside her now, Valentino."

Valentino's chest grew tight. Although he knew he was breathing, it felt like all the oxygen had disappeared from the air. "Are you saying you believe Faith is pregnant?"

"Of course that is what I have been saying. Weren't you listening? I should never have snooped. Now when she tells me, I will have to admit I already guessed. She will be let down."

His mother continued to talk, but Valentino did not hear what she said. He had surged to his feet and was trying to rush across the brickwork of the patio. But his movements were uncoordinated and jerky as his mother's words reverberated inside his head like clanging cymbals in a discordant rhythm.

Faith was pregnant?

His Faith? The woman who said she did not want to

see him anymore. The one who had ended their relationship, such as it was.

He shook his head, but the blanket of shock refused to be dislodged.

He was going to be a father again? Now? When he had thought never to remarry, when he had believed Giosue would be his only child. It was unreal but not. Part of him accepted the news with an atavistic instinct of rightness. He had no doubt the baby was his. Dismiss him though she had tried to do, Faith was his. She had been since the moment they met. Hell, a primal part of him claimed she always had been—even before they knew each other.

Even the most rational part of his mind accepted that she was his *now*. She had been with no one else since their first time together, and probably for a long time before that.

He yanked open the door of his Jaguar and climbed inside, slamming it again as he started the car with a loud roar of the engine, and then tearing out of the drive.

How was she pregnant?

They used birth control. Religiously. Rather, he did. Still, there had only been a handful of times that their protection had not been one hundred percent. After each slip, he would be beset by guilt, and work extrahard in future to make sure they were covered.

With a sense of inevitability, he realized one of those times had not been too long ago.

He'd taken Faith to dinner at a favorite trattoria. Instead of sitting outside, so they could watch people on the street—as Faith was wont to do—Valentino had asked for some privacy. They had been given a table in the back corner, the restaurant lighting barely reaching into the shadows that surrounded it. The light from the single candle in the center of the table set a romantic mood.

At least, he'd thought so.

Faith frowned as he helped her take her seat. "I know our relationship isn't common knowledge, but do we have to hide in the dark?"

He leaned down and whispered in her ear. "I thought we could entertain ourselves over dinner, rather than finding our amusement in watching other people."

The embarrassing truth was that Faith liked people-watching—sometimes too much. She paid more attention to the ones surrounding them than to him, and he did not like that. Tonight he was determined to have her entire focus. If it took seducing her publicly, so be it.

And that is exactly what he did, starting with a kiss just below the shell of her ear, using both teeth and tongue as well as his lips.

She was shivering and had made a small whimpering sound by the time he finished and took his own seat across the small table from her.

"Considering what you apparently have planned for our *entertainment,* I now understand why you asked for a table hidden away from curious eyes." Faith smoothed her top, accentuating the way the silky fabric clung to her breasts and exposing hardened nipples, despite two thin layers of fabric over them.

"You think you can survive one evening without people-watching?" he asked, his voice husky with the desire sparking his senses.

"I have a feeling you can make it worth my while."

"You must be psychic," he teased. "For I plan to."

"Call it an educated guess. I've been at the receiving end of your tender mercies too often to discount their effect."

"Good." He had every intention of lavishing those mercies on her tonight.

They teased each other over dinner, working their desire to a fever pitch. He was tempted to find an even darker corner and bring them both to completion right then and there. He refrained, determined to make the night a memorable one for his beautiful lover.

Her peacock-blue eyes were glazed with passion, her lips swollen as if they'd been kissed, and her breathing was shallow and quick. Her nipples were so hard they created shoals in the fabric over them and she'd squirmed in her seat more than once.

"Having trouble, *carina americana mia?*" He meant his voice to be joking, but it came out deep and sensual instead.

A competitive glint shone in her gaze along with the passion. "I think no more than you."

She'd definitely done her utmost to turn him inside out, and she had succeeded.

He reached across the table and brushed her cheek in a rare public display of affection. "I think it is time to make our way to my apartment."

"Yes."

Back in his apartment, they wasted no time in disposing of their clothing, but once they landed naked on the bed, he forced a slowing of the pace. It wasn't easy, he wanted nothing more than to bury himself in her wet, silken depths, but there was more to making love than reaching an orgasm.

There was the element of driving your partner out of her mind.

Her hands were everywhere in a blatant bid to side-track him from his silently stated intention, and he had to gather both her wrists in one hand and hold them above her head.

She gasped, her body bowing in clear need. "Kinky, Tino."

"Necessary, *tesoro*."

"Why?"

"I want you out of your mind with pleasure."

"I'm already there."

"No." He kissed her, sweeping her mouth with his tongue. He pulled back. "You can still talk."

And then he set about taking care of that. He kissed his way down her throat, sucking up a bruise in the dip right below her clavicle bone. His mark.

She shuddered and cried out, like she always did when his hormones got the best of him and he gave her a hickey like he was still an adolescent learning his way around a woman. Maybe that's why he regressed so often.

He moved to her breasts, taking one in his free hand and laving the other with his tongue. Eventually, after a lot of mewling and half-formed words from the dead-to-rights sexy woman below him, he zeroed in on her nipples. He didn't play. He focused. He plucked. And he pleasured.

She screamed.

She arched.

She came, her body going rigid and then shaking.

He released her hands and rolled on top of her, using the head of his penis to tease the swollen nub of her clitoris. She cried out incoherently and he kept it up. Her legs locked around his and she pressed upward, forcing him inside. He rocked and kissed her until he was on the verge of climaxing himself.

It was only then that he remembered the condom he wasn't wearing.

With more self-control than he thought he had, he pulled out and reached for the bedside drawer where he kept his supplies before surging back inside her.

When he came, she was screaming his name and convulsing around him in a second more-intense orgasm.

Remembering made him harder than a rock and twice as immovable.

That night had happened somewhere between two and three months ago. If he looked at his PDA, he could get an exact date. It was something he'd kept track of as zealously as he had their birth control itself. Only, the timing had never come to anything before. Maybe that was why he hadn't been worried along these lines in this instance?

The possibility that Faith might be carrying his child had not even occurred to him. Why would it? A woman didn't break up with the man whose child she carried.

He spit forth a vicious curse as he yanked the door open on his Jaguar. It was entirely too possible, though.

And rather than tell him, Faith had booted Valentino from her life.

Why? What was she thinking? Did she believe he would allow her to take his child back to America and raise it, ignorant of its Sicilian family?

Did she think he would not find out? That he would disappear from her life as easily as she dismissed him from hers?

She did not know him very well, if that was the case. It seemed they both had a great deal to learn about each other.

Something didn't make any sense, though. If she had wanted to marry him as she had hinted, why had she kept this a secret? Surely she knew he would never deny his child the right to his name and heritage. What was the matter with her?

Then he remembered how irrational Maura had gotten on a few occasions while she was pregnant with Giosue.

Faith was no doubt suffering the same emotional fragility. He would have to get himself under control. He could not allow the fury coursing through him a vent. Not in her current condition. He would have to remain calm.

And he would have to remember she was not thinking clearly.

It was his responsibility to make things right and that was something he was good at. Fixing things for others. Had he not taken a slowly sinking vineyard, at risk of closing its doors before the next generation was old enough to take over, and made it a diversified, multinational company?

He had saved the Grisafi heritage and when his younger brother and their father were at loggerheads, Valentino had salvaged the relationship by sending his brother across the ocean to run their offices in New York. The two strong-headed men spoke on the phone weekly and rarely argued any longer.

The only thing he had failed to fix was his wife's illness. He had not been able to save Maura, and he had paid the price for his inability, but he wasn't going to lose another woman who depended on him.

Loud knocking startled Faith from a fitful doze. She sat up, looking around her small apartment in disoriented semiwakefulness.

The pounding sounded again and she realized it was coming from her door. She stumbled to her feet and made her way toward it, swinging the door open just as Tino raised his hand to knock again.

He dropped his arm immediately, a look of relief disparate to the situation crossing his handsome features. "Thank the *madre vergine*. I tried knocking quietly, but you did not hear me." He reached out as if to touch her, but didn't—letting his hand drop to his side once again. "Were you working? Is that safe now? Do the clay or glazes have dangerous fumes? This is something we need to look into. I do not wish to demand you give up your passion, but it may be necessary for these final months."

"Tino?" Was she still too groggy to make sense of his words, or had her former lover lost his mind?

"Si?"

"You're babbling." She'd never heard him say so many words without taking a breath. And none of them made any sense. "You sound like your mother when she gets a bee in her bonnet."

"Mama does not keep insects in her wardrobe and she would not thank you for implying otherwise."

"It's an expression, for Heaven's sake. What is the matter with you tonight?"

"You need to ask me this?" he demanded in a highly censorious voice. His eyes closed and he groaned, just a little, but it was definitely a groan. "Excuse me, Faith."

"Uh, okay?" she asked, rather than said.

He took three deep breaths, letting each one out slower than the one before. Then he opened his eyes and looked at her with this Zen-like expression that was almost as weird as his babbling. "May I come in?"

"You're asking me?" Not demanding she invite him in. Not just forging ahead, assuming he was welcome? "What's going on, Tino?"

He didn't answer, simply giving the room behind her a significant look.

"Oh, all right. Come in." She stepped back.

It wasn't the most gracious invitation she had ever extended, but she was still disoriented from falling asleep after speaking to Agata on the phone. And Tino was acting strange.

Really. Really.

"Can I get you something to drink?"

"I could use a whiskey," he said in an odd tone. "But I will get it. You sit down."

"You've only been here once before, Tino. You don't know where I keep anything."

His hands fisted at his sides, but then the Zen thing was back and he said in a very patient tone, "So tell me."

She knew he wanted her back, but enough to sublimate his usually passionate nature? She would never have guessed.

"Why don't I just get us our drinks instead?"

"You aren't having whiskey, are you?"

She rolled her eyes. "I never drink hard spirits. You know that."

But he'd never acted as if he thought she shouldn't before. Though, considering how tipsy she got on a single glass of wine, perhaps his concern made a certain kind of sense. And honestly, she'd never implied she wanted to drink hard liquor before. But still. "What's the matter with you tonight?"

"We have things to discuss."

"We've done all the talking that needs doing." For right now, anyway. She was frankly too tired and too nauseous to rehash their breakup. She was feeling week and wishing he would just hold her.

She had to get a handle on these cravings. Or she was going to do something stupid, like ask him to fulfill them.

He didn't bother answering. He simply guided her back to the small love seat she'd been dozing on and pressed her to sit down. Bemused by his insistence on getting their beverages, she did. He then picked up her feet and turned her so that they rested on the love seat as well.

Apparently not content with that level of coddling, he tucked the throw she'd been sleeping under around her legs.

He nodded, as if in approval. "I will get our drinks now."

He was seriously working on getting back in her good graces. But no amount of tender care could make up for his refusal to see her as nothing more than a casual lover. Why couldn't he see that?

"If you insist on serving, I'd like a cup of tea." Something that hopefully would settle her tummy. "There is some ginger tea in the cupboard above the kettle. That's where you'll find the whiskey, as well."

An unopened bottle she had purchased in the hope that one day he would break his pattern and show enough interest in her life outside their sexual trysts to come see her.

He went to the kitchen area, nothing more than an alcove off the main living area, really. She watched him fill the kettle and flip the switch to heat the water. The domesticity of the scene tugged at her helter-skelter emotions. It was so much like something she wanted to experience all the time—for the right reasons—that stupid tears burned her eyes before she resolutely blinked them away.

He pulled down the box of tea and the bottle of whiskey from the cupboard. "I've never had ginger tea before."

She had. When she'd been pregnant before. And she was one of the lucky women it helped. "It's not something I drink often."

He gave her an enigmatic look but said nothing as he poured his own drink and waited for her water to boil.

She didn't ask him why he was there or what he wanted to talk about, because the answer was obvious. He wanted her back in his bed, but she'd do her best to avoid that particular conversation. "How is Gio?"

"You saw him only three days ago."

She shrugged. "I wish I taught more days a week," she admitted, before her brain caught up with her mouth.

"I understand."

"You do?"

"You hold my son in deep affection."

"He's easy to love."

"I agree."

"Um…"

"He wishes he could see you more often, as well."

"I know." Only, his father did not want them to grow closer. He'd made that clear.

"I think we can rectify that problem soon enough."

How? Was he going to up the ante of getting her back in bed by offering time with his family on a regular basis? Her rather creative and active imagination offered up a second option. One a lot less palatable.

Maybe he had decided to remarry after all. To find the paragon of Sicilian virtue he thought Gio deserved as a stepmother. Someone who would eradicate the child's fantasies about being his favorite teacher's son.

Faith went from weepy to annoyed in the space of a heartbeat. "I wouldn't rush into anything if I were you."

"And yet some things require quick action."

"Marriage isn't one of them."

Surprise showed clearly on Tino's face. "You believe I plan to marry?"

"Isn't that the way you plan to fix your son's desire to see me more?" Provide the little boy with a mother so he wouldn't miss the teacher he had decided he wanted in that capacity.

"It is, in fact."

Despite everything—knowing how he felt, knowing that he did not want her in his life like that—at Tino's words, unpleasant shock coursed through Faith. Somewhere deep inside, she had believed he would not go that far.

Her stomach tightened in a now familiar warning and she shot to her feet, kicking the lap blanket away. When she reached the commode, she retched. Though, since she had not been hungry earlier, she did nothing but dry heave. It hurt and it scared her. Though she knew that the cramps were in her stomach and not her womb, a tiny part of her brain kept saying it was one and the same.

Tino had come into the small room with her and she could hear water running, but she couldn't look up long enough to see what he was doing. Then a cold, damp cloth draped the nape of her neck while another one was pressed gently to her forehead. Tino rubbed her back in a soothing circular motion, crooning to her in Italian.

The heaving stopped and she found herself leaning sideways into his strength. He said nothing, just let her draw heat and comfort from his touch. She didn't know how long they remained like that—him crouching around her like a protective angel—her kneeling on the floor, but eventually she moved to stand.

He helped her, gently wiping her face with one damp cloth before tossing them both in her small sink. "Better?"

She nodded. "I don't like being sick."

"I do not imagine you do." He handed her a glass of water.

She rinsed her mouth before drinking some down. Placing the glass down by the sink, she turned to leave and weaved a bit.

Suddenly she found herself lifted in the strong arms she had been craving earlier. There was no thought to protest. She needed this. Even if it was a moment of fantasy in her rapidly failing reality.

He carried her to her minuscule bedroom, barely big enough for the double-size bed—another purchase made with hope for something that had never developed between them—and single bedside table that occupied it.

He sat her on the bed, reaching around her to arrange her pillows into a support for her back. Then he helped her to settle against them. It was all too much, too like what she secretly craved that she felt those stupid tears burning her eyes again.

Ignoring the overwrought emotions she knew were a result of pregnancy hormones, she teased, "How did you know where my bedroom was?"

"Instinct?"

She forced a laugh that came out sounding hollow rather than amused, but it was better than crying like a weakling. "Are you saying you have a homing device for beds?"

"Maybe beds belonging to you." He brushed her hair

back from one side of her temple and smiled, the look almost tender.

But she knew better. "This is the only one I have."

"For the last year, almost, you have been sharing the bed in my apartment in Marsala and you have shared my bed in my family home."

"Are you trying to say those beds belong to me in some way now?" she asked, unable to completely quell her sarcasm at such a thought.

"Yes."

She gasped but could think of nothing to say in reply until she spluttered, "That's— It's *ridiculous*."

He shrugged. "We will agree to disagree."

After everything he had said? She didn't think so. "We will?" she asked in a tone she used so rarely he'd probably never heard it.

He gave her that Zen look again and nodded, as if he had no idea he was in imminent danger of being beaned upside the head with a pillow. "It is the only rational thing to do. You clearly do not need to upset yourself."

"I..." She wanted to tell him he was wrong, but she couldn't. She didn't relish the thought of more dry heaves at all. She wanted to say she didn't know what was wrong, or that she had a touch of the flu or something...anything but the truth. Only, she could not, *would* not lie.

He patted her arm. "Rest here. I will get your tea."

"Fine, but your beds don't belong to me in any way, Tino. You made that clear."

Not a single spark of irritation fluctuated his features. What in the world was going on?

CHAPTER NINE

VALENTINO slammed back the scotch whiskey. It was his favorite brand. An unopened bottle before tonight. There was a message there he did not have time to contemplate.

Faith needed him.

It was worse than he had expected. She was obviously suffering from uncommonly bad morning sickness. After all, it was no longer *morning,* but she was definitely sick.

Maura had been lucky. She had only experienced the lightest amount. However Tino's mother had regaled him with stories of her own debilitating morning sickness when he had become worried during Maura's pregnancy. She'd said over and over again how relieved she was Maura's pregnancy nausea was so light and confined itself to mornings.

Faith's did not.

And that made Valentino feel guilty. After all, she was pregnant with *his* child. He did not want his *carina americana* to be sick.

He would not allow it.

There was only one thing to do.

* * *

Faith could hear Tino's voice, but couldn't imagine who he was talking to. She hadn't heard a phone ring.

Was he muttering to himself? He did that sometimes when he worked at his state-of-the-art laptop when they were together. Only he didn't have his computer and she had a hard time imagining him working instead of bringing her tea. Nor could she imagine him making a business call. He might not love her, but he was not heartless.

He'd actually proven himself to be a more than adequate nurse the one time she'd caught a cold the previous winter. Her illness had brought out a soft side to her stoic, businessman lover. Not quite as concerned as the one now, but then she hadn't been puking then, either.

He'd gotten plenty upset over her stuffy nose, fever and headache.

So, where the heck was he with her tea?

She was on the verge of going after it herself when he walked into the small room, filling it with his presence. Why had he decided to come see her *after* they'd broken up? Even this brief visit was going to haunt her when she tried to sleep in her lonely bed at night.

He placed a steaming mug and a small plate with crackers and mild cheese on it on the table beside her bed. Then he leaned down to adjust the pillows so she could sit up more fully.

"I'm not an invalid, you know." She winced at the crabby tone to her own voice. Ashamed, she laid her hand on his wrist as he reached for the tea again. "I'm sorry. Thank you for getting my tea."

"Do not worry about it. Moodiness is to be expected." He spoke with all the patience of a man bent on humoring the woman in his life.

Only she wasn't in his life. Was she? Right now, it sure didn't feel like they'd broken up.

And she *had* been moody when she'd been sick before. And he'd been patient. She was sure he had been the ideal husband during Maura's pregnancy. And even though he was only being so nice because he thought she was ill, she would take what she could get. "Thanks for being so understanding."

He settled onto the bed beside her, careful not to jostle and handed her the mug. "Drink."

"Bossy."

He shrugged.

She took a sip. "It's sweet." Very.

"The doctor said sugar might help with the nausea. He said the crackers and a nonpungent cheese might also help."

"What doctor?"

"The one I called."

"Overkill, Tino." But sweet. Even sweeter than the tea. She took another sip. The well-sugared beverage did seem to be helping with her upset stomach.

"Not at all. When in doubt, go to an expert."

She shook her head. "You're too funny sometimes."

"Right now I am not laughing."

No, he wasn't. He looked genuinely worried and *guilty*. "It's not your fault I got sick."

"I think it was."

"No. I…it's been like this for the past few days." That at least was pure truth, if not the entire truth.

"Only a few days. It was better before?"

"Naturally."

He examined her, as if he was trying to decide if he believed her or not. She ignored him and took a bite of cheese and cracker. Oh, that did hit the spot. Her empty stomach began to rumble for more sustenance.

"You have not eaten?"

"I wasn't hungry."

"You must take care of yourself. You cannot skip meals."

He was right, even if he didn't know how much. "I'll do better in future."

"I will see that you do."

"Right, because we spend so much time together. I mean before we broke up."

"I do not consider us broken up."

"Don't be arrogant."

"I cannot force you to stay with me, but surely circumstances dictate a certain level of leniency on your part?"

The admission shocked her. She'd always gotten the impression that Tino thought he could make anything happen if he worked at it hard enough. She supposed his words indicated a necessary level of respect for her. But she did not get where he expected tolerance from her.

If he knew she was pregnant, that would be one thing, but there was no way he could know. She didn't show any physical signs and she hadn't told anyone but her doctor. Even if by some weird stroke of coincidence, Tino and her doctor were friends, the older man was hardly likely to chat about his patients.

No, there was no way Tino could know, but he was acting very strangely.

"Uh, Tino, you're being really odd tonight."

"You think so?" he asked.

"Yes, but, uh…that's okay. No need to explain."

"You think not?"

"No, really. We all have our moments."

"Funny, I have never been accused of having *mine* before."

"You're serious?"

"Definitely."

"You need to get out more."

"Lately I have had little excuse for getting out."

"You mean you haven't started shopping for that new wife yet?" The words came rolling off her tongue, a ball of bitterness landing between them.

"I do not need to shop."

"You already know her?" Who was it? Faith tried to think of the women Agata had mentioned, but no one came forth as a potential candidate for Tino's new wife.

"Intimately."

"You bastard." Her hand shot out in an involuntary arc that ended in a crack against his cheek. Shocked at her own actions, she nevertheless cried, "We promised each other exclusivity!"

He grabbed her hand—and examined it for damage. "Did you hurt yourself? You should not get so worked up. You are going to be sick again."

"And whose fault is that?" She meant to sound accusing, but the words came out sounding weak. Bewildered.

Because that was what she felt.

Why wasn't he furious with her?

She'd slapped him. A lump lodged in her throat, and she did her best to swallow it down without giving vent to the emotions roiling through her. She wasn't a violent person. He knew that, but she'd broken her own personal code without thought. She would have imagined he would be spitting nails in anger right now, but he was looking at her with a peculiar expression of indulgence.

"Do you know my doctor?" she asked suspiciously.

"Not that I am aware of, no."

"You don't have psychic tendencies I don't know about?"

"Definitely not."

Okay, so he couldn't possibly know about the baby. "You just admitted to cheating on me," she said, her words laced with pain she couldn't begin to suppress in her current state.

His expression zoomed to total affront in less than a second and was tempered by concern only a half a second later. "I did no such thing. I am no liar. I do not cheat."

"You lied to your mom, about us being friends." She tugged her hand out of his grip.

"I have come to realize I know too little about you to call you a true friend. I will be rectifying this in the future, however. I have already taken some steps to do so."

"You expect me to be your friend when you marry another woman?" None of this was making any sense. He could not be so cruel.

"You are being irrational. This is to be expected, but please remember what kind of man I am before you start flinging such offensive accusations."

She stared at him, totally at a loss as to what to say.

"I did not say I was going to marry another woman."

"Yes, you did." Did he think she would ever have made something so painful up in her own mind?

"I did not."

"I'm nauseous, not nuts. I know what I heard you say." And it had hurt.

"I said I planned to marry."

"Exactly."

"I did not say I planned to marry *someone else*."

He could not mean it. She shook her head. "You don't... You won't... I'm not..."

It was his turn to roll his eyes. "I do. I will. You are."

"Are you asking me to marry you?" In what she might describe as the least-romantic proposal ever. Getting her so upset she had been sick was not the way to a woman's heart.

He flinched, just slightly, but she saw it. "More informing you that I am willing to meet your terms."

Terms. A sinking feeling drained the energy from her and she fell back against the pillows. "You want me in your bed so much you are willing to marry me?"

He didn't answer.

"No. I don't believe that."

"Does it matter what my reasons are?"

"Yes."

"You need me. I need you. We need to marry." He shrugged. "My family loves you already."

She ignored the bit about his family. He hadn't been so quiescent about their affection for her before. "You need my body, not me."

"Stop overanalyzing this."

"Then tell me why. The truth."

He sighed, looking away. "You did not ask me how my mother is."

"I spoke to her on the phone tonight. I know how she is."

"You noticed her upset?"

"She's upset?" No, Faith hadn't noticed. Had she gotten so wrapped up in her own challenges, she ignored a friend in need?

"Very. She feels she betrayed you."

What? Could this night get any more unreal? "How?"

"She came by to see you today at lunch."

"I know. I wasn't home."

"She has a key to your apartment."

"Yes." She'd given it to Agata in case of an emergency. It had made Faith feel like she had someone in the world who cared enough to check on her.

"She used it."

"So?"

"Her curiosity got the better of her."

Understanding washed over Faith in a wave of despair. He *did* know she was pregnant. Everything he had done and said in the last hour now made complete and total sense. Even that bit of tenderness she'd thought she'd seen in his eyes. It had been for the flicker of life within her womb.

"You know." Her voice came out a whisper, but it was the best she could do as those pesky tears she'd been fighting since his arrival redoubled their efforts to expose her weakness.

"I do." He laid his hand on her stomach, leaving no doubt about exactly what they were discussing.

"She guessed."

"Yes."

"I knew she would if she saw the statues."

"She saw only one, but it was enough."

"And she told you?"

"When Mama is upset, she vents. My father was swimming with Giosue."

"So, she vented to you."

"*Si.*"

"And you assumed you were the father."

"As you said, we promised exclusivity."

"You had no doubts about my integrity."

"No."

"And now you want to marry me."

"I have no choice." He took Faith's hand between both of his much larger ones. "*We* have no choice."

She shook her head.

"Be reasonable, Faith. It is the only way."

"No. It… We… There are other options."

Acute horror darkened his eyes to near black. "You would not abort our child."

"No, I wouldn't, and if you really knew me at all, *you* would know that."

"I told you that was something I planned to correct."

"Be still my heart."

"Do not mock me, Faith."

She took a fortifying sip of tea. "I don't have to marry you."

"You would deny my child his father?"

"Sheesh, Tino, you are so all or nothing. First you think I'm going to have an abortion and now you think I'm going to refuse you parental rights."

"Are you?"

So much for his trust in her integrity. "No."

"So, marry me."

"There are other choices."

"None that are as good."

"Right, because marriage for the sake of a baby is going to create a family that baby is going to love being raised in."

"We are compatible—there is nothing wrong with this picture."

"You left out one little aspect that is supposed to exist in marriage."

"What?"

Could he really be that dense? "Love, Tino. I'm talking about love."

"We care for each other."

So much that this was only the second time he had ever been to her apartment. "It's not enough."

"It is. Many people marry with less."

"I loved Taylish and he loved me." Maybe they hadn't felt the same kind of love for each other, but the love had been there.

Tino's jaw hardened. "I loved Maura, but she is gone as is your Taylish. *We* are here now. That is all that matters."

"Not even. You were completely unwilling to entertain the idea of marriage before."

"I did not know you carried my child."

Did he have any concept of the kind of damage his words were doing to her heart? Of course not. Love had not come up between them until she asked for it. He couldn't begin to understand how much his attitude hurt.

She hunched her shoulders, hugging herself, but the cold was seeping into her heart, anyway. "I knew it."

"Knew what?"

"That if I told you I was pregnant, you would insist on marriage. Do you even begin to see how feudal-lord your thinking is?"

"I am a Grisafi." As if that said it all.

"Well, I'm not and I'm not sure I want to be one, either."

His already-tense jaw developed a tic, but his voice remained even. "My mother's heart would be broken to hear you say that."

"I wouldn't be marrying your mother."

"I should hope not." He laughed, the sound low and sexy despite the topic of their conversation—or maybe because of it.

Marriage to Tino. A dream come true for all the wrong reasons.

He put his arm over her thighs in a proprietary gesture she did not miss the meaning of. "You say there are other options."

"There are."

"Name them."

"I didn't say you were going to like them," she felt the need to warn.

"If they do not include marriage between us, I think that is safe to assume." The Zen tone of ultimate patience was back.

"They don't."

He just waited.

"Fine, but I want to point out that I'm in no condition to argue."

Amusement flickered in his dark gaze. "I did not notice you having any trouble doing so up to this point."

"I mean it, Tino. I've had my limit of upset for the evening."

His expression went ultraserious. "I will not distress you again."

She nodded, knowing full well she was taking advantage. But the truth was? She *didn't* want to argue. Her emotional reserves had been in the negative totals for weeks now.

"I could go back to America and raise the baby there. You could visit."

She waited for the explosion, but it never came. He simply sat there staring at her.

"Nothing to say?" she had to ask.

He shook his head, and it was then she realized his jaw was clenched tight.

"I don't want to do that."

"Good." He bit the word out, but the sense of relief he felt was palpable.

"I was just pointing out that it was an option." And trying to hurt him back a little for the pain he had dealt her? The thought mortified her. She was not that kind of person.

"Noted."

"I want to stay in Sicily," she said quickly, wanting him to know right away she wasn't going to hurt him with the baby. "I love it here and I want our child to grow up knowing its family. The Grisafis are all he or she has in the way of extended relatives, and they're wonderful people to boot." She tried a tentative smile.

He did not return it. "So, marry me."

She wanted to, badly, but not merely for the sake of the baby. "I could stay here."

Appalled was the only word to describe his look. "In *this* apartment?"

"It is kind of small for a baby." She bit her lip, wincing when it drew blood. "I could find a bigger place."

"You can move into the family home."

"I considered that." She had, after examining every other alternative—living with the Grisafis was the only way she could give the baby the life it deserved. Not monetarily—she was set in that regard—but the daily access to people who would love the baby and the baby would grow to love. Including its father.

That didn't mean he would have access to her. That point was not negotiable. But she wanted her baby to have a family. The pain of growing up without her parents had dulled with time, but never disappeared. She wanted her baby to have its grandparents, its brother, its father close by—to live in a home filled with love and people who would enrich the baby's life.

The Grisafi home was big enough to accommodate her and the baby in a set of rooms that would be much like having her own apartment. And yet there would be easy and consistent access to familial ties important to the baby's well-being.

"So, you will marry me."

"That's not what I said. I can live in your family home without being your wife. It's definitely big enough."

"Why would you deny me my rightful place in my child's life?"

"I will not do that. You will be named on the birth certificate, the baby can have the Grisafi name."

"But you do not want it."

She was about to say no, but she could not force the word from her mouth. So she shook her head.

"Why, Faith? When you wanted marriage before I knew?"

"That's exactly why."

"I do not understand."

"I think you do."

"You feel slighted because I will marry you for the baby's sake and not your own."

"Yes."

"That is childish thinking, Faith." Not, *I care about you, too.* Not, *It's not the way it looks.* No, just an accusation of immaturity.

Faith's resolve not to be pressured into anything doubled. "Believe what you like, but I am not running to the courthouse for a quickie marriage."

His bark of laughter was mocking. "As if my mother would allow such a thing."

Faith just glared at him.

"You will move in, though?"

"I said it was something I was considering. That it was an option."

"It is the best option you have suggested so far."

"Actually, you suggested it."

"But you had considered it?"

"Yes."

"Favorably?"

"Yes."

"So, what is stopping you from agreeing?"

"I'm not sure I want to live in the same house as you," she answered honestly.

He reeled back as if struck. "You hate me so much."

"I don't hate you at all, but I'm not sure this is what is best for us."

"It is best for the baby and that is all that matters."

"On that point we agree."

"So, you will move in."

"You're stubborn."

"Very."

She sighed.

He took it as acquiescence, if the grim satisfaction on his face could be believed. "How soon?"

"I haven't agreed, Tino," she pointed out. "If I decide that's the best course of action, and provided your parents approve the idea, I would move in after the baby is born."

"You need looking after *now*. Tonight proves that."

"Tonight I thought you were telling me that the father of my unborn child wanted to marry another woman. *A suitable Sicilian woman*."

"Stress induced your stomach upset?"

"Yes, I think so."

"We will have to make sure you are not distressed in any way from this point forward."

"I would appreciate that." If she had known it would be so easy, she would have played the illness card earlier. Exhaustion overcame her, like it did sometimes lately. "I'm tired," she said, knowing he had to be able to see it. "We can talk more about this at a later time."

"Very well."

She reached up and brushed his cheek, needing to say one last thing before he left for the night. "I'm sorry I slapped you."

"I forgive you."

"Thank you," she slurred as sleep overtook her.

CHAPTER TEN

FAITH had fallen asleep. Just like that.

Thirty seconds later and her breathing had already leveled out into true somnolence. It always amazed him how she could do that, though the only other times he'd seen it was after they had made love. They hadn't done so tonight.

Yet, here she was—sleeping. Dark bruises marred the lovely skin below her eyes. Her pregnancy was taking it out of her. It bothered him to see her looking so frail. Was she taking her vitamins? Had she gone to a doctor? There were so many questions he needed answered, but she wasn't going to be satisfying his need to know right now.

It wouldn't be until morning, if he had his way and she slept the night through. He was careful not to jostle her unduly as he removed her clothes to increase her comfort. He could not help but stop and look at the changes her pregnancy had already wrought on her beautiful body.

With near reverence, he cataloged each one. Her breasts were slightly bigger and the aureoles had darkened. She had an exhausted air about her, but she glowed too, her skin reflecting an overall abundance of health. He could see no evidence of the baby within in the curve of her belly. It was no bigger.

The need to touch was intense and he carefully placed his hand over her lower abdomen, a sense of awe permeating him. It might not look different, but although he might be being fanciful, he would swear he could feel the presence of his child in her womb. Usually when he massaged her tummy, the flesh was soft with feminine give. Now below the silken skin, it felt hard, solid. Amazing.

She made a soft noise and turned on her side to curl into her pillow.

He found himself smiling, but then frowned in thought. He knew she expected him to leave, but he wasn't going to. He'd agreed not to argue; he hadn't agreed to vacate her apartment, leaving her alone, with no one to care for her needs.

He flipped out his cell and called home to tell his parents he would not be returning tonight. Thankfully, his father answered, so Tino was not subjected to a barrage of questions when he said he would not be home that night. His mother tried calling ten minutes later, but he let the call go to voice mail. He wasn't ready to speak to her yet.

He and Faith had some explaining to do and Tino was determined to do it on his own agenda and in his own way.

Faith woke up with a sense of well-being that had been missing for the past several weeks. The sense that she had been held in strong arms all night long tickled at her conscience, but she dismissed it as leftover dreams from the night before. Just like so many other mornings.

Her stomach was slightly upset, but nothing like the night before. Memories of Tino's visit beset her, but she wasn't ready to deal with the implications of his discovery. Not if she wanted to keep a handle on the physical side effects of her pregnancy. She would keep her mind blank, and if she moved slowly, hopefully she could avoid anything beyond the mild nausea.

She started with opening her eyes and orienting herself to her surroundings. The first thing she noticed was the mug of tea on her bedside table. Steam was coming from it. The cheese and crackers on the plate beside it looked fresh, as did the grapes accompanying it.

Trying to make sense of the fresh libations, she sat up carefully. No matter how curious she was, she wasn't going to jostle her queasy tummy.

As the sheets slid against her skin, she realized she was naked.

Completely and totally.

"Tino!"

Despite the evidence of his presence, she was still shocked when he came rushing in. And looking too damn good in nothing but his boxers, too. "Are you all right, *piccola madre mia?* Did you try the tea? It should settle your stomach. Do you need help to the bathroom?"

The babbling would be endearing if, well…maybe it was endearing regardless, but still. And calling her his little mother, that was…it was…she didn't know what it was. Cute? Maybe. "What are you doing here?"

"Caring for you, as you can see." He swept his hand out to indicate the mug and plate of food.

"I meant what are you doing here at all?"

"I spent the night."

"In my bed?"

"Your small sofa is much too short. Besides, you might have needed me in the night."

Once she got used to the fact he was there, with her, in her apartment, she had no problem believing he had spent the night in her bed. And while she knew it should bother her, it didn't. It made her feel cared for, darn it. He hadn't made sexual overtures after all, he'd just been there for her.

The sensation of having been held throughout the night was not her imagination, nor had it been yet another hollow dream. The fact that she wanted it so badly made her cranky. "You said you were leaving."

"I did not."

"You—"

"I promised not to argue with you last night."

Right, and she had assumed that meant he would accede to her wishes. "You are sneaky, Tino."

"I prefer to think of it as resourceful." He gave her the smile that had been melting her heart for almost a year. "You should drink your tea and eat. The doctor said it would be most helpful if you partake before getting out of bed."

"Taylish used to have soda crackers and a glass of flat Seven-Up ready for me in the morning." She sighed, looking around her small room. "I'd forgotten."

"Would you prefer that?" Tino asked with a flat voice. "Only the doctor recommended these items."

"This is fine."

He nodded and left the room.

Mentally shrugging at his strange behavior, she drank her tea. She'd eaten the crackers and cheese and several of the grapes as well before Tino returned. They did help. She felt almost normal, certainly not in any risk for a hasty trip to the bathroom to void her stomach.

Tino was still wearing nothing more than his boxer

shorts, a luxurious emerald-green silk she wanted to touch. Which was really, really stupid, but true all the same.

Her nipples tightened—aching a little because they were tender from the hormonal changes in her body—and reminding her of her total nudity beneath the sheet and blanket. "You undressed me last night. While I was sleeping."

"If I had done it while you were awake, I am sure the outcome would have been quite different." He gave her a heavy-lidded look that sent sparks of arousal straight to her core.

"No." She shook her head in further denial, trying to convince them both that what he was suggesting was not an option.

He sat beside her and cupped her nape, his hand warm and big against her neck. "Are you sure about that?"

"We can't. Tino, no sex." Though her body was aching for the feel of his.

"Why?" His expression grew worried and his entire body tensed. "Has your doctor identified a problem with your pregnancy."

"No," she admitted, knowing she was going to sound paranoid. "He says that I'm healthy and so is the baby." He'd also said that the vast majority of miscarriages in the first trimester could not have been avoided. It was simply a matter of an unviable pregnancy ending itself.

She wasn't that clinically detached.

"So, why no sex?"

"Do you know the risk of miscarriage in the first trimester, Tino?"

"No."

"It's 12.5 percent. The number is probably higher because some women miscarry before they even realize they are pregnant, but one in eight known pregnancies end in miscarriage in the first trimester. But even if it was only one in a million, I wouldn't do anything to risk it."

"Certainly, if making love increases the risk, we will not do so. I am surprised Maura's doctor never said anything." Tino sounded angered by that fact.

Faith had to be truthful. "Um, there's actually no evidence to suggest that normal sexual activity increases the risk of an early trimester miscarriage."

"But you are still afraid of taking the risk."

"Yes."

"So, we will abstain," he said with the air of a man making a great sacrifice if not with pleasure, without re-crimination. "It will make for an interesting wedding night, though."

"We aren't getting married." At least not right now.

"We shall see." He stood up. "Now I believe it is time to ready ourselves for the day. Do you need help in the shower?"

"I'm pregnant, not an invalid, Tino. I can bathe myself."

"That is probably for the best. Prolonged exposure to your wet, naked body would not be good for my self-control."

"You always talk like I'm some sort of femme fatale."

"Perhaps that is because you are death to the control I exercise over my libido."

She laughed, feeling pleased when she knew she shouldn't. After all, they were no longer a couple. But, like the night before, she had a hard time remembering that, when it felt so right to be with him.

Tino dressed while Faith was in the shower, and then he made a couple of business calls while she was getting ready. Anything to keep himself from going into her small bedroom and ravishing her body.

For some reason, Faith feared miscarriage. He refused to add to those fears, no matter how difficult it might be to abstain from intimacy with her luscious body. He had to admit, he had no idea that miscarriage was so prevalent in the first trimester.

He did a quick web search on his PDA while he waited for Faith to come out of the bedroom, and discovered some interesting facts.

When she came out, she was wearing a flowing sundress the same peacock blue as her eyes in a halter style that tied around her neck. The deep vee of the neckline accentuated her burgeoning curves, but the dress looked comfortable, as well. Its empire waistline had no binding around her tummy, he noticed.

It would look even more amazing once her stomach started to protrude with the baby. He could not wait.

"Did you know that the risk of miscarriage drops to less than one percent after the first trimester and that there are *no* studies linking normal sexual activity to the loss of the baby at all?"

She stopped and stared at him for a half second and then laughed. "Tino, you are too much. Did you call the doctor again while I was in the shower?"

Chagrined at the thought that doing so might have carried more weight with her, he shook his head. "Web research."

"I didn't realize you knew the password to my computer."

"I don't. I used my PDA."

"Trust you to go right to the heart of the matter, and yes, I did know that. I told you as much, remember?"

"I didn't know if you realized it held true throughout your pregnancy."

"I did."

"Good."

She just shook her head and went to sit on the love seat she'd used the night before. This time he sat down beside her and pulled her legs into his lap, starting to massage one of her feet.

She gave him a shocked little stare. "Why are you doing that?"

"To make you feel good."

"But…I'm not exactly huge with child and have aching feet yet, Tino."

"So, I am getting some practice in. If you do not like it, I will stop."

She glared. "Don't you dare. It feels wonderful."

He smiled, feeling smug. Faith had always loved a good foot rub. "Now, tell me why you are so afraid of losing this baby."

The look of ecstasy on her face changed to one of deep sorrow tinged with very real fear. "I lose the people I love, Tino. Every single one. I'm not taking any risks with this baby."

"You have not lost my mother…or my son." He didn't mention himself, because in truth, he wasn't sure she loved him. Even when she had asked him if he could love her, he hadn't known if she had those kinds of feelings for him, or was asking in the hopes of building something in the future.

"If you had your way, neither of them would be in my life."

"That is not true."

"You were angry when you found out I was Gio's teacher, that your mom is my friend."

"I was shocked—it made me respond badly—but I would not take them from your life. Even if you were not pregnant with my child." And he realized that given the choice, he would not have prevented Faith from forming the attachments with his family that she had.

She needed them.

"I believe you. I don't know why. I shouldn't, but I do."

"I am glad. I have never wished ill on you."

"I know." She reached out and brushed her fingertips down his arm.

It sent chills through him, but he ignored the stirrings of desire and said, "So you have not lost everyone you love."

"Every chance I had at family has been snatched from me, Tino." The remembered agony on her face was enough to unman him. "First my parents, then the one foster home I felt like I belonged. They were hoping to adopt a baby, and when the baby came, they let me go."

"That is terrible."

She shrugged, but her pain was there for him to see. "When I lost Taylish and our baby…" Tears filled her eyes and then slid down her cheeks while she tried to compose herself to continue. Finally she choked out, "I figured I must not be meant to have a family."

"I understand why you might feel that way." And it broke his heart for her. "But you must realize it is an irrational conclusion to draw. Though you have suffered more tragedy than any woman should have to, you are still alive—you have much to give to a family and much to receive from one." He took the hand still resting on his arm and kissed her palm, squeezing her fingers tightly. "You are my family now, Faith."

She pulled her hand away, with apparent reluctance, but did it all the same. "No, I'm not. If I manage to deliver this baby, *then* I'll have a family—someone who belongs to me." More tears and a final choking whisper, "Someone I belong to."

Her words sliced at his heart, leaving wounds he refused to dwell on in the midst of her sharing such a personal pain. "Marry me and you will have a ready-made son, mother, father and assorted aunts, uncles and cousins."

She shook her head, her eyes telling him she did not believe. "I won't have *you*, will I, Tino?"

"Of course you will have me. I will be your husband." He could not understand how that could mean not having him.

She just shook her head.

He couldn't stand it any longer. He pulled her into his lap, wrapping his arms around her. "I cannot imagine how you have survived losing the people you have. You are a strong, beautiful woman, Faith. A woman I would be proud to call my wife."

He could feel the edges cracking around his promise to Maura, but he could not pull back. Not in the face of Faith's sorrow.

"You only want to marry me for the baby's sake."

"And for your sake and yes, for my sake. I want you, Faith, and maybe you don't think that is very important, but I have never craved a woman physically the way I do you."

"Not even Maura?"

"No." It hurt to admit and shamed him, but Faith deserved the truth. As much as he had loved his wife, she had not elicited the same sense of soul-deep need for physical oneness that the woman in his arms did.

"I don't want to lose any more family," Faith said in a pained undertone.

"You will not lose this baby. You will not lose me."

"You can't know that."

"And you are not a person who gives up on life because of fear, or you would have given up already." He held her tightly to him. "There is also the baby to consider. We can give her more stability as a married couple, *cara,* than simply living as house mates."

"Her?"

"I can think of nothing I would like better than a daughter who takes after her spirited and beautiful mama."

"Don't say things like that."

"I cannot help it."

"But…"

"I am not only thinking of the baby." He had to convince Faith to marry him.

"Who else?"

"My mother. You carry her grandbaby inside you. She will not be happy if you do not marry me."

"Your mother knows you better than I do, she will understand."

Tino managed a laugh at the implied insult, despite the heavy emotions surrounding them. "No, she will take it quite personally and will be heartbroken if you refuse to make yourself her daughter-in-law."

"I cannot marry you because it will make Agata happy."

"What about Giosue?"

Faith flinched, her beautiful blue eyes clouding. "You said he deserves someone better than me."

"I did not."

"You did. You want to give him a *Sicilian* step-mother, so he will have someone at least that much like his real mother."

Hearing his own reasoning quoted back to him was not pleasant in this instance. How could he have said that to Faith, even if he had believed it at the time? Once again that morning, he felt shame. "My son does not agree. He does not want a traditional Sicilian woman for a stepmother. He wants a free-spirited artist who loves children enough to teach them though it is a mixed blessing for her because being around those children reminds her of what she has lost."

Faith buried her face in his chest. "You said you do not know me."

"Maybe I know you better than either of us thinks." That thought was *not* an unpleasant one. "Can you do it?"

She did not ask what he meant, but he explained anyway. "Can you marry for the sake of our child, for the sake of my mother and your dear friend, for the sake of Giosue's happiness, a little boy you already love? For the sake of your own inner strength that sees beauty and joy in a world that has already taken so much from you? Can you marry me because it is the right thing to do?"

She swallowed and spoke. "Ask me again in two weeks." Her voice was barely above a whisper, as if forcing the words out had been difficult.

"Why two weeks?" he asked, rubbing her back and marveling anew at her resiliency.

He had never known another person like Faith. She amazed him, never more so than today after he heard the short version of her life story.

"My first trimester will be over."

"What has that got to do with anything?"

She sat up and looked away from him, her gaze going to the view out the sunroom's floor-to-ceiling windows. "You only want to marry me because I am pregnant with your child. If that pregnancy ends, you would resent the fact we had married because of it."

"What is all this negative talk? You are not going to lose our baby. If you want to go without sex until you feel it is safe, I will not argue. But I refuse to consider the possibility of future miscarriage in making the decision about marriage. You are not going to lose us."

She was looking at him now, her eyes wide but no longer spilling over with tears. "You can't promise that."

"I can promise that baby, or no baby, I expect to marry you."

"No."

"Yes."

"That makes no sense."

"It does to me."

"It's an obligation thing." Horror cascaded over her features. "You pity me."

He laughed. He could not help it. It was not a sound of happy amusement, but a grim one. "You are too strong to pity."

"I'm not. I'm scared to death. That makes me a coward. I don't want to tempt fate."

"You are no coward."

"I don't know how we jumped to talk of marriage. Last night we were negotiating whether or not I'm going to move into the Grisafi villa."

"I go after what I want."

"And what you want is me to marry you?" She sounded disbelieving.

"Believe it." He tilted her chin with the edge of his hand, so their eyes continued to meet. "You are living scared and that is no way to live."

"Says you."

Instead of continuing to argue with her, he kissed her. It wasn't a passionate, let's-make-love kiss, but a tender salute of comfort. Then, leaning his head against hers, he spoke. "Faith, I want you to live up to your name. I want you to have hope in the future. I want you believe in the family we can make together."

"I don't know if I can."

"I believe in you."

She took a shuddering breath. "I want to show you something."

"Whatever you need."

She stood and he did, as well, wondering what she felt he needed to see. She was his, even if she did not yet acknowledge that fact. And the presence of their baby in her womb meant that no matter what promises he had made, the need to make her a permanent part of his life superseded them now.

He would not break the final promise and allow Faith to replace Maura in his heart, but he would spend the rest of his life proving to Faith that marriage to him was not a mistake. He had no doubts he would convince her of it.

She might not be in love with him, but she loved his mother and his son. And she loved teaching at the primary school. She would not be able to keep that job if she insisted on keeping a single status while pregnant. This was Sicily, not the more liberal UK or America.

He might not agree with all the cultural norms of his country, but he wasn't above taking advantage of them when he needed to.

Faith would marry him.

She stopped in front of a covered statue and met his eyes with hers. "You didn't look."

"No."

"Weren't you curious?"

"Very."

"But you respected my privacy."

"Si." Unlike his mother. But this one time he could give thanks for her excessive curiosity. With her pessimistic views regarding her pregnancy, she would probably have waited to tell him until she was inches from giving birth—if then.

Faith's fingers were on the cloth, but she had not lifted it, though he assumed that was her plan. "You didn't think undressing me compromised that?"

"I have mapped every centimeter of your naked body with my eyes, my fingers…my tongue. There are no secrets between us in that regard."

"And if I did not want you undressing me?"

"It has never bothered you before."

"But we broke up, Tino."

"Did we?" He stepped closer until they were sharing breathing space. "Or were we on hiatus while you worked out best when and how to tell me of our child?"

For he had no doubt she had planned to do so. He remembered comments she had made when they spoke of commitment that had made no sense at the time, but looking back had ominous import.

She looked chagrined, but did not answer.

"Even if I had been looking to marry again—which I was not—you would not have allowed me to do so without informing me of our child's existence, would you?"

"No."

"Nor would I have ever let you walk away, but admit it—you were biding your time before we reconciled."

"I wasn't." She bit her lip and sighed, her blue eyes troubled. "You seem to forget you were the one who was so adamantly opposed to marriage *to me*."

"If I could go back and change my responses to you in that regard, I would." Because even without the baby, he now admitted he could never have let Faith walk out of his life. He wasn't proud of his weakness, but he would not lie to himself about it, either.

"I am arrogant. I admit it, but truth is truth. You have never stopped belonging to me and vice versa."

"We were casual lovers, Tino. Bed partners. Not a couple." Bitterness and confusion laced her voice in equal measure. "We didn't belong to each other."

"That is not how I see it."

"Oh, really? That's why you refused my calls for two weeks while you were in New York." That was his Faith, still fragile from her admissions, but ready to speak her mind regardless.

"Yes."

Blue eyes went wide in shock. "What?"

"I was not comfortable with the depth our relationship had attained, and I attempted to retrench to a less emotionally intimate position." He took a deep breath and prepared to speak words that rarely passed his lips. "I am truly sorry that hurt you."

"I..." She looked lost for words, but then visibly regrouped. "It must have worked, or you would not have denied our friendship to your mother."

"You know that is not true." They would lay this to rest once and for all. "I explained why I said what I did, and if it makes you feel any better, I learned to regret it." Deeply.

"The big bad, business tycoon was afraid of his mother. Very convincing, Tino."

Just about as convincing as his Faith giving in to sarcasm. "Mocking me will not change the truth of our circumstances."

She sighed, as if her anger was deflating. "I know that."

"We belong to each other. My idiocy and your intransigency cannot change that. Admit it."

CHAPTER ELEVEN

FAITH shook her head. "You never give up, do you?"

"No."

"You are a piece of work, Valentino Grisafi."

"If you mean 'a piece of work' like those you create, I will take that as a compliment."

"Thank you."

"You are a very talented artist."

"I hope you continue to think so after seeing these pieces."

And then she showed him, one after another. Each one was a pregnant woman in a different situation and varying stages of pregnancy, from barely pregnant to one where the woman looked as if she was ready to give imminent birth to twins.

The most striking thing about the collection was the wealth of emotion it expressed—and elicited. There was one woman in a state of misery, clearly on the edge of losing her child. There was another who glowed with such joy it choked him. Another was a grouping, a man, a woman and a child. The man and child had their hands on the protruding belly of the mother-to-be. One of her more abstract pieces, their features were blank and the sex of the child was not clear. But Tino was sure it was a little boy and that both man and boy wore grins on their faces.

He was certain the statue represented something Faith hoped for, something Tino was determined he and Giosue could give her. Acceptance. And family.

He reached out to touch the woman who looked on the verge of final tragedy. "Is this how you feel right now?"

"Sometimes."

He pulled the emotionally fragile woman to him and kissed the top of her silky red curls, inhaling her scent and trying to imbue her with his confidence. "You will not lose this baby."

"I have to believe that, or I would go crazy."

"But you are still afraid." He rubbed her back, loving the feel of her smaller body so close to his.

"Terrified."

"You are also happy."

"Ecstatic."

Something inside him settled when she admitted that. "You want the baby."

"Very, very, *very* much." She hugged him tight as if that was the only way to express the depth of her feelings on the matter.

"Three *very*s. That *is* a lot." And he was glad.

"Yes."

He drew back a little, not pulling from her embrace but far enough that he could tilt her head and let their gazes meet. "But you do not want the father."

"That is not what I said." She pouted, just like she did when he told her it was time to go home after a night of lovemaking.

Remembering those occasions now caused an internal wince. "Certain things can be inferred."

"No, they can't."

He leaned back against her worktable, tugging her with him so she ended up plastered against him. "Oh, really?"

She seemed disinclined to move, snuggling against him trustingly. "Yes. I just…"

"What?"

"I told you…I don't want to tempt fate." She dipped her head, so he could not see her face.

He could not help himself from cupping her bottom and massaging it. Her curves were so damn enticing to him. "Why not try trusting in Providence instead of worrying about fate?"

"I never thought I could lose my parents."

"You did."

"Yes and believe me when I tell you that I was sure Taylish and the baby were my shot at a family. A family I was positive could not be taken from me. I knew he would never leave me."

"Then he did."

"It wasn't his fault, but it wasn't mine either, and I was alone again."

"Look at me."

She tilted her head back, her peacock-blue eyes shiny with emotion.

He felt like he'd been kicked in the gut with that look. "You are not alone now."

"You don't think?"

"I know. And so should you. Even without the baby, you had my mother, my son, your friends…me."

"Did I have you, Tino?"

"More than any other woman since Maura's death."

That fact was not a comfortable one for him, but it was something Faith deserved to know.

"You aren't happy about that," she said perceptively.

"If I could choose any woman on the planet to have awakened such emotions in me, it would have been you." He could wish he had not slighted his own honor, but never that another woman had been the cause.

He did not believe any other woman *could* have been.

"I don't know what to say."

"Say you will marry me." He dropped his hand to palm her hard stomach. "I need you to believe in the future, if not for my sake, then for the baby's."

"But—"

He lifted his other hand and pressed a finger to her lips. "No buts."

"I want to believe."

"Then do."

"It's not that easy."

"I know, but you must try."

"My first pregnancy was ectopic." The words were bald and emotionless, but he could feel more remembered pain radiating from her.

For a moment his vocal chords were paralyzed with grief for her. "You lost your first baby?"

"Yes."

"I had read that a tubal pregnancy could be very dangerous for the mother."

She nodded, her expression matter-of-fact. "I almost died."

"And you still risked pregnancy again." He was not sure that as her husband, he would have had the strength to allow her to do so.

Taylish had either been a saint or an idiot. Tino knew which one he preferred to believe.

"Absolutely."

He gave a hollow, self-deprecating laugh. "Do you know? I thought you did not want children."

"I did not think it would ever be an option. I believed I would not be able to get pregnant again. Tay and I had to resort to a fertility specialist before I could get pregnant the second time."

"So, this baby is a miracle."

"Yes."

Joy settled inside him. "Believe in the strength of that miracle, Faith."

"Meeting you was a miracle, Tino."

"What?" He could not accept she had said that.

"Wanting you shocked me. I had not expected to ever have another intimate relationship with a man." She rubbed her cheek against his chest as if she needed the contact.

She had been that in love with Taylish? Certainly, the couple had not had an intensely satisfying sexual relationship. Not like he and Faith did. Her reaction to the pleasure she felt when they first made love indicated she'd never experienced something like it before. "But you desired me."

"Yes."

He squeezed her close. "I want you, too, *bella mia*."

"I know." There was a smile in her voice, and she moved a little to let him feel that she could feel the evidence pressing against her belly.

"So marry me."

She laughed softly as if amused, not frustrated, by his persistence. "It's not that simple."

"It can be if you let it."

"You're so stubborn, Tino."

"You love that about me."

She was silent for a count of five full seconds, then she kissed him through his shirt, right over his heart. "Maybe."

Faith spent the morning working, feeling inspired and better than she had in weeks. Every brush with her palette knife was perfect, every gentle manipulation of the clay with her fingers resulting in just the effect she was looking for.

A loud beeping from her small alarm told her it was time to start getting ready for lunch with Agata. She was washing the clay from her hands in the kitchen sink when someone knocked.

Thinking Agata had decided to come by and pick her up instead of meeting at the restaurant as planned, Faith dried her hands and swung the door open.

To a frowning Tino. "You did not ask who it was. There is no peephole on your door. How did you know it was me?"

"Sheesh, arrogant much? I didn't know it was you."

"I believed we already established that that is a Grisafi family trait." He bent down and kissed her, his lips lingering just long enough to make it the kiss of a lover and not a typically warm Sicilian greeting. "If you did not know it was me, why did you open the door?"

"I thought it was your mother."

"I was under the impression your plans were to meet at the restaurant for lunch."

Faith didn't remember telling him the details of her lunch appointment, but just like with her first pregnancies, her short-term memory was just a tad compromised. "I thought she might have arrived in town early and decided to pick me up."

"But you did not know."

"Clearly not. After all, I was wrong, wasn't I?"

"And yet you opened the door."

"Is there a point to this interrogation?"

"A point?" He stepped inside and shut the door. "Yes, there is a point. I could have been anyone."

"But you weren't."

"Nevertheless, such behavior is reckless."

"Reckless? Opening the door?"

"Opening your door when you do not know who is on the other side puts your safety at needless risk."

"What are you? The arbiter of in-home security for pregnant women?"

"This has nothing to do with your pregnancy."

She believed him. "You look so fierce, Tino."

"Do not make fun of my concern for you, Faith. I should have visited you here long before this. No doubt, you have been behaving in a similar fashion all this time."

"This is Sicily, Tino, not New York City. I can open the door without worrying the person on the other side is set on robbing me."

"Or worse? I do not think so. Marsala is not such a small city as all that, and there are plenty of tourists with intentions you cannot begin to be certain of."

"Overprotective alert, Tino."

"I think not. Common sense is not overprotective behavior." But color burnished along his chiseled cheekbones.

"I like this side of you," she decided.

"Good. I am unlikely to change."

"That I believe." She grinned, then frowned. "Um, not that I want to kick you out or anything." She so didn't, no matter how little sense that attitude made. "But I'm supposed to meet your mother for lunch in less than an hour and I need to get ready. Was there something in particular you needed?"

"I am horning in on your lunch with my mother."

"What? Why?"

"You have decided to tell her about the baby, yes?"

"Yes." And she was more than a little nervous about doing so.

"As much as we both adore my mother, I am certain you could use my moral support."

"That's really sweet." Man, when he decided to take down the barriers, they crumbled with a crash. She was still glowing from the things he'd said when he'd been trying to convince her to marry him. Going back over the conversation had filled her with renewed hope and dead certainty that no matter what he had said before, Tino *wanted* to be with *her*.

She already knew she wanted to be with him. But maybe not this afternoon. "Won't your presence be suspect? Your mom isn't dumb, she's bound to guess there's more between us than a casual acquaintance."

"I am sure she drew that conclusion when I ran from the house without a word after she told me she thought you were pregnant."

"You didn't."

"I did."

"Tino!"

"I know. I was not thinking, *bella mia*."

"I didn't want to tell anyone I was pregnant until my first trimester was over," Faith lamented.

"What is done is done."

"Is that a Sicilian proverb?"

He grinned and kissed the tip of her nose. "I believe it is a universal one."

"I suppose." She headed to her bedroom. "I need to change my clothes."

He followed her.

"Tino, I'm getting dressed."

"So?"

"You really don't recognize personal boundaries, do you?"

"You wish to have a wider personal boundary as my wife than you have had as my lover?" He sounded confused and not a little upset.

"We're not married."

"Not yet, but it will happen."

"I haven't said yes." But she would. She loved him and now that she knew his feelings for her had always run deeper than he'd wanted to admit or acknowledge even to himself, she wasn't going to let him go.

He wasn't the only stubborn, possessive one in their relationship.

"You will."

"You are so sure?"

"I cannot allow myself to consider the alternative." And for just a brief moment, her Sicilian tycoon looked as vulnerable as any male on the planet. "For now I will be happy if you admit we are still a couple."

"Were we ever a *couple?*"

"We had our limits on our relationship, but that does not mean we were not together."

"Limits you set."

"I acknowledge it."

"You seem to have dumped them with efficient speed." And she was loving that reality.

"Circumstances change."

"Like finding out I'm pregnant with your baby."

"Believe it or do not, but the walls I imposed between us would have crumpled when you dumped me, regardless of your reason for doing so."

"I do believe it." Did he love her? She didn't have the guts to ask and risk getting shot down again, but the possibility warmed her heart as surely as her baby did. "So, you do admit that I dumped you, regardless of the reasons why?"

Pain darkened his expression for just a moment. *"Si."*

"Then I can admit that we are a couple."

Gorgeous white teeth flashed in a smile that turned her inside out.

He watched as she pulled off her clay-spattered jeans and top, his gaze going hot and hungry when her almost nude body was revealed.

"You're not wearing a bra." His voice was hoarse and his hand made an abortive move to touch her.

She smiled. "No sex, remember."

"How could I forget?"

"You look like you're in danger of doing so."

"I am not, but you would not deny me what pleasure I can have, would you?"

"You are going to get yourself all revved up with nowhere to go." Though knowing he still wanted her so much was nice. Really nice to know, in fact.

He laughed. "I think a tiny part of you enjoys knowing that."

"I think you may be right."

She turned to grab some clothes from the closet,

bending to get the gold and white Roca Wear sandals she wanted to wear with her white sheath dress.

He groaned.

She let her lips curve in a smile because he could not see. "You sure you're going to survive this."

"If Taylish could stand the abstinence, so can I."

"Ohh, competitive. You don't have to be. Tay and I didn't stop making love during either of my pregnancies."

Silence for a full five seconds. "I'll wait for you in the studio." He turned and left the room without another word.

She blinked, not sure what had happened there. One minute she'd been teasing him with her body, positive they were both enjoying it. And the next, he was gone.

He was quiet on the way to the restaurant to meet his mother, too.

"Tino," she said when they pulled up in front of the trattoria. "Is something wrong?"

"What could be wrong?"

"That's what I want to know."

He simply shrugged and got out of the car, coming around to open her door and help her to her feet. He kept his hand on the small of her back as they walked into the restaurant.

Agata was already seated at a table for four; Rocco was across from her.

She smiled at their approach. "Hello, Faith. My son. Why am I not surprised to see you as well?"

"Because you are intelligent enough to add two and two and get four. I, on the other hand, am a little shocked you brought Papa along without warning Faith first."

"Why, am I some ogre my soon-to-be daughter-in-law should need forewarning of my presence?"

"Do not be melodramatic, Papa."

Tino looked down at her to see how she was taking this development and she gave him and then his parents a reassuring smile. "I'm very happy to see you, Rocco."

"And I am very pleased to be expecting a new grandchild."

Tino didn't give her a chance to answer, but pulled her chair out for her. She sat down, glad there was already water at her place. She took a sip and wondered how best to break it to the older couple that she had not yet agreed to marry Tino.

"Faith has not consented to become my wife," Tino said bluntly, taking care of that little detail for her.

"You have not asked her?" Rocco asked in clear censure.

Tino waited to answer until he had taken his own seat at the table. Then he gave his father a look that would make most cringe. "Naturally, I have asked her. She turned me down."

"Flat?" Agata asked in a faint voice, her shock palpable.

Faith glared at Tino. So much for supporting her during this conversation. "I told him to ask me again in two weeks."

"I will start making plans immediately," Agata said with a smile.

"She did not say she would agree, then."

"But of course she will. You simply have to convince her." Rocco gave his son a significant look. "You've already seduced her into your bed, surely you can induce her to marry you."

Faith felt her cheeks going hot, but Tino did not look in the least bothered. "I intend to try."

"You will succeed," his mother said complacently.

"Will I?" Tino looked at Faith, his gaze trying to decipher something in hers. "That is my hope."

"You know why I want to wait."

"Yes, you do not wish to make the mistake of promising to spend the rest of your life with me in the remote chance it is not a necessary sacrifice."

"It's not me I'm worried about."

"And yet I have made it clear I do not wish to wait to make the commitment."

"You didn't want to marry me before I got pregnant. You didn't even want to be my friend."

"I want to marry you now and I was your friend, if too much of a coward to admit it to my mother." He focused on Agata and Rocco. "I am sorry I was less than truthful with you about my relationship with Faith."

"You lied," Rocco said. No compromise.

Tino nodded, looking pained. *"Si."*

"We forgive you, don't we?" Agata said, giving her husband a transparent look that clearly meant he'd better agree or risk being sent to a guest room for the night.

"Si. You are our son."

And that meant forgiveness. Faith smiled. Maybe Tino had been worried about this. She was glad his parents hadn't drawn it out the way he'd clearly been expecting.

Tino looked no happier, but he said, "Thank you."

"So, do you want a big wedding or something small?" Agata asked.

"I told you—"

Agata cut her son off. "I know what you said, but your father and I have complete faith in you." She looked at Faith expectantly.

"I always dreamed of getting married in a church,

with my family there to witness my happiness." She didn't know why she said it. It was a dream that could never be realized.

"I will talk to the father, unless you wish to be married in your Lutheran church?"

Faith shook her head. "I've been attending the Catholic Mass since coming to Sicily. It just felt right."

Agata's face lit up at that. "How wonderful. The father will be very pleased to hear this."

"No doubt," Tino said.

Faith looked at him, a question in her eyes.

He shrugged. "It is one more thing I did not know about you."

"Tino, you know me more deeply than anyone has since Taylish, maybe even better than he did."

Agata glowed at them, while Tino looked almost speechless.

Rocco nodded his head. "As it should be."

While they ate, Agata quizzed Faith on the progress of her pregnancy, wanting to know everything from what doctor she'd gone to see to what her due date was. Tino and Rocco left the conversation to the women for the most part.

They were finished eating when Tino spoke again. "I will be staying with Faith until she moves home. You will have no problem watching over Giosue for me?"

"Naturally not," Rocco said before Agata could answer.

"But Tino, Gio needs you."

"So do you, even if you will not admit it."

Faith opened her mouth to argue further, but Tino shook his head. "Trust me, I will not neglect my son. I will tuck him in at night and then come to your apartment. If you should be willing to join me in the evenings with Gio, we will both be pleased. I will make sure he knows to invite you."

"You're being sneaky again, Tino." No fair bringing his son into it. "You know I cannot refuse Gio."

"The term is resourceful."

Rocco and Agata laughed.

"I am only relieved my son carried more cache with you than his father."

"That's not true."

"Would you have accepted my invitation so readily?"

She wanted to say yes, if only to prove him wrong, but she couldn't. "We'll discuss this later."

"Already they are talking like an old married couple."

"Don't tease the children, Rocco."

Faith had to laugh at that.

CHAPTER TWELVE

TINO GOT OUT OF THE CAR when they arrived back at Faith's apartment building.

"I don't need an escort to my door, Tino."

"That is no surprise. You do not think you need me for anything."

"I didn't mean that, I just…you don't have to walk me up."

"Perhaps I want to."

She nodded, warmth unfurling through her when he placed his hand on the small of her back even though he was clearly upset with her.

"I do need you, Tino," she said as they climbed the stairs to her second-floor apartment.

"That is good to hear." There was something in his voice that she could not decipher, but he sounded sad…defeated.

Something was definitely wrong.

Hoping to find out what, she offered him a drink when they got upstairs.

But he shook his head. "I must get back to the office if I am going to get out of there at a decent hour tonight."

"Something is bothering you. I want you to tell me what it is."

"It does not matter." He looked away from her. "Life is what it is."

"I don't understand. Are you unhappy I'm pregnant? If you don't want to marry me, I'm not going to make you. And as much as they love you, your parents aren't going to, either."

"I am well aware you are all too ready to walk away from me."

"What? Tino, what has gotten into you? I'm not walking away."

"But you want to."

"No, I don't."

"Oh, you are happy enough to have my baby, but it is clear you would have chosen another father for your child. Only the man you would have chosen is dead."

"I don't want this baby to be Taylish's."

"I do not believe you."

"You are being ridiculous, Tino."

He simply shrugged. "I will see you tonight."

"You do not have to stay with me." She knew he would ignore her, but she had to say it.

"So long as you stubbornly refuse to move home, I do."

"Grisafi Vineyards is not my home."

"It became your home the moment you conceived my child and will remain that way until the day you die, should you wish it. Even if you can never bring yourself to marry me."

"You have no idea how much I want that."

"But not enough to commit to taking me along with it, unless it is proven necessary. Right?"

"Tino, what is going on with you today? That is not what I said and you know it. That is so far from what I feel, it isn't even funny."

"I know that I want you to marry me and that you will not do so."

"You're like a single-track CD programmed to repeat."

He didn't respond.

She had to take a deep breath so she would not yell. He could be so irritating. "Tell me something, Tino."

"*Si?*"

"If I miscarried tomorrow, would you still want to marry me?"

"Yes." His dark eyes gleamed with sincerity and something else. Oh, gosh…it looked like love. He meant it.

Really. Truly.

Her knees went weak, but she could not trust what her brain was telling her heart her eyes were seeing. "You don't mean it."

"I do."

"I…"

"Give us a chance, Faith. You may not love me like you did your precious Taylish, but I can make you happy. You said your attraction to me was a miracle to you."

"It was…it is."

"Marry me, *cuore mio.*"

My heart. He'd called her his heart. Was it a misspoken word, an attempt at manipulation…or did he mean it? "You…I…"

"Please."

She could not deny him. "Promise me something."

"What?"

"You will not regret it."

"This I can easily promise."

"Why?"

"Why would I promise you?"

"Why is it easy?"

"You have not figured it out yet? I have broken my promise to Maura. I love you. You fill my heart. You are my heart."

"You don't. You can't. You said."

"Many things I wished were true, but the only real truth is my love for you."

"But you aren't happy about it."

"I have never before broken a promise. I could not save Maura and now I cannot keep my last promise to her."

"She made you promise never to love again?" That didn't sound like the woman Agata had told Faith about.

"I promised her at her grave. I told her I would never replace her in my heart."

Faith felt the most amazing sense of release pour through her. And she laughed, the joy-filled sound stopping Tino's pacing. "You find the compromise of my honor amusing?"

Instead of answering, she said, "You're being all-or-nothing again. Loving me doesn't mean that Maura no longer has a place in your heart. She has a place in mine, too, because she loved you and because she gave birth to a little boy that I love very much."

"But not his father. I understand. You loved Taylish too much to love another. I should be grateful for what I have. You carry my child and that is a great gift."

"I loved Taylish, but nothing like I love you."

"What do you mean?"

"I loved Taylish, but I was never in love with him. I have been in love with you since the first night we made love."

"You mean that?"

"More than anything."

"I…this is hard."

She grinned. "Talking about your feelings?"

"*Si*. It is not something I like to do."

"You told me you loved me, that's all you needed to say."

"No. You deserve all of the truth."

"What did you leave out?"

"Maura was the love of my youth, you are the love of my life. It hurt when she died. I grieved a long time, but if I lost you, it would kill me."

Faith threw herself at Tino and he caught her, just as she knew he would. They kissed until they were both breathing hard. He pulled his head back, protecting them both from going too far.

She snuggled her head into his neck. "Just one thing, Tino."

"*Si?*"

"Promises made to dead people don't count. They're a way of dealing with our own grief, but when they cause more sadness than consolation, you have to let them go."

"You sound like you know what you are talking about."

"I do. I made a promise to Tay after he died."

"What was it?"

"That I wouldn't try to make a family with someone else." She sighed and kissed the underside of Tino's jaw. "The promise was for my protection, not his. I made it so I couldn't be hurt again, and when I realized that, I let it go."

"I am glad you were wiser than I."

"I'll remind you that the next time we argue you said that."

"You have my permission, just never remind me what a selfish bastard I was when we were lovers only. I will never forget. But I do not know if I could stand the thought that you won't."

"Tino, we all make mistakes, but real love forgives and forgets."

"You are more than I deserve."

"You just keep believing that, but remember, you are my miracle."

"I love you, *cuore mio*."

"I love you, Tino, more than life."

They married on their one-year anniversary.

Agata had managed to pull together an amazing church wedding and fill said church with family and friends. Faith didn't realize how many friends she'd made in the artistic community and at Gio's school until she saw them all sitting in the pews as she walked up the aisle.

Once her gaze locked on Tino, though, she looked neither to the right nor the left. His expression was filled with love and joy and peace.

It was the peace that made her feel so good. So right.

He was happy to be marrying her, and the guilt he'd felt at loving her was gone now. They'd visited Maura's grave together along with Gio. The trip had seemed to give both males a sense of closure.

Gio was his father's best man, and Agata was Faith's matron of honor. Rocco was giving her away, and the wedding was what she'd always dreamed of and had been sure she could never have. A ceremony celebrating the love and commitment between her and Tino, witnessed by their family.

He had been right about one thing—maybe more than one, but she wasn't telling him that and letting him get a swelled head—that she did have a family now. The Grisafis accepted her as one of their own and unconditionally. Even his brother who lived in New York came home to make her feel welcome and witness his brother's second marriage.

Calogero had insisted on helping Tino by overseeing the transformation of a first-floor room with lots of windows into Faith's new studio. Thereby managing to avoid the brunt of his mother's attempts at changing his single status since returning to Italy. Faith could only be happy that Agata had not made that effort with Tino. Perhaps the older woman had known instinctively her eldest son had already found his second love.

That was all before, though.

Right now Faith hesitated with her hand on the door between the en suite and Tino's—their—bedroom. They had not made love, even when her first trimester had officially ended two weeks before.

Tino had said he wanted to wait for their wedding night. He wanted it to be right. His patience despite his obvious arousal every night when they went to sleep had forever cemented Faith's trust and appreciation for this amazing man she now called husband.

She opened the door and stepped into the bedroom.

Tino stood beside the bed wearing a pair of white silk pajama bottoms.

"White?" she asked with a smile, even though her own lace peignoir was the color of fresh snow.

"It is our first time."

"As husband and wife."

"As a man and a woman who have admitted their love and promised to hold each other in their hearts for a lifetime."

Oh. "I'm going to cry."

"No…you are going to love."

She nodded, too choked up to speak.

He put his arms out. "Come here, *cuore mio*."

She went to him, straight into his arms. He held her there for the longest time, saying nothing. Doing nothing.

Except looking into her eyes, his that dark Hershey-brown that meant his emotions were close to the surface. Finally he said, "Thank you."

"For what?"

"For being mine. For putting up with me. For falling in love with me and not walking away with my baby. For being just who you are, you incredibly precious woman."

The tears rolled then, but they were filled with joy and she made no effort to stop them. "Thank you, Tino, for being mine. For giving me a family again. For being you, but mostly for loving me."

"I will always love you."

"I believe you."

Her fear that she could never have a family was almost completely gone now. His love had given her hope unlike any she'd known since the death of her parents. She'd loved Tay, but she was in love with Tino, and she couldn't help feeling Heaven blessed their union.

His mouth came down on hers, the kiss so incredibly tender and yet sensual, too.

Their tongues played a lazy dance together, getting reacquainted after so much time apart. Their bodies strained together of their own accord as if the very molecules that made up their skin and nerve endings could no longer stand any sort of separation.

Although they had slept curled together for the past few weeks, she felt the need to relearn his body. She let her hands roam freely over hot, silky flesh covering defined muscles. The hair on his chest rubbed her through her lacey peignoir, reminding her just how susceptible she was to the barest touch by this man.

His rapid heartbeat and heavy breathing said he was equally impacted.

He was no slouch in the caressing department, either, his big hands mapping her body in a way that made her ache deep in her core. She needed him.

He cupped the barely there bump in her stomach. "I have this image of you rounded with my baby, wearing one of my shirts and nothing else while you work on your art."

"Fantasizing, Tino?" she asked with a husky laugh.

"Prophesying, I hope."

"You are silly."

"Because I crave seeing you large with child?"

"It's not exactly sexy."

"So, this is not the time to tell you that the image makes my knees weak with lust."

"Are you serious?"

"I love you, Faith. Seeing you that way, seeing the evidence of our love changing your body—it's the biggest turn-on I've ever known."

"I'll remind you of that when I look like a balloon."

"Trust me, I'm not likely to forget."

"I do trust you, Tino."

"Thank you." Then he kissed her again.

They undressed each other slowly, each treating the other like a treasure to be unwrapped.

Then Tino carried her to the bed and laid her down with tender care. He kissed and caressed her body, gently manipulating her breasts since they were sensitive. She returned the favor, holding the velvet hardness of his arousal with both hands.

"I want you," she whispered.

He nodded, the moment profound as he gave in to her desire.

He made love to her slowly, pleasuring her body and building to the peak of perfect oneness with a measured rhythm that drove her insane and made her feel incredibly cherished all at the same time.

Despite the slow build, her climax surprised her, tightening her body and sending convulsions of pleasure through her. He came a second later, calling out his love.

It was the most perfect moment of Faith's life.

She belonged to him completely, just as he belonged to her.

"I love you, Tino. With all my heart and soul."

"*Ti amo,* Faith, who is my heart and reminds me I have a soul."

EPILOGUE

RAFAELLA AGATA GRISAFI was born six months to the day after her parents' marriage. A healthy eight pounds, four ounces, she caused her mother a bit of a problem in the delivery room. Faith was so happy her daughter was healthy and strong, she didn't care how hard the delivery of her precious child had been.

Giosue adored his younger sister and his new mother, often telling anyone who would listen that God must love him an awful lot to give him the best mommy and little sister in the world. Valentino couldn't help agreeing.

He'd lost his first love, but reveled in his second chance at happiness with a woman he looked forward to spending the rest of his life loving.

They were what Faith had always craved—a family.

MISTRESS TO THE MERCILESS MILLIONAIRE

ABBY GREEN

This is for Lorna Mugan and Anne Warter,
whose friendship I value so much.

PROLOGUE

KATE LANCASTER stood at the very ornate stone font where her two-month-old goddaughter was being christened. The holy water was being poured onto her forehead as the priest said a blessing in French. The ceremony was achingly beautiful, in a tiny ancient chapel in the grounds of her best friend Sorcha's new home, a stunning château just outside Paris. Kate had been at her wedding in this same chapel just nine months previously, as maid of honour.

And yet this moment in which Kate wanted nothing more than to focus fully on the christening was being upstaged effortlessly by the tall man who stood to her right. *Tiarnan Quinn.*

He'd also been at the wedding, as best man; he was Sorcha's older brother.

Kate tried to stem the pain, hating that it could rise here and taint this beautiful occasion, but she couldn't stop it. He was the man who had crushed her innocent ideals, hopes and dreams. The man who had shown her a moment of explosive sensuality and in the process ruined her for all other men. And yet she knew she had no one to blame but herself. If she hadn't been so determined to— She ruthlessly crushed that line of thinking. It was so long ago she couldn't believe it still affected her. That it still felt so fresh.

Despite her best efforts to block him out she could feel the heat from his large body envelop her, his scent wind around her, threatening to burst open a veritable Pandora's Box of memories. The familiar weight of desire she felt whenever she was near him lay heavy within her, a pooling of heat in her belly, between her legs. Usually she was so careful to avoid him, but she couldn't here—now. Not at this intimate ceremony where they were being made godparents in this traditional ritual.

She'd survived the wedding; she'd survive this. And then walk away and hope that one day he wouldn't affect her so much. But how long had she been hoping for that now? A sense of futility washed through her—especially as she recognised that if anything her awareness of him was growing exponentially stronger.

Her jaw was tight from holding it so rigid, her back as straight as a dancer's. She tried to focus on Sorcha and Romain. They were oblivious to all except themselves and their baby. Romain took Molly tenderly from the priest, cradling her easily with big hands. He and Sorcha looked at one another over their daughter's head, and that look nearly undid Kate completely. It was so private; so full of love and hope and earthy sensuality, that it felt voyeuristic to be witnessing it. And yet Kate couldn't look away or stop her heart clenching with a bittersweet pain, momentarily and shamingly jealous of what they shared.

This was what Kate wanted. This was all she'd ever wanted. A fulfilment that was so simple and yet so rare. Tiarnan shifted beside her, his arm brushing against hers, making her tense even more rigidly. Against her will she looked up at him; she couldn't *not*. He'd always drawn her eyes to him, like a helpless moth to the certain death of a burning flame.

He was looking down at her and her heart stopped, breath faltered. He frowned slightly, an assessing look in his gaze as he seemed to search deep within her soul for her secrets. He'd looked at her like that at the wedding, and it had taken all her strength to appear cool. He was looking at her as if trying to figure something out. Figure *her* out. Kate was so raw in that moment—too raw after witnessing Romain and Sorcha's sheer happiness and love. It was worse than the wedding. She had no defence here with a tiny baby involved—a tiny baby she'd held in her arms only a few moments ago. Holding that baby had called to the deepest, most primitive part of her.

Normally she coped so well, but with Tiarnan looking at her so intently her protective wall of icy defence was deserting her spectacularly, leaving in its place nothing but heat. And she couldn't do anything to stop it. Her eyes dropped betrayingly to his mouth. She quite literally yearned to have him kiss her, hold her. *Love her.* Look at her the way Romain had just looked at Sorcha. She'd never wanted that from any other man, and the realisation was stark now, cutting through her.

Against her volition her eyes rose to meet his again. *He was still looking at her.* Despite everything, she knew the futility of her secret desires; the feelings within her were rising like a tidal wave and she was helpless to disguise them, caught by the look in his eyes. She also knew, without being able to stop it, that he was reading every raw and naked emotion on her face, in her eyes. And as she watched his blue eyes darkened to a glittering shade of deep sapphire with something so carnal and hot that she instinctively put out a hand to search for something to cling onto, seriously fearful that her legs wouldn't support her.

He'd never looked at her with such explicit intensity…it had to be her imagination. It was all too much—and here she was, pathetically projecting her own desires onto him…

It was only after a few seconds that she realised Tiarnan had clasped her arm with a big hand. He was holding her upright, supporting her… And right then Kate knew that all her flimsy attempts to defend herself against him for years were for naught. He'd just seen through it all in an instant. Seen through *her.* Her humiliation was now complete.

CHAPTER ONE

One month later. Four Seasons Hotel, downtown San Francisco

KATE felt even more like a piece of meat than usual, yet she clamped down on her churlish thoughts and pasted on her best professional smile as the bidding continued. The smack of the gavel beside her made her flinch minutely. The fact that the gavel was being wielded by a well-known A-list Hollywood actor was not making the experience any easier. Despite her years of experience as a top model, she was still acutely uncomfortable under scrutiny, but she had learnt to disguise it well.

'Twenty-five thousand. Twenty-five thousand dollars to the gentleman here in the front. Am I bid any higher?'

Kate held her breath. The man under the spotlight with the unctuous grin was a well-known Greek shipping magnate. He was old, short, fat and bald, and his beady obsidian eyes were devouring Kate as he practically licked his lips. For a second she felt intensely vulnerable and alone, standing here under the lights. A shudder went through her. If someone else didn't—

'Ah! We've a bidder in the back—thirty thousand dollars from the new arrival.'

A rush of relief flooded Kate and she tried to strain to see past the glaring spotlights to identify who the new bidder was. It appeared as if the ballroom lighting technicians were trying to find him too, with the spotlight lurching from coiffed person to coiffed person, all of whom laughed and waved it away. The bidder seemed determined to remain anonymous. Well, Kate comforted herself, whoever it was couldn't be any worse a prospect to kiss in front of all these people than Stavros Stephanides.

'And now Mr Stephanides here in the front is bidding *forty* thousand dollars...things are getting interesting! Come on, folks, let's see how deep your pockets are. How can you turn down a chance to kiss this lovely lady *and* donate generously to charity?'

Kate's stomach fell again at Stephanides' obvious determination—but then the actor spied movement in the shadows at the back. '*Fifty* thousand dollars to the mysterious new bidder. Sir, won't you come forward and reveal yourself?'

No one came forward, though, and inexplicably the hairs rose on the back of Kate's neck. Then she saw the look of almost comic indignation on Stephanides' face as he swivelled around to see who his competitor was. The Greek's expression visibly darkened when someone leant low to speak in his ear. He'd obviously just been informed as to the identity of the mysterious fellow bidder. With an audible splutter Stephanides upped the ante by raising the bidding in a leap to one hundred thousand dollars. Kate held in her gasp at the extortionate amount, but her smile was faltering.

She became aware of the ripple of hushed whispers and a distinct frisson of excitement coming from the back; whoever this person was, he was creating quite a buzz. And then whoever it was also calmly raised their bid—to a cool two hundred thousand dollars. It didn't look as if her ordeal was going to end anytime soon.

Tiarnan Quinn wasn't used to grand, showy gestures. His very name was the epitome of discretion. Discretion in everything: his wealth; his work; his life, and most definitely in his affairs. He had a ten-year-old daughter. He didn't live like a monk, but neither did he parade his carefully selected lovers through the tabloids in the manner so beloved of other men in his position: a divorced heterosexual multi-billionaire male in the prime of his life.

None of his lovers had ever kissed and told. He made sure that any ex-partner was so well compensated she would never feel the need to break his trust. He always got out before any messy confrontations, and he always kept his private life very private. None of his lovers ever met his daughter because he had no intention of marrying ever again, and to introduce them to Rosalie would be to invite a level of intimacy that was reserved solely for his family: his daughter, sister and mother.

His lovers provided him with relief. Nothing more, nothing less.

And yet here he was now, bidding publicly, albeit discreetly for the moment, in the name of charity, for a kiss with Kate Lancaster—one of the most photographed women in the world. Because something in his mind and body was chafing, and for the first time in a long time he was thinking discretion be damned. He wanted this woman with a hunger he'd denied for too long. A hunger he'd only recently given himself permission fully to acknowledge and to believe it could be sated.

And it had been a long time building—*years*. He could see now that it had been building with a stealthy insidiousness into a subconscious need that was now very conscious—a burning necessity. His mouth twisted; those years hadn't exactly been uneventful or allowed much time for contemplation. A short-lived marriage and an acrimonious divorce, not to mention becoming a single parent, had taken up a large part of that time. If he'd had the luxury of time on his hands he might have realised a lot sooner— He halted his thoughts. No matter. He was here now.

His attention came back to Kate, focused on Kate, and he had the uncanny sensation of being in the right place at the right time. It was a sensation he usually associated with business, not something more emotional. He corrected himself; this wasn't about emotion. It was desire. Unfulfilled desire.

Perhaps it was because he'd finally allowed himself to think of it again—that moment ten years ago—but it was as if the floodgates had opened on a dam. It had been little more than a kiss, and yet it was engraved more hotly onto his memory than anything he'd experienced before or after. It had taken all of his will-power and restraint to pull away from her that night. Since then Kate had been strictly off-limits to him for myriad reasons: because that incendiary moment had shaken him up a lot more than he cared to admit; because she'd been so young *and* his little sister's best friend.

He remembered the way her startlingly blue eyes had stared directly into his, as if she'd been able to see all the way into his soul. As if she'd wanted him to see all the way into hers. *She'd looked at him like that again only a few weeks ago.* And it had taken huge restraint for him to allow Kate to retreat back into her shell, to ignore his intense desire. Until *now,* when he knew he could get her on her own, could explore for himself if what he'd seen meant what he thought it did.

His sister's wedding had sparked off this burgeoning need, this awareness. He hadn't been thrown into such close proximity to Kate for years. But all through the ceremony and subsequent reception she'd held him back with that cool, frosty distance of hers. It was like being subjected to a chilly wind whistling over a deserted moor. He'd always been aware of it—yet that day, for the first time in years, it had rankled. His interest had been piqued. *Why* was she always so cool, distant?

Admittedly they had a history that up until now he'd been quite happy not to unearth. He knew on some level that that night ten years ago had marked a turning point for him, and perhaps it was one of the reasons he'd found it so easy to relegate Kate to a place he had no desire to re-explore. Her studied indifference over the years had served to keep a lid on those disturbing memories.

And yet he knew he couldn't deny the fact that he'd always been aware of her—aware of how she'd blossomed from a slightly gauche teenager into a stunningly assured and beautiful woman.

He'd thought he had that awareness and desire under control, but one night some years ago a girl had bumped into him in the street: blonde, caked in make-up, and wearing an outfit that was only a hair's breadth away from a stripper's. The feel of her body slamming into him, her huge blue eyes looking straight up into his, had scrambled his brain and fired his libido so badly that he'd sent his date home that night with some pathetic excuse and hadn't been able to look at another woman for weeks—turned on by a girl in a tarty French maid's outfit because she'd borne some resemblance to—

Tiarnan halted his wayward thoughts right there. He chafed at the resurgence of something so minor he'd thought long forgotten—and at the implication that Kate had occupied a bigger place in his mind than he'd admitted to himself. He reassured himself that he'd had his own concerns keeping him more than occupied—and lovers who'd been only too warm and willing, making it easy to shut out the frosty indifference of one woman. Seeing Kate just once or twice a year had hardly been conducive to stoking the embers of a latent desire.

But just a few weeks ago…at the baptism…she'd turned and looked at him and that cool façade had dropped for the first time. She'd looked at him with such naked blatant need in those fathomless blue depths that he'd felt as if a truck had just slammed into him. For the first time Tiarnan had seen the heat of her passion under that all too cool surface. It was a heat he hadn't seen since that night, when it had combusted all around them. It could have ended so differently if he hadn't found a thread of control to cling onto.

In one instant, with one look, Tiarnan had been flung back

in time, and all attempts to keep her off limits had been made redundant. It was almost as if he'd been put to sleep after that night, and now, with a roaring, urgent sucking-in of oxygen, he was brought back to painful, aching life.

She'd clammed up again after a few moments, but it had been enough of a crack in her armour...

Blood heated and flowed thick through his veins as he took her in now. She was dressed in a dark pink silk cocktail dress, strapless, showing off the delicate line of her shoulders and collarbone, her graceful neck. Her long, luxuriant blonde hair—her trademark—hung in loose waves over her shoulders, a simple side parting framing her face. And even though he was right at the back of the room those huge blue eyes stood out. Her soft rose-pink lips were full, the firm line of her jaw and straight nose transforming banal prettiness into something much more formidable. True beauty. There was fragility in the lines of her body, and yet a sexy lushness that would have an effect on every man in that room—something Tiarnan was very aware of. Uncomfortably so.

He felt a proprietorial urge to go and sweep her off that stage and out of everyone's sight. It only firmed his resolve, strengthened his sense of right.

His eyes drifted down with leisurely and very male appreciation, taking in slender shapely legs, it was clear why she'd become one of the most sought-after models in the world. She was, quite simply, perfect. She'd become a darling of the catwalks despite their predilection for a more emaciated figure; she was the face of a well-known lingerie company among countless other campaigns. Her cool, under-the-surface sensuality meant that people sometimes described her as cold. But the problem was he knew she wasn't.

He had the personal experience to know that she was very, *very* hot.

Why had he waited so long for this?

Tiarnan clamped down on looking again at what had made him suppress his desire for so long—apart from the obvious reasons. He dismissed the rogue notion that rose unbidden and unwelcome that she'd once touched something deep within him. It must have been an illusion, borne up by the fact that they'd shared a moment in time, imbuing the experience with an enigmatic quality.

She'd displayed a self-possession at the age of eighteen that had stunned him slightly. He had to remind himself that he'd overestimated her naivety. She'd known exactly what she'd been doing then, and she was a grown woman now. Tiarnan's body tightened in anticipation. She was a woman of the world—the kind of woman he could seduce. She was no longer an innocent… A sharp pain lanced him briefly. It felt awfully like *regret,* and Tiarnan crushed it back down. He didn't do regret. He would not let her exert this sensual hold over him. He would not let her bring him back in time and reduce him to a mass of seething, frustrated desire with one look because of a *kiss!* He would seduce her and sate this lust that had been burning for too long under the surface. It was time to bring it out into the open.

All he could think about was how urgently he wanted to taste her again, touch her. She had once tried to seduce him. Now it was his turn. And this time they wouldn't stop at a kiss.

His attention came back to the proceedings. He saw Stephanides bid again. He had no intention of letting that man anywhere near Kate's lush mouth. But the Greek was stubborn and out to prove a point—especially now that he'd been informed who it was bidding against him. He and Stephanides were old adversaries. Tiarnan casually made another bid, oblivious to the gasps and looks directed at him, oblivious to the whispers that came from nearby as people speculated if it was really *him.*

People's idle speculation and chatter was of little interest to him. What was of interest was Kate Lancaster, as she stood there now, with her huge doe eyes staring straight at him but not seeing him. She would—soon enough.

Stavros Stephanides finally admitted defeat with a terse shake of his head. A sense of triumph filled Tiarnan and it was heady. He hadn't felt the sensation in a long time because triumph invariably came all too easily. With no idea as to how much he'd finally bid for a kiss with Kate, and not in the slightest bit fazed, he stepped out of the shadows and strode forward to collect his prize. Not just the kiss he was now due, but so much more. And he *would* collect—until he was sated and Kate Lancaster no longer exerted this mysterious pull over his every sense.

Kate simply didn't believe her eyes at first. *It couldn't be.* It just could not be Tiarnan Quinn striding powerfully through the seated awed crowd towards her, looking as dark and gorgeous as she'd ever seen him in a tuxedo. Her face flamed guiltily; he'd been inhabiting her dreams for weeks—and a lot longer— jeered a taunting voice, which she ignored. Only the previous night she'd woken shaken and very hot after a dream so erotic that she was sure it must be her rampant imagination conjuring him up now.

Fervently hoping that it *was* just her imagination, she took him in: the formidable build—broad shoulders, narrow hips and long legs—the loose-limbed athletic grace that hinted at his love for sports, his abhorrence of the gym. His hair was inky black, cut short, and with a slight silvering at the temples that gave him an air of sober maturity and distinction. As if he even needed it. Kate knew his darkly olive skin came from his Spanish mother. She felt weak inside, and hot.

His face was uncompromising and hard. A strong jaw and proud profile saved it from being too prettily handsome. He was intensely male—more intensely male than any man she'd ever met. Years and maturity had added to his strength, filled out his form, and it was all hard-packed muscle. But his most arresting feature was his eyes—the strongest physical hint of Celtic lineage courtesy of his Irish father. Icy blue and utterly direct. Every time he looked at her she felt as though he saw all the way through her, saw through the paltry defences she put up against him. She tried so hard to project a professional front around him, maintain her distance, knowing that if he ever came near her he'd see in an instant how tenuous her control was.

And he had. The memory sickened her. Just a month ago, at Molly's christening, he'd caught her in that unguarded moment when her naked desire for him had been painfully evident. It had been just a look, but it had been enough. He'd seen it, and ever since then she'd been having those dreams. Because she thought she'd seen a mirror of reaction in his eyes. And yet she had to be wrong. She wasn't his type—she might have been for a brief moment, a long time ago, but it had been an aberration.

A dart of familiar pain gripped her momentarily. She knew she wasn't his type because she'd seen one of his incredibly soignée girlfriends at close quarters, the memory of which made her burn with embarrassment even now. She'd been out with a group of girlfriends, visiting her in New York from Dublin, celebrating a hen night. Kate, very reluctantly, had been dressed in a French maid's outfit, complete with obligatory fishnet tights and sparkly feather duster, when she'd walked slap-bang into Tiarnan as he'd been emerging from an exclusive Madison Avenue restaurant, an arm protectively around a petite dark-haired beauty.

Kate had felt about sixteen and fled, praying that he hadn't recognised her. And then, to add insult to injury, one of her friends had chosen that moment to relieve the contents of her stomach in a gutter nearby... She'd never forget the look on Tiarnan's face, or his date's, just before they'd disappeared into the darkened interior of a waiting chauffeur-driven car.

Bitter frustration at her weak and pathetic response to him burned her inside. Would his hold over her never diminish? And now she was imagining him *here*, walking towards her, up the steps. Coming closer. Desperation made her feel panicky. When would the world right itself and the real person be revealed? Someone else. Someone who wasn't Tiarnan Quinn.

She was barely aware of the Hollywood actor speaking in awed tones beside her, but when he said the name *Tiarnan Quinn* everything seemed to zoom into focus and Kate's heart stopped altogether. Reaction set in. It *was* him—and he was now on the stage, coming closer and closer, his eyes narrowed and intent on her.

Kate's instinct where this man was concerned was always to run, as far and as fast as possible. And yet here and now she couldn't. She was caught off guard, like a deer in the headlights. And alongside the very perverse wish that she could be facing anyone else—even sleazy Stephanides—was the familiar yearning, burning feeling she got whenever this man came near.

'Kate.' His voice was deep, achingly familiar, and it impacted on her somewhere vulnerable inside, where she felt her pulse jump and her heart start again. 'Fancy meeting you here.'

Somehow she found her voice—a voice. 'Tiarnan…that was you?'

He nodded, his eyes never leaving hers. Kate had the strongest sensation that she'd been running from this man for a long time and now it was over. But in actual fact he'd caught her a long time ago. A wicked coil of something hot snaked through her belly even as she clamped down desperately on every emotion and any outward sign of his effect on her.

With a smooth move she didn't see coming, Tiarnan came close and put his hands around her waist, thumbs disturbingly close to the undersides of her breasts. His touch was so shocking after years of avoiding any contact beyond the most perfunctory that she automatically put her hands out to steady herself, and found herself clasping his upper arms. Powerful muscles were evident underneath the expensive cloth of his suit. Her belly melted and she looked up helplessly, still stunned to be facing him like this. Shock was rendering her usual defences around him useless.

He was so tall; he'd always been one of the few men that she had to look up to, even in the highest of heels. He towered over her now, making her feel small, delicate. She was aware of every slow second passing, aware of their breaths, but she knew rationally that things were happening in real time, and that no one was aware of the undercurrents flowing between them. At least she hoped they weren't.

'I believe you owe me a kiss?'

This was said lightly, but Tiarnan's grip on her waist was warm and firm, warning her not to try and run or shirk her duty. She nodded, feeling utterly bewildered; what else could she do in front of the wealthiest, most powerful people in San Francisco? How much had he paid in the end? She'd forgotten already. But it had been a shockingly high amount. Half a million dollars? She had the very strong feeling that he was claiming far more than a kiss, and that coil of heat burned fiercer within her.

He pulled her closer, until their bodies were almost touching, and all Kate could feel was that heat—within her and around her. It climbed up her chest and into her face as Tiarnan's head lowered. Overwhelmed at being ambushed like this, and feeling very bewildered, Kate fluttered her eyes closed as the man she'd failed so abysmally to erase from her memory banks pressed his firm, sensual mouth against hers. It had been ten years since they'd kissed like this, and suddenly Kate was eighteen again, pressing her lips ardently against his...

Kate put a shaky finger to her mouth, which still felt sensitive. As kisses went it had been chaste enough, fleeting enough, but the effect had been pure devastation. She'd been hurtled back in time and Pandora's Box was now wide open. A flare of guilt assailed her; she'd fled the thronged ballroom as soon as she'd had the chance.

They'd been grabbed for photos with the press pack behind the stage straight after Tiarnan had claimed his kiss. Dizzy with the after-effects, she'd stood there smiling inanely. His hand had been warm on her elbow, his presence overwhelming. It was still a complete mystery to her as to why he was here at all, but she hadn't even had the wherewithal to stick around and make small talk. She'd run. Exactly like that night in New York on the street.

Bitter recrimination burned her. She was falling apart every time she saw him now, and if she'd not already made an ass of herself in France, mooning at him like a lovesick groupie, then tonight would certainly have him wondering what on earth was wrong with her. How was it possible that instead of growing immune to him she was growing ever more aware of him? Where was the law of physics in that?

She'd fled, not really thinking about where she was going, and now she realised that she was in the hotel bar, with its floor-to-ceiling windows showcasing a glittering view of downtown San Francisco in all its night-time vibrancy. The sound of a siren wailing somewhere nearby failed to root her in reality. The bar was blissfully dark and quiet. A pianist played soothing jazz in the corner. Kate took a seat at a table by the window. After a few minutes someone approached her. She looked up, thinking it would be the waiter, but it was a stranger—a man. He was wearing a suit and looked a little the worse for wear.

'Excuse me, but me and my buddies—' he gestured behind him to two other men in crumpled suits at the bar, who waved cheerfully '—we're all agreed that you're the prettiest woman we've ever seen. Can we buy you a drink?'

Kate smiled tightly, her nerve ends jangling. 'Thanks, really…but if you don't mind I'm happy to get my own drink.'

He swayed unsteadily, with a look of affront on his face, before lurching back to his friends. Then she saw one of the other men make a move towards her, as if taking up the baton. She cursed her impulse to come here, and turned her face resolutely to the window, hoping that would deter him.

She heard a movement, a deep voice, and then a looming dark shape materialised in the glass. She looked up and saw the face of her dreams reflected above her own. Disembodied. Throat dry, she looked round and up. Tiarnan stood there, looking straight at her, eyes like blue shards of ice against his dark skin. Her heart leapt; her palms dampened.

A waitress appeared next to him, and when she asked if they'd like a drink Tiarnan just looked at Kate and said, 'Two Irish whiskeys?'

Kate nodded helplessly, and watched as Tiarnan took the seat opposite her, undoing his bow tie as he did so and opening the top button on his shirt with easy insouciance. His voice, that distinctive accent with its unmistakable Irish roots, affected her somewhere deep inside. It was a connection they shared—both being half Irish and brought up in Ireland.

He jerked his head back towards the men sitting at the bar. 'You could have sent me packing too. They must be devastated.'

A dart of irritation and anger sparked through Kate at Tiarnan, for being here and upsetting her equilibrium. Her voice came out tight. 'I know you. I don't know them.'

His brow quirked. A hint of a smile played around his mouth. Kate felt very exposed in her strapless dress. Her breasts felt full against the bodice. She strove for calm, to be polite, urbane. This was her best friend's brother, that was all. They'd bumped into each other. That was all. On the surface of things. She wouldn't think about what was happening under the surface, the minefield of history that lay buried there. She smiled, but it felt brittle.

'What brings you to San Francisco, Tiarnan?'

Tiarnan's eyes narrowed. He could see very well that Kate was retreating into that cool shell he knew so well. The shell that for years had deflected his attention, made him believe she didn't desire him. But he knew better now, and he saw the pulse under the pale skin of her neck beat hectically even as she projected a front so glacial he could swear the temperature had dropped a few degrees.

He fought the urge to say, *You,* and instead drawled, 'Business. Sorcha mentioned you were here for the annual Buchanen Cancer benefit.' He shrugged easily deciding not to divulge the fact that he'd specifically booked into the same hotel as her. 'I'm staying here too, so I thought I'd come look for you. It would appear that I found you just in time.'

A vision of being kissed and groped by Stavros Stephanides came back into Kate's head. She lowered her head slightly. Some hair slipped forward over her shoulder. She longed for something to cover herself up, and berated herself for not going straight to her room. What had compelled her to come here? She forced herself to look up. She couldn't go anywhere now.

'Yes. I never thanked you for that.' And then curiosity got the better of her. 'How much did you pay in the end?'

'You don't remember?

Kate burned as she shook her head, knowing very well why she didn't remember.

He seemed to savour his words. 'Seven hundred and fifty thousand dollars. And worth every cent.'

It would be. Tiarnan watched her reaction, the shock on her beautiful face, those amazing blue eyes framed with the longest black lashes. Saw the way the candlelight flickered over her satin smooth skin, the slope of her shoulders, the swell of her breasts above the dress. His body hardened and Tiarnan shifted, uncomfortably aware that he wasn't used to women having such an immediate effect on him. He enjoyed always being in control, and yet he could already feel that control becoming a little shaky, elusive… Sitting here with Kate now, the thrill of anticipation was headier than anything he'd felt in a long time.

He'd paid over half a million dollars, just like that. The amount staggered Kate, and yet she knew to Tiarnan it was like small change. That was a fraction of what he gave to charity every year.

'At least it's for a good cause,' she said a little shakily.

The waitress arrived then, with two glasses. She placed napkins down, and then the drinks, and left.

Tiarnan reached out a strong, long-fingered hand and raised his glass towards her, an enigmatic gleam in his eyes. 'A very good cause.'

Kate raised her glass too and clinked it off his. She had the very disturbing impression that they weren't talking about the same thing. Just then his fingers touched hers, and a memory flashed into her head: her arms wrapped tight around his neck, tongues touching and tasting. Tiarnan's hands moving to her buttocks, pulling her in tight so she could feel the thrillingly hard ridge of his arousal. She could almost hear their heartbeats, slow and heavy, then picking up pace, drowning out their breathing—

Kate jerked her hand back so quickly that some of her drink slopped out of the glass. Her skin felt stretched tight, hot. She couldn't believe this was happening. It was like her worst nightmare and her most fervent dream.

She took a quick sip, all the while watching Tiarnan as he watched her, hoping that he couldn't read the turmoil in her head, in her chest. The whiskey trickled like liquid velvet down her throat. She wasn't used to this, that was all. Tiarnan didn't seek her out. She only ever saw him with Sorcha, or when lots of people were around. When Sorcha had lived with her in New York and Tiarnan had called round or invited them out to dinner Kate had always made an excuse, always made sure she wasn't there as much as possible.

But facing him now…that kiss earlier… She was helpless to escape the images threatening to burst through the walls she'd placed around them. Tiarnan leant back, stretching out his long legs, cradling his glass as if this were completely normal, as if they met like this all the time. The latent strength in his body was like a tangible thing.

Kate had to close her eyes for a second as she battled against a vision of him pulling back from kissing her, breathing harshly—

'So, Kate, how have you been?'

Her eyes snapped open. What was *wrong* with her? Normally she managed to keep all this under control, but it was almost as if some silent communication was going on that she knew nothing about—something subversive that she was not in control of, messing with her head. She'd never been so tense. But she told herself she could do this—do the small-talk thing. And after this drink she'd make her excuses and get up and walk away—not see Tiarnan for another few months, or even a year if she was lucky.

So she nodded her head and smiled her most professional smile, injecting breeziness into her voice. 'Fine. Great! Wasn't Molly's christening just gorgeous? I can't believe how big she is already. Sorcha and Romain are so happy. Have you seen them since? I've been *crazy* busy. I had to go to South America straight after the baptism. I got back a few days ago and I flew in tonight for the benefit—'

She took a deep, audibly shaky breath, intending to keep going with her monologue, thinking *Just talk fast and get out of here even faster,* when Tiarnan leant forward and said with quiet emphasis, 'Kate—stop.'

CHAPTER TWO

KATE'S mouth opened and closed. With just those two words she knew that he was seeing right through her—*again*. Silly tears pricked the backs of her eyes. He was playing with her, mocking her for her weakness, as if he'd known all along. So she asked the question, even though she knew it would give her away completely,

'Tiarnan, what are you *really* doing here?'

His face was shuttered, eyes unreadable. The dim lights cast him half in shadow, making him look dark and dangerous. Like a Spanish pirate. His shoulders looked huge. Kate's insides ached as only the way a body recognising its mate ached. Its other half.

Her soft mouth compressed. She'd tried to tell herself that what had happened between them hadn't been unique, hadn't been as earth-shattering as she remembered, but…it had. Since that night, no one had ever kissed her the way he had—with such devastating skill that she'd never been able to get over him. He'd imprinted himself so deeply into her cells. Just one kiss, a mere moment, that was all it had been, but it had been enough.

She repeated the question now, a throb of desperation mixed with anger in her voice, even leaned forward, put her glass down. She wanted to shout at him to just leave her alone, let her get on with her life so she could realise her dream: find someone to love. Have a family. *Finally get over him.*

'What are you doing here, Tiarnan? We both know—'

'We both know why I'm here.' His voice was harsh. The piano player was between numbers, and the words hung almost accusingly in the soft silence. Time seemed to hang suspended, and then the piano player started again and so did Kate's heart, and she desperately tried to claw back some self control and pretend that he *wasn't* referring to that night.

'I don't know what you're talking about.'

Tiarnan took a swift drink and leaned forward to put his empty glass down on the table. The sound made Kate flinch inside.

'You know perfectly well what I'm talking about. That explicit look you gave me in France, and what *didn't* happen that night.'

Oh, God. Kate felt the colour drain from her face. She was officially in her worst nightmare. She *knew* he'd seen her weakness in France—but she just hadn't been able to hide it. And if Tiarnan Quinn was known for anything, it was for sensing weakness and exploiting it ruthlessly.

She forced herself to meet his gaze, even though it was hard, and her voice came out low and husky. 'That night was a long time ago—and you're right. Nothing happened—' She stopped ineffectually. What could she say? *If you're thinking if I still want you, even after a humiliating rejection, then you're right.* Bitterness rose within her.

He was still sitting forward—predatory, dangerous. He said softly, in that deep voice, 'I'd call that kiss something happening, and that look told me that you've been just as aware of this build-up of sexual tension as I have.'

Kate shook her head fiercely, as if that could negate this whole experience. Shame coursed through her again at her youthful naivety, and yet her body tingled even now, when humiliation hung over her like the Sword of Damocles.

Why was he bringing this up *now?* Was he bored? Did he think he'd seen an invitation in her eyes that day at the christening? She burned inside at the thought and rushed to try and fill the silence, the gap, to regain some dignity.

'Tiarnan, like I said, it was a long time ago. I barely remember it, and I've no intention of ever talking about it or repeating the experience. I was very young.'

And a virgin. That unwanted spiking of regret shocked Tiarnan again, and suddenly the thought of other men looking at her, touching her, made him feel almost violent…

He said nothing for a long moment. He couldn't actually speak as he looked into clear blue eyes not dissimilar to his own. They were like drops of ice but they couldn't cool him down. Tiarnan fought the urge to reach across the table and pull her up, crush her mouth under his, taste her again. Instead he finally said, 'You're a liar, and that's a pity.'

Kate felt winded, breathless. The way he was looking at her was so *hot*—but she didn't think for a second that it meant anything. She didn't know why he was bringing this up now. She just wanted to stay in one piece until she could get away.

'I'm not a liar,' she asserted, and then frowned when she registered what he'd said. 'And what do you mean, it's a pity?'

Tiarnan sat back again, and perversely that made Kate more nervous than when he'd been closer.

'You're a liar because I believe you *do* remember every second of that kiss, as well as I do, and it's a pity you don't intend repeating it because I'd very much like to.'

Kate sat straight and tall. Somewhere dimly she could hear her mother's strident voice in her head: *Kate Lancaster, sit up straight. I won't have you let me down with sloppy manners. Show your breeding. You're a young lady and you will not embarrass me in front of these people!*

Her focus returned to the room. She wasn't ten years old. She was twenty-eight. She was an internationally renowned model: successful, independent. She struggled to cling onto what was real: the pianist was playing a familiar tune, the dark, muted tones of the bar, the lights glittering and twinkling out-side. The waitress appeared again, and Kate could see Tiarnan gesture for another drink. His eyes hadn't left hers, and she thought that she might have misheard him. He might have said something entirely different. But then she remembered the way his hands had felt around her waist earlier, how close his thumbs had brushed to her breasts. The way he'd looked at her. The way he was looking at her now.

Ten years on from one moment with this man and she was a quivering wreck. Despite a full and busy life, despite relation-ships… If he had decided, for whatever reason, that he wanted her, and if she acquiesced, it would be like opening the door, flinging her arm wide with a smile on her face and inviting ca-tastrophe to move in for ever. If she was this bad after a kiss, what would she be like after succumbing to the sensual invita-tion that was in his eyes right now? Because that look said that a kiss would be the very least of the experience. And awfully, treacherously, any insecurity she'd harboured since that night about her own sexual appeal died a death in a flame of heat. But it was small comfort. He had rejected her clumsy, innocent advances and she had to remember that—no matter how he might be making her feel right now.

The fact that this moment was a direct manifestation of her most secret fantasies was making her reel. The waitress came and deposited more drinks, taking away the empty glasses. Kate shook her head, feeling her hair move across too sensi-tive skin. She knew all about Tiarnan Quinn—she'd always known all about him. One of the perks of being best friends with his sister. So Kate knew well how he compartmentalised women, how he inevitably left them behind. She'd witnessed his ruthless control first-hand. She wouldn't, *couldn't* allow that to happen again. Not even when his softly spoken words had set up a chain reaction in her body that she'd been ignoring for the past few earth-shattering seconds.

She shook her head harder, even smiled faintly, as if sharing in a joke, as if this whole evening wasn't costing her everything.

'I don't think you mean that for a second.' She took a drink from her glass, put it down again and looked at Tiarnan. 'And even if you did, like I said, I've no desire to re-enact that kiss for your amusement. If all you're looking for is a convenient woman, there are plenty available. You don't need me. I don't think I need to remind you that you made your rejection of my advances quite plain that night.'

Tiarnan chafed at her sudden assuredness—and at her reminder of his clumsy rejection. That feeling of regret spiked uncomfortably again. Her smile was almost mocking—as if she pitied him! He'd never been an object of pity, and he wasn't about to start being one now.

He smiled tightly and saw Kate's eyes widen, the pulse trip in her throat.

'I rejected you because you were inexperienced, too young, and my little sister's best friend.' His jaw clenched. '*Not* because I didn't desire you, as you may well remember. I'm looking for a lot more than a re-enactment of that kiss, and believe me, I don't expect it to be amusing. I'm not looking for a convenient lay, Kate. I'm looking for *you*.'

All of Kate's precious composure crumbled at his raw words.

'You can't possibly mean that…that you—'

'Want you?' He almost grimaced, as if in pain. 'I want you, Kate. As much as you want me.'

'I don't.' she breathed.

He arched a brow. 'No? Then what was that look about at the christening, when you all but devoured me with your hungry blue eyes? And the way you trembled earlier under my hands?'

Kate flushed brick-red. 'Stop it. I wasn't. I didn't.' This was too cruel. Her humiliation knew no bounds. The sword had fallen spectacularly.

Tiarnan grimaced again. 'Don't worry. It's mutual.' His blue eyes speared hers. 'You've never forgotten that night, Kate, have you? It's why you always freeze me out every time we meet.'

She shook her head, his intuition sending shockwaves through her whole body. 'Don't be ridiculous. It was so long ago…of course I've…' She hitched up her chin defiantly. 'I've more than kissed men since then, Tiarnan. What did you think? That I've hugged my pillow to sleep every night, dreaming of you?'

The awful thing was, she could remember the mortification that had led her to rid herself of her virginity as soon as was humanly possible after that night—and what an excruciating disappointment it had been.

His mouth had become a thin line of displeasure. 'I wouldn't imagine for a second that you haven't had lovers, Kate.'

He reached out and took her hand, gripped it so that she couldn't pull away, and Kate was caught, trapped by her own weak responses: lust, and the building of guilty exhilaration. Her heart beat frantically against her breastbone.

'But did any of them make you feel the way I did after just a kiss? Did any of them make you want them so badly that it was all you could think about? Dream about?'

Tiarnan felt momentarily shocked by his words and the emotion behind them; until recently, until he'd set on this course to seduce Kate, he'd never really allowed himself to acknowledge what her effect on him had been. Touching her now, confronting this for the first time, was bringing it all back in vivid detail. Her hand felt small, soft and yet strong. He could feel her pulse beating under the skin.

Kate saw a red mist descend. The exhilaration dissipated. His words were so close to the bone—*too* close to the bone. She pulled her hand from his grasp and curled it tight against her chest.

'How dare you? How dare you come back into my life like this, making assumptions? Judgements? Asking me about things you've no right to know?'

Tiarnan looked at her and felt more sure than ever.

'I have a right, Kate, because one kiss clearly wasn't enough. This has been building between us all these years…this *desire* to know what it might have been like.'

Anger rushed through her, gathering force, and she used it before she could dissolve again. She stood up on shaky legs and looked down as imperiously as she could. But then Tiarnan stood too, altering the dynamic, taking some of the fire out of her anger, making her remember just how tall he was, how broad and strong.

She hitched her chin. 'I think *dormant* is a more appropriate word, and dormant is how it'll stay, Tiarnan. What's brought on this revelation? The fact that you thought you saw something in France? You saw nothing except what you wanted to see. I've no intention of becoming a notch on your bedpost just to satisfy some belated curiosity on your part.'

She walked around the table, as if to leave, but Tiarnan moved too and blocked her way. Kate saw a couple of people looking at them in her peripheral vision. She stalled and looked up, tried to shut out the way looking into Tiarnan's eyes had always made her feel as if she was drowning. She gritted her teeth.

'Could you please move? You're blocking my exit.'

'Need I remind you,' he said silkily, 'that *you* were the one so determined to score that notch in the first place? We both know that if I hadn't stopped when I still could I would have taken your innocence on the rug in front of that fire…'

Those softly spoken words smashed through the last vestiges of Kate's dignity and defence. She looked up at him and beseeched with everything in her. 'Please. Get out of my way, Tiarnan.'

He shook his head. 'I'm walking you to your room.'

'I'm perfectly capable of walking myself, and have been for some time now.'

His voice had steel running through it. 'Nevertheless, I'll walk you to your room—or do you want me to make a spectacle of both of us and carry you out of here?'

One jet-black brow was arched. Kate didn't doubt him for a second. Tiarnan had never been one to give a damn about what people thought.

She felt unbelievably prim as she bit out, 'That won't be necessary. You can escort me to my room if you insist.'

He finally moved aside to let her pass, and Kate stalked towards the entrance of the bar feeling stiff all over, her shoulders so straight and tense that she felt as if she'd crack if someone even touched her. She pressed the button for the lift and looked resolutely up at the display above the door as she waited. Tiarnan stood beside her, a huge, impossibly immovable force. Heat and electricity crackled between them. There was such tension in the air that Kate wanted to scream.

No one reduced her to this. *No one.* She was dignified, calm, collected. She knew she had a reputation for being cool and it hurt her—she was the least cold of people. She could turn it on when it suited her, but it wasn't really her. Cold histrionics and dramatics had been the territory of her mother. Kate had learnt at an early age to be a pretty, placid foil for her mother's effervescent beauty.

The lift arrived and the bell pinged, making Kate jump and then curse silently. She hadn't thought about her mother like that for a long time; Tiarnan's disturbing presence and even more disturbing assertions were effortlessly hurtling her back in time.

He stepped into the lift with her, and the space contracted around them when the doors closed. Kate pressed the button for her floor and looked at Tiarnan irritably when he didn't make a move to do the same. 'Which floor?'

Tiarnan looked at her glaring up at him. She was so beautiful. All fire and brimstone underneath that icy façade. Her eyes were flashing, her cheeks were pink and her breasts rose and fell enticingly under the bodice of her dress. She was rattled, seriously rattled, and he had to admit he was surprised at what was so close to the surface.

In truth he'd imagined this happening much more easily. He'd imagined a sophisticated woman embarking on a well-worn groove, both of them knowing and acting out their parts. But right now he was rattled too. She was resisting him. He couldn't think. All he wanted was to stop the lift, drag her into his arms and plunder her soft mouth. It had been too long since he'd tasted that inner sweetness, and the brief all too chaste kiss earlier had only proved to make his desire even more pronounced. But he knew he couldn't. He had to tread carefully or he might lose Kate for ever—and he didn't like the panicky feeling that generated. He didn't *do* panic.

Kate turned and folded her arms crossly, inadvertently giving Tiarnan an even more enticing view of her cleavage. She was sending out desperate silent vibes: *Get away from me! Leave me alone!* And as the lift climbed the floors with excruciating slowness that was exactly what he did. He actually moved further away. Back towards the wall. And when Kate sent him a suspicious glance she saw that he was leaning back, hands in his pockets, looking at the ceiling. He was even whistling softly.

The lift finally came to a smooth halt and Kate all but ran out through the doors, taking her door key from her purse as she did so. She expected him to be right behind her. She'd seen a new side to him tonight: implacable, ruthless. Determined. It intimidated her. *It excited her.* She got to her door and slid the key into the slot, her hands barely steady after that revelation.

But if he thought for a second that she was going to meekly turn around now and invite him in— Kate turned and pasted on a bright smile, words trembling on her lips…only to find the corridor empty. For a split second she had the bizarre and terrifying notion that she'd imagined the whole thing. Dreamt it all up.

But then she saw him. Leaning against the open lift door nonchalantly, one foot stopping it from closing, his huge shoulders blocking the light inside. That was why she hadn't seen him straight away. He inclined his head,

'Goodnight, Kate, it was good to see you again. Sweet dreams.'

And with that he stepped back in and the doors closed with a swish. Kate's mouth dropped open. All she could see in her mind's eye was that nonchalance and the bright dangerous glitter of blue eyes under dark brows. All her pent-up fury dissolved and she literally sagged like a spent balloon. She stepped inside her door and closed it, stood with her back against it in the dark for a long moment. Her heart beat fast, her skin tingled and her lips still felt sensitive. And yet more than all this was the ache of desire. She felt raw, as if a wound had been reopened.

Damn Tiarnan Quinn. He was playing her—playing with her. She didn't believe for a second that he was going to meekly walk away. No more than she would have meekly let him into her room. He was undoubtedly the most Alpha male she'd ever known. He always had been. He'd been born Alpha. And she'd set him a challenge with her refusal to acknowledge what had happened between them. There was no sense of excitement in knowing this, no sense of anticipation. She'd been too badly hurt in the past. She'd spent too long disguising her feelings, pretending to herself that she didn't want him. Hiding it from others, even from Sorcha.

She couldn't help but feel—knowing his reputation, which was legendary albeit discreet—that she was posing a challenge to him in large part because he'd let her get away. Was this the banal satisfaction of some long-forgotten curiosity? Kate knew well that there would be a very small number on Tiarnan Quinn's list of women who had resisted his charms, for whatever reason. She had the uncanny prescience that hers might be the only name. And yet that night it had been *he* who had stopped proceedings, not her. He was absolutely right; if she'd had any say that night ten years ago they would have made love on that rug in front of the fire.

For whatever reason, he'd obviously decided that he wanted to carry on from where they'd left off. And Kate knew with every bone in her body that if she didn't resist him she would be the biggest fool on this earth. The one shred of dignity she'd clung onto all these years was the very fact that they hadn't slept together.

Tiarnan stood at the window of the sitting room in his luxurious suite. The best in the hotel. He felt hot and frustrated, hands deep in the pockets of his trousers as he looked out at the view, not seeing a bit of it.

All he could see was his own reflection in the window and the slightly tortured look on his face—tortured because Kate Lancaster was lying in bed some floors below him in the very same hotel, and right now Tiarnan would have gladly given over half his fortune to be in that bed with her. She'd emerged from the mists of memory to assume a place that no other woman had ever assumed.

He could smell Kate's light floral scent even now. And yet she'd walked away, resisted him. Tiarnan couldn't remember a time when any woman he'd wanted had resisted him. From the moment the divorced wife of one of his father's friends had seduced him as a teenager he'd seen the manipulative side to women and had been initiated into their ways.

His mother had dealt him his first lesson. Cold and martyred. He'd seen how she'd made life hell for his father. Not happy to have been brought to inclement Ireland from her native Spain, she'd subjected his father and him to the frost of her discontent, eventually driving his father into the arms of another woman who'd been only too happy to accommodate him. Tiarnan could remember his father's secretary, how she would cajole and plead with him to marry *her*. He'd witnessed those scenes as he'd played outside his father's office, listening to the crying and hysterics. And then she'd taken the drastic step of becoming pregnant in a bid to secure her own happiness, and Tiarnan had been forced to collude in a devastating lie.

He forced his mind away from dark memories. He'd witnessed too much as a child. He knew well enough that his father had been no innocent party, but the machinations of the first female role models in his life had inured him to their ways and moods as he'd grown up. He'd vowed long ago not to be at the mercy of any woman, and yet despite everything, all his lessons learnt, he'd been caught too. Rage still simmered down low in acknowledgement of that.

A ripple of cynicism went through him. Even in Kate's innocence ten years ago she'd been manipulative too, just like the rest. Her innocence had been hidden beneath a veneer of sophistication that had fooled him completely until the moment he'd felt that hesitation. A telling gaucheness, an untutored response. It had cut through the haze of lust that had clouded his judgment that night.

Tiarnan could remember the spiking of betrayal and desperation he'd felt. He'd believed her to be experienced. For a second he'd been seduced into believing them to be on equal ground, both knowing what was happening.

Certainly there'd been no indication when she'd found him alone in the library. He'd offered her a drink and she'd taken it… Her hair had gleamed like spun gold in the firelight. A storm had howled outside. There had been a Christmas party going on in the house. Tiarnan had been making a rare home visit…

She had been wearing a dark red silk dress. Ruched and short, it had clung to her breasts and the curve of her hips. Her long legs had been bare, she'd worn high heels. She had taken the glass of whiskey and smiled at him, and for the first time Tiarnan had allowed himself to really notice her. In truth he'd noticed her as soon as he'd arrived that evening, and he hadn't been able to take his eyes off her. Some defence of his must have been down.

He'd noticed her before—of course he had—he'd have to have been dead not to. But strictly as his sister's friend. They'd both been tall and gangly, giggling blushing girls, but that night for the first time Tiarnan had seen that Kate had become a woman.

It was a quality that his own almost eighteen-year-old sister still hadn't quite achieved. But he'd had to concede that Kate had always possessed a quiet air of mature dignity, of inherent sophistication. A quiet foil to Sorcha's rowdiness and effervescence. Sorcha, his sister, had just come through a traumatic time after the relatively recent death of their father, and Tiarnan had taken the opportunity to thank Kate for being there for her.

Kate had blushed and looked down into her glass before looking back up, something fierce in her eyes. 'I love Sorcha. She's the closest thing I have to a sister and I'd do anything for her.'

Tiarnan could remember smiling at her, seeing her eyes widen in response, and then the flare of his arousal had hit so strong and immediate that it had nearly knocked him sideways. The air around them had changed in an instant, crackling with sexual tension. Even though Tiarnan had tried to deny it, to regain some sanity.

Standing there with her skin glowing in the firelight, her lush body firing his senses… He could remember how choked his voice had felt with the need to push her away when all he'd wanted to do was kiss her into oblivion.

'You know I've always considered *you* like a sister too, Kate.'

For an infinitesimal moment Kate had just looked at him, and then she'd carefully put down the drink and come closer to him, her blue eyes glittering, pupils huge. And she'd said huskily, 'I don't see you as a brother, Tiarnan. And I don't want you to see me as a sister.'

His arousal had sky-rocketed. On some level Tiarnan hadn't been able to believe he was being so wound up by an *eighteen-year-old girl*. But in fairness she wasn't like other eighteen-year-olds. She'd already been a model for a couple of years, was already living independently in London. And he couldn't believe she was standing there and seducing him. Or how out of his depth he felt in that moment. At the age of twenty-eight he was no novice around women, but he'd felt like one then.

She'd stepped right up to him and placed her hands around his face. Then, stretching up, she'd pressed her mouth to his. He'd put his hands on her waist, to try and set her back—but he'd felt her curves, and then she'd leaned closer into him, her soft breasts pressed against his chest...and he'd been lost. From that moment Tiarnan had been overtaken for the first time in his life by pure, unadulterated lust. It had felt like the most necessary thing in the world to pull her even closer, to deepen the kiss, taste her with his tongue.

Things had become heated and urgent in seconds, and only that telling movement she'd made, which had brought him back to sanity, had stopped the night ending a lot differently.

Tiarnan's focus came back from the heat of that memory. The vividness of it shocked him. He knew if he was asked he wouldn't be able to recall his last sexual liaison with such clarity. He stepped away from the window with a jerky movement and did the only thing he could do to ensure he'd have a modicum of sleep that night. He took a cold shower and vowed to himself as he did so that very soon he'd have Kate Lancaster in his bed—once that had happened these provocative memories would return to where they belonged: in the past.

Madrid, one week later

'Signorina Lancaster, you have a call.'

The phone felt slippery in Kate's hand. She knew who it was, and her body was already responding as if he was right there in the room with her.

'Gracias.'

She heard a click on the line and then a voice, deep, authoritative. 'Kate.'

His voice reached right down inside her and caused a quiver. She pressed her legs together and gripped the phone even tighter.

'Tiarnan. What a surprise.'

'Hardly,' he responded drily. 'I live about ten minutes from your hotel, and Sorcha told me you'd got the messages I've left. Apparently you've been too busy to get back to me.'

'I did speak to her earlier—and, yes, I've been extremely busy.'

'But now you're finished working?'

'Yes.' Relief rushed through her. Escape was in sight. She was still getting over the shock of having been sent on this last-minute assignment to Madrid—right into Tiarnan's territory, and so soon after their last meeting. Which she had no intention of repeating.

'I'm going home tomorrow—'

'Evening,' Tiarnan finished smoothly for her. 'So you have plenty of time to let us take you for lunch tomorrow.'

'I'm afraid I—' Kate stopped. He'd said *us*.

'Rosie is here. She'd like to see you.'

The words of a lame excuse died in Kate's throat. As much as she hated him for doing this to her, she knew that he would never in a million years use Rosie in any kind of manipulative way. He would know that she'd spent time with Rosie, but probably had very little idea just how much. Kate liked Rosie. She'd used to help Sorcha look after her whenever Tiarnan was in New York on business—which had been frequently enough, as he had offices there. He had sometimes left Rosie with Sorcha for a night or two a couple of times a year when she'd been younger. It had always turned into a joint effort, as Sorcha had been living with Kate in New York until just before she'd met her husband.

Sorcha, up until her pregnancy and the birth of her own daughter, hadn't possessed a maternal bone in her body, so Kate had always been the one to make sure Rosie was wrapped up warm, had eaten well and was tucked in at night. Sorcha used to joke that Kate had been born with a double helping of maternal instinct to make up for the lack of her mother's. The three of them would go to Central Park on adventures, or to the movies and for ice cream afterwards. Kate had always felt a kinship with the small, serious dark-haired child, whose mother had all but abandoned her after her divorce from Tiarnan.

'I'd like to see Rosie too. It's been a while.' Kate's voice felt husky, and already in her head she was rationalising giving in. She *was* leaving tomorrow evening, and with Rosie at lunch too Tiarnan was hardly going to ravish her, was he? And then once she got back to New York she'd be safe again…it would be fine.

'Good. We'll pick you up at midday from the lobby. See you then, Kate.'

And with those softly spoken last words, almost like a caress, the phone line went dead and Kate had the horrible feeling that everything was *not* going to be fine.

CHAPTER THREE

THE following day at midday Kate sat in the lobby of the impossibly chic hotel where she'd been staying. She'd already said goodbye to the crew who'd been with her for the shoot. They were all leaving on an earlier flight, heading to London and their next assignment. Her nerves were coiled tight, making her belly constrict. The thought of the lunch ahead was daunting, to say the least.

And then, as if pulled by an invisible thread, Kate's head came up and she saw Tiarnan silhouetted in the doorway. A huge, imposing figure. Not even giving her time to collect herself, prepare herself. Kate's nerves intensified to a crescendo as she stood up jerkily. Tiarnan strode authoritatively towards her—a man clearly on his own turf. Confident, powerful.

He was dressed in black trousers and a white shirt, open at the neck, his dark skin visible and the strong bronzed column of his throat. Kate hadn't been sure what to wear, and her wardrobe was limited, so she'd gone for a plain black shirt dress and accessorised it with a bright red scarf around her throat. She'd pulled her hair back in a ponytail, trying to project an image that said *friend* and not *lover*. Except right now she felt as if her scarf was strangling her as Tiarnan came to a halt right in front of her. *Too close.* Especially when he took her hands and leant forward to kiss her on both cheeks.

His scent wound through her, and she felt that quiver between her legs again. He had his own very uniquely male scent. She'd always been aware of it. He was one of the few men she knew who didn't douse himself in cologne. Kate had developed an acute sensitivity to smell after years of having to promote various perfumes, almost to the point that strong scents made her feel ill. But Tiarnan's scent was simply soap and water and *him*. Headier than any manufactured scent.

He let her hands go and they tingled. He looked around her. 'Where are your things?'

Kate fought to sound calm, aloof. 'The concierge has my bag. I've arranged for a car to pick me up from here to go to the airport later.'

Tiarnan shook his head and took her by the elbow to lead her over to the desk. 'That won't be necessary.'

In shock, Kate heard him instruct the concierge to cancel the cab and get her bag. The man jumped straight away, clearly recognising Tiarnan. She rounded on him, incensed that he was already dictating. 'What do you think you're doing?'

He looked down at her, leaning nonchalantly against the concierge desk. 'I have to go to the airport later too. You might as well come with me. It'll give us more time together.'

Kate realised something then. Suspicion sparked from her eyes and she crossed her arms. 'Where's Rosie?'

Tiarnan straightened as Kate's small case was delivered by the concierge, who all but bowed to Tiarnan.

He took Kate's arm again, giving her no choice but to trot after him unless she wanted to create a scene. She felt slightly bewildered. She wasn't used to seeing this side of Tiarnan. They emerged, and Kate saw a Range Rover and realised that he still hadn't answered her question. He opened the passenger door and turned to her, the intense blue of his eyes rendering her speechless.

'Rosie's at home. I thought we'd have lunch there.'

She chafed at his easy dominance, at the feeling of being backed into a corner. Tiarnan still had a hand on her elbow and he helped her into the passenger seat. Then, after putting her case in the back, he came around and got into the front, pulling away from the hotel with smooth ease.

The journey to Tiarnan's home didn't take long. It was in the Salamanca area of Madrid, one of the oldest *barrios* and home to some of the most exclusive houses, shops and hotels. It was just off Calle de Serrano, near a charming park, where he turned into a set of huge wrought-iron gates which opened slowly.

Kate looked around her, seriously impressed. Madrid was one of her favourite cities—it always had been. She loved its vibrancy, its history, the café culture, and could spend days wandering around, taking in the museums and galleries. Even now, though it was well into autumn, people were strolling in the lingering warm sunshine. Tiarnan waited to let a woman pass with a baby in a pushchair, and Kate had a sudden vision of what it might be like to live here, have this life. *Be that woman with the pushchair.*

She glanced at Tiarnan's profile as he drove forward when the gates were fully open. He looked distant, and not a little harsh. A shiver went through her even as she felt hot inside. He'd never be part of a dream like that. He'd made it clear a long time ago that as far as he was concerned he'd done the family thing. Sorcha had often told Kate how strongly Tiarnan felt about never marrying again. How Rosie had fulfilled any need he might have had for children.

'Here we are.'

Kate's turbulent thoughts came to an abrupt halt when she realised that they'd stopped outside a huge baroque townhouse. The colour of warm sandstone, it had a crumbling grandeur, with wooden shutters held back from gleaming windows. Bright flowers burst from ornate wrought-iron window box railings and from pots set around the steps and door. Trees surrounded the house, so that it seemed to nestle into the foliage. It was beautiful.

Tiarnan came around to join her. He carried her case in one hand. Kate asked suspiciously, 'Why are you taking it out of the car?'

Tiarnan's blue gaze mocked her for her suspicion. 'Because my driver Juan will be taking us to the airport.'

'But how do you know what time I have to be there?' Kate was struggling not to give in to Tiarnan's effortless domination.

His mouth quirked and her belly flipped.

'Because I know everything, Kate. Stop worrying. I'm not going to jump on you like some callow youth. You're quite safe.'

Just then the massive front door opened, and Kate saw a small dark-haired figure appear. Genuine emotion rushed through her. Tiarnan was forgotten for a moment.

'Rosie!'

Kate started forward instinctively, but then faltered. Rosie wasn't running to greet her as Kate remembered she'd used to do. She was standing there looking very serious. In an instant Kate curbed her instinct to go and hug Rosie, sensing that the child had changed since she'd seen her last. And it *had* been a while. Rosie hadn't come to Molly's christening. Instead, when Kate reached her she just smiled and bent to kiss her formally. She pulled back and looked into dark, wary eyes, wondering what had made her so cautious.

'Rosie, you're all grown up since I last saw you. You're becoming quite the young lady.'

Kate couldn't help tucking a strand of long dark hair behind her ear. Rosie's cheeks flushed pink as she seemed to fight something, and then she mumbled an incoherent reply before turning and running back inside—presumably to her room.

Kate sensed Tiarnan behind her, sensed his impatience. 'I'm sorry about that. Rosie is going through a difficult patch. She spent time with her mother recently, which never ends well.'

Kate's heart went out to the child. She could remember her own trials and tribulations, how *her* mother hadn't wanted anything to do with the fact that her daughter was growing and developing into a young woman. She could remember the turmoil she'd felt. Maybe Rosie was going through the same thing? From what Kate could remember, Stella Rios, Rosie's mother, had never been warm.

She looked at Tiarnan. 'It's fine. You don't have to apologise.'

A buxom housekeeper bustled into the hall, and Kate tried to keep track of the rapid Spanish as Tiarnan introduced them. The woman's name was Esmerelda, and Kate greeted her warmly in Spanish. She could sense Tiarnan looking at her and turned.

'I forgot that you speak Spanish.'

Kate shrugged and coloured slightly. 'Enough to get by.'

She had spent a lot of time working in Spain some years previously, and had kept up Spanish classes when she'd returned to the US.

He regarded her for another long moment, and then gestured with an arm for her to precede him. 'We have some time before lunch is served—let me show you around.'

Kate duly followed Tiarnan through the house, her awe mounting as he revealed a sumptuously formal reception area that led into a dining room which could seat up to twenty people. But just when she was starting to feel too intimidated he drew them away, towards the other side of the house and a much more relaxed area: a comfortable sitting room, complete with overstuffed couches and shelves heaving with books, a widescreen TV, videos and DVDs on the shelves alongside it.

Something in Kate's chest clenched. This was truly a home. Warm and inviting, with colourful rugs on the exposed stone floor.

At the back of the house Tiarnan revealed an idyllic garden with sunlight glinting off an aquamarine pool set among the bushes. A slice of paradise right in the middle of one of the most cosmopolitan cities in the world.

'You have a beautiful home, Tiarnan.'

Kate said the words but they felt ineffectual, stilted. How many women had stood here and told him that?

Tiarnan was looking around them. 'Yes,' he said, almost absently.

Kate shot him a look but he was already moving, walking back towards the house. With a last lingering look at the stunning peaceful garden, Kate followed.

Tiarnan heard Kate's soft footfall behind him. Something forceful and inarticulate was rising in his chest. He'd stood outside and showed her his idyllic paradise, and yet for the first time since he'd bought it he was aware of something inherently empty about it. The image of Rosie appearing at the front door came into his mind's eye. There had been something so lonely about that image too…

He didn't know what it was that was suddenly making him so introspective. He had Kate here. He had no grand plan where she was concerned, apart from getting her into his bed. When it came to women he found it easy to detach. But right now he was feeling anything but detached. He assured himself that it was just because he knew Kate already—they had a connection. And that was why she was here. He was going to use whatever means necessary to show her that he wanted her, to get her to admit to her own desire…

Lunch was in a smaller, less formal dining room just off the huge kitchen. Esmerelda was bustling back and forth with delicious food and warm smiles, but that didn't help dissipate the slight tension in the atmosphere. Despite the fact that Tiarnan was being utterly charming and mesmeric in a way that made Kate feel extremely flustered.

Being the focus of his attention, albeit with Rosie there too, was nothing short of overwhelming. The coiled energy in his taut muscular body connected with hers and she felt jumpy. It was a monumental struggle just to try and keep up with the easy enough conversation.

Rosie was largely silent and monosyllabic when Kate tried to talk to her. Kate had realised that the faint underlying tension was between father and daughter, and she guessed it went deeper than Tiarnan had let on. Rosie was picking at her food, and when she asked in a small, ever so polite voice if she could leave the table, Tiarnan said tightly, 'You've barely said two words to Kate.'

Kate directed a quick smile at Rosie and said, 'I don't mind. She can go if she wants. I remember how boring it can be, listening to adults.'

Rosie immediately jumped up and ran out, her chair scraping on the ground as she did so, making Kate flinch slightly. Tiarnan made as if to go after her, but Kate caught his arm, jerking her hand away again when she felt the muscles bunch under the thin material of his shirt. 'Really, it's fine, Tiarnan. I don't mind.'

He sat down again and sighed heavily. 'When we moved here from the outskirts of Madrid I changed her school. It's not been the easiest of transitions, and I'm currently public enemy number one.'

Kate thought of Stella again—Tiarnan's ex-wife. She'd never really known why the marriage had ended, and Sorcha had never talked about it either, but then Tiarnan's marriage break-up and subsequent fatherhood had coincided with a hard time in Sorcha's life... Kate's attention had naturally been taken up with her friend. In all honesty she'd used every and any excuse to avoid talking or thinking about Tiarnan. And the fact that she was thinking about his marriage now irritated her intensely.

Just as that thought was highlighting the juxtaposition between how she'd always so carefully protected herself around this man and how much he'd already reeled her in, the door opened and a woman came in—someone Kate hadn't yet met. She was middle-aged, and her face was white and tense. She looked as if she'd been crying.

Tiarnan stood up. 'Paloma, this is Kate—an old friend.'

Kate stood and extended her hand. As the woman came in it was extremely obvious that she'd been crying. She shook Kate's hand and managed a distracted watery smile.

Tiarnan was looking from her to Kate. 'This is Paloma— Rosie's nanny.' Belatedly noticing Paloma's distress, he said, 'What is it? Something with Rosie?'

Kate could feel the tension spike, and guessed in an instant that Rosie had probably been giving Paloma a hard time too.

The woman shook her head and fresh tears welled,

'No, it's not Rosie, it's my son. He's been involved in an accident and he's been taken to hospital. I'm sorry, Mr Quinn, but I have to go there immediately.'

Kate put her arm around the woman's shoulders instinctively as Tiarnan quickly reassured her. 'I'll have Juan take you. Don't worry, Paloma, you'll be taken care of.'

'Thank you, Mr Quinn. I'm so sorry.'

He waved aside her apology, and with a look to Kate strode out of the room to make arrangements. Kate did her best to help out. They went to Paloma's room and Kate helped her pack.

A short while later, as they stood on the steps and watched Tiarnan's chauffeur-driven Mercedes pull away with Paloma in the back, he turned and ran a hand through his hair. 'I'm sorry, Kate. I invited you for a quiet lunch and it's been nothing but drama. I didn't intend for it to be like this.'

Kate looked up into those glittering blue eyes and felt out of her depth. Tiarnan had taken control of the situation and despatched Paloma with an assurance that she must have as much time off as she needed. She'd heard him make a call to the hospital where Paloma's son was to make sure that he was getting the best of treatment, arranging for him to be moved to a private room.

Kate knew that he would personally oversee any payment. His innate goodness and generosity made her feel vulnerable.

She shrugged a slim shoulder. 'That's OK. It couldn't be helped.'

A shadow passed over Tiarnan's face and he swore softly under his breath. He looked out past her to where the car had disappeared.

'What is it?'

He looked back to her. 'I'm due in Dublin this evening, for the AGM of the board of Sorcha's outreach programme. I promised Sorcha and Romain I'd do it for them while the baby is so small.'

'Oh...' Kate would instinctively have asked what she could do to help, but she was due on her flight back to New York herself. She knew how important Sorcha's outreach youth centre was to her. And while she'd no doubt Romain would jump on a plane to Dublin for an important meeting like this for his wife, she knew Tiarnan wouldn't want to let them down.

'Can't Esmerelda help out?'

Tiarnan shook his head. 'She's a lot older than she looks, and while she does live here, in an apartment out the back, her husband is old too and needs taking care of... I couldn't ask her to take on Rosie.'

'Your mother?' Kate knew that Mrs Quinn had moved back to her native Madrid as soon as Sorcha had left home.

'She's down in the south, staying with her sister until the spring.'

'Oh...'

'The other problem is that I'm due to fly straight to New York from Dublin tomorrow. I'm taking part in talks with a senator, the mayor and one of the major banks. It's something I couldn't get out of even if I wanted to...'

Kate's conscience pricked her. She had to say something, because she knew when she got back to New York she didn't have any work lined up. She'd told her formidable agent, Maud Harriday, that she wanted to start scaling back her work commitments, and Maud with typical brusqueness had declared that all she needed was a holiday. So now, for the first time in a long time, Kate had a few clear weeks of...nothing.

'Look, I don't have any work lined up for the next...' she stopped herself revealing too much '...the next while. I could stay here and watch Rosie if you want. I mean, if that's OK with you?'

Kate couldn't decipher the expression on Tiarnan's face. She knew he was fiercely protective of his daughter. Perhaps he didn't trust her? That thought lanced her.

'I'd enjoy having an excuse to stay in Madrid—and a chance to see Rosie properly again...'

Tiarnan looked down at Kate, taking in her clear blue gaze. She was surprising him again. Offering to take on responsibility for Rosie like this. A few lovers after his divorce had hinted at wanting to get to know Rosie, to try and become more intimate. He instinctively wanted to say no to Kate's suggestion, but found himself stopping. The immediate feeling that he could trust her with Rosie surprised him.

Kate saw him deliberate, and felt compelled to insist on helping him. She refused to investigate *that* impulse.

'Tiarnan, you're stuck. If you want to go to Dublin in two hours and New York tomorrow, who can you get to mind Rosie at such short notice? And you know if you say you can't go then Romain will have to leave Sorcha on her own with the baby.'

She was right. Tiarnan knew if Kate wasn't here, offering this solution, he would have to take Rosie with him on his trip—and that was never ideal. Especially when her routine was of paramount importance right now. And Kate wasn't some random stranger. Tiarnan knew that she'd spent time with Rosie whenever Sorcha had looked after her for him before, and his discreet security team would make sure that Rosie and she were well protected. Rosie was an independent, mature girl for her age, so she really just needed to have company. Esmerelda would be on hand too. But…

He seemed to be considering something—and then he took Kate by surprise, moving closer. She froze.

He cocked his head slightly. 'You wouldn't be doing this just to avoid me, would you, Kate? Now that you know I'm going to New York? Or even because you're hoping that this will foster some kind of longer-lasting position in my life?'

Kate clenched her fists, surprised by the strength of the hurt that rushed through her at this evidence of his cynicism, and felt anger at his arrogant assumption that her capitulation was a foregone conclusion. His mention of New York hadn't even registered—*or had it?* The evidence that she might have been faced with his relentless determination again within days sent a flare of awareness through her. She damped it down, hating that he might see something.

'No, Tiarnan. Believe it or not, I'm just trying to help.'

She saw a suspicious light flash in his eyes, as if he didn't trust her assertion. He came even closer and lifted a hand, trailing a finger over the curve of her cheekbone and down to the place where her jaw met her neck. Since when had that small area become so sensitive that she wanted to turn her face into his hand and purr like a cat?

'Good,' he said softly. 'Because I had been planning on asking you out for dinner in New York. We can discuss it when I get back.'

Suspicion slammed into Kate, clearing her lust-hazed mind as she remembered the frenetic call from Maud about this assignment, the apparent urgency. She reached up and took down Tiarnan's hand. It felt warm and strong and vital, but she forced herself to let it go and glared up at him. 'Did you have anything to do with my being sent here for this impromptu shoot?'

Tiarnan crossed his arms and looked down at Kate, completely at ease. Smug. He shrugged minutely. 'Not…exactly…'

Kate crossed her arms too, as suspicion turned into cold certainty and not a little fear at how Tiarnan was determined to manipulate her. 'What's that supposed to mean?'

His eyes turned steely. 'It means that I *might* have encouraged the CEO of the luxury brand Baudé, who is a personal friend of mine, to hire you. I was aware he was looking for a suitable model…'

Shock spread through Kate—his influence had meant that within a week of seeing him in San Francisco he had managed to get her all the way across the world to Madrid, practically gift-wrapped on his doorstep. The realisation stunned her. Evidence of his determination made her feel funny inside—confused.

'How dare you use me like that? I'm not some pawn you can just move around—'

Tiarnan took her hand, and her words halted and died.

'Kate. You know I want you. I will do whatever it takes to convince you of that and get you to admit that you want me too.'

'But…but…' Kate spluttered. The effect of him just holding her hand was sending her pulse into overdrive. 'That's positively Machiavellian.'

He came closer and lifted her hand to his mouth, pressed a kiss to the underside of her wrist. 'No. It's called desire—and it's a desire I've denied for a long, long time…'

Ten years. It hung there between them like an accusation.

'Tiarnan,' Kate said weakly. 'It was so long ago…it was just a kiss…we're not the same…'

'So why does it feel like it was only yesterday, and that it was more than just a kiss?'

And right then, with Tiarnan holding her hand and standing so close, it slammed back into Kate with all the intensity as if it had been yesterday. It was exactly the same for her. The only problem was it had never diminished for her, while he'd been busy getting married, having a baby. Forgetting her. Until now. Because he was bored, or intrigued to know what he'd refused?

Kate tried to pull her hand away, but he was remorseless, wouldn't let go. She glared up at him, feeling panic rise, feeling inarticulate.

Tiarnan's voice was eminently reasonable. 'I may have suggested you to someone for a campaign. That's all I did. I wanted to meet you here, show you that I meant what I said in San Francisco…and then in New York I was hoping that you'd agree to go out with me. Give us a chance.' He grimaced. 'What happened with Paloma today was out of even *my* control.'

Kate flushed and looked down for a moment. The panic was still there, but she fought it down. 'Of course it is. You couldn't have known that would happen.'

She looked up then, and finally managed to pull her hand from his. She stepped back to give herself space. But she knew it was useless. Tiarnan Quinn was fast filling every space within her and around her—as only he could.

'Look, I'm offering to stay and watch Rosie till you get back. Apart from that…' She shook her head. 'I—'

Tiarnan put a finger to Kate's mouth. 'Just…think about it, OK?'

Kate looked into his eyes for a long moment, and what she saw there alternately scared the life out of her and made her want to wrap her arms around his neck and have him kiss her— exactly as she'd been wanting him to since the christening in France. Eventually, feeling weak, she nodded. It was only a small movement, but it seemed that Tiarnan was happy enough with that. She was afraid he'd seen some capitulation in her eyes that she wasn't even aware of.

'Good. And thank you for offering to stay.' He stepped back too, and gestured for her to precede him back into the house. 'I'd better see if Rosie's OK with this, and fill you in on all the details of her routine.'

Kate walked back into the house and felt as if she was stepping over a line in the sand. She just hoped and prayed that someone would come along and divert Tiarnan's attention in New York. And yet as soon as she had that thought the acid bile of jealousy rose. Kate was very afraid that when Tiarnan returned she wouldn't have the strength to resist him...

Kate's eyes were tired. She put down what she was working on and sat back in the couch for a moment, closing her eyes, pinching the bridge of her nose. She was waiting up for Tiarnan. He was due home at any time now. He'd been gone for three days.

Kate was all geared up to be clear and firm. She fully intended flying back to New York first thing in the morning. The thought of Rosie, though, made her heart clench. It had taken some time—a couple of days of Kate walking her to and from her new school nearby, chatting easily about this and that—for a sense of the familiar old accord to come back. And while it wasn't exactly the way it had been, things were definitely thawing. Rosie clearly had a lot going on in her serious little head.

Earlier that evening, after Kate had bent down to kiss her goodnight, she'd been surprised and touched when a pair of skinny arms had crept around her neck and held on tight for a second. Rosie had said nothing, and Kate hadn't pushed it, just crept out of the room, her heart swelling with emotion. Emotion she shouldn't be allowing herself to feel for the little girl. *Or* her father.

Kate was surprised to admit to herself that in the past few days she'd felt an increasing sense of relaxation stealing over her. It had been so long since she'd slowed her pace. Stopping at the local café on her way home from seeing Rosie off to school each day, taking time to just read the paper had reminded her of how long it had been since she'd devoted any time to herself.

Sorcha had phoned earlier, and Kate hadn't missed the open curiosity in her voice. Kate hated misleading her friend, keeping the real nature of what was going on with Tiarnan from her, but Sorcha was just too close, so she'd passed off the chain of events that had led her to Madrid as just coincidence. But it was no coincidence that she was sitting curled up on Tiarnan's couch, waiting for him to come home, and no coincidence that was causing this churning mixture of excitement and turmoil in her belly...

Tiarnan stood at the door of the living room. The house was silent, warm. A sense of peace washed over him—the same peace he always felt when he got home and checked that Rosie was safe, tucked up in bed asleep. And yet tonight, after checking on her, that quality of peace was deeper, more profound.

One dim lamp was lit and on the couch was the curled-up figure of a woman. Kate. Here in his house. *His.* Satisfaction coursed through him. He walked in, the rug muffling his steps. She was asleep, hair tumbled over one shoulder in a bright coil of white-gold. His eyes travelled over her lissom form—what he could see of it in faded jeans and plaid button-down shirt. Her feet were bare, delicately arched, toenails painted with clear gloss. Desire was instant and burning within him.

He shrugged off his jacket and threw it onto the edge of the couch, sitting down beside Kate. She moved slightly in her sleep, sliding towards him, towards the depression he'd made. Tiarnan put an arm across the back of the couch and leant towards her face, which was turned towards him.

'Kate,' he whispered softly. She didn't stir.

He'd never been turned on by sleeping women, usually preferring them awake and willing, but there was something so perfect about Kate in sleep, her cheeks flushed a slight pink, her mouth in a little *moue,* that he couldn't resist the temptation to bend even closer and press his mouth to hers.

Kate knew she was dreaming, but it was too delicious a dream to wake herself from just yet. A man's mouth was moving over hers enticingly, softly, as if coaxing a response.

And, as if watching herself from outside her own body, she gave full rein to her imagination and let it be Tiarnan; let it be *his* hard, sensual mouth. It felt so good, so right, and on a sigh that seemed to draw in pure lust she opened her mouth against his.

She felt his deep moan of approval. It rumbled through her whole body, sensitising every point, making her breasts tighten, the tips harden into points. When his tongue sought entry to explore and tease, she smiled against his lips, her own tongue making a bold foray, tasting his, sucking it deep. She arched her body, wanting to feel more…

On some level, even while Kate knew she was dreaming, she was also very aware of the fact that she was in Madrid, in Tiarnan's house, waiting up for him to come home from the US… As if she'd climbed too high in consciousness to stay where she'd been, the shocking realisation came that she was no longer dreaming…what was happening was very real. *Tiarnan!*

Kate's eyes flew open, and at the same time she became aware of her heart racing and her breath coming hard and fast. She also became aware of slumberous blue eyes looking directly into hers. As if he'd sensed her wakefulness before she did, Tiarnan had moved back slightly. Her hands were on his shoulders, *clutching them to her,* not in the act of pushing him away. Her mouth felt bruised, sensitive. She remembered the hunger of that kiss just now. And yet amongst the shock and dismay that splintered her brain was pure joy at seeing him again.

It was all too much for her to process for a minute, seeing him here like this. She reacted against that feeling of joy and tried to push him away with all her might.

'What do you think you're *doing?*'

She gave another huge push, but Tiarnan was like a rock and still far too close. His mouth quirked sexily and everything seemed to slam into Kate at once: the dimness of the room, his scent, his body so close to hers. *Her wanton reaction.*

'Waking you with a kiss.'

She reacted violently to his voice, feeling acutely vulnerable—he'd taken deliberate advantage of her, and the more he did it, the less she could argue to him or herself that she was immune to him. If he knew how close this was to the fantasy she'd had for a long time...

She pushed again, feeling heat rise in her face. 'Finding me asleep did *not* give you the right to molest me.'

Tiarnan finally rolled back and away, releasing her, but a mocking look on his face cut right through her flimsy attack.

'Kate, believe me, I wasn't— *What the—?*' He suddenly jumped up like a scalded cat, holding something in his hand.

Kate immediately saw what it was.

'What the hell is that?' Genuine pain throbbed in his voice, and Kate allowed herself a small dart of pleasure; that would teach him.

She stood up and took the offending article from him. 'It's a knitting needle.' She indicated the couch and the pile of knitting that had rolled off her lap when she'd fallen asleep. 'I'm knitting a jumper for Molly, for Christmas.'

His mouth opened and closed. Kate saw a genuine lack of comprehension in his eyes, and then she looked down to where his hand still held his side, just above his trousers. A dark shape was flowering outwards through a small rip in his shirt, under his hand.

Shock slammed into Kate, turning her cold in a second. 'Tiarnan—you're *bleeding*.'

His mouth was a tight line. 'It went right into me.'

Acting on pure instinct, and feeling a shard of fear rush through her, Kate reached out and ripped open the bottom of his shirt. The wound was a small puncture, but it was pumping blood, and when she looked up at Tiarnan he'd gone white. Too panicked to feel bemused at his obvious distaste for blood, Kate held his shirt to the wound and led him out to the kitchen, where she found the first aid kit under the sink.

She made him rest back on the huge wooden table as she opened his shirt all the way to tend to him. She felt shaky. 'I'm so sorry, Tiarnan. I'd no idea you were leaning on the needle…'

He just grunted, and Kate busied herself stanching the blood. She applied pressure to a piece of cotton wool over the wound for a long moment, and looked at him warily. Colour had come back into his cheeks and his eyes were now glittering into hers.

He arched an incredulous brow. 'Knitting?'

She smiled weakly. 'It's a hobby. Something I took up to pass the time backstage at the shows.'

'Reading would have been too boring, I take it?' His tone was as dry as toast.

She smiled again. 'And smash the stereotype that all models are thick?'

A glint of humour passed between them, and suddenly Kate became very aware of the fact that Tiarnan was lounging back, lean hips resting on the table, shirt open, impressive chest bare. In a surge of awareness, now that the panic was gone, she unthinkingly applied more pressure, making Tiarnan wince.

'Sorry,' she muttered, lifting the cotton wool to check if the bleeding had stopped. To her relief it had, and it didn't look as if the needle had gone too deep. But now all she could think about was the fact that she was right between his splayed legs. The material of his trousers was pulled taut over firmly muscled thighs. His belt buckle glinted and a line of dark silken hair led upwards over a hard flat belly, like an enticement to his chest, which was covered with more dark hair. She had a sudden burning desire to know what it would be like to have her bare breasts pressed against his chest…

She grew hot again as she busied herself cleaning the wound and getting a plaster to hold it in place. Her hands didn't feel steady, and she prayed that Tiarnan wasn't noticing her meltdown.

What Tiarnan *was* noticing was the tantalising display of her breasts, just visible as she moved, in the vee of her shirt. From what he could see she wore a plain white bra, and her breasts looked soft and voluptuous. Perfectly shaped. He could remember how they'd felt, crushed against his chest. Her soft, evocative scent wafted up from her body as she moved. Her legs looked impossibly long in the faded jeans. He shifted on the table as she bent down and unwittingly came closer to where he was starting to ache unmercifully. The pain of where the needle had lanced him faded in comparison. The incongruity of finding that she'd been knitting in the first place—not a hobby that he associated with a woman like her—had faded too, in the heat of his arousal.

If she looked down… He gritted his teeth, trying to control his body, a muscle throbbing in his jaw as her soft small hands worked. Her hair slid over her shoulder then, and whispered against his belly. Everything in him tightened, and he couldn't help a groan. Immediately Kate looked up with wide, innocent eyes, inflaming him even more.

'Did I hurt you?' He shook his head. She was finished putting on the plaster. He could hear the tremor in her voice when she said, 'There—all done.'

He reached out and held her elbows, dragging her imperceptibly closer, and closed his legs around hers slightly. He could see her widening eyes, pupils enlarging, and it had a direct effect on his arousal levels. She was tantalisingly close to where his erection strained against his trousers. But not close enough.

His voice felt as if it was being dragged over gravel. 'Not all done yet… I think you should kiss it better.'

Kate's insides seemed to be melting and combusting all at once. She was unable to look away from Tiarnan's gaze. It held her like a magnet. Time stood still around them. She was so close now. One little tiny step and she'd be right there, captive between his legs, and she would be able to feel… She had to stop this madness. She had to remember that he'd deliberately set out to get her to Madrid to seduce her—had to remember her vow to be strong, resolute. She *couldn't* let this happen. She struggled to swallow.

'Tiarnan, you're not four years old…' Her voice sounded pathetically weak and feeble.

'You stabbed me with your knitting needle,' he growled. 'The least you can do is kiss me better.'

What they were saying should have had a thread of easy humour. But humour was long gone. This was deadly serious.

Kate's heart was pumping so fast now she felt sure he would be able to hear it. His hands on her elbows were strong, rigid. He wasn't going to let her go, and she didn't even know if she would have the strength to step away without falling down. This was the most erotically charged moment she could ever remember experiencing. Her throat was as dry as sandpaper.

'One kiss and then you'll let me go?'

Without taking his eyes from hers, he nodded.

Kate pulled away slightly and Tiarnan let go—cautiously. He leant back a little farther and rested his hands behind him on the table. It made him appear vulnerable and even more sexy, his torso long and lean, shoulders broad. Kate looked down at where the wound was. She put her hands behind her back, as if she couldn't trust herself not to run her fingers over the ridges of muscles that rippled over his belly. She felt weak inside—hot and achy.

She bent down over his chest, and down further, her mouth hovering over where the plaster was. His skin was dark olive, taut and gleaming, begging to be touched, kissed. She imagined it to be hot to the touch, and pressed her mouth just above the plaster. Without having consciously intended it, her mouth was slightly open. She could feel and hear his indrawn breath. Acting on pure instinct, Kate darted her tongue-tip out for the tiniest moment. His skin was warm, and slightly salty on her tongue. Lust coiled through her like a live flame. She could smell the musk of arousal and didn't know if it was hers or his.

She wanted with a desperate urgency to explore further, to press herself close and feel if he was aroused...

With every atom of strength Kate possessed, she managed to straighten up and look Tiarnan in the eye. Her hands were still clenched tight behind her back. She felt feverish. His eyes burned into hers, and suddenly Tiarnan's hands gripped her upper arms and he pulled her right into him. Caught off balance, she fell forward. He caught her full weight, and her hands came out automatically to splay across his chest. Desire flooded her belly and between her legs with traitorous urgency.

'Your wound...' she gasped.

'Will be fine.'

She was desperate now. As desperate for him to keep holding her as she was to get away—and that killed her. 'You said one kiss.'

He looked at her for a long moment. Kate felt her breasts crushed to his chest and, worse, felt his arousal hard against the apex of her legs. She was right in the cradle of his lap, unable to save herself from falling headlong into the fire. Her whole body was crying out to mould into his, to allow it to go up in flames.

She repeated herself, as if that might change the direction things had been taking since he'd walked up to her on that stage in San Francisco.

'You said one kiss.'

Tiarnan snaked one arm around her back, pulling her in even tighter. The other went to the back of her head. She was his captive, and she couldn't move even if she wanted to.

'I lied.'

CHAPTER FOUR

TIARNAN'S mouth came down onto Kate's with all the devastation of a match being put to a dry piece of tinder. Ten years of build-up exploded inside her. Her hands curled into his chest and he pulled her so close to his body that all she could feel was rock-hard muscle and his arousal. Kate could feel moisture gather between her legs and she moved unconsciously, as if she could assuage the need building there.

With a move she wasn't even aware of Tiarnan shifted them, so that Kate was now sitting on the table and he was leaning over her. Eyes closed, Kate could only feel and experience, and give herself up to the onslaught on her senses. Tiarnan's hands were in her hair, around her face. His mouth was relentless, not breaking contact, his tongue stabbing deep—and she was as insatiable as he.

Her arms wound up around his neck, clinging, hands tangling in his short silky hair. She finally broke her mouth away for a brief moment, sucking in harsh breaths. Her heart hammered as she felt Tiarnan's hands move down, moulding over her waist, cupping under her buttocks, pulling her into him even more.

She opened her eyes, but they felt heavy, Tiarnan's face was close, his breath feathering across her face, his mouth hovering. Feeling bereft, Kate reached up again and pressed her mouth feverishly to his, her whole body arching into Tiarnan's, revelling in his hard strength. No other man had ever made her feel so hot, so sensual.

Tiarnan's hands went to her shirt and she could feel him open the buttons, fingers grazing her skin, the curve of her breasts. She didn't protest—she couldn't. Impatient to touch him too, she pushed his shirt off completely, so his chest was bare, and ran her hands over the smooth skin of his shoulders. She felt the muscles move under his skin as his hands pushed aside her shirt. His mouth left hers and blazed a trail of kisses down over her jaw and neck. Kate's head fell back. All she was aware of was here and now and how badly she craved this touch. *His* touch.

Tiarnan's arm supported her as he tipped her off balance slightly so she leant further back. His mouth was on the upper slope of her breast and all her nerve-endings seemed to have gathered at the tip, so tight it hurt.

When she felt him pull down her bra strap and then her bra to expose her breast, her breath stopped. Tiarnan cupped the voluptuous mound with one hand, his thumb passing back and forth over the hard aching tip. Kate bit her lip and looked down. She was breathing fast, one hand behind her, trying to balance, clenched into the table as if that could stop her tipping over the edge of this sensation. Between her legs she burned, and she could feel herself fighting the urge to push into Tiarnan's body.

'So beautiful...' he breathed, looking down at her cupped breast with its pouting dusky peak.

Before Kate could gather her fractured thoughts and steady her breathing he lowered his head and his mouth closed over her nipple. She let out a long moan somewhere between torture and heaven as he drew it into the hot cavern of his mouth and suckled.

This felt so right—as if they had been transported back in time and this was a natural progression of that kiss. And yet...it shouldn't be. Not after ten years. How could ten years of other experiences be obliterated so easily? Wiped out as if they hadn't even existed?

It was that tiny sliver of rationality seeping into her head that woke Kate from her sensual trance. She became aware of the fact that she was practically supine on the kitchen table, and when she felt Tiarnan's hand search for and find the button on her jeans, about to flick it open, she struggled upwards, battling a fierce desire to just give in.

'No...*no,* Tiarnan. *Stop.*' Her hands were on his arms, pushing him back.

After a long moment he stood up, chest heaving, cheeks flushed, eyes glittering. Kate knew she wasn't much more composed. She dropped her hands. Her voice felt raw.

'We can't do this. Rosie might wake and find us...or Esmerelda.'

He looked at her for a long moment and finally took a step back, raking a hand through his short hair. He emanated veritable waves of danger, his face stark with a raw masculine beauty that nearly made Kate throw herself back into his arms. But she didn't.

She stood from the table on shaky legs and pulled her bra up, her shirt together, turning her back to him for a moment. She felt dizzy.

His voice cut through her dizziness. 'A few moments more and here would have done fine... But you're right. This isn't the time or the place.'

She rejected the almost violent need that beat through her body. She knew he was right; a few more moments and here *would* have been fine. Anywhere would have been fine. *The rug in front of the fire.* Any feeling of exhilaration that their desire had been mutual was lost in the humiliation that burned her again. Her voice was fierce.

'There won't *be* a time or place, Tiarnan.'

Kate felt a hard hand on her arm and she was pulled around to face him. His face was glowering down at her, taut with a frustrated need that had to be reflected on hers too.

'How can you deny what just happened here?'

Tiarnan saw Kate's eyes widen and he let her go. The force of need running through him was so strong he was actually afraid he couldn't contain it. She'd felt like nothing he could describe or articulate in his arms. Soft and fragrant and pliant…and so passionate. But he was shocked to come to his senses and acknowledge that if she hadn't stopped him he would be taking her right now on the kitchen table, overhead lights blazing down, like some overgrown teenager who couldn't wait.

Where was his sophistication? His cool logical approach to such matters? *She'd* had to remind *him* about Rosie. She stood, holding her shirt together, hair tousled over her shoulders, her cheeks flushed, lips red and engorged with blood. His hormones were already raging back to life. He had to get a grip.

Kate struggled to close her shirt. She felt as though she'd just been through some kind of seismic earth shift. She watched as Tiarnan's face closed down. He bent to pick up his shirt, muscles rippling across his back, and when he put it on her eye was drawn to the rip and the dark stain of blood. Her belly clenched. She couldn't answer his words. Couldn't deny what had happened.

She looked down, struggling with her bottom button, feeling tears threaten. *God.* How could she have been so un-utterably weak?

'Kate.'

She composed herself and finally closed the button before looking up. She hoped her face was blank, her eyes giving nothing away. She couldn't count on her years of training around Tiarnan any more. Her control was shot to pieces.

His shirt was back on, haphazardly done up, making Kate's heart turn over and making her want to do it up properly for him. She clenched her hands by her sides, fought the urge to tidy her hair, which was all over the place.

His eyes snared hers. She couldn't look away. Her mind blanked.

'I never meant to leap on you the minute I walked in the door...but you can see what happens between us...'

'I—'

His face tightened. '*Don't* deny it, Kate. At least don't do that.'

Kate shut her mouth. She hadn't been sure what she was going to say, but he was right. She'd been about to try and make some excuse for what had happened.

Tiarnan turned away and paced for a moment, before coming back to stand right in front of her. He looked grim. 'I was going to ask you tomorrow, but it seems as if now is as good a time as any.'

'Ask me what...?' Kate said nervously.

'Rosie's school is giving them some holidays from the day after tomorrow while they do some unavoidable renovation work. We're going to our house in Martinique. I'd like you to come with us.'

Kate could feel herself pale. She took a step back and started shaking her head, her heart beating fast.

Tiarnan watched her. 'You know why I'm asking you, Kate. You know what will happen if you say yes. But know this—if you say no, if you insist on returning to New York tomorrow, it won't change anything... I'm not letting you go. Not when we have unfinished business between us. Not when we have *this*.'

He reached out a hand and cupped her cheek. Immediate heat suffused her whole body and electricity made the air between them crackle. He was determined. Nevertheless, she had to hang onto some control. She pulled down his hand and stepped back.

'I need to leave here by eleven to catch my flight. I'd appreciate it if you could call a cab for me in the morning.'

Kate saw Tiarnan's jaw clench, but he just said, 'You won't need a cab. I'll take you if you want to go. *If* you want to go.'

'I will—'

Tiarnan cut her off, changed tack, and surprised himself when he said, 'When I went in to check on Rosie earlier she looked more peaceful than she's done in weeks.'

Kate shook her head, her heart constricting. 'Tiarnan, don't do this.'

Surprise at that admission, and at the way Kate was reacting, made him sound harsh. 'Look, you did me a huge favour minding Rosie. You've got time off, and you probably haven't had a holiday in months…'

Years, she said in her head, and right now it felt as if she'd been running from something for years. That sense of peace that had been stealing over her these last couple of days was elusively seductive, but there was no way she would relax around this man.

'I *would* like you to come on holiday with us. I spoke to Rosie on the phone about it earlier, and she said she'd love to have you come. I asked her not to say anything until I'd spoken to you… Just sleep on it, OK? And let me know in the morning.'

His tone brooked no argument. Pure arrogance. Kate felt tense.

'Fine. Tell yourself what you want. I know what I'll be doing tomorrow.'

Escaping from you again.

Kate backed away while she could and turned away. And felt as if she were being hounded by jeering voices all the way to her room.

Tiarnan watched the space Kate had left for a long moment. She'd rapidly taken up a place in his life he wasn't used to women occupying. He'd already drawn her into an intimate space that no other woman had occupied just by inviting her here, by letting her take care of Rosie. Apart from family, his wife was the only other woman who'd been that close; familiar darkness filled his chest. *She* didn't count.

And even his wife had never taken such control of his every waking and sleeping thought as Kate was beginning to. He tried to rationalise that moment in New York when in the middle of an important meeting his mind had wandered helplessly and he'd had the lightbulb inspiration of asking Kate to join them on holiday. How right it had felt.

He'd tried to tell himself that it was for Rosie as much as himself; he was becoming more and more acutely aware, as she grew older, of the lack of a solid female role model in her life. Yet he'd never introduce anyone into their intimate circle who Rosie wasn't completely comfortable with. When he'd mentioned asking Kate along on holiday to Rosie she'd been more excited about the prospect than she'd been about anything in weeks. The fact that they'd obviously bonded merely comforted him that he'd made the right decision. And he *did* genuinely feel grateful to Kate for stepping in to care for Rosie at such short notice. But he knew that for all his high-minded intentions a much baser desire lay behind the sudden impetus to ask her to come. He just wanted her in one place: in his bed, underneath him.

He recalled her obvious shock at the suggestion and felt curiously vulnerable before he quashed it ruthlessly. He had to wonder if this playing hard to get was just a game. Punishment for his earlier rejection? Or foreplay because she knew she was going to give in? A stab of disappointment ran through him; he didn't want that, but couldn't articulate why he couldn't accept that calculated behaviour from her when he might expect it from another woman. Conflicting emotions rose up, muddying the clarity of his thought, his intention.

One thing was clear: he wanted to keep Kate close until such time as he could let her go again, and he knew that day would come. He couldn't fathom any woman ever taking up that much space *for ever.* He'd never felt that way about anyone.

His conscience pricked. There had been one moment—that night ten years ago, when Kate had all but admitted she was a virgin. The realisation had tapped into something within him and he'd felt compelled to pull back, push her away. He'd found himself reacting from a place of shock—shock at how immediate and raw his response had been. And he'd been more curt than he had intended. The flare of wounded emotion in her eyes had seared through him, but after a moment it had been as if he'd imagined it.

And then her cool response had been all the proof he'd needed that she was exactly the same as every other woman. That momentary weakness he'd felt had been a lesson learnt— a lesson he'd needed in those months afterwards when he'd dealt with his duplicitous wife. If anything, what he'd experienced with Kate and subsequently with Stella had merely reinforced his own cynical belief system.

No, all he and Kate had was history—unfinished business. Thinking of how much he wanted her made him feel ruthless, and he never usually felt ruthless when it came to women. They didn't arouse such passionate feelings. Grim determination filled him as he refused to look any deeper into those feelings. Bed Kate and get her out of his system. There was nothing more to it than that. And if she said yes tomorrow she'd only be proving to him that all this was a playful front. And that was fine. It was all he wanted—wasn't it?

Kate lay on her back as the pre-dawn light stole into her bedroom, a tight knot low in her belly. She'd tossed and turned all night. And now she lay gritty-eyed, staring up at the ceiling.

Turmoil couldn't even begin to describe what she'd been going through in the wee small hours. As if she even had to *think* about Tiarnan's offer: of *course* she would not be going with him to some tropical island paradise to indulge in an affair. Yet, instead of feeling at peace with her decision, she was back in time and standing before Tiarnan in that library, with nothing but the firelight illuminating the room.

At the age of eighteen Kate, despite the fact that she'd been modelling on the international circuit for a couple of years and living in London, had still been unbelievably gauche and unsure of herself. But she'd learnt the art of projecting a cool, dignified façade from an early age, and she used it like an armour.

Kate had accepted Sorcha's plea to come and spend Christmas with her and her mother in Dublin; her own mother had been on holiday with a new husband. When Tiarnan had shown up unexpectedly for the family Christmas party, Kate's world had instantly imploded. She'd been in awe of him since he'd dropped her and Sorcha off at school one Sunday evening in his snazzy sports car. *All* the other girls in the boarding school had swooned that day. But Kate, as Sorcha's friend, had got to see a lot more of Tiarnan than the others. And as the years had progressed she'd developed a crush of monumental proportions.

The night of that party, after only seeing him fleetingly at his father's funeral some months before, and not for quite a while before that, to her he'd become even more handsome, more charismatic, with that cynical edge he still possessed today. Kate had been wearing a dress borrowed from Sorcha, far too tight and short for her liking, and had spent the evening avoiding Tiarnan's penetrating speculative gaze, trying to pull the dress down to cover her thighs. Feeling utterly over-whelmed, and not a little dismayed at her reaction to seeing him again when she'd hoped she would have grown out of such feelings, Kate had slipped away to try and compose herself.

She'd gone into the library, ran smack-bang into Tiarnan, and all good intentions had disappeared instantly. Her crush had solidified there and then into pure grown-up lust. But then something amazing had happened. Alone in that darkened room…looking into his eyes…she'd sensed instinctively that he was looking at her for the first time as an adult. She'd seen it in the quality of his gaze when he'd arrived to the party—it was what had made her feel so self-conscious.

Realising this had been headier than the most potent drink.

An electric awareness had sprung to life between them and she'd experienced a feeling of confidence for the first time in her life. A heady *female* confidence. The kind of confidence she faked for photographers and on the catwalk every day. She was tired of faking it. She wanted to *know* it. And she'd known that the only man who could teach her—who she *wanted* to teach her—was standing right in front of her. She'd known if she didn't seize the moment then, she never would. With that brand-new confidence something reckless had gripped her, and she'd stepped up to Tiarnan and boldly told him she wanted him. And then she'd kissed him.

Kate cringed now in the bed, ten years later, as it all flooded back. To have Tiarnan respond to her untutored kisses had been the most potent aphrodisiac. He'd pulled her close and she'd gone up in flames, pressing herself even closer to him. It had only been when his hand had found the hem of her dress and started to pull it up that reality had intruded for a rude moment. She'd instinctively frozen, becoming acutely aware of her lack of experience and the fact that a very aroused Tiarnan Quinn was about to make love to her. In an instant he'd pulled back and put her away from him with hard hands on her shoulders, looking down at her with glittering angry eyes.

Her heart thudded. So much had happened that night. Whatever romantic notions she might have entertained for a brief moment had been ruthlessly ripped apart within minutes.

She'd looked down, mortified and he'd ruthlessly tipped up her chin and asked brutally, 'Kate, are you a virgin?'

The flare of colour she had felt rising in her cheeks had told him her answer as eloquently as speaking it out loud. He'd spun away towards the fire, turning his back to her for a long moment. Their breathing had been harsh in the quiet room. She could remember how loudly her heart had been beating.

In that moment while he'd turned away Kate had struggled

to claw back some composure. Some semblance of dignity. The fact that he was rejecting her was blatantly obvious.

He'd finally turned back to face her, tall and proud, every line in his body rigid. Kate had forced herself to face him, and the coldly speculative gleam tinged with concern in his eyes had been an instant master class in making her realise just how naïve she'd been.

And then he'd said, 'Kate—look. I'm not sure what just happened—*hell*.' He'd run a hand through his hair and his expletive had made her flinch. His eyes had speared her again. 'I don't sleep with friends of my sister. You're just a kid, Kate, what the hell were you thinking?'

Tears had pricked behind Kate's eyes at the unfairness of that statement. Until just moments ago he'd been with her all the way... And then for an awful moment she doubted that it had even happened the way she'd thought. Had he in fact been trying to push her away all along, and she'd been so ardent she hadn't even noticed? A sensation of excruciating vulnerability had crawled up her spine and she'd called on every single bit of training she possessed. All the years of her mother instructing her not to show emotion, to be pretty and placid.

'Look, Tiarnan, it's no big deal. I just wanted...'

She'd racked her shocked and malfunctioning brain for something to say—something to make it seem as if she didn't care. As if kissing him hadn't been the single most cataclysmic thing that had ever happened to her. Because he was Tiarnan Quinn, and he didn't *do* tender kissing scenes with his little sister's best friend and she should have realised that...

She repeated her words and shrugged. 'I just wanted to kiss you.' She felt exposed and numb. Cold. 'I wanted to lose my virginity, and you...well, I know you, and it seemed—'

Tiarnan had jerked back as if shot, staring down at her with eyes as cold as ice. 'What? As if I'd do because I was handy and available? You don't pull your punches, Kate...'

His face was stonily impenetrable. 'Do you know, it's funny,' he said, almost to himself. 'I might have actually assumed for a moment that you were different...' He shook his head. 'But women never cease to amaze me. Even an innocent like you.'

He'd come close, making a violent tremor go through her whole body, before he'd casually picked up his dinner jacket from where *she* had pushed it off his shoulders onto the floor. His voice had been so cold it had made her shiver, her hands clench tight.

'Go and find yourself a boy your own age, Kate. He'll be much more gentle and understanding than I ever could be.'

And then he'd cupped her chin with his big hand, forcing her gaze upwards to his. She'd gritted her jaw against his fingers.

'And when you've finished with him, go easy on the others...you're undoubtedly a consummate seductress in the making. I've already met the mature version of the woman you'll undoubtedly become.'

And within a scant week of that soul-destroying little speech, before Kate had had time to gather the tattered shreds of her dignity, news had broken of Tiarnan's impending parenthood with his South American ex-girlfriend. Rumours had abounded of upcoming nuptials, which had shortly afterwards been confirmed. Evidently his most recent association with the dark beauty Stella Rios had resulted in more than a kiss goodbye. And, even more evidently, renowned playboy and bachelor Tiarnan Quinn was happy to settle down overnight and avoid the clumsy moves of a woman *like her*.

Kate sighed. Raking up the past was no help, but the memories were still so fresh, the hurt still like a deep raw wound. That night she'd attempted to play with fire and had been badly burnt. She'd been shocked at how deeply Tiarnan's cynicism had run. His easy cruelty had dealt her a harsh first lesson in allowing herself to be vulnerable. And the fact that he'd read her so wrong had hurt more than she could say.

When would she *ever* be free of his hold over her? Especially now that he'd made it obvious he still desired her? At least before she hadn't had to contend with being the target of Tiarnan's attention…and she knew how determined he could be. He hadn't made his fortune and become one of the most influential men in the world through lack of determination. Now that he knew her weakness for him he would pursue her with single-mindedness until she gave in. Until she was powerless before him.

A flutter of traitorous excitement snuck into her belly, cancelling out the knot of tension even as Kate tried to reject the accompanying thought—a mere dark whisper of a suggestion: *What if she gave in?* She immediately rejected the audacious thought outright, aghast that her sense of pride had even let it surface.

But it wouldn't go, staying and growing bigger in her mind with obstinate persistence. And with it came an awful feeling of rightness, of inevitability. A surge of desire flared in the pit of her belly, between her legs, all the stronger because she'd been so desperately suppressing it.

But what if she looked at it as Tiarnan was so obviously looking at it? He had no idea she'd never really got over that night—had no idea and never *would* know that he'd hurt her so deeply. He had no idea that she'd all but believed herself to have become frigid. And he had no idea that last night had proved to her that she wasn't frigid; she was just inexplicably bound to one man. *Him.* A playboy who could never give her the stability she needed, who would undoubtedly hurt her all over again.

Kate clenched her fists, a sense of anger rising at his implicit power over her. Maybe she needed to play him at his own game? Perhaps the only way she could ever truly get over Tiarnan would be to give in? Allow this seduction. Render his hold over her impotent by sating her desire. It had to be because that kiss that night had assumed mythical proportions in her head. Despite her reaction to him just last night, who was to say if it went further he wouldn't have exactly the same effect as every other man had had? Ultimately one of disappointment.

If she slept with him—if she got him out of her system and negated his hold over her, restored the balance of his initial rejection—perhaps then she could walk away, not look back, and find the peace and happiness she craved in her life. Find someone to love, settle down with.

She'd had a fantasy vision of the life she wanted to create for herself ever since she'd been a small girl and had realised that her mother loved herself far more than she loved her, and that her father cared only about his work—to the point where it eventually killed him prematurely. Her life would be as far from her emotionally barren childhood as she could get, and while she knew that a man like Tiarnan Quinn was never going to play the starring role in that scenario, was this in fact an opportunity to gain closure? His words last night came back to her: *Unfinished business.* Wasn't that all he was to her too?

For the first time all night, as dawn broke in earnest outside, Kate felt peace steal over her like a complicit traitor.

'Are you going to tell me what's *really* going on?

Kate sat down heavily on her bed and bit her lip. Her knuckles were white around the mobile phone she held to her ear. Her open suitcase, half packed on the floor, said it all, and she didn't have to look at the clock to know she'd already missed her flight to New York.

She closed her eyes. 'Tiarnan's invited me to go to Martinique with him and Rosie for a holiday, and I've said yes.'

'Yes, I know that, Kate.'

Kate's belly felt queasy. Sorcha *never* called her Kate unless she was upset.

Her friend continued. 'I've just been talking to Tiarnan, and—oh, I don't know—a few things aren't exactly adding up: like the fact that little more than a week ago my brother paid a fortune to kiss you in front of hundreds of people when he avoided a public display of affection even on his wedding day; like you're still in his house in Madrid and tomorrow you're heading to a tropical paradise together.'

'With Rosie too,' Kate quickly asserted—as if that could save her now.

'Kate Lancaster, please give me some credit.'

The hurt in her friend's voice was unmistakable, and Kate's heart clenched painfully.

'Don't you think it's always been glaringly obvious to me that you're never exactly overjoyed when Tiarnan is around? You close up tighter than an oyster protecting a pearl.' Sorcha's voice changed then, became more gentle. 'Look, I know something happened between you two all those years ago in Dublin.'

Kate could feel the colour drain from her face. 'Sorcha, I—'

Sorcha sighed audibly. 'It's OK, you don't have to say anything. I just knew…and when you never said anything I didn't want to push it. But I just… Katie, you were there for me when I needed you, and I always wished that you'd trusted me enough to be there for you too.'

Kate's stomach had plummeted to the ground. 'Sorch, I'm so sorry. I *do* trust you—of course I do… I just—he's your brother, and I was just so mortified. It wasn't that I didn't trust you…'

'OK, look, we can talk about it again—but right now just tell me: do you know what you're doing?'

What could Kate say? She felt a bubble of hysteria rise. She was lurching between excoriating confusion and being absolutely sure that this was what she should be doing every two seconds. When she'd gone down to see Tiarnan in his study, after he'd come home from dropping Rosie to school, all rationality had flown out of the window. Yet despite her early-morning revelations, she'd been so determined to resist the awful temptation to give in and bring to life her greatest fantasy.

He'd stood from behind his desk, tall and intimidating, and

so gorgeous that her mouth had dried up. Like watching a car crash in slow motion, she'd heard herself blurting out, 'You said that night that you don't sleep with your sister's friends—so what's changed?'

Instantly she'd cringed at how she'd given herself away so spectacularly, proving that she remembered every word he'd said.

Tiarnan had come around the desk slowly, to stand lethally close. His eyes so blue it had nearly hurt to look at him.

'Everything. You're no longer an innocent eighteen-year-old. You've matured into a beautiful woman and the boundaries I would have respected before around your friendship with my sister have changed too. She's married, getting on with her own life… Don't you want to do the same, Kate? Haven't you always wondered what it would be like?'

Hurt lanced her at his uncanny ability to strike at the very heart of her most vulnerable self. And the fact that what he said underlined the biggest understatement of her life had rankled unbearably.

'So I'm good enough to take to bed now, just to satisfy your curiosity, Tiarnan? From what I recall there were two of us in the room that night, and there was a significant amount of time before you called a halt to proceedings. To be perfectly honest, I don't think I *do* want to give you the satisfaction of filling a void in your memory.'

And right at that moment Kate had felt as if she really *did* have the strength to walk away. The pain of his rejection was vivid all over again—right up until Tiarnan had hauled her into his chest, captured her close and kissed her, turning her world upside down and all her lofty intentions into dust. Desire had quickly burnt away any remaining paltry resistance.

He'd pulled back finally, when she'd been pliant and dazed in his arms, and said mockingly, 'What about giving *yourself* the satisfaction, Kate? Can you be honest enough with yourself to do that?'

Shockingly aware of his arousal, and knowing with an awful sense of futility that she didn't have the strength to walk away, she'd just said shakily, 'If we do this, Tiarnan, it's going to be on *my* terms. This affair ends when the holiday ends…'

'Katie? Are you there? Did you hear me?'

Kate came back from the memory of the bone-shattering intensity of that kiss. 'I heard you, Sorch. I know what I'm doing.'

She just hoped she sounded convincing.

'Katie, you know Tiarnan almost as well as me. He's always been adamant that he's not going to settle down again. And I just don't want—'

'Sorcha.' Kate cut her off before she could go any further. 'Look, I know what to expect. I'm going into this with my eyes wide open. Please just trust me. It's something we both need to…get closure on.' She winced at how trite that sounded, even though they were exactly the words she'd used to rationalise all this to herself only hours before.

Kate heard a baby's mewl in the background.

'You'd better go, Sorch. Molly sounds like she's waking up.'

Sorcha finally got off the phone, grumbling about the fact that she should have noticed that there'd been more to the tension between Kate and Tiarnan over the years than mutual antipathy.

Kate sat looking into space for a long moment. She knew that she couldn't turn away from this now. She knew that this was the only likely way to even *begin* getting over Tiarnan properly. But she was very afraid that Sorcha was right: that as distant as she planned to keep herself from emotional involvement with Tiarnan, she was already fighting a losing battle…

CHAPTER FIVE

THE following day Kate followed Tiarnan across the tarmac of the airport in Madrid to his private jet. He was hand-in-hand with a still serious-looking Rosie. As he'd said, Rosie had welcomed the news that Kate was coming with them—much to Kate's relief—but she still couldn't quite figure out the tension between father and daughter. Tiarnan looked back at her in that moment, making Kate's breath catch in her throat. He was wearing jeans and a plain polo shirt which made him look astoundingly gorgeous.

'We're flying to New York. I'm leaving my plane there and we'll be taking a smaller plane down to Martinique.'

Kate just nodded and forced a smile. What she also knew was that, far from just leaving his plane in New York, he was leaving it to be used by the philanthropic organisation he'd set up, which covered a multitude of charities he chaired or had set up. It was a very public move he'd made some years ago, to try and discourage the unnecessary use of private aircraft. Kate also knew he took commercial flights wherever possible.

She cursed him under her breath, her eyes drawn with dismaying inevitability to the perfection of his tautly muscled behind in the snug and faded jeans. The man was practically a saint, which made it so much harder to keep herself distanced. But from now on that was what she had to be—distanced. She was a woman of the world, sophisticated and experienced. Not shy, gauche Kate who quivered inwardly at the thought of what lay ahead.

Once they were settled onto the plane and it had taken off, Kate was relieved to see Tiarnan take out some paperwork. She and Rosie set up a card game at the other end of the plane. They were served a delicious lunch, after which Kate and Rosie had exhausted all the card games they knew—so Rosie started reading and Kate went back to her seat to try and get some sleep.

Tiarnan glanced over at her and Kate noticed that he looked tired. Her heart clenched, and she had the bizarre desire to go over and sweep away all his paperwork and force him to relax. Her cheeks warmed guiltily when she thought of how she'd like to make him relax. Already that precious distance was disappearing into the dust.

His head gestured towards the back of the plane, a glint in his eye. 'You can lie down in the bedroom if you want.'

Kate shook her head and tried to stem the heat rising in her body, which had reacted to that explicit glint. 'No, it's fine. Rosie's in there reading; she'll probably fall asleep.'

He just looked at her. After a moment he shrugged minutely and went back to his work. Kate reclined her chair and curled up, facing the other way.

Eventually the tension left her body. She was relieved that since that kiss in his study he'd been the personification of cool, polite distance. For all the world as if she were nothing more than a family friend joining them for a holiday. She would have been scared off if he'd been any other way: triumphant or gloating. But Kate didn't doubt that Tiarnan was a master in the handling of women, and even though that realisation hit her in the solar plexus she was too exhausted after a couple of sleepless nights to feel enraged.

When Kate's body had stopped moving, and it was obvious she was asleep, Tiarnan put down his paperwork and looked over. A tight coil of tension seemed to start in his feet and go all the way to his head. He allowed his eyes to rove over her form, taking in the deliciously round provocation of her bottom as it stuck out, straight at him, encased in linen trousers through which he could see the faint outline of her pants. Her legs were curled up, shoes off. Golden hair billowed out across the cushion and her head was tucked down into her chest. He got up silently and took down a blanket from overhead, spread it out over her body. In profile her face was relaxed, with none of that wakeful watchfulness that she seemed to subject him to, her big blue eyes wary.

He'd had to fight to control himself since he'd kissed her in his study. He'd expected to feel a certain level of disappointment in her acquiescence, which was such a contradiction when all he'd wanted was for her to say yes. And yet she hadn't been coquettish, she hadn't been calculating. When she'd stood in front of him in his study, strangely defiant, she'd had faint bruises of colour under her eyes, and if anything he might have guessed that she'd spent a sleepless night.

He stood straight and looked down at her. A surge of possessiveness gripped him. None of that mattered now. What mattered was that she was here, and very soon he would be discovering all the secrets of that luscious body. He turned abruptly before he did something stupid, like kiss her while she slept, and went to check on Rosie.

Kate woke to the sound of heated voices. Rosie and Tiarnan. She sat up and felt thoroughly dishevelled. She pushed her hair back from her face as she heard Tiarnan's voice emerge from the bedroom at the back.

'Rosalie Quinn, I will not continue this discussion until you can talk to me in a civil manner.'

Kate looked around, and her eyes widened as she saw Tiarnan standing in the doorway with hands on hips, obviously facing Rosie. And then she heard a tearful, 'Go *away!* I hate you, Tiarnan. Why should I listen to you when you're not even my real dad?'

And then a paroxysm of crying started. The door slammed in Tiarnan's face. He sighed deeply and jiggled the knob.

'Rosie, come on…'

Then, as if he could feel her eyes on him, he looked around and saw Kate. He ran a hand through his hair and walked up the cabin towards her, dwarfing everything around him as he did so.

'I'm sorry—we woke you.'

Kate just shook her head. 'It's fine…is everything OK?' Patently it wasn't.

Tiarnan sat in his seat, tipped his had back for a moment. 'Not really, no.'

He looked at her then, and Kate felt speared by the intensity of his eyes and the pain she could see in the blue depths.

'I should be honest with you, Kate. Rosie—well, it's a little more complicated than just moving schools—'

Just then the captain's voice interrupted, to announce that they were approaching New York and to get ready for landing. Kate had no idea she'd slept that long.

After the steward had come to make sure they were all awake, Kate said softly, 'Do you want me to go and—?'

Tiarnan shook his head. 'No, I'll get her. It's not your problem, Kate, and I'm sorry you had to hear anything. I'll explain later.'

After a few minutes a white-faced and obviously upset Rosie came out with Tiarnan and strapped herself into her seat.

As they landed and went through the formalities to change planes, Kate did her best to be upbeat and chirpy, to try and take Rosie's mind off whatever tension was between her and her father. She'd said that Tiarnan wasn't her real dad. Kate had no clue what that could be about. Sorcha had never mentioned anything.

By the time they'd boarded a smaller yet equally luxurious plane for Martinique, Rosie was obviously wrung out, and after picking at a meal she let Kate put her to bed in a small cabin in the back. Kate stayed with her till she fell asleep, feeling a very inappropriate level of maternal concern.

When she emerged to take her seat again Tiarnan asked, 'Do you want a drink?'

Kate shook her head, and then changed her mind abruptly, 'Actually, a small Baileys might be nice.'

Within seconds it was being offered to her by the steward on a tray. Once they were alone again, she could feel Tiarnan looking at her.

She turned to face him, and finally he said, 'I've decided to go to Martinique now with Rosie not only because of the school closing but also because we both need a break, and our house there is her favourite place in the world. It always has been. It's where she gets all the maternal love and affection I can't give her.'

Or her mother, evidently, Kate thought to herself. But she said nothing. Tiarnan was looking into his glass, swirling the liquid. Outside the window beside him the sky was a clear blue, strewn with white ribbons of clouds.

He looked at her and smiled a small smile. 'Mama Lucille and Papa Joe are like grandparents to Rosie. They've been the caretakers of my house since before I owned it, and they have five children and dozens of grandkids—all around Rosie's age. When we go there Rosie can disappear for days and I know she's fine. She turns into something almost feral with all her adopted family... I'm hoping that perhaps—'

He stopped, and the word *adopted* struck her. Kate asked quietly, 'What did she mean about you not being her real dad?'

He looked at her, and something intensely bleak crossed his face for a second before it was gone, making Kate think she'd imagined it.

'I'm not.'

Kate shook her head, frowning. 'But you are. I mean—'

He shook his head and downed his drink. His jaw clenched.

'No, I'm not. I believed I was until a couple of years ago. And I'd probably have never found out if Rosie hadn't got ill and had to have some blood tests done.'

He glanced at Kate. 'It was nothing serious, but we found out that her blood type didn't match mine. That isn't unusual in itself, but other tests were done and, to cut a long story short, I found out that Rosie is not my biological daughter.'

Kate just shook her head, frowning. 'But if you're not, then—'

'Who is?' He laughed sharply. 'Take your pick. It could be any one of the three or four men that Stella slept with around the time we split up.'

'Oh, Tiarnan, I'm sorry.'

His mouth was a grim line. 'The others weren't as wealthy or well set-up as me, so when Stella found out she was pregnant she decided to make me the father. A gamble that paid off. She had all the evidence, doctor's notes, and the dates seemed to match up. And I, who'd never wanted to find myself in that predicament, suddenly discovered a hitherto unknown paternal instinct, a sense of moral responsibility to do the right thing, so I proposed to Stella.'

Kate felt as if a stake were being driven into her heart. She tried to keep her face as bland as possible, not to allow that pain to surface—the pain she'd felt as a vulnerable eighteen-year-old who'd dreamed for a second that perhaps Tiarnan Quinn might fall for her in the space of one kiss.

'Stella married me and milked that paternal instinct for all it was worth. And then as soon as Rosie was born she was off—back to her current lover. We divorced soon after, she got a nice settlement—and the rest, as they say, is history.'

Kate knew that was an understatement. Stella Rios had made a small fortune out of Tiarnan. It had been all over the news at the time. Her head pounded with questions: Had he loved her, though, despite that reluctance to settle down? Was that why he'd married her, apart from wanting to do the right thing? Had she broken his heart?

Kate's throat felt dry. 'When did you find out about the other men?'

Tiarnan closed his eyes for a moment and rubbed a hand over his face. 'When I confronted Stella with the fact that Rosie wasn't mine.' He looked at Kate again. 'I officially adopted Rosie as soon as I discovered the truth. Luckily Stella had signed complete custody over to me on our divorce. There was no way I was going to allow her any opportunity to use Rosie as some kind of pawn in an effort to get more money. Which was exactly what she did as soon as she realised that I knew. But thankfully by then Rosie was mine, and Stella knows well that taking on a small child would disrupt her hedonistic lifestyle, so she's never contested.'

Kate could see that, despite finding out Rosie wasn't his daughter, in every sense she obviously meant as much to him, if not more, than if she *had* been biologically his. It made her feel an ache inside. This wasn't the Tiarnan she was used to—calculating and ruthless and a little intimidating. This Tiarnan was far more human.

'I only allow Rosie to see Stella because she wishes it. Invariably she returns upset every time, but no matter what happens she always wants to go back.' Tiarnan shook his head incredulously, clearly not understanding the apparently masochistic instinct of his ten-year-old daughter. 'Over a year ago I went to Buenos Aires to pick Rosie up from a visit. She overheard Stella and I arguing…she heard every word…unfortunately it was all about the adoption. At first Rosie refused to come home with me, but when Stella told her in no uncertain terms that she wasn't welcome to stay with her any longer, she had no choice…'

Horror coursed through Kate that a mother could be so cruel. She put a hand to her mouth. 'Oh that poor, poor child.'

Tiarnan looked grim. 'And yet Rosie still goes back. Still wants to see Stella even though she's been so unutterably cruel.'

Kate shook her head. She could feel Rosie's pain acutely. In some ways it was similar to what she'd endured with her own mother for years.

Tiarnan looked bleak again. 'I haven't even told Sorcha yet because I don't want to rake up her own painful memories.'

Kate knew what Tiarnan was referring to. When Sorcha and Tiarnan's father had died, Sorcha had found out that she'd actually been born to the mistress of her father—his secretary. She'd died in childbirth, and Tiarnan's Spanish mother had taken Sorcha in as her own. But they'd never really got on, and finding out the truth had sent Sorcha into dark turmoil which could have resulted in a tragedy but thankfully hadn't. Unfortunately Sorcha and Tiarnan's mother had had an even more estranged relationship ever since.

Tiarnan's voice cut through Kate's memories. 'Rosie is punishing me for this…'

Kate looked at him and answered instinctively. 'Because she can. She knows deep down that you love her, so she's lashing out at you when she really wants to lash out at her mother, for rejecting her. She just wants her mother to love her…that's all.'

Tiarnan's mouth thinned. 'I hope you're right. I could cope with anything if I knew that for sure. It's been a tough year.'

Looking into Kate's eyes, Tiarnan had a sudden sense of being out of control. He'd only ever revealed the truth of his marriage to one or two people, and that had been out of pure necessity. His own sister didn't even know about Rosie. And yet here he was, blithely spilling his secrets to a woman whose presence in his life was solely down to the desire he felt for her.

As if to drive away his disturbing thoughts, and an unwelcome feeling of vulnerability, he reached over and with effortless strength pulled Kate from her seat.

She landed on his lap, off balance, her hands against his

chest. Breathless, she said, 'Tiarnan, stop—we can't…not here. What if Rosie—?'

'Rosie could sleep through a bomb going off.' He quirked a sad smile. 'I used to think that she got that from me…'

An unbidden wave of tenderness and compassion came over Kate, taking her by surprise. 'Well maybe she did in another way. Biological ties can be highly overrated, you know.'

A dark brow arched. 'You sound like you speak from experience. Anything you'd like to share? What skeletons are in *your* closet, Kate?'

She shook her head and ignored the dart of pain that struck her. Her skeletons were dull and boring. She thought of her stressed-out, harassed father and her vacuous, narcissistic mother. Kate hadn't seen her flighty mother, currently on rich husband number four, for nearly a year—and that wasn't unusual. She didn't want to allow that old familiar pain to rise now. It would make her think of her yearning to create a solid, loving family base. She couldn't think of that here and now, feeling so raw after what Tiarnan had just shared.

Kate became very aware of being cradled in Tiarnan's lap. And very aware of a shockingly hard piece of his anatomy. When he tugged on her hair to pull her face closer she was powerless to resist. She felt as if a layer of skin had been stripped away, leaving her even more vulnerable to him. She touched her open mouth to his, breaths intermingling and weaving together. Their tongue-tips met, retreated. Breathing and heart-rates increased. Kate could feel his other hand drag her body even closer, and in an instant the kiss had changed from tentative and exploratory to full-on passion, mouths fused, tongues dancing an erotic dance.

After long, heady seconds Kate could feel the whirlpool of pleasure threatening to suck her down. Tiarnan pulled back, his chest still hard against hers. She made a sound of frustration when he broke away. She felt flushed, dizzy, breathless.

Smoky blue eyes glittered up into hers. 'You're probably right. Now is not the time…'

Sanity returned, and Kate pushed herself away from his chest with trembling hands. 'No, it's not.'

She stood up unsteadily and wobbled back to her own seat, snapping her belt shut across her lap, as if it might afford her some protection from the man she would have allowed to make love to her sitting right there in the seat if not for the fact that he'd stopped. In that moment she knew she had to protect herself—had to make Tiarnan see that this affair was on *her* terms and had limits.

She took a deep breath and looked at him, forcing herself not to notice the way his flushed cheeks, tousled hair, the almost feral glitter in his eyes that connected to something deep inside her with visceral intensity.

'Tiarnan, look—'

'That sounds ominous.'

Kate cursed him. 'We need to talk about…*this*.' She cast a quick look back to the closed cabin door, even though there was no way anyone could hear their softly spoken words. 'This has to end when we return home.'

His eyes flashed. Kate knew he probably wasn't used to his lovers dictating terms. Well, tough. This was the only way she knew would be able to get through this. This would be her great indulgence. She knew better than anybody after those revelations that Tiarnan was not the marrying or settling down kind. Once these ten days were over she would be getting on with the rest of her life. No matter how hard. She had to. She couldn't contemplate another moment of this lingering pain.

She forged on. 'I mean it, Tiarnan. I don't want to add to Rosie's woes by causing her more turmoil.'

Tiarnan's whole body bristled at that. 'Neither do I, Kate. I wouldn't have asked you here in a heartbeat if I thought it might result in upsetting Rosie. She wants you here too, and she won't see anything to upset her. If she'd expressed the slightest doubt about you coming I wouldn't have asked you.'

Kate immediately felt chagrined. 'Of course not. I know you wouldn't do anything— But I'd just be afraid of her seeing…something.' How could she not, Kate wailed inwardly, when all she had to do was look at Tiarnan and feel herself going up in flames…

Tiarnan finally looked away, after a long, intense moment, and seemed to spot something out of Kate's window. He came out of his seat to lean over her. Kate squirmed backwards, terrified he'd feel the peaking of her nipples against his arm, the evidence of how easily he could turn her on.

He pointed at something. 'Look—there it is.'

Kate looked down and, sure enough, an idyllic-looking island of forested green rose out of the unbelievably azure water around it. Mountain-tops and peaks were visible through the clouds.

Just then the cabin door opened, and Kate felt Tiarnan tense. Acting on pure instinct, she took his hand for a moment and squeezed it before he stood up to greet Rosie. He flashed her an enigmatic look. Immediately she felt silly, exposed. Who did she think she was? His wife?

'I was just showing Kate Martinique. We'll be landing soon.'

Tiarnan was barely aware of Rosie ignoring him as she came and sat on Kate's lap, pointing things out to her through the window. He sat down and could still feel the press of Kate's fingers around his. A show of support. He'd never had that— never had that sensation of someone sharing his experience. It made him feel— He didn't want to think about how it made him feel. Or how it felt to see Rosie sitting on Kate's lap with such trusting ease, their two heads close together.

Kate's assertion that she wouldn't want Rosie to be hurt had made all sorts of hackles rise. *He* was the one responsible for his daughter's well-being and security, and he had the uncustomary sensation of having allowed himself and her to be put in a vulnerable position. With an effort, he let himself tune into Rosie's chatter to Kate about Mama Lucille and Papa Joe, and her best friend Zoe.

Still feeling exposed, and studiously avoiding looking anywhere near Tiarnan, Kate hugged Rosie's skinny frame close until she had to take her own seat. Kate hated that her heart ached so much for Rosie and Tiarnan's distress. She shouldn't be allowing them to get too close. But as the plane touched down in a bright tropical paradise, all she could feel was a bittersweet joy so intense that she had to shield her face with her hair, terrified that Tiarnan or Rosie might see it.

With the time difference, it was afternoon when they arrived. The sun beat down, and it must have rained shortly before as the ground was steaming. The air was heavy and humid, warming right through to Kate's bones and already making sweat gather at the small of her back and between her breasts.

A smiling young local man met them off the plane, with a small open-top Jeep, and Tiarnan drove it now on a narrow road along the coast. They were heading south, and Kate was happy just to take in the scenery and listen to Rosie chatting non-stop about everything and anything. It was good to see her so animated.

Before too long they came into a charming fishing village, Anse D'Arlet with a white church dominating the seafront and a long wooden promenade that stretched out over the water, where colourful boats bobbed up and down. Shops were strewn along the main street. Some of the buildings were crumbling and had a faded grandeur that just added to the appeal of this slow, peaceful-looking place.

'This is it—our local village.'

Kate looked at Tiarnan briefly. Even he already looked more relaxed.

Rosie was standing up behind his seat, pointing a finger, and she said excitedly, 'That's Zoe's house—there, Katie, look! Tiarnan, please can I get out and go see her now?'

Kate could see Tiarnan's jaw clench, and she felt his pain at Rosie's insistent use of *Tiarnan*. He looked for a moment as if he was going to say no, but then he slowed the Jeep at the bottom of a small drive and Rosie jumped out. Another small girl appeared, and the two started squealing and running towards each other. Tiarnan waved at the woman who had appeared in the doorway of the house, and Kate guessed it must be the little girl's mother.

He turned then and shook his head at Kate. 'See? We'll be lucky to get her back for dinner, but she'll want to see Mama Lucille…'

Tiarnan kept driving southwards out of the small town, and after a couple of minutes turned right towards the sea into an open set of gates that were wildly overgrown with frangipani and exotic flowers. They emerged from under a dense canopy of foliage into a small forecourt in front of an idyllic white-painted villa.

It was old colonial French-style, and had a wooden deck wrapped around it and what looked like a long balcony above, with an intricately carved railing. Shutters were painted bright blue, and everything looked pristine and lovingly cared for. A shape appeared in the open front door, and Kate saw a huge, buxom woman with the biggest, whitest smile she'd ever seen in her life.

Tiarnan had stopped the Jeep, and as he helped her out he smiled and said, 'May I present the inimitable Mama Lucille…?'

The woman came to the top of the steps and put her hands on ample hips. She looked from left to right. 'Where is my baby girl?'

Tiarnan took the steps two at a time and gave her a huge hug before standing back, 'Where do you think? She had to stop and see her partner in crime—*your* granddaughter Zoe. No doubt they're already driving Anne-Marie crazy.'

Mama Lucille shook her head and laughed a big belly laugh,

and as Kate came shyly up the steps behind Tiarnan she could see that this woman truly was some sort of universal earth mother. She looked ageless.

Mama Lucille set Tiarnan aside and put her hands on her hips again. 'And who is *this* vision?' She glanced at Tiarnan with a wicked gleam in her dark eyes. 'Is she an angel come to save us all?'

Before Tiarnan could answer, Kate stepped forward and smiled. 'No angel, I'm afraid—just Kate. I'm an old friend of Tiarnan and Sorcha's.'

Kate's innate humility struck Tiarnan forcibly. She was one of the most famous models in the world, but she had absolutely no evidence of an ego to reflect that; no expectation that people should *know* her. The realisation unsettled him for a moment, and he had to concede that Kate was surprising him—exactly as she'd done in San Francisco, when he'd imagined things going differently. He was somewhat belatedly aware that he didn't really know her that well at all, and with that awareness came a tingling sense of anticipation.

Kate was holding out her hand, but Mama Lucille waved it away and dragged Kate into her massive bosom. 'Any friend of theirs is a friend of mine.' She pulled back then and held Kate away from her slightly, looked her up and down critically. 'Are you a model, the same as that sister of his?'

Kate nodded.

'Hmph. Thought so. Too skinny—just like that other one— but I'd say she's bigger now, after the baby!' Mama Lucille guffawed again and pinched Kate's cheek. 'Don't you worry, angel. A few days of my cooking and we'll put some fat on those hips…'

Kate had to laugh as she imagined her agent's horrorstruck face if she arrived back a few pounds heavier, and with that came the familiar yearning to just let go and stop being so aware of things like her weight.

Before she knew it, Mama Lucille had disappeared in a flurry of movement, with a promise of some dinner in a couple of hours. A young girl with a shy pretty smile appeared and took their bags into the house.

Tiarnan took Kate by the hand. She would have pulled away, but he held her with easy strength, looking at her with an assessing gaze that made her toes curl.

'Come on, I'll give you the tour.'

Kate felt dizzy by the time Tiarnan was leading her upstairs. The house was completely charming. All dark polished wooden floorboards, white walls and beautiful old furniture. White muslin curtains fluttered in the breezes that flowed through open sash windows, with latticed shutters wide open. She'd seen a butterfly dart in one window and out through the next with a flash of bright iridescence. It was truly a home. Kate could imagine the doors always open, people coming and going all day, and yet it had a tranquil air that beguiled and seduced…

'Do Mama Lucille and Papa Joe live here too?' Kate asked as she followed Tiarnan up the stairs and tried not to look at his bottom. He glanced back and she coloured guiltily.

'No. Even though I've been trying to get them to move in for years. They're on the other side of the property. There's a back entrance, down by the private beach, and they live in the old gate lodge. Mama Lucille says she prefers it because there's not enough room for her family to come and stay, and it's the only way she and Papa Joe get peace and quiet to themselves.'

Clearly, from the warmth in his voice, Tiarnan was as crazy as Rosie was about this place and the people. It made Kate's heart do a funny jump in her chest. And what also made her heart feel funny was that the same impression she'd had on the plane: she'd never seen this more relaxed side of Tiarnan before. There'd always been something slightly aloof about him, distant and distinguished. Formidable. And here all that was being stripped away. *Distance—keep your distance,* she repeated like a mantra in her head, futile as she knew it was.

She got to the top of the stairs to see a wide open corridor, doorways on each side, and a huge window seat at the end with what she could imagine must be a spectacular view over the garden. Tiarnan was leaning nonchalantly against a door that led into a bedroom.

'This is your room.'

Kate looked at him warily as she passed him and went in. Her bag had already been deposited inside. The same lovingly polished floorboards were echoed in the antique furniture. Old black and white photographs hung on the walls. A huge four-poster bed was in the centre of the room, its muslin drapes pulled back. A small door led to a white-tiled bathroom with a huge stand-alone bath and shower in the corner. It screamed understated luxury. A pair of open veranda doors led out to the second level wooden balcony, along which trailed vine-like flowers of colours so vibrant it almost hurt to look at them. And beyond that lay the unmistakable clear blue waters of the Caribbean. This truly *was* paradise.

She turned at the open door and looked back at Tiarnan, her heart thumping heavily. 'It's beautiful. Really.'

He walked towards her with all the grace and danger of a dark panther, and Kate could feel her eyes grow bigger as he came closer. Her loose linen trousers and shirt suddenly felt constricting, but he just took her hand and led her outside and to the left, where she could see an identical set of open doors. He stopped at the entrance and Kate could see another room, a little bigger and obviously decorated along much more masculine lines. *His room.*

He didn't even have to say it. The understanding was heavy between them. Within this stunning house and these two rooms they were as effectively cut off and private as they wanted to be. He let go of her hand and looked down at her. Kate felt unbearably hot right then, and it had nothing to do with being in the tropics.

He gestured with his head back to her room. 'That used to be Rosie's room when she was smaller, so I could hear if she woke during the night, but she hasn't slept there for a few years. Her room is on the other side of the villa. This balcony isn't accessible except by these two rooms.' He took her hand and raised it to his mouth, kissing it briefly, his eyes searing down into hers. 'All you have to do is let me know…'

Kate gulped. 'Tiarnan, I…' She stopped. She couldn't fight the inevitable—couldn't *not* own up to her own desire. So finally she just said weakly, 'OK.'

Sudden trepidation assailed her. He must be assuming that she'd had plenty of practice in the last ten years, and while she hadn't been celibate, she hadn't exactly been swinging from the rafters either. He certainly wouldn't be getting the sophisticated seduction he was no doubt used to and expecting!

He let her hand go and stepped back. 'Why don't you rest up and settle in? Mama Lucille will be serving dinner in a couple of hours…'

He stood there, silhouetted by the sun, looking taller and leaner and darker than she could ever remember him being, and Kate felt almost paralysed by the strength of her desire. When she finally could, she just nodded, and turned and fled.

CHAPTER SIX

THAT evening Kate looked blankly at her clothes laid out on the bed. Luckily she'd been able to go shopping in Madrid to pick up some more things. Tiarnan had offered to buy them for her, but her withering look at that suggestion had made him throw his hands up and step back saying, 'Fine—I've just never known a woman to turn down a chance of a free shopping trip.'

Kate's hackles had risen—and a sense of having made a monumental error. 'Well, I'm not every other woman out there, and I can afford to dress myself—thank you all the same.'

Her mind returned to the present, but with a lingering after-taste of the jealousy she'd felt when he'd alluded to dressing other women. She forced it from her mind. She was well aware that she was going to be the latest in a long line of Tiarnan Quinn's conquests. He was nothing if not discreet about his lovers, and Kate knew that was to protect Rosie—but, coming from the world she came from, she was well aware of the gossip that told of the countless beauties he'd bedded over the years, all of whom had been left with extravagantly generous gifts. Kate vowed there and then that she would not be the same. No trinket, no matter how expensive, would be lavished on her at the end of this. Even the thought of it made her burn with humiliation.

She finally focused on the clothes in front of her again. What did one wear to dinner with the man who'd stolen your heart for what felt like all your life? Kate felt the colour drain from her face and she pressed a hand to her chest, feeling suddenly constricted. He hadn't stolen her heart. *He hadn't.* How could he have? She'd had a teenage crush that had culminated in the single most shattering moment of her life. That was all. She hadn't spent enough time with him to fall in love with him. That night had ripped away any rose-tinted views she might have had of love. And she certainly hadn't come close since.

She couldn't love someone like Tiarnan. He was too hard, too forceful. Too obviously driven to succeed—like her father. She'd always pictured herself with someone kind, gentle...unassuming.

This was just going to be a brief interlude. A completion of something that *she* had started a long time ago. She was doing this so that she could move on with her life and banish Tiarnan Quinn from all the corners of her mind in which he still lingered. She wasn't in love with him, she was in lust. That was all.

The constriction in her chest eased, Kate breathed deep. And finally managed to choose something to wear.

When she came downstairs and approached the door leading out to the wooden terrace at the back of the house a short while later, she could hear Tiarnan's deep rumble of a voice and Mama Lucille's infectious belly laugh. Kate felt unaccountably self-conscious all over again, and resisted the urge to smooth sweaty palms on the dress she'd chosen. It was plain and simple, as only the best designer clothes could be. She'd picked out something that helped her to feel covered up—a deep royal blue silk maxi-dress. She knew how lucky she was that because of her profession she'd never lacked for beautiful clothes, and she was glad of the armour now—as if she could somehow project an image that Tiarnan would be familiar with: an elegant and nonchalant lover.

But when she took a deep breath and walked out Tiarnan looked up. His eyes locked onto hers, and she immediately felt undressed, despite the ankle-length dress, and regretted pulling her hair back into a low ponytail, wishing she had it loose, to cover her face. The silk seemed to cling and caress her body with indecent eagerness. All nonchalance fled and the churning turmoil was back with a vengeance as every step brought her closer and closer to that glittering blue gaze that swept up and down her body, leaving what felt like a trail of fire in its wake.

For a second, as Kate walked towards him, Tiarnan's brain went completely blank and every coherent thought was replaced with heat. She was a vision in blue silk that seemed to waft around her body and yet cling to every curve with a lover's touch. He looked down, and his chest tightened with an indefinable emotion when he saw that her feet were bare. The heat in his brain intensified, and only Mama Lucille pointedly clearing her throat stopped him from turning into a drooling speechless idiot. Some of the most beautiful women in the world had appeared similarly dressed before him, for his pleasure, yet they had never had this paralysing effect on him. He managed to stand just as Kate got to the table, her delicate scent reaching his nostrils as he pulled out her chair and she sat down with a warm smile directed at Mama Lucille.

Her colour was high and she was avoiding his eye, making Tiarnan feel unaccountably flustered. He ignored Mama Lucille's explicit look, which seemed to bore a hole in his head, and thankfully she bustled off with her young assistant in tow.

Kate struggled to get her heartbeat and her breathing under control. The dress which had felt so appropriate now felt like the most inappropriate thing she could have chosen. When she felt sufficiently calm she flicked a glance to Tiarnan. He was staring at her with hooded eyes. Against her volition, her eyes dropped, taking in the snowy-white shirt, open at the neck, and the dark trousers. His hair was damp, as if he'd showered not long ago, and Kate could feel heat climbing upwards over her chest. She grabbed her napkin and clung onto it, twisting it under the table.

'Where's Rosie?'

Tiarnan's eyes didn't move from hers. 'She came back here earlier with Zoe, for dinner with Mama Lucille. Zoe's mother, Anne-Marie, collected them just before you came down. She's spending the night at their place. It's something of a tradition. She'll be back in the morning.'

Kate looked down for a moment. *They were alone all night?* Her heart was thudding heavily, unevenly. Right then she wished for Rosie's comforting presence, even with the tension between father and daughter. 'She's having fun, then…'

Tiarnan nodded. 'Yes. She's surrounded by people who love her like their own, and it's important for her to have that while she's determined to reject me.'

Kate looked at him, unable not to, touched deeply by his concern that Rosie feel loved even while she was determined not to accept love from him. In her experience parents either ignored their children or resented them. And yet he was doing his utmost to make sure Rosie was secure.

'You're a good father, Tiarnan.' She cursed herself for sounding so husky and trite. And cursed herself again when she could feel that armour she'd put up around herself crumble ever so slightly. In an instant he had smashed aside her assertion that he was a man like her father—too career-orientated to care about his daughter.

To her relief Mama Lucille returned with a steaming bowl, followed by Eloise, the girl who'd helped with the luggage and who Mama Lucille now introduced as one of her older granddaughters. Kate got up instinctively to help, but Mama Lucille ordered her to, 'Sit! Let us serve you now.'

Kate watched as more plates arrived, with what looked like an impressive array of fish and roasted vegetables and rice and potatoes and salad. Her eyes were wide, watching as Tiarnan poured white wine into glasses so cold they still had mist on them.

'I've never seen so much food in my life.'

He took her plate and proceeded to heap it high with the succulent food, saying drily, 'Don't tell me you're one of these women who prefer to push a lettuce leaf around your plate and watch it wither and die rather than eat it?'

'No,' Kate said quickly, taking the plate he handed her. 'I couldn't think of anything worse. My problem has never been lack of appetite, it's stopping myself eating.' She grimaced for a second. 'Unfortunately, unlike your sister and presumably you too, I can't eat everything around me and stay the same size. All I eat has to come off again.'

Tiarnan fought down the urge to let his eyes rove over her curves. She was right. Where Sorcha was lean and athletic, Kate had a more natural voluptuousness, a sexy lushness. He picked up his glass and waited for Kate to do the same.

Kate was intensely aware of the way the dusk was claiming the setting sun, turning the sky smoky mauve. The breeze was warm and the sound of the sea came from nearby. Small flaming lights nearby lit up the table and surrounding area. It was idyllic.

Tiarnan held up his glass and said, 'I thought it would be nicer to eat out here. I hope it's not too rustic for you?'

Kate shook her head, mesmerised, and picked up her glass. 'It's perfect. I love it.'

He touched his glass to hers and it made the most subtle chime.

'Welcome, Kate, and *bon appetit*.'

'*Bon appetite,*' she mumbled, her face flaming, and she took a quick sip of the deliciously dry wine.

Tiarnan made sure she had everything she needed, and then proceeded to fill up his own plate impressively. Kate didn't doubt for a second that a man like him would have a huge appetite. When she thought of that, the heat which had begun to recede surged back. She groaned inwardly and then groaned out loud as she tasted a langoustine and it nearly melted on her tongue with an explosion of exquisite tastes.

'This,' she said, when she could. 'Is amazing.'

Tiarnan smiled and nodded. 'Mama Lucille's cooking is legendary. She's had countless offers to work for others, even from the best restaurants here on Martinique, but she's turned them all down.'

Kate smiled too, and picked up her wine glass. 'And no doubt you keep her very well...compensated?'

He inclined his head modestly. 'But of course. I look after everyone I love.'

Kate's heart clenched, and she speared some more food to distract him from what might be in her expression. Was he also talking about the way he compensated his lovers so well? Did he, on some level, love them all too? In that easy superficial way that some men did? Only to let them go easily when they got too clingy? Was he capable of truly falling in love?

'What about you, Kate? Would you like children some day? You're good with Rosie—you seem to have a natural affinity...'

She just about managed not to choke on her wine, and put down the glass carefully, a little blindsided by his swift change of subject. Normally, with such a question from someone else, her natural inclination to reply honestly that she'd never wanted anything more would make answering easy. But here, now, with Tiarnan, she had to protect herself.

She shrugged one shoulder and looked down. 'Yes, I've thought of it. What woman my age doesn't?' Her voice was light, unconcerned, but her womb seemed to contract as she battled a sudden vivid image of holding a dark-haired baby in her arms, Tiarnan's head coming close to press a kiss against the downy, sweet-smelling skin.

In complete dismay at her wayward imagination, and in rejection of that image, she looked up almost defiantly, feeling brittle. 'But not yet. I'm not ready to be tied down. I'm sure it'll happen some day, though, when I meet the right person.'

Tiarnan lounged back. Kate could imagine his long legs

stretched out easily under the table. In comparison she felt incredibly uptight and tense.

'And you haven't met the right person yet, I take it?'

'Well, I'd hardly be here now if I had, would I?' She cursed herself for letting him get to her, making her sound snappy. Tiarnan's eyes had become assessing. Looking deep.

He shrugged too. 'I wouldn't know, Kate. To be honest, it wouldn't surprise me in the least. Let's just say that in my experience women are perennially unsatisfied—either with themselves or their lives—and will do whatever it takes to relieve their boredom.'

'That's a very cynical view to have.'

He shrugged and took a sip of wine. 'When the first relationship you witness has deep flaws, it tends to colour everything else.'

Kate's prickliness dissolved in an instant. 'I know your parents didn't…get on.'

Tiarnan's mouth tightened. 'To put it mildly. I don't have to tell you what it was like… But if none of that had happened I wouldn't have Sorcha for a sister.'

Kate said quietly, 'The fact that your mother took Sorcha in as her own was pretty selfless.'

He made a rejecting motion with his hand. 'A selfless act which drove the wedge between her and my father, and ultimately Sorcha too, even deeper. My mother was—still is—a devout Catholic. She took Sorcha in more out of a sense of religious duty than anything else.'

They both fell silent for a moment, very aware of how that had caused such pain and hurt to Sorcha when she had found out. Kate knew instinctively that there was very little likelihood that Tiarnan would discuss this with anyone else—it was just because of who she was, and the fact that she knew already. Any intimacy she was feeling now was false.

Something rose up within Kate, compelling her to say quietly, 'I do believe, though, that it's possible.'

'That what's possible?'

'For people to be happy. I mean, look at Sorcha and Romain; they're happy.'

Tiarnan's face looked unbearably harsh in the flickering light of the candles for a moment. 'Yes, they are.' He sounded almost surprised, and then his voice became hard. 'I, however, learnt my lesson a long time ago. I indulged in the dream for a brief moment and saw the ugliest part of women's machinations, and how far they're prepared to go to feather their nest.'

Kate's heart clenched. He was talking about Stella, of course—and every other woman too, it would appear, by proxy.

Tiarnan looked into his wine glass, tension gripping him. He cursed himself again for allowing this woman to loosen his tongue, and forced down the tension. He looked up and caught Kate's eye, allowed himself to dive into the deep blue depths. He saw her exactly as she was: a woman of the world, successful, confident, single. Not afraid to take what she wanted. She was like him. Immediately he felt on a more even keel. He snaked out a hand and caught hers, revelling in the contact, the way her skin felt so warm and firm and silky. Revelling in the sensual anticipation.

'For people like us, however, things are different... We won't be caught like that, seduced by some empty dream.'

Kate's heart clenched so hard at that she had to hold in a gasp. She stung inside that he believed her to be the same as him. Ironically enough, out of his sister and Kate, Sorcha had been the more cynical of the two, constantly teasing Kate for her innate romantic streak, for her maternal instinct. Sorcha had been the one with the high walls of defence erected around her, and Romain had been the only man capable of gaining her trust, opening her heart...

Yet, despite her own largely loveless upbringing, Kate had somehow emerged clinging onto those maternal instincts and that romantic dream. And a very secret part of her was still doggedly clinging onto it, despite witnessing the cynicism of the man to whom she was willingly, *stupidly* planning to give herself, in the hope that perhaps it would cure her of this obsession. The fact that he believed her to be as jaded as he was surely had to be in her favour? Protection for when she would walk away? He would believe her to be in one piece, unmoved, moving on with blithe disregard to her next lover. And she would be, she told herself fiercely now. She'd be blithe if it killed her.

She wanted to ask him about his wife—ask if *she'd* managed to break through his cynical wall to make him believe in love for a brief moment. But even if she had, considering how she had deceived him about Rosie, it could only have reaffirmed his beliefs, made them even more entrenched.

Kate forced down all her questions and leaned forward to start eating again, even though her appetite seemed to have vanished. She smiled brilliantly.

'Well, then, we can rest easy in the protection such beliefs can offer us: no expectation, no disappointment.'

The words seemed to score through her heart like a serrated knife, they so went against her own personal philosophy. A philosophy she couldn't share with Tiarnan.

Tiarnan smiled lazily, eyes narrowed on hers. 'A kindred spirit. I couldn't have put it better.'

As Kate forced herself to eat and sip the wine, engage in conversation that moved away from darker topics, she told herself that at least now she was under no illusion that some kind of fairytale would happen here. Tiarnan was utterly content with his life and there was no way he was going to let in Kate to shake things up.

The plates were gone, Mama Lucille had bade them goodnight, and Kate had kissed her in thanks for the meal, making the older woman look embarrassed but happy. Papa Joe, her handsome husband, had come to collect her to walk her home. Being bowed with age didn't diminish his charm. He seemed as naturally friendly and happy as his wife, and they heard them laughing and conversing loudly in local French patois all the way down the garden path. Witnessing their happiness made Kate's conversation with Tiarnan over dinner feel all the more unbearably poignant.

The heavy perfumed air was alive with the sounds of insects. Kate felt almost painfully sensitive to everything. All too aware of what she yearned for and what she was prepared to settle for with Tiarnan. He reached out and took her hand, and predictably she tensed.

'You don't seem very relaxed.' He stated the obvious.

Kate shrugged and forced down her tangled thoughts of yearning. 'Despite what you might believe, I'm not used to being whisked halfway across the world to become a rich man's mistress for a few days.'

Tiarnan's jaw clenched. She kept talking about the time limit. And she certainly wasn't just a rich man's mistress. She was going to be *his* lover. Her words over dinner, her reassurance that she was like him, should be making him feel at ease, confident, and yet they weren't. Not entirely. He didn't trust her. And he didn't know why that rankled. What woman *did* he trust? He was used to not trusting women.

He drove away the questions. He had no need to question anything. Kate Lancaster was here, his for now, and that was all that mattered. They were wasting time. He studied her downbent head, the gleaming blonde hair, the satin smooth skin of her bared shoulders under the straps of her dress, the swell of her breasts…and he knew just how to drive away those thoughts, the tenseness which made ambiguous feelings run through him.

Tiarnan kept a hold of her hand and stood, tugging her up with him. Kate's eyes met his and the world seemed to stop turning momentarily. 'I know just what we need.'

'You do?'

Kate's voice came out like a squeak. She cursed her inability to sound insouciant when she needed to. He nodded, and started to walk back into the house, taking her with him, his grip strong and sure. Her legs felt like jelly. Panic started to rise up, strangling her. She had to tell him, had to say something. He thought she was something she wasn't...

'Tiarnan, I—'

He turned and pressed a finger to her lips.

'I'm taking you out.'

Confusion cut through the panic. The scarily vivid images of their naked limbs entwined on his bed faded.

'What? Where?'

He looked at her for a long moment, and then just said, 'Dancing.'

Kate's hand was still in Tiarnan's as he led them into a dimly lit bar not too far from the house. A throbbing pulsing beat of music enveloped them instantly, along with the heat of bodies and muted conversations.

He'd waited till she had put on some shoes and had obviously made a call, as an open-top Jeep with a smiling driver had been waiting for them outside the villa. He led her to the bar now, only letting go of her hand to put an arm around her waist and draw her in close. Kate saw the bartender spot him and come over with a huge smile on his face.

'Tiarnan, my man! It's good to see you.' The barman's openly curious and very flirty glance took Kate in with blatant appreciation.

She felt embarrassed, and very out of her depth. Tiarnan kept surprising her at every turn, and the thought that he might have read her trepidation and done this to somehow make things easier for her made her feel vulnerable.

'And your beautiful guest...'

For the first time in his life Tiarnan felt the intense spiking of jealousy as his old friend Luc looked Kate up and down with what seemed to be insulting impunity. He'd noticed every other man's head swivelling too, as they'd walked into the bar. Kate stood out like a magnificent bird of paradise.

Resisting the unfathomable urge to walk straight back out again, he forced himself to sound civil and say, 'Luc, good to see you too. We'll have two of your best rums.'

He looked down at Kate and was surprised to see her looking almost…self-conscious. He tugged her in closer and she looked up, a flare of colour racing across her cheekbones.

'Is that OK?'

Kate felt almost disembodied, looking up into Tiarnan's eyes. 'Is what OK?'

'Martinique rum—you should try it.'

She just nodded, still barely aware of what he was saying. Their solicitous host insisted on showing them over to a secluded booth with a view over the faded grandeur of the bar, which was open to the street, and the dark inkiness of the sea in the distance. They were in the ground floor of an old colonial building. The crowd were local, the music was a kind of sexy upbeat Salsa. And then it changed smoothly to something slow and *very* hot. Some of the couples on the dance floor certainly looked as if they were just moments away from disappearing to a dark corner where—

Kate willed down the intense blush she could feel on her face as she looked at the couples, and just then Tiarnan's hand cupped her jaw, turning her to face him. She felt feverish.

He shook his head, and a thumb moved back and forth across her cheek. 'Enchanting. I don't think I've ever seen anyone blush the way you do.'

Kate burned inside and out. The enormity of where she was and who she was sitting with was hitting her anew all over again. 'It's just my colouring.'

Their eyes stayed locked for a long moment, until Kate felt as if she was melting inside. Just as she was about to beg to be released from that intense gaze, Tiarnan suddenly broke it and looked away, making Kate feel absurdly bereft all of a sudden. She was a mass of contradictions and warring desires.

Tiarnan's friend approached with two glasses, and left again with a mischievous smile and a look that Kate didn't miss. When Tiarnan had introduced them briefly she'd thought he'd been uncharacteristically curt to the other man, but Luc didn't seem to mind. She took a sip of the dark liquid and coughed immediately, her eyes smarting.

Tiarnan quirked a brow and smiled. 'Strong stuff.'

Kate grabbed for some water and drank it down. 'You could have warned me.' She watched as Tiarnan took another sip himself, watched the way the strong column of his throat worked. At that moment the music changed back to an infectiously upbeat rhythm.

Tiarnan extended a hand across the table. 'Come on, let's dance.'

Kate shrank back with genuine fear. She could see couples dancing with effortless grace and style, making moves she could never even hope to mimic. She shook her head desperately, 'I can't dance, Tiarnan.'

He left his hand where it was.

'Seriously,' she said pleadingly. 'I'm really, really bad, I'll just embarrass you.'

He stood up and took her hand from her lap, pulling her up.

She tried to resist. 'I'll watch you dance with someone else—honestly.'

He wasn't listening. He pulled her remorselessly after him. Kate was having flashbacks to excruciating moments on other dance floors where she'd shuffled around, invariably much to Sorcha's hysterical amusement. Or memories of standing on various hapless men's feet and apologising profusely.

She tried to pull away again. 'Tiarnan, you don't understand. I've two left feet—just like my father. I've never been able to—'

Tiarnan turned and pulled her into his arms, and Kate shut up instantly at the feel of his body so close to hers, one hand low on her back and the other held high. She could feel Tiarnan's hips move sinuously against hers, his legs making hers move in tandem with his.

His voice came low near her ear, making her tingle, 'Just feel the beat—let it go through you.'

All Kate felt was boneless, with an indecent need running through her.

Tiarnan moved them apart and put both hands on her hips. 'See? Look at my feet. Copy what I'm doing.'

She could barely function. Tiarnan's broad chest and those lean hips were hypnotising her. She didn't know if what she was doing was anything like dancing, but she did feel the deeply sexy beat in her blood, and when Tiarnan turned her around and pulled her back against him, his arm across her midriff, she didn't even care that she couldn't dance. She had to close her eyes and try not to let out a low moan of pleasure.

Then the music changed again to slow and sexy. Tiarnan twirled her around with effortless ease and pulled her into him, so close that she could feel the imprint of his body all along hers. He tipped up her chin. Her head fell back.

'See? Anyone can dance.'

'I wouldn't go that far,' Kate said huskily, her eyes seemingly riveted to Tiarnan's mouth, and as if to prove her point she stumbled and stood on his foot. She looked up to see him wince slightly and smiled sweetly. 'See?'

'It'll take a lot more than standing on my foot to diminish this.'

His voice was low and dark with promise as he pulled her even closer, and Kate's eyes widened on his when she felt the hard thrust of his arousal just above the apex of her legs. The silk of her dress was no barrier to the size and strength of it.

Hot liquid seemed to pool southwards in answer to his body's calling. Her hand clenched on his shoulder, as if to stop herself falling.

'See?' he asked mockingly, his smile dangerous with sensual intent.

Kate could barely hold it together. A bone-deep tremor was starting to build up through her whole body. She felt Tiarnan's hand go to her neck, massaging the delicate skin, undoing her hair so that it fell down her back. A shudder of pure desire ran through her, making her move instinctively against him, eliciting a deep growl from his throat. She turned her face into his neck, her hand resting on the hair at the back of his collar. He brought their joined hands in close to his chest. Her lips were so close to his hot skin. The slightly musky smell was an overwhelming temptation to snake out her tongue and taste, just for a second. She could feel the kick of his pulse under her tongue and exhilaration fired her blood.

Tiarnan stopped dead on the middle of the dance floor and pulled her even closer, urgency in his movements. 'Let's get out of here.'

Kate could do nothing but nod silently. Now she knew she was ready. Now she knew that nothing could hold her back.

Everything happened quickly. The smiling driver took them home. Tiarnan took her by the hand and led her into the house and up the stairs. One or two dim lights lit the way.

All Kate was aware of was the burning need inside her, the prospect of fulfilment more heady than anything she'd ever known. Since the moment she'd stepped up to Tiarnan to kiss him boldly on the lips all those years ago it had never been enough.

So now, when he halted outside her bedroom door and turned to face her, saying with a low voice, 'Kate, I want you. But I'll wait if I—' It was the easiest thing in the world to step close and put a finger to his lips.

'So have me…I'm yours.' She couldn't play games, couldn't

deny the need that had given her the impetus to say yes to coming here. She'd been waiting for this moment for so long.

Tiarnan emitted a guttural sound of satisfaction and pulled her in so tight against him she didn't know if it was his heartbeat or hers she could feel thumping so loudly and heavily. His mouth seemed to hover over hers for a long moment, as if relishing the anticipation, the moment, and then, with one hand spearing her hair possessively, his mouth slanted down onto hers, and Kate gave herself up to the maelstrom that erupted instantly around them.

Without really knowing how they'd got there, Kate found herself standing in Tiarnan's bedroom, facing him. Both were breathing harshly. Her universe had contracted to this moment and this man. It felt utterly right, as necessary as breathing.

She held her half-removed dress to her chest, not even knowing how it had become undone, and with a deep ragged breath let it go. It pooled at her feet in a swirl of vibrant blue silk. She kicked off her shoes and stood before Tiarnan in nothing but lace pants.

'Come here,' he said throatily.

Kate moved forward and started to undo his shirt, fingers grazing and revealing dark olive skin covered in a smattering of dark hair. He was so masculine, and it resonated with something deep within her. Recognition of a mate. Her belly quivered. He hadn't touched her yet, and it was all the more erotic for that. Her breasts felt full and aching and tight, the tips tingling painfully. Kate pushed his shirt off his shoulders and down his arms, and it too joined her dress in a pool of white on the floor.

She trailed her hands down across his defined pectorals, felt his indrawn sharp breath as her fingers trailed lower. She looked down, and amidst the haze of heat that seemed to surround them saw the small cut where her knitting needle had stabbed him just a few nights ago. She traced it lightly, and then bent forward to press a soft kiss to it.

Tiarnan sucked in a breath at the feel of her lips and her breath there. Her hair fell over one shoulder, and when she stood again he looked greedily at her lush form in all its glory. The tiny waist, feminine hips, impossibly long legs…up again to surprisingly full breasts. He quite literally ached to touch her, but this sweet anticipation was too exquisite.

With a voice he barely recognised as his own because it was so full of raw need, he said, 'Undress me. Please.'

Kate looked up into Tiarnan's face. She read the restraint and silently thanked him for it. He was giving her time, letting her dictate the pace. Yet she knew if he threw her on the bed right now and took her with no further ado she'd be ready. She felt indecently damp between her thighs. With other men since Tiarnan she'd always felt self-conscious, awkward, but with him it felt natural, *right,* and that gave her confidence. She had the fleeting wish that she could eradicate all other experiences and make this moment her first time all over again…

Feeling unbearably emotional for a second, she stepped forward and reached up to put her arms around his neck, bringing her breasts into contact with his chest. A shudder of reaction ran through both of them, and it took all of Kate's strength to stay standing and say somewhat shakily, belying her outward show of confidence, 'I'll undress you—but first…a kiss.'

Tiarnan couldn't resist. He smoothed his hands over her slender arms, then down over the bare curve of her waist and hips, settling on her behind, drawing her close. He dipped his head and met Kate's mouth with his, and within seconds the flames of desire were igniting around them, their tongues dancing feverishly. Kate forgot about teasing and restraint. She strained upwards on tiptoe to try and get even closer, pressing herself against Tiarnan blindly, seeking more, seeking to assuage the urgent need building deep in her core.

Without breaking contact she brought her hands down between them to his trousers, found the opening, careless in her haste, dragging his trousers down impatiently over lean hips. His hands had gone under her panties, moulding the cheeks of her bottom, making her arch into him, thwarting her attempts to drag down his trousers.

'Tiarnan…' She almost sobbed with frustration, not even sure what was hampering her, only knowing that she didn't want to stop touching him for a second. To lose contact with that hot skin, that heavenly musky scent, would be like depriving herself of oxygen.

His hands came up to her arms and put her back slightly. She felt dizzy, and they were both breathing as if they'd just been running.

'Kate…' He sounded hoarse, surprised and slightly bewildered. 'How could I have denied myself this for so long…?'

With indecent haste he brought his hands to his trousers and finished what Kate couldn't do. Finally he stood before her, naked and proud, virility oozing from every pore. Kate looked down and her throat went dry as she took him in in all his glory. She looked up again, and even though the room was dark she could see the expression on his face, the look in his darkened eyes. Passion and desire blazed forth—*for her.*

She was feeling suddenly weak, and as if he sensed it Tiarnan took her hand and led her over to the bed, through the muslin curtains that had been drawn down to protect against the stinging night insects. Surrounded by the gauzy material, the bed was like a cocoon, an oasis of pleasure.

Kate lay back and watched as Tiarnan stretched over her. He smoothed back her hair and it felt unbearably tender. Then he looked down her body, and wherever his eyes rested seemed to throb in response. He cupped one breast and Kate arched her back, eyes widening in a mute plea. She heard a dark chuckle, and felt his breath feather on her hot skin before he took the turgid tip into his mouth and suckled mercilessly, inciting the most intense response Kate could ever remember. She was gasping, grabbing his shoulders, his arms, hands clenched tight around bulging hard muscles as his mouth moved from one breast to the other, torturing her with pleasure. And then he moved down, and down again. The breeze whispered over the wet tips of her breasts and her stomach, where his tongue had touched her.

He pulled down her pants, throwing them aside, and then with ruthless intent pulled her legs apart. Kate stopped breathing for a long moment, her belly sucked in as she watched Tiarnan looking at her with such intimacy that she almost couldn't stand it.

Rising desire drowned out her mortification. Instinctively she moved on the bed, hips lifting slightly. 'Please...' She wasn't even sure what she was asking for.

Tiarnan looked at her, his hands travelling back up her legs, coming ever closer to her centre, thumbs massaging the tender inner skin of her thighs. His hands stopped at the very top of her legs, thumbs resting on the curls that covered her. They started moving slowly, back and forth, seeking, exploring, kneading her flesh.

Kate sucked in a breath that felt like a sob. *'Tiarnan.'*

'What? Tell me what you want?'

As if it was the easiest thing in the world.

'I...' Kate began brokenly. 'I want you to touch me... I want you inside me...'

One hand moved, and Kate felt long fingers thread through the damp curls, exploring ever inwards until he felt her slick heat for himself. She felt his reaction run through him. His erection lay thick and heavy against her thigh. She moved restlessly.

'Like this? First I touch...'

And he did. He touched her intimately. Fingers moving in and out, testing her, drawing out her response, his thumb finding that small hard nub and massaging it until Kate's hands clenched in the bedsheets so tight that her knuckles were white.

She felt all at once helpless, wanton and insatiable. And mortified at how he was turning her into someone she didn't even recognise. He bent his head, his chest close to hers, brushing against sensitive breasts, and kissed her deeply, erotically, as his hand and fingers caressed her intimately.

But just as she could feel the elusive peak she'd rarely reached with anyone else come like a vision through the haze of desire Tiarnan broke the kiss and removed his hand.

'Now *you* touch…'

He brought her hand down to cover his shaft. Kate's eyes grew big and round, glued to his as she allowed herself to feel and explore as he had done. It was his turn to shift restlessly, colour slashing his cheeks as she moved her hand, tightened her grip, feeling the satin smooth skin slip up and down over the steel-hard core. She could feel their heartbeats thudding slowly and heavily.

When he looked down at her with tense jaw and fever-bright eyes she took her hand away, and shifted herself so that she lay under him. She spread her legs, opening herself up to his welcome heat and heaviness.

'Now… I want you…' She reached up and pressed a hot kiss to his mouth, her tongue slipping inside with seductive innocence for a moment before she said, '…inside me.'

Tiarnan had lost all sense of time and place. At the last second before desire sucked him under completely he reached for protection and smoothed it on with all the finesse of a novice. This scene was so reminiscent of a dream he hadn't even acknowledged. He could feel Kate move beneath him. Her hair was spread in a golden halo around her head, and her eyes, like two huge pools of blue, looked up at him. Her legs parted a fraction more, and because it was the most necessary thing in the world he slid his erection, which felt engorged to the point of pain, into her silken heat, and died a small death of pleasure at the exquisite sensation.

He felt her move her hips, drawing him deeper. Exerting extreme control, he slowly started to thrust in and out. His eyes were locked on hers. Twin flags of colour stained her cheeks, her lips were plump and red...her teeth bit them as she fought to keep her moans back. It was all Tiarnan could do not to explode there and then. Seeing her like this was a fulfilment of something he'd so long suppressed.

Their skin was slick with sweat, their heartbeats no longer slow and heavy but frantic. The tempo increased. Tiarnan could feel Kate's legs wrap around him, urging him even deeper, harder. The pinnacle came in a blaze of white light and pleasure so intense they both stopped breathing for a long moment, hung suspended in time. And then came the fall, tumbling down and down all the way, their bodies releasing and pulsing for an age as Kate accepted Tiarnan's weight onto her, wrapped legs and arms around him even tighter, binding him to her.

Tiarnan woke at some point and felt an empty space beside him. Immediately a low hum of panic gripped him that he did not like. He lifted his head. Dawn was touching the sky outside and Kate stood on the balcony, leaning on the railing looking out to sea, dressed in nothing but his white shirt. The outline of her body was silhouetted enticingly under the material. Relief surged through him—which he also did not like.

Tiarnan got out of bed. As if linked to him by an invisible thread, Kate stood and turned around, pulled the shirt together over her chest haphazardly with one hand. Her hair was tumbled around her shoulders. Tiarnan prowled towards her. She was the only thing filling his mind, his vision in that moment. Seeing her dressed in nothing but his white shirt should have been a cliché. But it wasn't. Plenty of women had dressed like this for him, as if in an effort to do the contrived sexy thing, and all it had incited within him was mild irritation. Right now, though, irritation was the last thing he was feeling.

What he was feeling was a surge of primal possessiveness rushing through him.

Kate stood straighter as he came closer, put her hands out behind her on the railing. The shirt fell open, revealing tantalising glimpses of the twin globes of her breasts and then, down further, the ever so soft swell of her belly and the apex of her thighs, where golden curls hid paradise. Tiarnan reached her and pulled her into him, his arms around her naked back under the shirt. Even though they'd barely slept all night, he was ready to take her again.

He felt her lift one leg to hook it around his hip…knew instantly that she was ready again too. It was the most powerful aphrodisiac. They didn't even make it back to the bed. Tiarnan slid into her there and then. And with the dawn breaking somewhere in the east, tingeing the sky with pink, he and Kate entered another realm of the senses.

CHAPTER SEVEN

KATE had never felt so lethargic in her life—as if every limb was weighted down with a delicious warm stone. She couldn't even open her eyes. Vague flashes of memory came back: her dress pooling at her feet; kissing Tiarnan until she had to break away to suck in air; his body moving into hers, taking her breath away all over again, slippery with sweat; Tiarnan drawing her on top of him and watching her face as she took him in, then flipping her onto her back, driving in and out with such exquisite and ruthless precision that she'd been begging for release, near to tears.

Kate tried without success to shut the images out. Heat was already flaring through her just thinking about what they'd shared. She remembered getting up at some point and standing on the balcony, as if to try and make sense of it all, and then she'd heard him get up and he'd joined her there. Within seconds of touching they'd been burning up all over again. She squeezed her eyes shut tight, as if that might block out the wanton image. She could vaguely remember him lifting her up into her arms…after that a bath…and then oblivion. An oblivion touched with the peace that came from a long-held desire finally fulfilled. Her somewhat pathetic concern that sleeping with Tiarnan might prove to be disappointing had been blown into the stratosphere.

Just then a sound came from somewhere near—a door opened, small feet ran in.

'Katie, Katie—come on, get up, sleepyhead!'

Immediately she was alert. She was in her own bed, dressed in the T-shirt and boxer shorts she'd laid out on her pillow the previous evening. Rosie and her friend Zoe were standing looking at her, holding back the muslin curtain that was around the bed. Kate sat up and pushed down the clamour of questions. Tiarnan must have put her to bed here and dressed her after the bath. Had she really been so exhausted that she hadn't even been aware?

Heat suffused her face, and she tried to hide it by throwing back the covers and climbing out of bed. She smiled at the girls, hoping they wouldn't notice her discomfiture.

'What time is it?'

Rosie rolled her eyes at her friend, who giggled shyly. They were both dressed in shorts and vest tops, feet bare. Kate could see a trickle of sand had followed them into the room.

'It's *really* late, Katie. Nearly midday! Come on—we're going to the beach. Tiarnan wouldn't let us wake you for ages. He said you were jet-lagged…'

The two girls ran out of the room again, shouting that they'd see her downstairs in ten minutes. Kate sagged back onto the bed and pushed her hand through her hair. The thought of seeing Tiarnan after last night made her tummy flip. Was it even real? Or had she dreamt it? But her body was the evidence. She was glad he'd had the foresight to put her into her own bed. She'd obviously been barely capable of moving. The fact that *he'd* managed to retain a cool measure of control and was clearly marking the boundaries between them made her feel vulnerable.

As she stood under the spray of her shower a few minutes later, Kate's movements suddenly halted. She remembered that moment on the balcony; they hadn't used protection. Tiarnan had been so careful to protect them up to that point, and she hadn't missed the horrorstruck look on his face when he'd realised. The pain of seeing how violently he'd castigated himself had led her to reassure him quickly that it would be fine—she was at a safe stage in her cycle. And she *was*. But still, it shocked her how easily they'd been careless, and he'd vowed vociferously to make sure it didn't happen again. She had no desire either, to risk bringing a child into a very temporary moment of madness. And the thought of what such a scenario would mean to Tiarnan made her go cold.

'Morning. Or should I say *afternoon?*'

Kate took a deep breath to steady herself against the bone-tingling effect of the deep, sexy drawling voice before she looked up from tying her flat sandals, sitting on the bottom stair. But she couldn't stop her heart beating wildly. Mortification twisted her insides anew as the enormity of what had happened hit her. She'd been so easy. She'd shown him with bells on how she'd hungered for him for years... She should try to hide that vulnerability from him. She had to somehow make him think he was just another in a long line of lovers. She had to protect herself from him.

Gathering all her training, that armour she'd perfected over the years, she looked up and steeled herself not to react to seeing him—but it was hard. He stood leaning nonchalantly against a doorjamb, dressed in a white T-shirt that strained across the biceps of his arms and faded loose khaki shorts. Battered sneakers on his feet.

She finished fiddling with her sandals and stood, self-conscious even though she was dressed similarly, in long shorts and a vest top. Perfectly respectable. She saw that they were alone and came close to him. Trying not to falter, she tipped her face up to his and said, *sotto voce,* 'Thanks for last night, I really enjoyed it.'

She saw his smile fade ever so slightly. A hard gleam came into his eyes and she wanted to gag. Those words were so meaningless, when she really wanted to say that the previous night had been the most exquisite experience of her existence. That she'd already stored away every single moment in her memory. But she had to remember who she was dealing with— *had to.* Or he'd destroy her.

He took her hand before she knew what he was doing and raised it to his mouth, pressing a kiss to the underside of her wrist, causing heat to flood her belly and her breath to catch.

'I enjoyed it too. I'm already looking forward to tonight.'

Kate's eyes were snared by his. She was terrified that he would see that she was putting on a desperate act. She smiled and it felt brittle. She could do this if she had to.

'Me too.'

Just then sounds came from outside, and they moved apart just as Rosie burst into the hall. 'Come *on,* you guys. We'll be late!'

Tiarnan bent down to pick up a big basket that seemed to be bursting at the seams.

'Where are we going?' Kate asked as Rosie hopped around, impatient to go.

Mama Lucille came into the hall then, wiping her hands on an apron, and dragged Rosie close for a big hug and kiss.

Tiarnan looked back at Kate as he dodged around Rosie and Mama Lucille. 'We're going to the beach with a picnic. Zoe's family will be there too.'

Kate followed them out to the Jeep, which was laden down with things. This was obviously a bit of a ritual for them, and she realised belatedly that it was Sunday. It must be a traditional family day out for the locals.

Mama Lucille surprised Kate by giving her a big expansive hug too, and then they set off, the two giggling girls in the back reminding Kate bittersweetly of herself and Sorcha when they'd been young.

Disconcertingly, as if able to read her mind, Tiarnan said while gesturing to the back, 'Remind you of anyone?'

Kate smiled. 'I was just thinking about that.'

'Thinking about what?' Rosie piped up from the back, proving that her ears were very keen.

Kate and Tiarnan shared a complicit smile, and Kate couldn't stop her heart feeling as if it was about to burst. But she turned around and started to tell the two girls stories about her and Sorcha when they'd been young.

That evening, when they were in a very bedraggled and sandy Jeep returning home as night fell, Kate knew she hadn't enjoyed a day so much in ages. She felt deliciously sunburned, her skin tingling in the aftermath of a day spent outdoors. They'd gone to a beach that was obviously a local secret as it had been empty but for them and Zoe's extended family, all Mama Lucille's children and grandchildren, nieces and nephews. She could see what Tiarnan meant. Rosie was as much a part of that family as their own kids—she could even see that there was a fragile and gradual thawing in Rosie and Tiarnan's relationship. She hoped that the holiday would prove to give Tiarnan the breakthrough he sought with Rosie.

Earlier in the day Kate had given up trying to keep track of everyone she'd been introduced to, and Zoe's mother Anne-Marie had taken her under her wing. She was a beautiful woman in her early thirties, who had three children including Zoe, the eldest.

They'd been watching an impromptu football game, with everyone chaotically involved, toddlers and all in the mix, when Kate had impulsively confided, 'I envy you.'

Anne-Marie had looked shocked. 'Are you mad? You'd give up a glamorous lifestyle travelling around the world to live with *this* kind of mayhem?'

But the other woman's sparkling eyes had told another story. Kate had felt her heart clench. She'd hidden the true extent of her desire to get out of modelling and settle down even from Sorcha. Somehow here, with this woman who was little more than a stranger, it had been easy to smile wryly and say with feeling, 'In a heartbeat.'

Anne-Marie had leant close then, and said conspiratorially, 'He's a good man.'

Kate had blushed immediately and realised to her horror that her eyes had been greedily following Tiarnan as he'd run bare-chested down the beach with the ball, a gaggle of children running after him, adults laughing. It was a world away from the austere image he projected to the world of finance and high-powered achieving. In truth, she was slightly shocked to see this side of him—and shocked at the feeling it caused deep inside her. A deep yearning for family, *love,* for belonging. With him. When she should be getting over him…

Kate tried to be cool. 'Oh, I've known Tiarnan for years. His sister Sorcha's my best friend. And, yes, he *is* a good man.'

Anne-Marie hadn't looked fooled for a second. She'd just said, 'He's never brought anyone else here, you know…and no man is an island.'

Kate's face had been burning by then, but thankfully Anne-Marie had deftly defused the situation and stood, reaching down to haul Kate up too.

'Come on—let's show the men a thing or two.'

Kate's attention returned to the present. It was just the three of them in the Jeep—Rosie sleepy in the back, Tiarnan driving. She snuck a look at his proud profile as he drove. Anne-Marie was wrong, Tiarnan most certainly *was* an island, and there was no room on it for her except as a temporary bed companion. The sooner she could come to terms with that, the better.

After dinner Kate offered to go and see if Rosie was tucked into bed. Tiarnan caught her hand to pull her back and said with a seductive drawl, 'I didn't bring you here to act as a nanny to Rosie.'

Kate looked down at him and her heart twisted. They'd all showered and changed as soon as they'd got back, and Tiarnan looked heart-stoppingly handsome with damp hair, in a clean shirt and worn jeans. His blue eyes were even more intense against the slight tan he'd already acquired in one day.

She pulled her hand free. 'Don't worry. I know exactly why I'm here, Tiarnan. We both do.'

Something in her voice or expression caught him and caused an ache in the region of his chest, but he had no idea why. He watched her walk out, her sexy cut-off shorts effortlessly showcasing her long lissom legs. She wore a peasant-style top and her hair was loose down her back, slightly darker as it was still a little damp. Her scent hovered on the air and he had to fight not to close his eyes and savour it.

Slightly irritated with himself for this moonstruck streak he wasn't used to, he turned back to the table and drank down the rest of his wine. Along with the heat of desire that washed through him in waves was a much more ambiguous feeling.

He'd expected Kate to suffer somewhat through the day, having to spend it *en famille*. But she had smiled and gelled with everyone immediately. She'd seemed to genuinely enjoy herself—and the rambunctious nature of Mama Lucille's family. He'd seen her talking to Anne-Marie, laughing easily, as if they'd known each other for years.

She'd been quite happy to muck in and help out with the food and children too, assuming a natural gentle authority which had taken him by surprise. When they'd been playing football he'd seen her go to pick up one of the smaller children who'd been accidentally knocked over without a moment's hesitation, and even though she didn't even know him, she'd hugged him close and kissed him better, so that by the time the father had rushed over the child had been clinging to Kate and playing happily with her blonde hair.

As if to distract his line of thinking from going down a dangerous path he had no desire to explore, he recalled her body in its petrol blue bikini. The other men had had the nous not to stop and stare, but he'd been aware of their interest when she'd first stripped off to go into the water with Rosie and Zoe and the others. Immediately he'd irrationally regretted bringing her with them, and not locking her up in the house or back in his home in Madrid. And yet her bikini had been no more or less revealing than Anne-Marie's, or any of the other women's...

Despite that, he could recall only too easily his intense relief when she'd put on her shorts and top again to come and play football. He'd been afraid that he wouldn't have the restraint not to insist that she cover up. He rationalised it: having slept with her only the night before, after such a long build-up, his desire still felt raw. He was just realising how hard it was to share her with everyone else so soon.

The lingering traces of that desire were making him hard again. He'd spent the day in a perpetual state of near arousal, taking frequent swims to disguise it. And he couldn't block out or forget that he'd been so hot for her last night, that for the first time in his life *ever,* he'd forgotten about protection. He hadn't even been careless with Stella Rios. She'd assured him she'd been on the pill, and even knowing that he'd insisted on using protection. But one time it had broken, and *that* had been her chance for convincing him he might be Rosie's father—especially after she'd revealed that she'd lied about taking the pill...

Tiarnan assured himself now that Kate was *not* Stella Rios. He would not be caught again. He forced himself to relax, and waited to hear her footfall coming back downstairs. He couldn't help thinking of that indecipherable expression that had flashed in her eyes just now, and her behaviour today. Most of the women he'd sought out for affairs in the past would have been clinging to him like a limpet, complaining vociferously about the rustic nature of the entertainment. Quite apart from the fact that he had to concede that he wouldn't have brought them here in the first place.

A feeling of vulnerability swamped him. Was he allowing Kate to play him? In a way that no other woman had done before? Not even Stella Rios?

Enough! Tiarnan chastised himself for his introspection. They were effectively alone again, and he could spend the night punishing her for making him feel so uncharacteristically vulnerable. He heard her coming back down the stairs and stood jerkily, his usual grace deserting him as he turned and went to meet her halfway…

Two days later Kate sat in the shade in the garden, knitting. No sound warned her she wasn't alone, so when she heard a softly drawled, 'I come in peace; I'm not armed,' she nearly jumped out of her skin. She looked up to see Tiarnan standing there, his hands up in a comic gesture of surrender, looking expressively at her knitting.

He'd taken her by surprise in more ways than one because, predictably, he'd been occupying her thoughts. In particular, vivid images of last night in his bed, and the moments of ecstasy she'd experienced in his arms. She felt as though he'd be able to see that straight away and looked down again, feeling cross, putting the knitting away.

'Don't worry—I'll restrain myself.' She knew she must sound cool. But it was the only way she could stem this constant state of heat she seemed to be in. Escaping for quiet moments was keeping her semi-sane. And she was also consciously trying to give Tiarnan time alone with Rosie.

He came and sat down in the wicker lounger chair beside her, long bare legs stretched out, making her eyes drop betrayingly to linger on their perfectly formed muscles. She couldn't help but remember how it felt to have those strong

hair-roughened thighs between her own, and a quiver of heat
made her clench her legs together. He was wearing his usual
Martinique uniform of casual shorts and T-shirt, looking as
relaxed as any local. Whereas she felt as tightly wound as a
spring.

'I thought Rosie was with you?' Kate said, as much to know
as in an effort to fill the silence.

Tiarnan had put his head back and closed his eyes. The
dappled sunlight coming through the leaves of the tree above
them caught his skin in patches. He was looking more tanned
by the day, and with it more devilishly handsome.

He opened his eyes and looked at her, shaking his head,
putting his arms behind it to cushion it. Supremely relaxed.
'She went into town to go shopping with Papa Joe.'

'Zoe…?'

He shook his head again. 'They're still in school here, so
Rosie has to do without her partner in crime during the day.'

'Oh…' Kate felt unaccountably awkward. She still hadn't
got used to dealing with Tiarnan during the day, after nights
which were filled with such passion. She was slightly overwhelmed. And, if she was honest, she was afraid of spending
too much time with him, getting closer, seeing even more
aspects of his fascinating character.

He leant forward and reached out a hand. Kate looked at it
suspiciously.

'Come for a drive with me. I want to show you something.'

Tiarnan could see the reluctance on Kate's face and irritation
spiked through him. She'd been keeping her distance the past
couple of days and he didn't like it. During the night she was undeniably his—more passionate than anything he'd ever experienced. But apart from that… It was as if there were two different
Kates. She gave off an air of insouciance he knew and expected.
And yet she wasn't constantly seeking his attention or moaning
about the lack of civilisation. She was here knitting quietly in the

garden. As much as he hated this compulsion to get to know her better, he couldn't ignore it. He hungered for her, and he realised now that he hungered just to spend time with her—a novel desire, and one that didn't sit entirely well with him.

'What about Rosie? Won't she be home soon?'

Tiarnan shook his head. 'Papa Joe is taking her over to the other side of the island afterwards to a market. They'll eat there and won't be back till late. Rosie's been to the place I want to take you a hundred times already. Come on, Kate. Or are you going to tell me that knitting is more exciting than taking a mystery tour with me?'

He quirked a brow. Kate's insides liquefied. How could she resist this man? She made a show of seriously contemplating for a moment whether she'd prefer to sit and knit the day away, and squealed when Tiarnan moved like lightning and put her over his shoulder, lifting her as if she weighed no more than a bag of sugar. She was wearing a relatively short sundress, and his warm hand was disturbingly close to the tops of her bare thighs and her bottom.

'Tiarnan Quinn—put me down this instant! What if someone sees us? Mama Lucille...'

She felt Tiarnan swat her bottom playfully and say loudly, 'Mama Lucille has seen plenty in her lifetime—haven't you, Mama? I'm taking Kate out for the afternoon. Don't worry about dinner for us.'

Kate's face burned and her fists clenched when she heard the familiar full-bodied chuckle and saw Mama Lucille's feet in their flip-flops pass them by.

She spied something out of the corner of her eye, put out a hand. 'Wait! My camera.'

Tiarnan obediently halted and retraced his steps, picking up Kate's camera which lay on a hall table. Then they were out through the front door and down to the Jeep, where he deposited Kate in the passenger seat with surprising gentleness. He handed her her camera before coming around and getting into the driver's seat.

They were pulling away from the villa within seconds, and Kate couldn't help a bubble of excitement rising within her. Tiarnan looked at her and smiled, and it was so carefree that she couldn't help but smile back. Her armour and her resistance were melting in a pool at her feet and there was nothing she could do to stop it.

She sat back in the seat and said mock-sulkily, 'I was quite happy knitting quietly, you know. This is meant to be a holiday.'

For a second Tiarnan had to reconcile that image of such domesticity with the woman he'd expected Kate to be. It was an anomaly he ruthlessly diverted his attention away from.

'I'm sure…' he said then, slanting her a mischievous look. 'I could see how fast you were knitting—feverishly, one could say, almost as if your mind was filled not with thoughts of casting on and single back cross stitches, but rather something more…elemental…'

Kate burned—because he was absolutely right. Though she didn't know what was more shocking—that or the fact that he knew any knitting terminology.

She turned to face him in her seat. The sea was an amazing backdrop behind him. 'Don't tell me you've had to put up with *other* women being more enthralled with knitting than you?' She opened her eyes wide, acting innocent.

He shook his head. 'You're on your own there, Kate Lancaster. No, it was my mother. You don't remember all those hideous Christmas jumpers we got every year, until Sorcha was discovered giving hers away to a homeless person?'

Kate laughed out loud. 'How could I have forgotten? Your poor mother was so insulted—and if I remember it had a lovely holly and mistletoe pattern, which I must say in her defence would not have been easy to do…'

Tiarnan smiled ruefully. 'I'm sure. I was just relieved that

Sorcha had unwittingly saved us from a lifetime of lurid Christmas jumpers.'

Kate was tempted to return with a quip that *she* could fill that gaping hole in his life, but stopped abruptly when she realised how it might sound. As if she expected to be a part of his life after this holiday was over.

He looked at her curiously, and she could feel that she'd gone slightly pale. 'What is it?'

She shook her head and smiled brightly. 'Nothing. Nothing at all. So—where exactly are you taking me?'

'Ah, that's for me to know and you to see.' He glanced at the camera nestled on her lap, her hands over it protectively. 'That looks pretty professional. I saw you taking pictures in the garden earlier…'

Kate lifted up the camera and looked at it. She felt self-conscious.

'The photographers at work told me which one I should buy if I was seriously interested in learning.'

'And are you? Seriously interested?'

Kate shrugged one slim shoulder. 'I've done some photography courses. Travelling around the world so much I get to see so many things, and I wanted to start documenting them… It's a hobby, I guess you could say.'

Tiarnan cast her a look. She was avoiding his eye, studying the camera. He guessed intuitively that she must be very good. She seemed to have the kind of personality that would be utterly respectful of anything or anyone she wanted to photograph.

They drove on in silence for a bit, and eventually Kate read out the name of the town they'd come into, where Tiarnan started slowing down.

'Saint-Pierre…'

Tiarnan stopped the Jeep and parked up, and they got out. He immediately came and took Kate's hand. She didn't pull away, and a surge of something went through him.

Her hand felt so good in Tiarnan's. She loved the way he was so tactile. With other men when they'd tried to maintain contact she'd always felt uncomfortable. She looked around curiously at the streets. It was a pretty enough town, but...

'What are you thinking?' Tiarnan looked at her intently.

Kate stood still. 'I don't know,' she answered after a long moment. 'It's weird. It's almost as if the buildings don't fit the town, or something...' A shiver went down her spine. 'And there's something eerie about it too...'

Tiarnan pointed at a mountain in the distance. 'See that?'

Kate nodded.

'That's Mount Pelée. In 1902 it erupted, and within minutes this town and its thirty thousand or so inhabitants were decimated. The only survivor was a man who was locked in a prison cell below ground.'

'Those poor people,' Kate breathed, and then looked at Tiarnan. 'It's almost inconceivable to imagine.'

He nodded, and noticed that she was shading her eyes from the sun with her hand. He felt a dart of guilt. He'd rushed her out of the house so fast she hadn't had time to pick anything up. He spied a shop across the road and led her there.

Two minutes later they emerged, and Tiarnan handed Kate a pair of lurid pink sunglasses, complete with pineapples on each corner, and a big floppy straw hat with a ring of fake flowers around the base.

She sighed and took them from him. 'Just what I've always wanted. To look like a clown.'

But she took them and put them on, and smiled up at him so beautifully that he couldn't resist taking her face in his hands and pressing a kiss to her lips. Only when someone wolf-whistled nearby did he let her go, slightly in shock at how turned-on he was already—and how easy it had been to kiss her like that when he normally had an absolute abhorrence for public displays of affection. He took her by the hand and led her away.

Kate's heart was beating quickly in her chest as she held onto the ridiculous hat and followed Tiarnan. That kiss had been so impromptu and so devastating. He'd taken her completely by surprise, buying the hat and glasses too. Right then she wouldn't have wanted their designer equivalent in a million years.

They walked for a bit, then came to the local museum where Tiarnan showed her the exhibits. Outside in the car park they looked down over the town. It was obvious where the lines of destruction still lay, despite the new buildings and life going on.

It gave Kate a sense of how fragile life was—how quickly everything could be ripped away. She felt as though she were falling off a high precipice. Unconsciously she gripped Tiarnan's hand tighter and he turned to look at her,

'OK?'

Kate tried to drive down the overwhelming sense of making every moment count with this man, because she knew now it would be all that she had, and she turned and looked up, pasting on a bland smile. 'You certainly know how to show a girl a good uplifting time.'

He smiled dangerously and drew her into him tightly. Kate held in a gasp at the potent feel of his rock-solid body against hers. The other tourists milling around them were forgotten.

'We'll discuss good uplifting times when we get home.'

'Promises, promises,' Kate said somewhat shakily, and Tiarnan let her go again, but kept a hold of her hand.

Later, eating ice creams he'd bought them outside a shop, they walked back to the Jeep. They stopped near the harbour wall for a moment, to finish eating, and something in Tiarnan's stance caught Kate's eye. He was looking out to sea, his profile so beautiful that she couldn't resist lifting her camera and taking a quick snap. He turned when he heard the shutter click and Kate smiled. 'For posterity,' she said. And felt inordinately guilty—because she knew it would be for *her*.

* * *

They took the road back the way they'd come, returning south, and Kate felt acutely aware of *everything*. Tiarnan turned left off the main road at one point and all of a sudden they seemed to be in the middle of a lush rainforest. Kate put out her hand as they drove, to try and touch the branches by the side of the road.

'This is so beautiful. I'd never have imagined this kind of scenery here.'

'Wait till you see what's up here…'

Kate felt a bubble of pure joy rise upwards within her as she watched Tiarnan drive against this backdrop. She was truly content, for the first time in a long time, and she wouldn't allow thoughts of the end of this holiday, and inevitably this affair, to cloud the moment.

They pulled up outside an impressive church and Tiarnan said, 'Remind you of anything?'

Kate looked up and gasped. 'It's the Sacré-Coeur!'

'A replica,' Tiarnan confirmed, and got out. 'Come on— there are some amazing views over Forte-de-France below…'

A short while later, as they drove back towards the coast, Kate's head was bursting with images—and a lingering sense of peace from the church that had been built as a smaller replica of the iconic Parisian landmark.

She could recognise the route now. They weren't too far from home. But Tiarnan surprised her by taking a winding road down towards the sea, and pulling in outside a beautiful old colonial-style house, half buried in thick bougainvillaea and hibiscus flowers. Martinique was certainly living up to its name as 'the isle of flowers'.

It turned out that the house was actually a converted restaurant, and when they walked in Kate wasn't surprised to see Tiarnan greeted like an old friend. As was the custom she was getting used to, she was greeted effusively, and they were led to a stunning white-clothed table in a wrought-iron balconied alcove that looked directly out to the sea and the setting sun.

Kate leant forward, a small frown creasing her forehead. 'Aren't we dressed a little...well, casually for somewhere like this?'

Tiarnan looked around then, and noticed a few men sitting with partners and looking at Kate with brazen appreciation. Jealousy rose swiftly. He turned back to Kate. She looked all at once so demure and so incredibly sexy that he had to bite back a completely irrational urge to tell her to cover up. And how could she, when he'd all but manhandled her out of the house earlier? Her hesitation before, in the garden, came back to him, made something inside him twist.

'You're fine,' he said gruffly.

She'd been a good sport today—happily wearing the ridiculous hat and glasses, taking snaps, eating ice cream at the side of the road. Once again he'd been hard pushed to think of any of his previous mistresses in those surroundings, happy to sightsee.

He gestured to her shoulders. 'You got a bit burnt today.'

Kate grimaced. 'Oh it's nothing.'

She looked at him with something almost like shyness in her expression, but Tiarnan had to reject that thought. It couldn't be. He wanted to keep seeing her as a cool, sophisticated woman of the world.

'It feels good, in all honesty. I usually have to be so careful of my skin. And my weight.' She rolled her eyes then, and imitated her agent's broad New York drawl.

'"Kate, honey, you're known for your porcelain skin. So don't gimme a heart attack and come back looking like me. I can take the sun. You can't. And whatever you do watch your weight. I'm always telling you, you don't have it as easy as the other girls, you're not naturally skinny. It's a shame, but we have our crosses to bear and yours is pasta..."'

She stopped and blushed when Tiarnan laughed out loud.

She knew he knew Maud well. She was Sorcha's agent too. Kate felt foolish all of a sudden. 'I'm sorry…Sorcha calls them my Maud monologues.'

He caught her hand, smiling widely. 'You mimic her brilliantly. I could have sworn she was here.'

Kate's hand tingled in his, and he only let go when a pristinely dressed waiter arrived and addressed Tiarnan in French while handing them menus.

Tiarnan replied fluently, and Kate made a face when the waiter left. 'No throwing of food allowed here, I'd guess?'

Tiarnan looked mock stern. 'Certainly not, young lady.'

Kate had to catch herself. She'd never have guessed she'd feel so at ease with Tiarnan, so comfortable. This day was in danger of becoming incredibly special, and she drove that thought down, to some deep and dark place. She took up the menu and made a great show of studying the indecipherable French.

After a long moment she heard an amused, 'Would you like me to translate?'

Drat the man. She had the grace to smile self-deprecatingly and put the menu down. 'Would you please?' she said. 'I don't particularly want frog's legs or snails.'

'So, the photography…tell me about it. Did you do a degree?'

Kate watched as Tiarnan speared a morsel of fish and ate it, and felt the familiar shame grip her. She nervously tucked her hair behind her ear.

'No…I couldn't do a degree because I never completed school…' She shrugged slightly and avoided his eye. 'I was already working in London and then New York…earning money…and then it was too late.'

She heard him put down his knife and fork. Compelled against her will, she met his eye.

'Kate, it's nothing to be ashamed of. I didn't go to college myself.'

She smiled tightly. 'Maybe, but in a world like this men are judged far less harshly than women if they've proved themselves in the interim—qualifications notwithstanding.'

He inclined his head and took a sip of wine. 'You're right. Unfortunately. But if it means that much to you why didn't you complete when you had a chance?'

'Like Sorcha, you mean?' Kate and Sorcha had both started modelling at the same time, but Sorcha had made the effort to get her Irish leaving certificate qualification, and had then had done a degree in psychology in New York.

Tiarnan nodded.

Kate shrugged again. How could she admit her even more secret shame, of constant years of her mother telling her that her looks were all that mattered and why should she worry about working? She took a fortifying sip of wine and looked at Tiarnan.

'You remember my mother?'

He nodded. He remembered a brash woman who had grated on his nerves—a woman who cared more for her appearance and her social standing than anything else. He also remembered that she would flirt outrageously with *him* at any given opportunity. He knew that on some level when Kate had approached him that night ten years ago he'd assumed she was of the same ilk as her mother—forward. And yet, despite her cool assurance after he'd put a stop to their lovemaking, he'd glimpsed a vulnerability that was at odds with her seemingly confident actions. He'd dismissed it that night and in the intervening years—especially as he witnessed her blooming into the stunning beauty she now was—and her cool exterior confirmed for him that she'd become accustomed to a certain kind of attention. But, despite all that, right now that vulnerability seemed to be back, and it jarred with his assessment of her character.

He tried to bring his focus back to the conversation, feeling as if he were treading on dangerous ground.

'How *is* your mother?'

Kate was glad to be stalled for a moment. She smiled tightly and looked at him. 'Oh, I'm sure she's fine. She's on a cruise with rich husband number four and blissfully happy, no doubt.'

Tiarnan frowned. 'You don't see her, then?'

Kate shook her head. 'Very infrequently. If she's shopping in New York for a few days or going to the shows… But in general she doesn't like to be reminded of her mortality, and I'm afraid that's what I do.'

Tiarnan winced inwardly. That didn't surprise him.

'My mother is a great believer in a woman surviving on her looks. After Sorcha and I were discovered by the model scout that day in Dublin she saw no real need for me to stay at school. I was never the most academic anyway, so in later years the thought of completing studies as an older student and failing was somewhat daunting.'

Tiarnan reached across and tipped up her chin from where she was studying the table. She felt excruciatingly exposed. She'd never admitted this to anyone. And now to *him* of all people? But with his hand on her chin she was forced to meet his gaze.

'Kate, you are most certainly not stupid, if that's what you're afraid of. You have an innate intelligence that anyone would recognise a mile away. And lack of qualifications hasn't stopped some of the world's most successful people from succeeding. I bet half the world-famous photographers you work with are self-taught.'

Kate gulped and reddened. Tiarnan had sounded almost angry.

As if he realised this, he took his hand away and said, 'Sorry…I just wouldn't want you to put yourself down like that.' He shook his head. 'Parents can be so cruel, and do so much damage.'

Kate felt a well of emotion rise up and had to blink away the prickling of tears. She put her hand over his and said huskily, 'Thank you for that. I know intellectually everything you say is right—and you're right about parents…' She smiled shakily, 'Rosie is lucky to have you for a father.'

He grimaced. 'You wouldn't think so at the moment. She goes out of her way to avoid me.'

Kate squeezed his hand. 'She'll come round. You'll see.'

Tiarnan just looked into the blue depths of Kate's eyes and felt unaccountably as if he were drowning.

That night when they returned to the villa Kate felt as though something had changed between her and Tiarnan. It felt dangerous. And yet heady.

She'd just come out of her bathroom, having washed her face, when Tiarnan appeared at her bedroom door. Her breath stalled in her throat and she felt her nipples respond with wanton eagerness. Aghast at her reaction, she reached for a wrap and pulled it on over her singlet and boxers, knowing it was slightly ridiculous to feel so self-conscious.

'Rosie wants to say goodnight to you.'

'Of course.'

Kate went to go out through the door, but Tiarnan blocked her way. His hands cupped her face and tipped it up, threading through her hair. He was huge, his shoulders blocking out the light, his face cast in shadow, and he looked so darkly handsome that Kate couldn't catch her breath again. Every part of her body reacted to his proximity.

'I enjoyed today, Kate—and this evening.'

'Me too,' she said huskily. The image of the sun setting over the sea beside them as they sipped wine and ate delicious food would be forever engraved on her memory.

He pressed the most fleeting and yet earth-shattering of kisses onto her mouth and said simply, 'I'll be waiting for you.'

Then he stood back and let her go.

Kate walked to Rosie's room on very wobbly legs, and when she got there she told Rosie all about where they'd gone. Rosie chattered about her day with Papa Joe, suitably satisfied that she'd missed Saint-Pierre, telling Kate that she'd been there, 'Like, *tons* of times.'

When Kate bent forward to kiss her goodnight, she said, 'Thank you, Rosie, for letting me share your holiday with you and your dad. This is such a special place.'

She was almost at the door when she heard a soft, 'Katie, did your daddy love you?'

Kate stopped dead and turned slowly. She could see Rosie's pale little face in the soft glow of the one lamp. She came back over and sat on the bed. 'What makes you ask that?'

The little girl shrugged. 'My dad—' She stopped and then started again. 'Tiarnan doesn't love me. I'm adopted…he's not even my real dad.'

Kate knew she had to tread carefully. 'Well, sweetie, my dad died a long time ago. I think he loved me—I mean, I'm sure he loved me…even if he didn't really show it.'

Rosie looked at Kate suspiciously. 'What do you mean?'

'Well, he was always very busy. He used to come home late at night, after I'd gone to bed.' She wrinkled her nose. 'And he was worried about work a lot, and money…things like that.'

Rosie looked contemplative for a moment. 'Tiarnan's busy a lot too…but he always tucks me in at night and takes me to school, and if he's away he calls me all the time.' Kate saw her bottom lip quivering. 'But it still doesn't mean he loves me. My mother doesn't love me either…not like Zoe's mum loves her.' A sob broke free and Rosie started crying in earnest, her little shoulders shaking.

Kate gathered Rosie up into her arms and let her cry it out, guessing she'd needed to do this for a long time. She rocked her back and forth, rubbing her back, her heart breaking for the child's pain and confusion.

When the crying had become big hiccupping sighs, Kate pulled back and smoothed Rosie's hair from her flushed face.

She got a tissue from the box nearby and wiped away her tears, made her blow her nose. 'Sweetheart, don't think that. Your dad loves you *so* much.'

'How do you know?' Rosie asked chokily.

Kate tucked some hair behind her ear. 'I know because he always talks about you, and he worries about you and tells everyone about you.' Kate took a bit of poetic licence and mentally crossed her fingers. 'And he's so proud of how well you're settling into your new school. How brave you are to make the change.'

Rosie's face twisted. 'He *made* me change schools and I've no friends now.'

Kate feigned shock. 'What? A stunningly beautiful and funny girl like you? Not possible.' She laid Rosie back against her pillow and then came down close, resting on an arm. 'Do you know? I had to change schools too, when I was just a bit older than you.'

'You did?' Rosie visibly perked up.

Kate nodded. 'And not only that I had to change countries as well. I was living in England, and after my father died my mum moved back to Ireland—right next door to where Auntie Sorcha lived. That's how she and I became best friends. And if I'd never moved country or changed schools I wouldn't have met her...and we wouldn't know each other and I certainly wouldn't know *you,* or be here now.'

'Wow...' Rosie breathed.

'It is hard when things change, but sometimes they change for the better. I bet you're going to have such good friends at the new school. You just have to give it a chance.'

Rosie was plucking at the sheet, looking down. 'Katie, my mummy doesn't want me to go and see her.'

Kate had to hide her visceral reaction. 'Rosie, I'm sure your Mummy loves you...but sometimes adults can be a bit confusing. It's not always easy to understand why they do certain things.' Kate took her hand. 'And you know what? You're lucky to have Tiarnan for a dad, because he loves you twice as much as any other dad.'

'What do you mean?' Rosie looked up with a wary light in her huge brown eyes.

'Even when he found out he wasn't your real dad he made sure to adopt you, so that no one could ever take you away from him. He wanted everyone to know you were his. And I know you still love him, even though you're angry with him.'

Rosie's face got red, and she looked down again.

Kate smoothed her hair. 'It's OK, sweetheart—really it is. Nothing you could do or say will make him stop loving you. He is always going to be there for you, no matter how angry you get, or if he annoys you or if you annoy him, because that's what fathers do.' Kate caught Rosie's eye and made a funny face, tweaking her nose. 'He didn't send you to a horrible nasty cold boarding school in the middle of nowhere, did he?'

Rosie giggled and shook her head. 'No… Katie, tell me a story about you and Auntie Sorcha in school—the one about the midnight feasts.'

Kate kissed her on the forehead and hugged her tight again for a second. 'OK. Just one story and then time for sleep?'

Rosie nodded and gave a big yawn, and by the time Kate was halfway through the first sentence the little girl's eyelids were already drifting shut.

When Kate walked into Tiarnan's room a short while later he lay sleeping on the bed, bare-chested, with the covers riding indecently low on lean hips. Even in sleep he dominated the space around him. She knew she should leave, go to her own bed despite what he'd said, but she felt so full of emotion in that moment she literally couldn't.

She dropped her wrap and went and curled up next to him. Automatically his arm came out and hugged her close to him with a vice-like grip, and Kate knew right then that all her attempts were for naught. Just like that day in the church in France. She could see through her own paltry attempts to protect herself, and she had the awful suspicion that they were failing spectacularly.

A couple of mornings later they were eating breakfast on the wooden terrace. Papa Joe was discussing the garden plants with Tiarnan, Mama Lucille was bustling back and forth, and suddenly Rosie appeared, dragging her bike up the steps from the garden.

'Daddy, can you look at my chain? It's falling off again,' she said.

Kate went completely still, and wondered if Tiarnan had noticed. He and Papa Joe stopped talking. Papa Joe walked away unobtrusively, with an expressive wink at Kate. Kate was about to take the hint and leave too, but Tiarnan shot her a look which told her to stay put.

He went and had a look at the bike and Kate's heart went out to him. He was trying to be so casual. He was fiddling with the bike, but even from here Kate could see the chain looked fine. And then Rosie said, ever so casually, 'Daddy, can we go hiking in the mountains today?'

He looked at Rosie. Kate could see that Rosie was avoiding his eye, scuffing her flip-flop off the ground, as if all this was normal.

Tiarnan's voice was husky. 'I thought you didn't enjoy doing that any more?'

Kate held her breath and to her relief Rosie said, 'I know, but I was thinking I wouldn't mind—and Zoe's in school so I've no one to play with.'

Rosie looked at Kate then and came over, jumping onto her lap to give her a big hug. 'Katie can come too! We can show her all the spiders' nests and things.'

Kate shuddered expressively, and made a face that had Rosie

giggling, 'Yuck! No, thank you very much. I think I can do without seeing where spiders live. I'm not good with creepy-crawly things. You can take pictures.'

Rosie jumped off her lap. 'Silly Katie—it's fun. But it doesn't matter. Me and Daddy can go this time, and you can come next time.'

And with that Rosie hared off into the house, shouting for Mama Lucille to help her pack a picnic for them. Kate's heart had clenched at Rosie's assertion of *next time*.

Tiarnan was standing looking stunned. In shock. He came and sat down and looked at Kate. 'I can't believe it. She hasn't called me Daddy in over a year.'

Kate shrugged. 'Children don't hold grudges for ever.'

He stood again and came around to her seat, hands on either arm of it, trapping her, eyes roving over her face, assessing. 'Why do I have the overwhelming suspicion this has something to do with you? You said goodnight to her for a long time the other night, and she's been unusually quiet these past two days…'

Kate shook her head. Tiarnan's voice had an edge to it that unsettled her. He didn't sound entirely happy with this development. She felt compelled to keep Rosie's counsel, knowing in her heart of hearts that it wouldn't help to divulge how upset she had been.

'We just talked, Tiarnan. She likes hearing stories about me and Sorcha in school. You should go and enjoy the day with your daughter.' Kate forced a smile and tried to shake off the sense of unease that she'd done something wrong. 'I've got a plan to bribe Mama Lucille for some of her secret recipes.'

Despite the fact that he still wasn't smiling, she could sense his relief and sheer happiness. The joy she felt for him scared her, and the realisation hit her like a thunderbolt: she was so deeply in love and bound to Tiarnan Quinn now, and to his daughter, that all she would be able to settle for in her life would be a very pale and insubstantial imitation.

Seeing him just now with Rosie, sensing his innate protectiveness, had rendered any lingering prejudice she might have had about him void. He was nothing like her father. He had a capacity for deep and abiding love, for putting his daughter first. Just no place for a woman or partner in his life... Desolation gripped her like a physical pain.

He spoke then, jerking her out of her reverie, and she was shocked that he didn't seem to see the emotions written all over her face.

'Are you sure you'll be OK here on your own for the day?'

Kate nodded emphatically. Suddenly she wanted nothing more than to be away from the pull of this man's orbit. 'Absolutely.'

Tiarnan seemed to search her eyes, as if looking for something, and then he finally spoke, sounding very stiff and unlike the man who seduced her so ruthlessly every night. 'Very well. We'll be back later—don't wait up; it'll probably be late.'

Kate's sense of unease deepened and lingered right up until the moment she waved Tiarnan and an ecstatic Rosie off in the Jeep.

Late that night Kate found herself waking from a fitful sleep to see the powerful outline of Tiarnan's build as he leant nonchalantly against the doorframe leading out to the balcony, silhouetted by the moonlight. Her first reaction was not of surprise or fear, just immediate joy, and a surge of desire so powerful she shook inside. She sat up.

'Tiarnan...' Her voice was husky from sleep and from that burgeoning desire.

Tiarnan looked at Kate and fought down the intense, nearly overwhelming urge to stop the clamour of voices that mocked him, silence them by going and laying her flat, stripping her bare, taking her so hard and fast that he'd have immediate satisfaction.

Despite the fact that today had proved to be a welcome turning point in his and his daughter's relationship, it had been overshadowed by the bitter realisation that he'd underestimated Kate. He'd put Rosie in an unforgivably vulnerable position. Since the other night, and before Rosie's *volte face* that morning, he'd noticed her introspection, seen how clingy she'd become with Kate, practically overnight. Without looking into it too deeply he'd been thankful that Rosie and Kate got on so well, and had noticed that lack of a central female figure in his daughter's life for the first time in a very concrete way. But that morning everything had been brought into sharp focus, and the time spent away from Kate and her seductive presence had provided the necessary distance for him to see things as they really were.

At first he'd tried to reassure himself that he was being ridiculous. But in his mind's eye all day he'd seen flashes of tender little moments between Rosie and Kate, the easy intimacy that had grown stronger each day, until he couldn't deny the evidence any more—not what it pointed to.

He couldn't *believe* he'd ignored his own instincts and that sensation of vulnerability he'd felt numerous times. He knew with an intense conviction now that Katie had been playing him masterfully all along. From the moment she'd looked at him in France and told him silently of her desire to the feigned reluctance to come with them on holiday and her false concern for Rosie. He'd played into her hands beautifully, all rationality gone in the grip of a lust so powerful he'd been rendered momentarily weak. But not any more.

He'd given her an opportunity and she'd adroitly taken every chance to inveigle her way in. He had no one to blame but himself. She'd admitted only the other night that she had no intention of settling down any time soon, and yet she'd obviously seen a way to assure herself a strong position as his mistress by using Rosie. And it was entirely his fault. He simply could not see another reason for her behaviour. His own mother and Stella had both proved to be woefully inept mother figures—

how could someone like Kate, an international model, possibly be any different? Especially with a child who wasn't even her own? Self-recrimination burned him deep inside.

Kate watched as Tiarnan straightened from the door and walked towards her slowly. Tension and that sense of unease was back with a vengeance. He stopped at the foot of the bed, his legs in a wide, unmistakably dominant stance. Arms folded. None of the teasing, lazily smiling seductiveness he usually displayed.

'We're leaving tomorrow.'

His words fell like shards of glass. Kate was completely nonplussed, had no clue as to what he was talking about or why it felt like a slap in the face.

'But…I thought we had at least another four days here? Has something happened?'

He shook his head, and then laughed harshly. 'You could say that. I've realised that I made a grave error of judgement in bringing you here.'

Pain lanced Kate, and she felt unbelievably vulnerable in her plain T-shirt, her head still a little fuzzy from sleep. 'What do you mean?'

Tiarnan came around, closer to the bed. Kate fought not to shrink back and looked up. The blue of his eyes was intense despite the dim light.

'I shouldn't have trusted that you wouldn't use Rosie in some kind of manipulative effort to gain a more intimate place in our lives—my life. A more permanent position. I can see now that that's *exactly* what you were doing in your own quiet little way.'

Suddenly Kate was wide awake. Without really thinking she sprang out of the bed to stand beside it, her heart hammering. 'What on earth are you talking about?' She shook because she was in such shock, so affronted. 'I would *never* use Rosie like that. How could you think such a thing?'

Tiarnan's face was harsher than she'd ever seen it. 'Because you said something to her the other night and she's now developed a sense of devotion to you that you've undoubtedly engineered for your own ends.'

Tiarnan thought again of the day he'd just spent with his daughter—her easy chatter about everything and anything that he'd missed so much, and how it had been interspersed with countless references to Katie this and Katie that. He'd had no idea that Kate had insinuated herself so subtly into their lives—and more importantly into Rosie's life. The child clearly had a case of hero-worship—no doubt fostered by Kate herself.

Kate drew herself up to her full height, unbelievably hurt that Tiarnan could think such a thing. And yet she knew she couldn't, *wouldn't* betray Rosie's confidence.

'I'm very fond of Rosie, and I'm flattered that she likes me. She's a very lovable little girl. But I would never foster intimacy with her just to get some kind of closer relationship with you, as you're suggesting.'

Tiarnan unfolded his arms and made a slashing gesture that forced Kate to take a step back. She'd never seen him look so angry, and realised that it was an intense anger at himself. Her heart ached in the face of his blatant mistrust, that he could believe that he had put Rosie in any kind of danger.

'There's a good reason I've never invited a woman into my life on such an intimate level. For you I made an exception, because we have a shared history and because you're not a stranger to Rosie. But it was a grave error, and it's one I'm going to rectify immediately—before Rosie can grow any more attached to you. I take full responsibility. I should never have allowed you to look after her in Madrid in the first place, or invited you here.' *Why had he thought for a second that she would be any different from any other woman?*

Kate folded her arms, willing the hurt from her voice. 'So you're going to banish me from your sight and from Rosie's presence? What about Rosie? What is *she* going to think if I suddenly disappear?'

He came close and put a finger under her chin to tip her face up. Kate clenched her jaw, refusing to let him see how badly he was affecting her.

'I've told Rosie that you've been called home for work. You can say goodbye to her in the morning. I'll escort you back to Madrid. I have some urgent business to attend to there for a couple of days, and then I'll return here alone to spend the rest of the holiday with Rosie.'

Anger rushed through Kate at his high-handed manner and she bit out, 'You don't have to escort me anywhere, Tiarnan. I'm not going to steal the silver on my way out. Need I remind you that I never wanted to come here in the first place?'

Tiarnan quirked his brow. His voice was like steel, reminding her of how intent he'd been on seducing her that night in San Francisco. It grated across Kate's nerves.

'I'll escort you because, as I said, I've business to attend to. And need I remind *you* that it took just one night to act out your charade of playing hard to get before you agreed to come here?'

Shame coursed through Kate. He was right. But it had been no charade.

Before she knew what was happening Tiarnan was pulling her close, reaching for the hem of her T-shirt to pull it up. Kate slapped his hands away ineffectually, incensed that he would think he could speak to her like this, accuse her of this, and still seduce her.

'What do you think you're doing?'

'I'm taking you to bed—which is what I should have remembered is the primary focus of this relationship.'

Kate pulled back within the tight band of steel of his arms, trying desperately to avoid his head as it lowered, his mouth intoxicatingly close to hers. She shook her head from side to side, felt Tiarnan catch a long skein of her hair, holding her head still.

'*No!* I won't do this. I don't deserve this, Tiarnan. It was your decision to ask me here. I did not manipulate you in any way. And I did *not* take advantage of Rosie.'

Her words sliced into Tiarnan with the precision of a knife, reminding him of his misjudgement once again. He drew back, but held her close. Angled his hips and moved them against hers so that she could feel his arousal. He saw the flare of helpless response in her eyes, saw it race across her cheeks in a blaze of colour. Triumph surged through him. He felt as if he was back in control.

'Well, then—if, as you say, you've no intention of using Rosie, and never wanted to be here in the first place, you can't possibly object to going home, can you?'

Kate stilled in her struggle, and felt an empty ache spread outwards from her heart. She might not have wanted to come here initially—but she had, and she'd seen a slice of paradise that had more to do with the family idyll she'd always craved and less to do with the stunning surroundings. But of course Tiarnan could never know that. So she hitched her chin and said, coolly and clearly, 'No. I couldn't think of anything I'd like more than to go home.'

'Good.' Tiarnan's voice was grim, and rough with barely leashed desire.

Kate heard it and her treacherous body responded. She knew at that moment that this was it. Once they returned to Madrid the next day she was going to walk away from Tiarnan and move on with her life.

So now, when he pulled her closer and his mouth found hers, she emitted a growl of angry, hurt capitulation, but she allowed him to sweep her along in the tide of desire that blew up around them because it would be for the last time.

CHAPTER EIGHT

THE journey back to Madrid was uneventful. Kate looked out of the window and saw that they were approaching landing. Relief should have flooded her, but it didn't—only heaviness. Tiarnan was immersed in paperwork and Kate was glad of the reprieve. She'd been terrified that he'd attempt to seduce her on the plane and that she wouldn't be able to hold her emotions back. She'd barely managed to hold them back last night after they'd made love and, despite the tension tinged with anger on both sides, Tiarnan had brought her to a point of such transcendence that she'd cried silent tears afterwards. He hadn't seen, though, and she'd feigned sleep, waiting for and willing him to return to his own bed, which he eventually had done, leaving her mortifyingly bereft.

The plane landed and the stewards escorted them out. Kate spied the car she'd ordered from Martinique waiting in the distance, and finally the relief she craved flooded her. Tiarnan's own car was pulled up by the steps. He gestured for her to give the driver her bag but she clung onto it. He frowned at her, a man clearly not patient with being made to wait for anything. He held out his hand.

'Your bag, Kate.'

Kate shook her head and backed away, looked over her shoulder to the other car. 'That's my car there, Tiarnan. I'm booked on a flight back to New York from here, I don't have much time.'

His eyes speared her and she quivered inwardly.

'Don't be ridiculous. You can stay with me until I have to return to Martinique.'

Kate smiled, and it felt brittle and false. 'Is that what you see happening? Now that I'm safely out of Rosie's way we can continue this affair until such time as you or I get bored?'

Tiarnan frowned even more deeply, an uncomfortable prickling sensation running over his skin. He wasn't used to women articulating his inner thoughts. That was exactly how he'd envisaged things going. He'd removed what he'd seen as a threat to Rosie from her life, which allowed him to continue his affair with Kate. He made a discreet gesture and knew that his driver had melted away into the car behind him.

He gestured with his hand again, and didn't like the sense of desperation gripping his innards. 'Come on, Kate. Let's not waste time.'

She shook her head again, more emphatically. 'No. I told you before this affair was only going to last for the holiday, and it's over now.' She forced the words out, even though they were like broken glass lacerating her tongue. 'Thank you for taking me. I had a nice time.'

A nice time? Tiarnan felt so incandescent his vision was blurred for a moment. He had the strongest, most primal urge to pick Kate up, throw her in the back of his car and instruct Juan to drive and keep driving until his head was clear of this gnarled heat.

'Kate, you don't have to act out this charade. I want you. But I'm not going to play games pursuing you all over the world. I'm quite happy for you to be my mistress. I just won't have you use Rosie as a pawn to get there.'

The pain was intense, but Kate forced herself to stay standing. 'I'm not playing games, Tiarnan. I don't do that. I meant what I said. This is over.'

The quiet intensity of her voice suddenly told him that she spoke the truth. And in that instant unwelcome and burning came the suspicion that he'd grossly misjudged her motives where Rosie was concerned. He couldn't deny that he'd acted out of a knee-jerk sense of panic that he'd done something wrong—that he'd allowed someone into their intimate sphere who could harm Rosie exactly as Stella had. The truth was, he'd simply never seen Rosie trust a woman so implicitly who wasn't either Sorcha, her grandmother, or Mama Lucille and her family...

Kate stood in front of him and she'd never looked lovelier. Her flawless skin had taken on a warm honey glow, and her hair had streaks of platinum among the blonde strands. She was dressed in a simple white shirt and jeans, and he noticed the straw hat she held in one clenched hand. It was the tacky hat he'd bought her in Saint-Pierre. Suddenly a memory hit him right between the eyes: the evening they'd returned from that outing she'd caught him about to throw it away, with the sunglasses. She'd grabbed them from him with surprising force and said, 'Don't!'

And then jokingly, as if to diminish it, 'I plan on showing them to one of my designer friends. You never know—they could inspire his next collection.'

But it was her eyes that had caught him. They hadn't been joking. They'd been deadly serious.

Right then, standing by his car, a lot of things seemed to be clicking into place. Everything that had happened between them seemed to merge into one memory, and he recalled how she'd looked at him when he'd pulled back from their kiss ten years ago—the light that had shone out of her just before he'd asked her what the hell she was thinking. He could see now that he'd forgotten how that light had dimmed...but the memory of her vulnerability was suddenly vivid.

He backed away, the compulsion to drag her off by her hair

curiously fading. And yet he felt empty inside. Twisted with conflicting emotions.

'Yes,' he said, not even sure what he was replying to. 'Thanks for coming with us, Kate, I'm sure I'll see you soon.'

Kate paled and she looked uncertain—as if she'd expected more of a fight, as if she were almost disappointed. 'Yes. No doubt. And, Tiarnan?'

He stopped and looked at her, feeling numb.

'Please don't feel that you have to give me anything…like a token… If you do, I'll just send it back.'

And then she turned and walked away quickly, that hat in one hand, her case in the other. Tiarnan watched as a driver leapt out of the other car and took her case, then waited till she sat inside and closed the door behind her. Then the car was pulling away and she was gone.

Two weeks later. The Ritz Hotel, Central Park, New York

'I'm afraid I'm not a very good dancer, William.'

Kate forced a smile at the man whose arm was far too tight around her waist as he led her to the dance floor through the throng. He was her date for the evening and, as for how getting on with her life was going, things were pretty dismal.

He breathed in her ear—far too close for her liking, 'I don't believe it for a second. It's impossible you can't dance well.'

Kate mentally told him, *You've been warned.* She'd been invited to this glitzy charity function by the honourable William Fortwin the Third, the pampered son of a well-known media mogul. And she'd come because she had to at least give him a chance. Now she wished she was anywhere but here. Her feet ached from working all day and her dress was too tight. She put it down to Mama Lucille's cooking, and then abruptly diverted her mind from that dangerous avenue of thought.

Her breasts felt almost unbearably sensitive too—and, come

to think of it, she felt sensitive all over, and bloated. It had to be down to her overdue period... She was practically bursting out of her dress, which wasn't a good thing as it was strapless and had a provocative slit to the thigh. She really didn't need William to have any more encouragement to look at her cleavage.

She sighed deeply as he swung her a little too enthusiastically onto the dance floor, and resolutely moved his hand back up to her waist from her bottom—*again.*

Tiarnan watched Kate move the man's hand from her bottom and unclenched his own hands a little. But everything else stayed clenched. He hadn't expected to see her here tonight; how many functions had he been to in New York over the years and never bumped into her?

And yet ever since he'd touched down in New York she'd filled his mind so completely that at first he'd thought he was hallucinating when he'd seen her. All thoughts of the business deal he was meant to be wrapping up were gone. And he had to concede now that she'd been filling his mind constantly in the last two weeks. Returning to Martinique and Rosie should have been a balm to his spirit. But it had proved to be anything but. It had seemed lacklustre, empty. Even his improved relationship with Rosie had failed to lift his spirits, and at every turn people had seemed to mention Kate and ask about her, ask when she might come back. She'd created an indelible impression in just a few days.

That sense that he'd misjudged her had been compounded even more so when Rosie had finally revealed what she and Kate had talked about that night. He could see now that Rosie had needed that outlet desperately—someone independent that she could confide in, someone who wasn't him. And from what he could gather Kate had reassured her with a gentle intuition that had done anything *but* take advantage of the vulnerable little girl.

He took her in. She looked stunning. Her dress was a champagne colour, and her skin glowed with the remnants of her tan even from where he stood. Her hair was swept up and kept in place with a diamanté pin, baring her neck, which made Tiarnan feel inordinately protective. There was something about her tonight that he hadn't noticed before—a kind of *glow*. She was undeniably beautiful, but it seemed to be radiating right out of her in a way he'd never seen before.

The crowd cleared for a moment, and Tiarnan saw the man's hand descend to Kate's bottom again—just as the thigh-high slit in her dress revealed one long shapely leg. It was too much. Restraining himself from physically throwing people aside, he went out to the lobby, where he spoke briefly to the reception-ist and then went back into the ballroom.

As he walked towards her now, with one goal in mind, all the nebulous tendrils of revelation and doubt he'd felt that evening standing before her at Madrid airport were conveniently forgot-ten in the mist of this lust haze clouding his vision. Also forgot-ten was the fact that he'd felt that instinctive need to let her walk away. He couldn't fathom right now how on earth he'd let her go.

Kate felt a prickling on her neck, and as she apologised to William for what seemed like the umpteenth time she wondered if perhaps she was coming down with flu. Then she heard a deep drawling voice behind her, and would have fallen if not for the fact that she was being held in such a grip.

'She really is a terrible dancer—I'm sure you won't mind if I cut in.'

It wasn't a question, it was a thinly veiled threat, an impera-tive, and William Fortwin recognised a superior male when he saw one. He dropped Kate like a hot coal, much to her chagrin and relief.

'Of course. Here…'

And before she knew what was happening Tiarnan Quinn had smoothly inserted himself into William's place. Suddenly

Kate's evening exploded into a million tiny balls of sensation. Her head felt light, she no longer felt constricted...or she did, but it was a different kind of constriction. Shock rendered her momentarily speechless. Lust and heat were intense and immediate after a two-week absence. All efforts to forget about this man and his effect on her were shown up in all their pathetic ineffectiveness.

And with that shaming realisation, as if she hadn't done the hardest thing she'd ever done in her life just walking away from him two weeks ago, she allowed anger to rise. She would *never* forget the way he'd so grossly misjudged her, letting his innate cynicism distort her innocent friendship with Rosie. Or the way he'd let her walk away from him in Madrid and, even more shamingly, the way that despite all her precious efforts to self-protect she'd longed for him to haul her back to him and demand she stay. He'd morphed in an instant that evening from hot and astounded to cool and distant, and she'd been terrified that he'd seen something of her real feelings. Her eyes flashed what she hoped were real sparks.

'What do you think you're doing?' she spat. 'That man was my date.' This was punctuated with an accidental stepping on Tiarnan's toes. He didn't even wince.

'You need to dance with someone who can handle your lack of...shall we say...skill?' He quirked his beautiful mouth.

Kate saw red at his easy seductive insouciance. 'You can't just order him off like a dog.'

Tiarnan's mouth thinned. 'I just did. That man wasn't fit to clean your shoes and you know it. You would have put up with the dance, feigned a headache and insisted you had to go home alone.'

Kate gasped, aghast. It was exactly what she'd been planning on doing. She coloured, and Tiarnan looked triumphant.

She smiled sweetly. 'Well, then, you can save me the bother of saying the same to you.'

He didn't respond, just seemed to be transfixed by her mouth—which made her groin tingle and her breasts tighten even more painfully. She began to feel desperate. He had to go.

'*What* are you doing here? Or did you somehow manipulate it so that I'd be asked here on a date just so you could cut in?'

He didn't look in the least bit insulted, and Kate tried valiantly not to notice how stupendously gorgeous he was in his tuxedo, even darker and more dangerous-looking after the holiday.

'I'm here on business. But the business side of things paled into insignificance the minute I saw you across the room.'

The uncomfortable realisation struck him that the business side of things had paled into insignificance long before tonight.

Kate stood on his feet again, but he merely whirled her further into the dance floor. She had to acknowledge that along with a sense of exasperation that he was here was also—much more treacherously—an intense joy she couldn't deny. To be in his arms again was such heaven, and even more so when contrasted with her hapless date.

Kate struggled not to let her eyes close as she repeated in her head like a mantra: *Just get through the dance...just get through the dance.* She had the awful feeling she wouldn't have the strength to walk away from him again, even if he was cool and distant. A humiliating image rose in her mind of her clinging onto his feet like a whipped puppy.

And then he bent his head low and whispered with bone tingling intimacy, 'I want you, Kate. You've kept me awake for two weeks.'

Kate jerked back and looked up, her eyes growing wide. She was shaking all over—and inside. She felt so torn that she was close to tears, unbelievably raw at seeing him here like this, taken by surprise. As if sensing weakness, Tiarnan kissed the edge of her mouth fleetingly, his tongue making the merest dart of sensation against her lips. It was enough to set off a chain reaction of desire throughout her body so strong that she could only look at him helplessly and follow him, her hand in his, as he strode off the dance floor and through the crowd. Desire transcended everything, and it eclipsed Kate's need to self-protect.

He didn't hesitate or deviate for a second, as if knowing how close Kate was to turning tail and running. They got into the lift, neither one looking at the other, just at the numbers as they ascended. Kate's hand was still in a tight grip with Tiarnan's much larger one.

The lift came to a smooth halt and the doors opened with silent luxuriousness. Tiarnan led them into a plush corridor and took out a room key to open a door. Kate vaguely took in the sumptuous room, with its grand view over the darkened outlines of Central Park lit up by moonlight in a clear sky. The lights of the city glittered and twinkled.

But she didn't care about views or luxurious rooms or any of that. She only cared about Tiarnan, and the fact that he had to touch her now or she'd die. As if reading her mind he threw off his jacket with an almost violent movement—and then she was in his arms and his mouth was on hers. And it felt so right. So good. So necessary.

They were still standing. Kate kicked off her shoes. She felt Tiarnan snake a hand up under all the chiffon folds of her dress. She gasped against his mouth when he reached her pants. He pulled them down; she kicked them off, urgency making her clumsy.

She struggled with and finally tore off his bow tie, opened his shirt to bare his chest, reached down between them to open his belt and release him. All the while their mouths were fused, as if it was too much to break apart even for a second.

Kate felt the clip being pulled from her hair, and the heavy mass fell down around her shoulders. Tiarnan's hand luxuriated in the strands, massaging her head in an incongruously tender gesture amidst the passionate urgency.

She finally managed to pull down his trousers, freeing his

heavy erection. His hands were under her dress, lifting it up. Kate raised her leg and cried out when she felt Tiarnan lift her against the door and thrust up into her in one smooth move.

For a moment, as if savouring the intensity, neither one moved or breathed, and then, because it was too exquisite not to, they moved. Kate wrapped her arms around his neck and clenched her buttocks. Tiarnan let out a long hiss of breath. They moved in tandem, surrounded by nothing but their breathing and their frantic heartbeats as Tiarnan drove in and out, taking them higher and higher, his chest heaving against Kate's which felt unbearably swollen against her dress.

When the pinnacle came, it seemed to go on for ever. Tiarnan had to soothe Kate, tell her it was OK to let go, before she finally allowed herself to fall, let the release sweep her away. Tiarnan joined her, and when they were finally spent he buried his head in her neck. It had been fast and furious. Shattering.

After what seemed like ages, Tiarnan finally let Kate down. Her legs were unbelievably wobbly. She muttered something and went to find the bathroom, locking herself inside with relief while she tried to gather her wits and come to terms with what she'd just let happen.

Her mind was barely able to function, but uppermost was a need to protect and survive. She had to get away from Tiarnan. After a few minutes she stood and looked in the mirror. She was wearing more make-up than she normally would and was glad of it now. Somehow she'd had the wherewithal to pick up her pants and hair clip. With shaking hands she stepped back into her underwear and pinned her hair back up—a little untidily, but it would have to do. And then, taking a deep breath, she went back out to the suite.

She came out to see Tiarnan smile at her with sexy laziness, in the act of taking off his cufflinks. His trousers were open at the top, shirt undone. All her good intentions nearly flew out of the window. *Nearly.*

She called on the cool reserve that felt so alien and hard to muster now and said, 'I meant what I said in Madrid, Tiarnan. It's over. And that—' she looked accusingly at the door '—shouldn't have happened.'

'Well, it did,' he drawled, and indicated to the bed. 'I've got the suite for the night.'

Kate looked at the bed. She was angry, because a very big part of her was tempted to just give in, throw caution to the wind and indulge in another ten hours of bliss. But then when and where would it stop? She had to be strong—had to do this now once and for all.

She shook her head and stood her ground. 'No, Tiarnan. I'm not staying the night. Much as I might be tempted, it's not going to happen.'

He stopped what he was doing and looked at her. She didn't look as if she wanted to hang around. Irritation and frustration prickled under his skin. He wanted her already again. Painfully. Urgently. The frustration of the past two weeks still shocked him with its intensity.

He couldn't stop the impatience lacing his voice. He was a man used to getting what he wanted, when he wanted. 'Look, Kate, you want me—I want you. We're good together. What's the problem?'

Kate wanted to scream; was it always this simple for men? She answered herself: it was if they didn't have feelings invested. Tiarnan started to walk towards her and panic made her jerky. She flung out a hand. 'Stop! Don't come any closer.' She knew if he so much as touched her she'd be a mess.

He stopped and frowned.

'Whatever we are is neither here nor there, Tiarnan. I'm not in the market for an affair. I just won't do it.'

'Well, I wouldn't call what we're doing an *affair*—we know each other, we're friends…it's more than that.'

He didn't even trust her with his daughter. Sadness and pain gripped Kate. 'It's *not* more than that because you don't trust me, Tiarnan. But that's beside the point—because it's going to come to an end, isn't it?'

Tiarnan wasn't sure where this was going. 'Well, of course it will—at some stage. But does it have to be tonight? Right now?'

Kate nodded and held back a sob. 'I can't do this. With you.'

She started walking to the door. Before she got to it Tiarnan reached her and turned her around.

She looked up, stiff all over, feeling more constricted than ever. 'Please, Tiarnan—just let me go.'

A muscle clenched in his jaw. She could see the confusion in his eyes. And then he said, 'Tell me why—just tell me why you don't want to do this.'

She looked at him for a long moment and knew that there was only one way he would let her walk away. She would have to bare her soul. Even so, she asked, 'Do you really want to know?'

He nodded. Grim. Determined.

She pushed past him back into the room, putting space between them. She paced for a minute, and then stopped and looked at him, summoned all her courage. 'Because that night ten years ago took way more out of me than I revealed to you at the time.'

He frowned, his black brows creasing over those stunning blue eyes.

Kate continued, but every word was costing her an emotional lifetime. 'That night…I'd no intention of trying to seduce you. I…' She faltered and looked away, then back again. 'I'd had a crush on you for a long time, Tiarnan, and that night I thought I saw you notice me as a woman for the first time. I somehow got the courage to kiss you…and you kissed me back…'

'So…?'

Kate could see he was trying to figure it out. 'I guessed you believed I was more confident that I really was. But then, when you rejected me, I wanted to protect myself—pretend that I'd been in full control. I felt humiliated, and I hated that you might see how much it had meant to me.'

Tiarnan had the strangest sensation of the earth shifting beneath his feet, but he stayed standing. He'd had that instinct, but then when she'd seemed to sure...so mature...so cool... he'd doubted it. But he shouldn't have. It was the vulnerability he'd sensed in Martinique. And at the airport in Madrid, when it had compelled him to let her walk away.

He tried to cling onto something. 'What does that have to do with *now?*'

'Everything!' Kate wailed, throwing up her arms, taking him by surprise.

Colour was high in her cheeks. Her eyes sparkled like jewels and he felt a chasm opening up between them.

Her chest rose and fell with agitation. 'I've been aware of you for the past ten years, Tiarnan. Every time I've looked at you I've remembered that kiss. The pitifully few and far between men I've been with have all come a far distant second to the way I imagined *you* might have made me feel.' Her voice cracked ominously. 'How pathetic is that? They fell short of little more than my imagination. I couldn't even form a decent lasting relationship because the shadow you'd cast made everyone else pale in comparison.'

Her mouth twisted bitterly, making Tiarnan want to kiss the bitter line away, hating that he had caused it.

'Over the years I learnt to protect myself. I never wanted you to know how I'd failed to get over you. But at the christening that day it was so hard to stand there and witness Sorcha and Romain's joy and love with you right beside me...and then in San Francisco...I couldn't hide it any more.'

She shrugged again, and it made something lance Tiarnan's heart, but he couldn't move.

'I agreed to go to Martinique with you because I thought it might help...that by sleeping with you it might somehow make you fall off your pedestal. Reduce what we had shared to something more banal. But it didn't, Tiarnan. It's made things worse. I can't do this. And I would never have used Rosie in any kind of manipulative way. I *hate* that you would think that.' She shook her head and made for the door again.

Feeling panic surge, Tiarnan gripped her shoulders and pulled her around, tipping her chin up. Her eyes were closed. He grabbed her hands and brought them up, holding them tightly, manacled in his. 'Kate—look at me.'

She shook her head, and he could see her press her lips together in a desperate attempt at control. A tear trickled out from under the long lashes that rested on her flushed cheek. He felt weak inside. Utterly helpless. And like the biggest heel.

'Kate—please, don't cry. I owe you a huge apology. I'm sorry for accusing you of using Rosie. I can see how wrong I was.'

The full extent of his own cynicism hit him forcibly. It was so clear now. He'd lashed out as much in an effort to protect himself as Rosie, and the realisation disgusted him. Kate had just got too close too quickly. She opened her eyes then, and the naked emotion in their swimming depths put him to shame. But he couldn't let go of her wrists. He felt the frantic beat of her pulse and it reminded him of a caged bird.

In a hoarse voice filled with emotion she said, 'This is who I really am, Tiarnan, and what I really want: if I never had to stand in front of a photographer again to have my photo taken or parade down a catwalk I'd be ecstatic. My idea of a good Saturday night is staying in and baking bread. I like knitting— and I like to crochet if I'm really going out on a limb. I make homemade soup. What I want more than anything in the world is to find someone to love who'll love me back and to have babies with them—lots of babies—and raise a family. That's what I want and need. I've no idea if that's as a result of my emotionally barren childhood or conditioning or whatever. All I know is that it's what I want in the deepest core part of me.

I'm not the kind of person who can have an affair and not get involved. And I would never ask any of this from you because I know you've done it. You've got it. You're happy. But I'm not, Tiarnan, and as much as we might have *this*...' she jerked her head to the bed '...it's not enough for me.'

She pulled her hands to try and free them, but he held on with something like a death grip.

'*Please* let me go, so I can get over you and get on with my life.'

Tiarnan stood in silence, stunned to his very depths. Shocked. In awe of this passionate Kate—a different kind of passionate that he'd never seen before. A huge block prevented him from speaking. She was looking up at him defiantly, as if daring him to seduce her again, knowing everything he now knew. She'd give in if he just kissed her. He knew she'd give in. They both knew. It permeated the air around them. But how could he do that?

The revelations he'd acknowledged when he realised that she *hadn't* been a dim and distant memory for him throughout the past ten years seemed so pathetic now, compared to her feelings. He knew he couldn't even begin to articulate that without sounding as if he was making excuses. It would be like trying to placate her—or, worse, patronise her.

She looked so young at that moment, so beautiful. His instinct had been right that day at the airport when he'd seen her holding onto that ridiculous hat. He'd seen something momentarily unguarded in her eyes. He realised now that it had been her attempt to make the break.

She was right. She deserved her happiness. She deserved to find a good man who would love her the way she wanted to be loved and give her all the babies and joy she wanted. Something in him reacted forcibly to that image but he forced it down. He had no right to it. No right to feel jealous.

All of a sudden he felt tired and jaded and cynical. He'd been there and had been badly burned in the process. He had always vowed never to expose himself like that again. He had Rosie. He had Sorcha and her family. Kate deserved more. He had to let her go.

Kate dropped her head. She couldn't keep looking Tiarnan in the eye, seeing the myriad emotions as he finally came to the realisation, as she knew he would, that he wouldn't be able to get rid of her fast enough. She sensed it before it even happened. He dropped her hands from his grip and stepped back. He was letting her go again. And this time she knew it was for good.

She couldn't look up. 'Thank you,' she said faintly.

His deep voice impacted like a punch in her solar plexus. 'You deserve to find what you want, Kate. I wish you all the best.'

A couple of days later Tiarnan stood in his office in Madrid, staring out of the window with his hands in his pockets. The fact that he *never* stood staring vacantly out of the window was not something that impinged on his consciousness. His eminently professional assistant knocked on his door and came in. He didn't notice the fleeting look of alarm cross her face just before he turned to face her. 'Maria?'

She came towards him and held out a brown padded envelope. 'This came for you just after you'd left for New York. It's marked "Private". I didn't want to open it.'

Tiarnan took it and had a strange feeling. He dismissed Maria and turned the envelope over. On the back, in the same clear, neat writing as on the front, was a familiar New York address and the name K. Lancaster.

He sat at his desk and opened it. Out fell a sheaf of glossy black and white photos. With his hands none too steady he looked through them, becoming more and more amazed and seriously impressed. They were stunning, and all taken completely off guard: pictures of him with Rosie, pictures of Mama

Lucille and Papa Joe, moments snatched. And he hadn't even been aware of her taking the pictures.

There was another smaller envelope, marked for Rosie. Tiarnan couldn't help himself. He had to open it. So far there were no pictures of Kate. The photo that fell out was of Kate and Rosie making funny faces at the camera, which must have been on a timer. And on the back was a note.

Rosie, I miss you already. Please know that I'd love you to come and visit me any time, and the next time I'm in Madrid we'll go out for ice cream—I'll be looking forward to hearing all about your new friends. In the meantime take care. Love, Katie.

It was only after a long moment that he realised he'd been holding his breath. He carefully put the photo back into the envelope. He stood up abruptly and went again to the window.

He couldn't want her this badly—so badly that a photograph of her pulling a funny face made him feel weak. Grim determination settled around him like a weight. She was gone. He had to let her be. She was right. He had his life. He had Rosie. He didn't need anything else, didn't want anything else. Maybe if he kept repeating it he'd start to believe it.

CHAPTER NINE

Six weeks later. Madison Avenue, New York.

KATE huddled deeper into her long padded coat and wrapped her scarf tighter around her neck. It was coming up to Christmas, and the shops were alive and bright with decorations and lights. They twinkled merrily in the dusk. She felt removed from it all, though—she was in total shock. She'd just come from an evening clinic with her doctor. Her awful growing suspicion of the last few weeks was now confirmed. There was a reason the bloated feeling had never gone away, and a reason for the fact that her breasts were so sensitive it hurt to touch them. And a very good reason for the fact that she hadn't had her period yet.

She was pregnant.

Over two months pregnant.

She stumbled on the sidewalk and someone automatically put out a hand to steady her, Kate smiled her thanks and kept going. But she felt as though everything was starting to disintegrate around her. She had to get home. She unconsciously started walking faster, sudden tears blurring her vision, and looked down to avoid people's eyes. Right in that moment she'd never felt so alone in all her life.

On the one hand, despite the shock, she felt the pure ecstatic joy of being pregnant, and on the other hand she felt the sheer desolation of knowing that the father would only see this as a burden or, worse, as something planned to trap him in some way. How could he not when it had happened before?

Why, oh why, had she blurted everything out to Tiarnan that night? Kate had remonstrated bitterly with herself ever since. The only thing she could give any thanks for was the fact that she hadn't come straight out and told him that she loved him.

But, she reminded herself, she hadn't needed to. She'd all but prostrated herself at his feet.

Kate unseeingly followed the mass of humans who were walking down Madison Avenue, her mind and belly churning sickly. All of a sudden, out of nowhere, she hit a brick wall. But it was a brick wall with hands and arms, steadying her. God, she couldn't even manage to walk down the street without avoiding mishap.

She looked up to apologise and her world stopped turning. She had the absurd impulse to laugh for a hysterical moment, before cold, stark reality set in.

'No,' she breathed painfully. 'It can't be you.'

'Kate? Is that you?'

It *was* Tiarnan. Looking down at her with dark brows pulled over piercing blue eyes. In a dark coat. Kate cursed fate and the gods, and at the same time had an awful soul-destroying awareness of how impossibly handsome he looked. How was it that she'd managed beautifully for ten years to avoid him and suddenly he seemed to be around every corner? And yet even amongst the shock and despair of seeing him she couldn't control her body's response, the awful kick of her heart.

'Yes, it's me. Sorry, I wasn't looking where I was going.' She attempted to be civil, normal, and completely and conveniently blocked out the fact that she'd just found out that she was pregnant and that the father stood in front of her right now. An extreme urge to self-protect was strong. 'How are you, Tiarnan?'

He was still holding her, looking at her strangely. Almost absently, he answered, 'Fine. Fine…'

It was only at that moment that Kate noticed someone hovering behind him. A woman. A petite, very beautiful, very soignée brunette, who smiled icily at Kate. It was all the impetus she needed. She was raw with the news she'd just received. Too raw to cope with this.

She stepped away, dislodging Tiarnan's hands, and noticed for the first time where they were. Kate had bumped into Tiarnan as he'd been walking into a restaurant. The same exclusive restaurant outside which she'd bumped into him dressed as a French maid some years before. With another dark-haired beauty. He'd obviously reverted to type.

Before she could lose it completely there on the path, in front of the man she loved and his lover, she fled. Exactly as she'd done before. Except this time Tiarnan had seen her and recognised her. The humiliation was so much worse this time, and the awful irony of coming full circle was nearly too much to bear.

Tiarnan watched as Kate strode away, her bright hair like a beacon among the sea of anonymous people. He still felt the force of her body slamming into him, full-on. He still saw her upturned face, those huge eyes. She'd looked pale—too pale. And tired. Concern clutched him. And a sudden feeling of *déjà vu*.

'Tiarnan? Are we going in? And who was that woman? She looked incredibly familiar.'

Tiarnan finally noticed his date again for the first time. He'd only asked her out in some kind of pathetic attempt to regain something close to normal in his life, but he knew now that he'd just watched his only hope of being normal again walk away. When he'd held Kate steady for those brief moments just now he'd felt at peace for the first time in weeks. A deep sigh of relief had moved through him.

He tried to focus on his date. 'Melinda, I'm sorry, but something's come up. I'm going to have to cancel dinner.'

He was already urging her back to his car at the kerb. He heard a very piqued, 'It's *Miranda,* actually—'

He opened the car door and ushered the woman in with little finesse, saying to his driver, 'Please take Miranda—sorry, Melinda—wherever she wants to go.'

Tiarnan slammed the door and watched the car pull away with an inordinate sense of relief. He started walking in the opposite direction to the one Kate had taken; as much as he wanted nothing more than to go to her straight away, he knew he had to handle this carefully. Impatience and urgency coursed through him, but for once in his life he had to control it. He had some serious thinking to do.

Kate felt as washed out as a dishrag. It was as if hearing from the doctor that she was pregnant had kick-started her body to react, and morning sickness had arrived with a vengeance. She finally emerged from the bathroom with her hand on her belly, which was feeling hard and surprisingly big already, now that she knew she wasn't just bloated. But she knew why that was. Her mind just shied away from thinking too much about it at the moment.

She was finding it hard to process everything, and also the fact that she'd bumped into Tiarnan last night. The pain of seeing him with that woman was buried deep. She still couldn't even begin to think about how she was going to tell him...and Sorcha... A welcome numbness came over her and she knew it was some kind of protective barrier, stopping the pain and hurt from impinging too deeply. She gave up silent thanks that she didn't have to work today, and then her head hurt at the thought of breaking the news to Maud too that she was pregnant. Her lingerie contract would be out of the window—not that Kate would be sorry.

A knock came on her door, and Kate started. She couldn't deny the fact that after seeing Tiarnan in the street she'd half expected him to turn up at her door behind her. And when he hadn't…the shame of how much she'd wanted it and the pain that he hadn't had been indescribable. She reassured herself now that it could only be someone from inside the building, as the concierge usually rang up if there was a visitor. It was probably the super—or Mrs Goldstein from next door.

As she approached the door she pulled a cardigan from the chair by the door and put it on. She was only dressed in ancient sweatpants and an old T-shirt of Sorcha's.

She opened the door, and when she took in who was on the other side she could feel the colour drain from her face. Her hand tightened on the knob. She instinctively clutched the cardigan around her belly, ridiculously glad she'd had the foresight to put it on.

'Tiarnan.'

'Kate.'

For an absurd moment neither spoke. They just looked at one another. Kate heard Mrs Goldstein's door creak open, and a voice with a thick New York accent asked, 'Kate? Are you OK?'

Kate dragged her gaze from Tiarnan's and stuck her head out. Her heart was hammering, and she was very tempted to say *No, I'm not OK!* But she didn't. She just said, 'Fine Mrs Goldstein. It's just Sorcha's brother. You can go back inside.'

'All right, dear.'

Mrs Goldstein's door closed and Tiarnan said drily, 'Security system? Together with your knitting needles, I'd say you and Mrs Goldstein could pack quite a punch.'

For some reason Tiarnan's comment hurt Kate terribly. She bit her lip and tried to swallow past the huge lump in her throat. 'What do you want Tiarnan? I'm busy.' She knew she sounded choked and could see Tiarnan's eyes flash in response.

All of a sudden he looked incredibly weary, and Kate could see lines on his face that hadn't been there before. His eyes looked a little bloodshot. Even so, he was still absolutely gorgeous, and she firmed her resolve. Thankfully her composure seemed to come back slightly.

'Kate, can I come in?'

'I'd prefer if you didn't.'

'Please.'

Her composure threatened to crack again, and Kate felt the weight of inevitability fall around her like a cloak. She was pregnant, and she had to tell him sooner or later. In truth, she was terrified of facing this on her own.

Eventually she stood back and held the door open.

Tiarnan walked in, past her, and Kate had to grip the doorknob tight again and close her eyes momentarily as his scent washed over her.

When she'd gathered herself enough after closing the door, she turned to face him. He had taken off his long dark overcoat and she saw that he was wearing a dark sweater and jeans that moulded lovingly to his long legs and hard thigh muscles.

Immediately her belly felt quivery. She felt weak, and moved jerkily to sit on the couch, very aware of his eyes on her.

Kate was as prickly as a porcupine. Tiarnan's eyes drank her in hungrily as she sat down. Her hair was tied back in a high haphazard knot and he longed to undo it. She still looked unbelievably pale, making concern spike through him again. And she looked different, somehow. Even though her cardigan and sweatpants hid her body, he remembered the feel of her slamming into him the previous evening. Every curve and contour.

He felt himself stir to life and cursed. Now was not the time. He had to hold it together—but he couldn't help reacting like a sex-starved teenager. She looked somehow more bountiful, and despite her paleness, more beautiful than he'd ever seen her. It shone right out of her, just as he'd noticed in the ballroom.

'Tiarnan, what is it you want?'

Her husky voice caught him and his eyes met hers. He'd been ogling her like a teenager.

Where to start? Uncharacteristically stuck for words, feeling all at sea and more terrified than he could ever remember feeling, Tiarnan paced up and down, running a hand through his hair. How did he come out and say it? He wanted her—he wanted *it*—he wanted everything. For the first time in his life.

Kate watched Tiarnan pace and saw the look of torture on his face. For the first time she had the awful abject fear that this had nothing to do with *them*. Something else must have happened. She stood, and he stopped pacing and looked at her. She almost couldn't frame the words she was so scared.

'What is it? Is it Rosie? Did something happen? Is it Sorcha or Romain?'

He looked completely nonplussed for a moment, and then comprehension dawned. Kate realised she must have looked terrified, because he was beside her in an instant and sitting her back down, coming with her to sit on the couch.

He shook his head quickly. 'No, nothing's happened to anyone. They're all safe. I'm sorry, Kate, I didn't mean to scare you.'

Relief flooded her—along with the scary realisation that Tiarnan was too close and touching her. She moved back to the corner of the couch. He let go.

She kept silent, but inwardly she was screaming at him to just tell her what he wanted and then leave. She'd even forgotten about telling him of her pregnancy.

Finally he spoke, and it sounded as if it was being torn out of him. 'Kate, I want you.'

Her stomach plummeted. She stood up and moved away, crossing her arms. When would this torture end? She turned to face him. 'Tiarnan, I've told you. I can't do this. I know you want me.' Bitterness laced her voice. 'And you know I want you. But I'm not going there.'

A vivid memory of that woman's face last night outside the restaurant came back into Kate's mind's eye like poison seeping into a wound. Acrid jealousy burned bright within her. 'I'm sure that woman you were with last night can give you what you need.'

Tiarnan stood, and the pain on his face was stark. His hand slashed the air in a gesture of absolute rejection.

'Kate, I couldn't even remember that woman's name after bumping into you—and in truth I was hard pressed to remember it at all. That was my pathetic attempt to try and get back to what I knew, to pretend that you don't exist. To try and block out the fact that I haven't been able to stop thinking about you for a second, the fact that it's taken me weeks of torture to finally realise that I can't live without you. And to block out the fact that I've been haunted with images of you meeting someone else, falling in love with someone else, making love to someone else. Having babies with someone else.'

His eyes burned so intensely blue they held Kate in absolute thrall, unable to move or speak.

His voice sounded rough. 'I wanted to follow you home straight away last night, but I forced myself to wait. I knew that I had to come to you and make you believe what I said— believe that I wasn't just saying it to get you into bed. I was going to be calm, rational, but it's the last thing I feel now. I need *you,* Kate. I don't just want you. *I love you.* And I'm terrified that you won't give me a chance to try and prove to you how much I love you. I'm terrified it might be too late for you to give me a chance to try and make you happy, because I know you want to find someone else. You deserve someone who isn't tainted with mistakes from the past, with an already grown daughter…but I'm selfish, and I don't want you to be with someone else. I want you to be with *me.* For ever.'

Tiarnan's words seem to hang suspended in the air for a long time. Kate didn't know if she was breathing, and then she felt something in her belly quiver. Even though she knew it couldn't be the baby yet, it seemed to inject the life force back into her system.

All the pent-up emotion she'd been keeping down and suppressing for so long seemed to rush up. The fact that she'd all but bared her soul to *him* and yet he'd let her walk away. The torture she'd been going through. She took a jerky step towards Tiarnan, tears prickling, and was so utterly confused and overwhelmed that she hit him ineffectually on his chest, lashing out at the pain he'd caused her. He stood there and let her hit him again, and that made her even more upset. Because even now she couldn't bear to hurt him.

Tears blurred her vision completely and made her voice thick. 'How can you just come in here and say those things? *How?* It's not possible. You can't do this to me, Tiarnan. You can't just walk in and offer me everything I've ever wanted and dreamt of for ever like it's the easiest thing in the world. I've spent a long time getting over you. I don't need you. I've tried so hard to forget you. But now you're here, and you're saying...you're saying...'

She put her hands to her face in turmoil and despair, sobbing her heart out. She sobbed even harder when she felt strong arms wrap around her and pull her close, holding her so tight that somewhere a spark of hope ignited—and the very scary thought that perhaps she wasn't dreaming this. That maybe he had actually said those things and meant them.

Kate had never felt so exposed and raw and emotional in her life. Eventually the sobbing stopped, and she felt her hands being gently pulled away from her face. She was too weak and limp to do anything but look into Tiarnan's eyes, uncaring of how awful she must look. His eyes were full of concern, and something else she'd never seen. *Love.* Tears blurred her vision again.

With the utmost tenderness he cupped her jaw and wiped the tears as they fell with his thumbs.

He sounded tortured. 'Katie, sweetheart. Please don't cry. I'm so sorry for making you cry. I don't ever want to be the cause of making you cry again.' He went very still, and tipped up her chin so she'd look him in the eye. 'I can't bear to see you so upset. If you want me to leave, to walk away, then I'll leave right now.'

She could see the stoic resolve in his eyes. His jaw was clenched, as if to ward off a blow, and a muscle twitched. Kate wiped the back of her hand across her cheek, unaware of the heart-achingly vulnerable image she portrayed. She shook her head and then said softly, shakily, 'If I was stronger I'd make you walk away, so you know what it feels like… But the truth is I'm not that strong. I don't want you to go anywhere. I don't want you to leave my sight ever again.'

Tiarnan put his hands on her upper arms and Kate could feel them shaking. 'Kate, are you saying…? Will you let me try and make you happy?'

Kate finally felt a sense of peace wash through her, diminishing the pain, and with it came trust that this was real. She couldn't keep back a wobbly smile. She put up a hand and touched his jaw. 'Tiarnan, much as I hate to admit this to a man of your supreme confidence, unfortunately you're the only person on this earth who has the power to make me happy. I need *you* so much. I think I've loved you for ever.'

With an unusual lack of grace Tiarnan pulled Kate into him again, then took her face in his hands and kissed her with small feverish kisses saying, *'Thank you…thank you…'* over and over again.

Kate finally stopped him and took *his* face in *her* hands, pressed a long lingering kiss to his mouth. Desire swept up around them, all consuming. Tiarnan's hands roved hungrily over her form, down her back, her hips, her bottom, pulling her in close.

She felt her belly press against him, and had to gasp at the painfully exquisite sensation when he cupped one throbbing and too-sensitive breast. Immediately he pulled back, concern etched on his face.

'What is it?'

Sudden trepidation trickled through Kate. *The pregnancy.* She searched his eyes, terrified that telling him would burst this bubble. But she had to tell him and deal with his response— no matter what it would be.

She pulled back and his hands fell. But she took hold of them tightly.

'When I bumped into you last night I'd just been to see the doctor. That's why I was so distracted…'

Immediately tension came into Tiarnan's body. She'd been so pale. Her cheeks were flushed now, but it could be a fever. 'What is it? Are you OK? Is something wrong?'

She shook her head and said quickly, 'No, nothing's wrong. Everything is fine.'

She smiled shyly then, and all Tiarnan could see was tousled strands of hair falling around her face, her lips plump from his kisses. He wanted to kiss her again so badly, to hold her tight and never wake up from this moment.

He squeezed her hands. 'What is it, Kate?'

She bit her lip and looked down for a moment. Even before she spoke a trickling of awareness came into his body and his consciousness. He recalled how hard her belly had felt just now, how her breasts had felt bigger, more voluptuous. They were obviously sensitive. An incredible joy started to bubble through him even as she looked up and said the words, with naked vulnerability on her face.

'I'm pregnant, Tiarnan. I found out last night. Nearly ten weeks. It must have happened that first night in Martinique…'

Tiarnan could see her start to become nervous.

'I know I said it would be OK—and I really thought it would. It's entirely my fault.'

He immediately shook his head. Anything to stop her talking. He put a finger to her mouth, watched her eyes widen.

'Stop. It's OK. I know what you're thinking, and what you're scared of: that I'll think it's Stella Rios all over again?'

She nodded her head slowly.

'That it's too soon and I might not be ready for this news when we haven't even discussed it?'

She nodded again, her eyes huge and intensely blue.

'Well, don't be. I was halfway to guessing the minute you mentioned the doctor but said you were OK.'

Tiarnan led Kate over to the couch and sat down, pulling her onto his lap. He lifted a hand and kissed it, and then covered her belly with their joined hands, looked into her eyes. 'I never imagined a day when I would be feeling this way about anyone. I'm so in love with you the only time I feel normal or rational or sane is when I can see you and touch you. I've never felt that way about anyone—not even Stella. Never Stella. My association with her was always about the baby, about my responsibility to an unborn child. Stella and I never even consummated the marriage.' He quirked a smile. 'I used her pregnancy as an excuse to hide the fact that I didn't desire her any more. For some reason a blonde-haired blue-eyed witch I'd just kissed kept distracting me.'

His smile faded. 'I should never have rejected you so cruelly that night. The truth is that you'd shocked me out of every arrogant and complacent bone in my body. The desire I felt for you that night was urgent enough that if I hadn't realised how inexperienced you were and remembered *who* you were I would have made love to you there and then, like a randy teenager. I lashed out at that. And then, when you were so cool and blasé, I felt stupidly insulted that you weren't bothered.'

Kate felt pure joy rip through her at his words, at the acknowledgement that it had meant something more for him too. She saw the regret in his eyes, on his face, and smoothed the back of her hand across his cheek. 'We were both young—I was far too young.' She smiled ruefully. 'I don't think I would have been able to handle an experience so intense. And perhaps it's as simple as the fact that Rosie needed you. She wouldn't be in your life now if it hadn't been for Stella.'

Tiarnan felt subtle tension snake into Kate's body and her eyes clouded. He took her hand again. 'What is it? You're closing up on me.'

She shrugged and avoided his eyes. 'It's just that you've only just developed these feelings for me, and you never wanted more children, and I'm just scared... You changed so quickly on Martinique. It scared me how easy you found it to think the worst...'

He pulled her face back to his, forcing her to meet his intense gaze. 'It was easy because I'd never let another woman in so close before. For the first time since Rosie was born I put my needs first and assured myself that Rosie would be OK. When I saw the evidence of her trust in you I panicked. I was terrified I'd lost all sense of judgement and was about to let another woman take advantage of her. I didn't stop to think.'

Kate looked at him, searching as if to see whether she could trust him, and finally said, 'I believe you. I can see how it might have looked... But are you sure you're ready for a baby? You've always—'

He put a finger over her mouth, stopping her words. 'Kate, I've never wanted children again *with anyone else*. But now— with you.' He shrugged with endearing vulnerability. 'I feel like I've been given a gift. A chance to experience something I denied myself for a long time. My background and Stella Rios poisoned my attitudes. You've healed that. These feelings have been brewing for a long, long time. Seeing your desire at the christening that day was merely the catalyst. I've been aware of you all these years, even though I might have denied it to myself. I kept you strictly out of bounds. But you intrigued me with your studied indifference and your coolness. It was just a matter of time before I would have been unable to fight the urge to discover why I couldn't stop thinking about you. I've never felt that same desire for another woman until the moment we kissed again.'

Kate blushed furiously, and Tiarnan tenderly caressed her cheek and said wonderingly, 'Even now you can blush.'

She was still serious for a moment. 'What about Rosie? I mean, does she know about this?'

He nodded, smiling. 'It's one of the two things I did last night, while I tried to restrain myself from coming over here. I told Rosie I was going to come and ask you to marry me, and after she stopped squealing she said, "Does this mean you'll go back to normal now and stop being so crabby?" I assured that I would as long as you said yes, so she's been praying all night that you would say yes.'

He got serious then. 'She cares for you, Kate, and even more importantly she obviously trusts you enough to confide in you. You've already been more of a mother to her than her own mother has been her whole life. She has the picture you sent her in a frame by her bed. A picture I'm extremely jealous of, I might add.'

Kate flushed with pleasure and buried her head against his neck for a moment, hugging him tight. Relief and joy flooded her, because she knew she would never have been happy taking up such a big role in Tiarnan's life unless Rosie was happy too.

She pulled back and pressed a lingering kiss to Tiarnan's mouth. 'You can tell Rosie I said yes. What was the other thing you had to do?'

His eyes flashed in response to her yes, and his hands tightened around her. 'I had to ask Sorcha for her blessing, of course. She told me that if I hurt a hair on your head she'd break my legs—or words to that effect.'

'Great,' Kate grumbled good-naturedly. 'Everyone knew about this before me.'

He looked at her sheepishly. 'There's something else I haven't been able to get out of my mind. You're going to think this sounds crazy, but bumping into you last night made me think of it again. A few years ago I bumped into a girl outside that same restaurant—'

Kate groaned and buried her face in her hands. She mumbled from behind them, 'In a French maid's outfit?'

Tiarnan took down her hands and looked at her, shocked. 'That *was* you?'

She nodded and smiled. 'It was a hen night. I ran away. I was so mortified.'

He shook his head and laughed out loud, head thrown back. 'I thought I was going mad—turned on by some anonymous girl in a tarty costume. Do you realise that after that night I couldn't look at another woman for weeks…months? And at night all I could dream about was you, and wonder what the hell was going on?'

Kate smiled. 'Good! I'm glad I tortured you a little too. It's not entirely fair that I had to endure hearing about your endless parade of women down the years—'

Tiarnan suddenly flipped them, so that Kate lay on the couch underneath him. He undid her hair until it flowed out around her head. He ran a hand over her burgeoning breasts, causing her breath to catch, and down to her belly, caressing the growing mound.

Kate put her hand over his and felt the exquisite quickening of desire that only this man could engender. She pulled his head down and said throatily, 'First, before I kiss you all over your body to within an inch of your life, Tiarnan Quinn, I have to tell you something else.'

Tiarnan had already started kissing her, pulling her top up.

Kate stopped him and looked at him mock sternly. *'Wait.'*

She smiled, then brought his hand back to her now bare belly and looked at him with shining eyes. 'How do you feel about twins?'

He stopped and looked down at her, eyes widening in wonder. 'Seriously?'

Kate nodded. His hand tightened on her belly. An unmistakably proprietorial gleam lit his intense gaze, making Kate rejoice inwardly.

He growled softly. 'Tell me how much it's going to cost to buy you out of every job contract and campaign you're booked for—because you and our babies are mine now, and I'm not letting another person have the right to touch you or photograph you without my say-so.'

Kate smiled and revelled in his innate possessiveness. She shifted easily under him, feeling the heavy weight of his arousal pressing against his jeans. She moved sinuously. Colour stained his cheeks.

'Kate,' he said warningly.

She made a quick calculation and said a round figure. He paled slightly under his tan, but didn't miss a beat. 'I paid a fraction of that just to kiss you, so I figure it's worth it to marry you, to be the father of your children and live happily ever after.'

'Sounds good to me.' Kate smiled, and pulled him back down to where she wanted him for ever—in her arms.

EPILOGUE

Two and a half years later, Martinique

KATE stood in the dim light and looked lovingly at the two small sprawled forms in the big double bed, protected by a muslin net hanging from above. Dark-haired Iris was on her back, thumb stuck firmly in her mouth and sucking periodically. Blonde-haired Nell was on her front, arms outstretched, her head resting on one chubby cheek and looking angelic. Kate smiled. She'd been anything but angelic a few hours ago.

Pure joy rose up within her, and she had to press a hand to her chest to try and contain it. And then she felt a big solid presence behind her, strong arms wrap around her waist. She leant back into the familiar embrace and smiled wider when she felt firm lips press a hot kiss to her neck.

They were in the room that had been hers the first time she'd come to Martinique. Now it was a nursery for the girls. She heard Tiarnan whisper close to her ear, 'We'll have to put bars around the room. I caught Nell making a near-successful bid for freedom earlier.'

Kate stifled a giggle at the image.

Tiarnan took her hand to lead her out and back to their own room along the balcony. He was in nothing but boxer shorts, and Kate's eyes ran over him appreciatively. Tiarnan caught her looking. He stopped and pulled her into his arms.

'Why, Mrs Quinn,' he said mock seriously, 'I think I'm feeling a little violated by your very explicit look.'

Kate leant into him luxuriously, loving the feel of his body, and especially the way it was reacting. She wrapped her arms around him and pressed a kiss to his neck. 'I'm very sorry, Mr Quinn. I know how sensitive you are.'

He groaned softly when he felt her move her hips, bringing the apex of her legs into close contact with his rapidly hardening arousal.

Kate looked at him, revelling in the intimate moment. Revelling in the bliss to come and the bliss she felt every day. She took his hand to lead him into their bedroom.

He asked on the way, 'What was wrong with Rosie earlier? Apparently I "wouldn't understand".'

Kate looked back and smiled. 'It's nothing, really—just girlie issues. She likes one of Zoe's cousins, but he likes someone else…'

Tiarnan groaned, and said with feeling, 'I knew there was a reason I married you. I could never deal with all this puberty stuff.'

Kate hit his arm playfully and said something—but it was indistinct as they disappeared into the bedroom, and then everything faded into the beautifully warm and fragrant tropical darkness.

PRINCE OF MONTÉZ, PREGNANT MISTRESS

SABRINA PHILIPS

With thanks to Penny,for her art expertise
and her much-valued friendship.
And to Phil, whose enduring patience
continues to astound me.

CHAPTER ONE

HER heart was beating so loudly in her chest that Cally Greenway was convinced the whole auction room could hear it. Drawing in a deep breath, she uncrossed then recrossed her legs for the umpteenth time and tried to dismiss it as a flurry of anticipation.

After all, tonight *was* the night she had been waiting for. She looked at her watch. In less than ten minutes, the dream she'd worked so hard for would finally be a reality.

So why did it feel like her whole body was going into meltdown?

Cally closed her eyes and trawled her mind for a legitimate explanation as the penultimate lot, a heavily sought-after Monet, reached astronomical heights. Yes, that was it. She might be a restorer of art, but the art world—epitomised by nights like this, where beauty and expression became about money and possession—left her feeling out of her depth. She didn't belong at Crawford's auction house at the most prestigious art auction in their calendar, she belonged in overalls in her studio.

That was why she couldn't concentrate, she argued inwardly as she tried to encourage the hem of the silky black dress she'd borrowed from her sister back towards her knee. It absolutely, categorically, had nothing to do with the fact that *he* was here.

Cally castigated herself for even having noticed him arrive, let alone entertaining the idea that he had anything to do with the physical symptoms that were assailing her. There was no way any man could have that kind of effect on her, least of all one she'd never met before.

Well, technically. She had seen him once before, when she'd attended the sale preview two days ago, but she hadn't actually *met* him. 'Met' implied that there had been some interaction between them, which of course there hadn't been. He was classically handsome, and the expensive cut of his clothes—along with his very presence at an event like this—suggested he was filthy rich. He probably had some meaningless title like 'duke', or 'count', which altogether added up to him being the kind of man who wouldn't give a woman like her a second glance. Which was absolutely fine, because she had no desire to meet someone that arrogant and conceited anyway. One man like that had been enough to last her a lifetime; she had no desire to meet another.

So why was it she hadn't been able to drive the intensity of his deep blue eyes from her thoughts, ever since she'd walked into that sale room and had seen him standing there like Michelangelo's famous statue come to life? And why was it taking all her willpower not to steal another glance over her shoulder to the second row in the back right-hand corner of the room? Not that she had plotted the layout on an imaginary piece of graph paper and knew his exact co-ordinates, or anything. Why would she? *Because every time you look round he slants you an irresistible, one-sided smile which sends the most extraordinary shiver down your spine?* an unfamiliar and thoroughly unwelcome voice inside her replied, but immediately she silenced it.

'And finally we come to lot fifty. A pair of paintings by the nineteenth-century master Jacques Rénard, entitled *Mon Amour par la Mer* from the estate of the late Hector Wolsey. Whilst the paintings are in need of some specialist restoration in order to return them to their original glory, they are undoubtedly the two most iconic pieces Rénard ever painted.'

Cally drew in a deep breath as the auctioneer's words confirmed that the moment she had been waiting for was finally here. She closed her eyes again, trying to visualise the air travelling up her nostrils and blowing her errant thoughts aside. When she opened them, the wall panel to the right of the bespectacled auctioneer was rotating in a spectacular one-hundred-and-eighty-degree turn to reveal the stunning paintings, and the breath caught in her throat in awe.

She remembered the first time she'd ever seen them, or rather a print of them. Not long after she'd started secondary school, her art teacher, Mrs McLellan, had held them up as an example of how Rénard dared to push the boundaries set by his contemporaries by having a real woman as his subject rather than a goddess. The rest of the class had been lost in a fit of giggles; between the two paintings, Rénard's *Love by the Sea* went from fully clothed to completely naked. But for Cally it had been a defining moment in her life. To her the pictures spoke of beauty and truth, of the two sides of every story—of herself. From that moment on, she had known unequivocally that her future lay in art. A certainty matched only by her horror when she had discovered that the original paintings were shut away on the country estate of a pompous aristocrat getting damp and gathering cigar smoke, rather than being on public display for everyone to enjoy.

Until now. Because now they were owned by Hector Wolsey junior, whose horse-racing habit had caused him to demand that Crawford's auction house sell his late father's paintings immediately, before they'd even had the chance to say 'in-house restoration team'. Which meant the London City Gallery had been frantically trying to raise enough money to buy them, and had been lining up a specialist conservator to undo the years of damage. To Cally's delight, her enthusiasm, impressive CV and her expert knowledge on Rénard had eventually convinced the gallery team that she was the right person for the job. The job she had wanted for as long as she could remember, and the break in her career she desperately needed.

Cally glanced around the room as the bids took off, starting reassuringly with Gina, the gallery's agent, who was seated just along from her. There was a low hubbub of hushed, excited voices in every row of seats. Telephonists packed around the edges of the room were shaking their heads and relaying bids to eager collectors the world over. Within seconds, the bids exceeded the estimate in the sale catalogue, so much so that Cally was tempted to use her own catalogue as a makeshift fan to combat her soaring temperature—but she refrained, partly because she was rooted to her seat in anticipation, and partly in fear that it might inadvertently be taken for a bid. The moment was tense enough.

Unless you were Mr Drop-dead Gorgeous, Cally observed, her pulse reaching an unprecedented pace as she stole another look in his direction and caught him leaning back with a casual expression, his body utterly at ease beneath the blue-grey suit. She could do with a bit of that—composure, that was. Because, whilst she saw Gina raise her hand in between every figure the auctioneer repeated at speed, it did little to ease her nerves. Even if the gallery had promised her it was a dead cert.

But no doubt that was what Wolsley's son said about the races, she thought, caught between recalling the dangers of trusting anything too blindly and willing herself to relax. No, however convinced the gallery team had been that they had secured enough funds, the only time you could truly relax in a situation like this was if you had nothing riding on it—as *he* clearly didn't, she justified to herself. So what was he doing here when he hadn't bid on any of the previous eleven paintings since he'd entered the room at lot thirty-eight? Just as Cally was about to make a list of possibilities in her mind, something happened.

'That's an increase of—wait—ten *million* on the phones,' the auctioneer said uncharacteristically slowly, taking off his glasses in astonishment as he looked from the gallery of telephonists back to the floor. 'That's seventy million against you, madam. Do I have seventy-one?'

The rest of the auction room went ominously still. Cally felt her heart thump madly in her chest and her stomach begin to churn. Who the hell were they bidding against? According to the gallery team every serious collector with their eye on the Rénards should have been sitting in this room. Gina's horrified expression said it all. Cally watched on tenterhooks as she looked discomposedly at the paperwork in her lap. Eventually, Gina inclined her head.

'Seventy-one million,' the auctioneer acknowledged, replacing his spectacles and looking back to the phones.

'Do I have seventy-two? Yes.' He moved his head back and forth like a tennis umpire. 'There, do I have seventy-three?'

Gina gave a single, reluctant nod.

'Any advance on seventy-three?' He looked up to the gallery.

'We have eighty on the phones.'

Eighty?

'Any takers at eighty-one?'

Nothing. Cally squeezed her eyes tightly shut.

'Last chance at eighty-one—no?'

Cally stared helplessly at Gina, who shook her head apologetically.

'Closing then, at eighty million pounds.'

The sound of the hammer, and the auctioneer's cry of 'Sold,' echoed through her body like a seismic tremor.

The London City Gallery had lost the Rénards.

Horror ripped through her gut. The paintings she loved were to be shipped off to God knew where. Her hopes of restoring them were dead, and the door to the career she'd been on the cusp of walking through slammed in her face. The wall panel revolved another one hundred and eighty degrees and the paintings disappeared.

There *was* no such thing as a dead cert. It was over.

As the people began to gather their things and make their way out into the anonymity of the London streets, Cally remained in her chair, staring blindly at the empty wall. She didn't see the way that Mr Drop-dead Gorgeous lingered behind, and barely even noticed Gina's whispered apology as she crept away. She understood; the gallery's funds were not limitless. Even if they could have raised enough retrospectively, they had to weigh up their expenditure against the draw of the public. At a few million over the estimate, the paintings were such a prolific attraction they'd considered them still worthwhile. But almost double? She knew Gina had been taking a risk to go as high as she'd gone.

So, someone else had wanted the Rénards more. Who? The thought snapped her out of her paralysis. Surely whichever gallery it was planned to get someone to restore them? She knew it broke every unwritten rule of auction-room decorum there was, but suddenly finding out was her only hope. Launching herself from her seat, she rushed over to the back of the room where the row of telephonists was filing away.

'Please,' she cried out to the man who had taken the call. 'Tell me who bought the Rénards.'

He stopped and turned to look at her along with several of his colleagues, their faces a mixture of curiosity and censure.

'I do not know, madam. It is strictly confidential between the buyer and the cashier.'

Cally stared at him in desperation.

The telephonist shook his head. 'He said only that he was bidding on behalf of a private collector.'

Cally stumbled backwards and sat down in one of the empty chairs, resting her head in her hands and fighting back her tears. A private collector. The thought made her blood boil. The chances were they would never be seen by anyone again until *he* died of over-excess.

She shook her head. For the first time since David she'd actually dared to believe her life was going somewhere. But her only ticket out had just been torn into a million pieces. Which left her with what? A night in the cheapest London hotel she'd been able to find, and then back to the cramped town house-cum-studio in Cambridge. Another year of sporadic restorations which would barely cover her mortgage, because on the rare occasions a career-altering piece like this came up it only ever seemed to matter who you knew and never what you knew.

'You look like you could use a drink.'

The accented voice was French, and to her surprise it sent an even more disturbing tremor through her body than the sound of the auctioneer's hammer. Perhaps because she knew immediately who the voice belonged to. Though she had told herself that if he came near the alarming effect he had on her would inevitably diminish, the reality was that it seemed to double in strength. She ran her hands through her hair as if she'd really just been fixing it all along and turned around to face him.

'I'm fine, thank you.'

Fine? Cally laughed inwardly at her own words. Even if she'd been asked to restore every painting in the auction she doubted it would have been possible to describe her mental state as 'fine', with all six-foot-two-inches of him stood before her, filling her body with sensations she barely even recognised and which she certainly had no desire to confront.

'I'm not convinced,' he said, looking at her altogether too closely.

'And who are you, Crawford's post-auction psychologist?' Cally replied, unnerved by his scrutiny. 'Brought in during the final ten lots ready to mop up the disappointed punters after the show?'

A wry and thoroughly disarming smile crossed his lips. 'So you did notice me as soon as I walked in.'

'You didn't answer my question,' Cally retorted, colouring.

'So I didn't.'

Cally scowled. There was only one thing she hated more than people who oozed wealth, and that was people who were selective with the truth. She picked up her handbag and zipped it shut.

'Thank you for your concern, but I have to get back to my hotel.' She turned to walk towards the open doors at the back of the room.

'I'm not,' he countered. 'A psychologist, that is.'

She turned, no doubt just as he'd known she would. It was arrogant, but at least it was honest. 'Then who are you?'

'I'm Leon,' he replied, stepping forward and extending his hand.

'And?'

'I'm here in connection with my university.'

So, he was a uni lecturer? Her first and utterly shameful thought was that she should have done her degree in France. The art professors she'd known had all been pushing sixty, and had looked like they hadn't seen a razor, and smelled like they hadn't used a can of deodorant, for just as long. Her second was pure astonishment; he seemed to exude too much wealth and sophistication. But then all Frenchmen were known for being stylish, weren't they? And it did explain why he'd simply been observing, not buying. She castigated herself for being too quick to judge.

'Cally,' she said, extending her hand in return, then wondered what the hell she'd been thinking when the touch of his fingers made her inhale so sharply that speech deserted her.

'And *are* you a disappointed punter?' He raised one eyebrow doubtfully.

'You think I'm not the type?' she rebounded defensively, finding her voice again, though she didn't know why she was arguing with him when as a lecturer he was no more likely to have the spare cash to buy a priceless painting than she was.

'I think you didn't make a single bid.'

'So, you noticed me right back?' Cally replied with more pleasure than she ought to have felt. He hadn't given her a second glance two days ago, when she'd been wearing her usual work clothes instead of dolled up as tonight's occasion demanded. Besides, why should it matter if he had noticed her? It would only be a matter of time before he noticed someone else.

He nodded. 'Indeed. And, since you haven't answered my question about whether or not you are a disappointed punter, it seems we're even.'

She stared at the wall where the paintings had been only moments before and was hit by a renewed sense of failure. 'It's complicated. Let's just say tonight should have changed my life for the better. It didn't.'

'The night is young,' he drawled with a supremely confident grin.

Cally dragged her eyes away from his lips and made a show of looking at her watch, horrified to find that she was almost tempted to find out what he meant. Ten-fifteen. 'Like I said, I have to get back to my hotel.'

She turned to walk towards the door.

'Do you have a better offer waiting at your final destination, or are you just the kind of woman who is scared of saying yes?'

Cally froze, not turning round.

'No. I'm the kind of woman who is well aware that asking someone you've only just met out for a drink is really asking for something else entirely, and I'm not interested.'

Leon whistled through his teeth. 'So you prefer a man to cut to the chase? Detail exactly what he has in mind before you agree?'

She blushed. 'I would prefer it if a drink only meant a *drink.*'

'So you *are* thirsty, *chérie?*'

Cally swallowed, her mouth going inconveniently dry. Was she the kind of woman who was scared of saying yes? she wondered, suddenly both horrified and aggrieved that he might actually be right. No, she justified, she wasn't afraid—she'd just learned from experience that *that* kind of yes inevitably led to disappointment. Which was why—unlike other girls she knew, who invariably spent their evenings making out with random guys in clubs—she'd spent the last seven years sitting at her desk into the early hours of every morning memorising the chemical make-up of conservation treatments, practising each and every technique for the sake of her precious career. But look where it had got her now! Precisely nowhere.

Cally took a deep breath. 'Yes' might very well lead to disappointment, but right now it didn't get much more disappointing than the thought of returning to her hotel with nothing but her misery and the overpriced minibar for company. At least accepting the offer of one drink with a perfectly normal man for once in her life would take her mind off what had just happened.

'On one condition, then…' she began confidently, but the instant she raised her eyes she caught sight of his devastating smile, and remembered too late that there was absolutely nothing remotely normal about the way he made her feel. If anything, that was what she should be afraid of. 'The topic of work is off the agenda.'

'Done,' he answered decisively.

'Right.' Cally's head began to spin. 'Then…where did you have in mind?'

CHAPTER TWO

LEON didn't have anywhere in mind. He hadn't had anything on his mind for two full days—except her. He'd come to Crawford's to view the pre-auction exhibition of the paintings the world wanted to get their hands on, and had found himself wanting to get his hands on something else entirely: the narrow waist and shapely hips of the woman with lustrous red-bronze hair, who'd been transfixed by the paintings he'd suddenly forgotten he'd come here to see. The wave of desire had come out of nowhere, for it was certainly unprovoked. Though the luscious curves of her figure were obvious, she couldn't have been dressed any less provocatively, in a drab, crinkled blouse and olive-green skirt that reached her ankles. He'd wanted to dispose of them both there and then.

And he would have done, if he'd known who she was and that she could be trusted to be discreet. But he hadn't. Standing there, all misty-eyed before the paintings, she'd looked—most inconveniently—like exactly the kind of woman who would cloud everything with emotion and make discretion an impossibility. But the knot of heat in his groin had demanded he find out for certain. How fortuitous, then, that when he'd asked a few discreet questions of his own it turned out that she was the London City Gallery's choice to restore the Rénards. For once in his life, a twist of fate had amused him. She would have to be fully vetted anyway. Suddenly it made perfect sense for him to stay on for the auction and undertake the investigation personally.

Leon watched her as she walked beside him, oblivious to the sound of taxicabs and buses that filled the tepid June evening. To his pleasure, she looked a world away from the olive-green drabness of just over forty-eight hours before; she was luminescent in black silk, the halter neck revealing an ample cleavage, and her striking hair, which had previously been tied back, now fell over her shoulders in waves. Tonight she looked exactly like the sort of woman capable of the kind of short and mutually satisfying affair he had in mind.

'Lady's choice,' he said, realising they had reached the end of the street, and he still hadn't answered her question as to where they were headed.

Cally, whose nerve was evaporating by the second, looked around the street and decided that the sooner this was over the better. 'The next bar we come to will be fine, I'm sure. After all, its only requirement is that it serve drinks, is it not?'

Leon nodded. *'D'accord.'*

As they turned the corner of the street, Cally heard a low, insistent drumbeat and saw a neon sign illuminating darkness: the Road to Nowhere.

'Perfect,' Cally proclaimed defiantly. It might look a little insalubrious, but at least it was too brash and too noisy for there to be any danger of lingering conversation over an intimate table for two.

Leon looked up, to see a young couple tumble out of the door and begin devouring each other up against the window, and he stifled a grin.

'It looks good to me.'

Cally did a double take, doubting he was serious. Then she wished she hadn't, because the sight of his impossibly handsome face beneath the soft glow of the street lights made her whole body start with that ridiculous tingling again.

'Fabulous. And my hotel is only two streets away,' she said, as much to convince herself that after one drink she could return to the safety of her room as to remind him.

'What could be better?' he drawled, the look in his eyes explicit.

She swallowed down a lump in her throat as they passed the couple, who were yet to come up for air, and entered the bar.

It was dark inside, the sultry vocals of a female singer stirring the air whilst couples absorbed in one another moved slowly together on the dance floor. *Oh yes, great idea, Cally. This is much safer ground than a quiet bar.*

'So what will it be, a Screaming Orgasm or a Pineapple Thrust?'

'I beg your pardon?' Cally swung round and was only partially relieved to see that Leon was reading from a cocktail menu he'd picked up from the bar.

'I'll just have a mineral water, thanks.' Leon raised his eyebrows in disapproval before the words were even out of her mouth. 'OK, fine,' she retracted, briefly running her eyes down the menu. 'I'll have a…Cactus Venom.'

When was the last time she'd had a drink? A glass of wine at her nephew's christening in January. God, she really did need to get out more.

Leon slipped off his jacket and ordered two of the same, somehow managing, she noticed, to look exactly like he fitted in. She, on the other hand, crossed her arms awkwardly across her chest, feeling horribly overdressed and self-conscious.

'So, don't tell me—you come here all the time.' Cally said, marvelling at how quickly he seemed to have got the waitress's attention, although on second thoughts she could guess why.

'Well, you know, I would, but I live in France. What's your excuse?'

She laughed, relaxing a fraction as they found themselves a table and sat down. 'I live in Cambridge.'

'You mean you didn't know that the Road to Nowhere was waiting just around the next corner?'

'No, I didn't.' Cally shook her head, remembering the auction and thinking that the bar's name was altogether too apt.

Leon seemed to sense her despondency and raised his glass. 'So, what shall we drink to?'

Cally thought for a moment. 'To discovering hard work doesn't pay off in the end, so why bother?'

Something about his company, the atmosphere, made her realise that maybe she did need to talk about it after all. She hoped it was that, and not that she couldn't go five minutes without mentioning work.

'Sorry,' she added, suddenly aware of how discourteous that sounded. 'To…the Road to Nowhere.'

Leon chinked his cocktail glass against hers and they both took a sip of the yellow-green liquid, smarting at the sour taste.

'So, tonight didn't exactly go to plan for you?' Leon ventured.

'You could say that. The London City Gallery promised

me the restoration job on the Rénards if they won them.
They didn't.'

'Maybe you should offer your services to whoever did.'

'According to the guy manning the phone, it was an anonymous private collector.' Her voice rang with resentment.

'Who's to say a private collector won't commission you
to complete the restorations?'

'Experience. Even if I could find out who he or she is,
they'll either choose someone they know or the team who
can get it done fastest. The rich treat art like a new Ferrari
or a penthouse in Dubai—an acquisition to boast about,
instead of something everyone deserves to enjoy.'

Leon went very still. 'So if you *were* approached, your
morals would stop you from working on them?'

Cally turned away, emotion pricking at the backs of her
eyes. 'No, it wouldn't stop me.'

She was aware how unprincipled that sounded—or
more accurately how unprincipled that actually *was*—but
it wasn't just because of the opportunities that working on
them was bound to lead to. It was because she could never
turn down the opportunity to work on the paintings that had
determined the direction of her entire life, even if that life
now seemed to be one big road to nowhere. She shook her
head, too mortified to admit as much.

'I'd be a fool to turn it down if I ever got the opportunity.
If I worked on the Rénards, I'd be known across the world.'

Leon gave a single nod. So, whatever impression she'd
given at the pre-auction, what she wanted was renown.
But of course, he thought cynically, what woman didn't?
And, going by her protestations that she didn't want to talk
about work, followed by her emotional outpouring on the
subject, she didn't seem any more capable of sticking to

her word than the rest of her sex. Well, there was one way to be sure.

He leaned back in his chair. 'So, was the pre-sale the first time you'd seen *Mon Amour par la Mer?*'

Cally shivered. 'I...I didn't think you'd noticed me that day.'

He waited for her eyes to lift and meet his. 'On the contrary, that was when I decided that I wanted to make love to you. In fact, that was why I came back to the auction.'

Cally gawped in shock at his nerve, whilst at the same time a treacherous thrill zipped up her spine, which surprised her even more than his words. Words which told her that, unbelievably, he had wanted her when she'd been dressed like *Cally,* not just tonight when she felt like she was playing dress-up to fit in with the art world. The world which, contrary to her initial impression, he wasn't a part of either. He who had only been there tonight because of her. How was that possible? Wasn't it obvious that she lacked that sexual gene, or whatever that thing was that most other women had? She didn't know, but suddenly all the reasons she'd amassed for loathing him toppled over, taking her defences with them.

'I ought to walk out of here right now.'

'So walk.'

'I...I haven't finished my drink.'

'And do you always do exactly what you say you are going to do, Cally?'

She was sure he turned up his accent when he said her name on purpose, sure he knew it made her stomach flip. Even surer that she didn't have the strength to walk away.

'I hate people who go back on their word.'

'As do I.' He looked at her sharply. 'However, there

were some parts of this agreement we didn't specify—like whether this drink included a dance, for instance?'

Cally drew in a sharp breath as she looked to the grinding mass of bodies on the dance floor, now slowing to a more languorous pace as the soloist with the heavy eyeliner and the husky voice began a rendition of *Black Velvet*.

'You're not serious?'

'Why not? Isn't seizing the moment one of life's beauties that art celebrates?'

Art, Cally thought. It was a celebration of life. But when was the last time she'd actually stopped to remember that and allowed herself to live it? She drank him in—his dark blond hair falling over his forehead, his eyes smouldering with a fire that both terrified and excited her—and for a split second she didn't feel as though she'd lost anything at all tonight.

She offered him her hand and answered him in a voice she didn't recognise as her own. 'You're on.'

As she stood up the alcohol went to her head, and for a second she closed her eyes, breathing deeply. The air felt thick, the heady beat of music vibrating through every cell in her body. She'd loved this song as a teenager. David had hated it. Why had she never played it since?

'Come on.' Leon snaked his hand around her waist and pulled her to him before he had time to consider whether or not this was such a good idea. He wanted her with a hungriness that unnerved him. He watched her mouthing the words of the song and, unable to drag his eyes away from her full lips, wondered if for once in his life he was going to be incapable of sticking to his own rules.

Always wanting more, he'd leave you longing for...

The lyrics seemed to reach into her soul. *He* seemed to

reach into her soul. She had never met anyone like him. She had only known him five minutes and yet—clichéd thought it sounded—it almost felt like he knew her better than she had known herself, about everything she'd been missing out on. Being pressed up against him was intoxicating, the smell of him, the touch of him. She ran her hands up his muscular back, locked them behind his neck and allowed the tension to leave her body as he moved easily, her body following every movement his made.

'Did I tell you how sexy you are?' he whispered in her ear, the warmth of his breath sending an inordinate level of heat flooding through her.

He did this all the time; she was sure he did. Which was why it was crazy. She'd never done anything like this in her life, and she didn't know what she was playing at now. But, though in her head she knew she was probably a fool to continue, right now her body was the only thing she could hear—and it was thrumming with a whole host of new sensations, all clamouring to be explored.

'Did I tell you how sexy *you* are?' she whispered nervously, grateful that she couldn't see his face, hoping he couldn't sense that she was trembling all over.

'No,' he whispered, drawing back to brush his lips just below her ear. 'You most definitely didn't mention that.'

She couldn't bear it. His mouth was playing havoc with the sensitive skin of her neck. She needed to kiss him. Properly. Shakily, she guided his head with her hand until their faces were level, not knowing where her confidence had come from. Had he known if he touched her like that she wouldn't be able to resist him? Probably. But right now she didn't care. She just wanted to kiss him.

His lips brushed hers, painfully slowly, then opened

hungrily. He tasted decadent, like dark chocolate and cinnamon. He ran his hand gently down her spine, slowing over the curve of her bottom. It was the kind of kiss that would have been utterly inappropriate in an exclusive little wine bar. To Cally's shock it had a lot more in common with the display of primal need they had witnessed in the street outside, but to her astonishment she wanted more. She told herself it was down to the charge of the music, the distinctive scent of his hypnotic, balmy cologne. But she could blame it on exterior forces all she liked; the truth was that it was kissing *him* that was explosive. Suddenly she forgot everything else—the fact that he was a man she had only just met, the fact that she was bound to disappoint him, that this could only lead to heartache— because her need for him was overwhelming, and he seemed to feel it too.

'You want to get out of here?'

She took a deep breath. 'Yes, I do.'

So, Leon thought, fighting his own desire, there was the concrete proof that her word could not be trusted. That was the rule.

Cally's cheeks were hot and her heart was pounding as he threaded her through the other couples on the dance floor and out onto the pavement, hailing a cab.

He opened the door for her as it rolled up. Then he coolly shut the door behind her and remained standing on the pavement.

She wound down the window, her brows knitted together in bewilderment. 'I thought we were getting out of here?'

His face was grim. 'No, *you* are. One drink was all you wanted, wasn't it, Cally?'

Cally felt a new fire burning in her cheeks as Leon signalled for the driver to go and she suddenly realised what was happening.

'Bastard!' she shouted.

But the driver had already pulled away, and all she could hear was the climax of the song as it poured down the street.

In a flash he was gone. It happened so soon, what could you do?

CHAPTER THREE

As CALLY rested her head on the window of the train from King's Cross back to Cambridge, the sky-rise landscape shrinking to a patchwork of green, she gave up sifting her memories for debris and concluded that, no, she had never felt more ashamed than she did right now.

She, Cally Greenway, had almost had a one-night stand with a total stranger.

And, what was worse, a tiny part of her almost wished she had.

No, she argued inwardly, of course she didn't. She just wished he hadn't subjected her to that hideous rejection, or at the very least that she'd been able to understand why he had.

Had the earth-shattering heat of their kiss, which she'd thought was mutual, actually been so one-sided that he'd realised she would be useless in bed? Or was it all part of a game he played to prove that he was so drop-dead gorgeous he could make any woman abandon her morals if he chose?

Cally spent the next week wavering between the two theories, subsequently caught between reawakened insecurities and fresh anger. In the end, frustration with herself for even caring made anger prevail. She should be glad that she'd had a lucky escape, and the reason for his insulting behaviour shouldn't even matter when he was no one to her, a no one whom she was never likely to see ever again.

So why, whenever she thought back to that night, did that moment in the taxi hurt even more than losing the commission had done? Cally pressed her lips together in shame, but then released them. It was simply because up until that point she had thought that what she'd lost was her dream job. He had made her see that she'd spent so long with her eye on that goal alone that she'd sacrificed every other aspect of her life in the process. Yes, she thought, unwilling to dwell on the other broken dreams his rejection had resurrected, that was it. Finding herself devastated that she would never have Leon's arms around her again just proved how long it had been since she'd actually got out there and spent any time in the company of anyone but herself, and occasionally her family.

Well, he might have reinforced her belief about the futility of trusting the opposite sex, but she had to acknowledge that maybe it was about time she accepted the odd invitation to go out now and again, instead of always having a well-rehearsed list of things she had to do instead. Particularly since the short list of restorations she had lined up for the next three months was hardly going to claim all of her time, she thought despondently as she booted up her computer to see whether her inbox heralded any new enquiries on that front today. It was all very well, deciding to get a social life whilst she worked out what to do next, but it was hardly feasible if it meant not being able to eat.

Three new mails. The first was a promotional email from the supplier she used for her art materials, which she deleted without opening, knowing she couldn't afford anything above and beyond her regular order. The second was from her sister Jen, who was back from her family holiday in Florida, desperate to know if the little black dress she'd leant her had been as lucky for Cally as it had been for her when she'd worn it to the journalism awards last month and scooped first prize. Cally shook her head, wondering how her sister managed to pull off being a high-flying career woman as well as a wonderful wife and mother, and resolved to reply with the bad news when she felt a little less like a failure in comparison.

The third email was from a sender with a foreign-sounding name she didn't recognise. She clicked on it warily.

Dear Miss Greenway
Your skills as an art conservator have recently been brought to the attention of the Prince of Montéz. As a result, His Royal Highness wishes to discuss a possible restoration. To be considered, you are required to attend the royal palace in person in three days' time. Your tickets will be couriered to you tomorrow unless you wish to decline this generous offer by return.
Yours faithfully, Boyet Durand
On behalf of His Royal Highness, the Prince of Montéz

Cally blinked at the words before her. Her first reaction was disbelief. Here was an email offering a free trip to a luxurious French island, so why wasn't she pinging it straight off to her junk-mail folder, knowing there was a catch? She read it again. Because it wasn't the usual generic trash: *You've won a holiday to Barbados, to claim just call this number....* This sender knew her name and what she did for a living. It was feasible that someone could have seen one of her few restorations that had ended up in smallish galleries and been inspired to visit her website—but a prince?

She read it a third time, and on this occasion the arrogance of it truly sunk in. If it was real, who on earth did the Prince of Montéz think he was to have his advisor summon her as if she was a takeaway meal he'd decide whether or not he wanted once she arrived?

Cally opened a new tab and typed 'Prince of Montéz' into Wikipedia. The information was irritatingly sparse. It didn't even give his name, only stated that in Montéz the prince was the sovereign ruler, and that the current prince had come into power a year ago when his brother Girard had died in an accident aged just forty-three, leaving behind his young wife, Toria, but no children. Cally cast her mind back, roughly recalling the royal-wedding photos which had graced the cover of every magazine the summer she'd graduated, and hearing the news of his tragic death on the radio in her studio some time last year. But there was no further information about the late prince's brother, the man who thought that she, a lowly artist, could drop everything because he commanded it.

Cally was tempted to reply that, attractive though the offer was, the prince was mistaken if he thought she could fit him into her busy schedule at such short notice. But the truth was he *wasn't* mistaken. Hadn't she only just been wishing she had more work lined up, and thinking she ought to start saying yes to something other than Sunday lunch at her parents' house?

Which was why she decided she would let the tickets come. Not that she really believed they would, until the doorbell rang early the following morning, thankfully interrupting a fervid dream about a Frenchman with a disturbingly familiar face.

Nor did she really believe she'd dare to use them until the day after, when she heard the voice of the pilot asking them to please return their seats to the upright position because they were beginning their descent to the island.

The last and only time Cally had been to France was on a day trip to Le Touquet by ferry whilst she'd been at secondary school, most of which had been spent trawling round a rather uninspiring hypermarket. She'd always fancied Paris—the Eiffel Tower and the galleries, of course—but she'd somehow never got round to taking any kind of holiday at all since uni, nor felt she could justify the unnecessary expense. So when she stepped out of first class and was greeted by the most incredible vista of shimmering azure water and glorious tree-covered mountains sprinkled with terracotta roofs, it was no wonder it felt like this was all happening to someone else. For the first time in years she felt the urge to whip out a sketch pad and get to work on a composition of her own.

A desire that only increased when the private car pulled up to the incredible palace. It almost looked like a painting, she thought as the driver opened the door of the vehicle for her to depart.

'Please follow me, *mademoiselle*. The prince will meet you in *la salle de bal*.'

Cally frowned as he led her through the impressive main archway, trying to remember her GCSE French in order to decipher which room he was referring to. He must have caught her perplexed expression.

'You would say "the ballroom", I think?'

Cally nodded and rolled her eyes to herself as they

passed through the courtyard and up a creamy white staircase with a deep red carpet running through the centre. There was a very good reason why she hadn't needed to know the word for ballroom for her project on *'ma maison'*.

The thought reminded her just how hypocritical it was to feel impressed by the palace when the man who lived here was guilty of the excess she loathed. She was even more ashamed to look down at her perfectly functional black jacket and skirt, teamed with a white blouse, and wish she had brought something a little more, well, worthy. Why should she be worried what clothes she was wearing to meet the prince? Just because he had a palace and a title didn't mean she ought to act any differently from the way she would with any potential client. Any more than he should judge her on anything but her ability as a restorer, she thought defiantly, hugging her portfolio to her chest.

'Here we are, Mademoiselle Greenway.'

'Thank you,' Cally whispered as the man signalled for her to enter the ballroom, bowed his head and then swiftly departed.

She entered tentatively, preparing to be blown away by the full impact of the magnificent marble floor, the intricately decorated wall panels and the high, sculpted ceiling that she could see from the doorway. But, as Cally turned into the room, the gasp that broke from her throat was not one of artistic appreciation, it was one of complete astonishment.

The Rénards. Hanging, seemingly innocuously, right in the centre of the opposite wall.

Cally rushed to them to get a closer look, momentarily convinced that they must be reproductions, but a quick appraisal told her immediately that they were not. She felt her heart begin to thud insistently in her chest, though she couldn't accurately name the emotion which caused it. Excitement? She had wanted more than anything to discover the identity of the mysterious telephone-bidder, to have the chance to convince them she was the best person to carry out the restoration. Now it seemed that somehow *he* had found *her*.

Or was it horror? For wasn't this exactly the fate of the paintings she had feared—shut away in some gilded palace never to be looked upon again? She closed her eyes and pressed her hands to her temples, trying to make sense of it, but before she could even begin a voice behind her cut through everything.

'See something you recognise?'

A voice which made her eyes fly open, every hair on the back of her neck stand on end and every thought fly from her mind. Every thought, except one.

Leon.

Stop it, she scolded herself. The Prince of Montéz is French, of course he's going to sound a little like him. God, she really did need to get out more if that one meaningless episode had the power to make her lose all grip on reality every time she heard a man with a French accent. The voice belonged to the Prince of Montéz, who had brought her here as his potential employee, so why was she still staring rudely at the wall? She turned sharply to face him.

The sight before her almost made her keel over.

Her imagination hadn't been playing a trick on her at all. It was him. Irritatingly perfect him, his impressive physique all the more striking in a formal navy suit.

Her mind went into overdrive as she attempted to make sense of what was happening. Leon was a university professor; perhaps he'd been invited here to examine the paintings in more detail; perhaps this was just one of life's unfortunate coincidences?

But as she stared at his wry expression—impatient, as if waiting for her tiny mind to catch up—she suddenly understood that this was no coincidence. Her very first appraisal of him in that sale room in London—rich, heartless, titled—had not been wrong. It was everything else that had been a lie. Good God, was Leon even his real name?

'You bastard.'

For a second his easy expression looked shot through with something darker, but just as quickly it was back.

'So you said last time we met, Cally, but now that you know I am your potential employer I thought you'd be a little more courteous.'

Courteous? Cally felt the bile rise in her throat. 'Well, since I can assure you I am not going to be capable of courtesy towards you any time this century, I think I should leave, don't you?'

Leon gritted his teeth. Yes, he did think she should leave, the same way he'd thought he should in London. But after countless hot, frustrated nights, when all his body had cared about was why the hell he hadn't taken her when he'd had the chance, Leon was through with thinking.

He blocked her exit with his arm.

'At least stay for *one drink*.'

'And why the hell would I want to do that?'

'Because, yet again, you look like you need one.'

Had he brought her here purely to humiliate her further, to revel in how much he had got to her? She fixed a bland expression on her face, determined not to play ball. 'I'll have one on my way back to the airport.'

'You have somewhere else to be?' he replied, mock-earnestly.

She knew exactly what he implied—that she had nowhere else to be today any more than when she had protested the need to return to her hotel room that night. It was the same reason he'd known she would come at short notice. And exactly why staying here could only quadruple the humiliation she already felt.

'No, you're absolutely right, I don't. But anywhere is preferable to being on this dead end of an island with some lying product of French inbreeding who has nothing better to do than to toy with random English women he meets for sport.'

'*Woman,*' he corrected. 'There is certainly only one of you, Cally Greenway.'

'And yet there is one of you in every palace and stately home on the planet. It's so predictable, it's boring.'

'I thought that you liked things to turn out exactly the way you expect them to—or perhaps that is simply what you pretend to want?'

'Like I told you, all I want is to leave.'

'It's a shame your body language says otherwise.'

Cally looked down, pleased to discover that if anything she had stepped further away from him, whilst her arms clutched her portfolio protectively to her chest.

'And do you always take a woman's loathing as a come-on?'

'Only when it's born out of sheer sexual frustration,' he drawled, nodding at the gap between them and her self-protective stance.

'In your dreams.'

'Yours too, I don't doubt.' He looked at her with an assessing gaze.

Cally felt her cheeks turn crimson.

'I thought so,' he drawled in amusement. 'But think just how good it will be when we do make love, *chérie*.'

'I might have been stupid enough to consider having sex with you before I knew who you were,' she said, trying not to flinch at the memory of her own wantonness. 'But I can assure you I am in no danger of doing so again.'

'You have a thing for university employees?' he queried, raising one long, lean finger to his lower lip thoughtfully, as if observing an anomalous result in a science experiment. 'Mediterranean princes just not your thing?'

No, men that self-important couldn't be any further from her thing, Cally thought, not that she had 'a thing'. So why in God's name was she unable to take her eyes off his mouth?

'Liars aren't my thing. Men who lie about who they are, who pretend not to be stinking rich and who profess to lend a sympathetic ear when—' Immediately the auction, which had slipped her mind for a moment, came back to her. The auction room. Leon the only one with the nonchalant glance. Not because he had nothing riding on it, but because he was so rich that he'd just instructed one of his minions to make the highest bid by phone on his behalf. That was why he had been there that night, to stand back and watch smugly whilst he blew everyone else out of the water. It had had nothing to do with coming back because he wanted her, and suddenly that hurt most of all. 'When all the time you were the one responsible for wrecking my career!'

Leon raised his eyebrows. 'Are you quite finished? Good. Firstly, I told you my name. You didn't ask what my surname was, nor did you give me yours. All I said was that I was in England in connection with my university. I was. The new University of Montéz has just been built at my say-so, and I was there to purchase some pieces for the art department. Since you chose where we should go, I can hardly be blamed if the bar you selected gave no indication of my wealth. Which brings me to your accusation that I offered to lend a sympathetic ear with regards to your career—on the contrary, it was you who insisted we should *not* discuss work. You simply chose to, I did not.'

'You consider being a prince a career choice?'

'Not a choice,' he said gravely. 'But my work, yes.'

'How convenient, rather like arguing that omitting the truth does not constitute a lie. If you and I were married—' Cally hesitated, belatedly aware that she couldn't have thought of a more preposterous example if she'd tried '—and you happened to be sleeping with another woman but just didn't mention it, would such an omission be tolerable?'

Leon's mouth hardened. Hadn't he just known that she was one of those women who had marriage on the brain?

'Tolerable? Marrying anyone would never be a tolerable scenario for me, Cally, so I'm afraid your analogy is lost.'

'What a surprise,' Cally muttered. 'When it proves that I'm absolutely right.' How utterly typical that he wasn't the marrying kind, she thought irritably, though she wasn't sure why she should care when she'd lost her belief in happy-ever-afters a long time ago.

'But surely a welcome surprise?' Leon seized the moment. 'For, rather than being the one responsible for wrecking your career, I think you'll find yourself eternally indebted to me for beginning it. What an accolade for your CV to be employed to restore two of the most famous paintings the world has ever known?'

Indebted to him; the thought horrified her. Yet he was also offering exactly what she had always wanted—well, almost. 'You said you were in London to purchase some pieces for the university's art department. Do you mean that once the Rénards are restored they will go on public display there?'

Leon lifted his arm sharply, the motion drawing back the sleeve of his shirt to reveal a striking Cartier watch. 'I would love to discuss the details now, but I'm afraid I have a meeting to attend with the principal of the university, as it happens. Much as I'm sure that, given your predilection for university staff, you'd find meeting Professor Lefevre *stimulating,* it is something I need to do alone. You and I can continue this discussion over breakfast.'

'I beg your pardon?'

'Breakfast. *Petit déjeuner.* The first meal of the day, *oui?*' He stared at her face, which was aghast. 'It is also a painting by Renoir, I believe—but, of course, you're the expert.'

Could he have any more of a cheek? 'I am well aware of the concept of breakfast, thank you. Just as I am well aware that I will be eating mine back in Cambridge tomorrow morning. You invited me here to discuss this *today.*'

'And I subsequently discovered that unfortunately today is the only day Professor Lefevre can have this meeting. But since you have nowhere else to be this can wait until tomorrow, *oui?*'

Cally seethed. 'I have a plane to catch. Home.'

'But how can you make the most important decision of your career without knowing all the facts?'

There was nothing to decide, was there? How could she even contemplate working for a man who had humiliated and lied to her? Because the job was everything she'd strived for, she thought ruefully. She recalled the hideous boss she'd once had at the gallery gift shop who'd paid her a pittance for running the place single-handedly, how she'd ignored him and had just knuckled down. She could do it again for her dream commission, couldn't she? But somehow she wasn't sure that ignoring Leon would be so easy. Unless she could do the restoration without his interference. Rent a studio by the seafront and work on the paintings there, only return here when she'd completed them. The idea seemed almost idyllic without the threat of his presence.

'If I stay for—for *breakfast*,' she repeated, the concept still ludicrous to her. 'You'll be open to discussion about how I would wish such a project to be completed?'

'Discussion? Of course.'

Cally did a mental calculation of whether she could afford one night in a French guesthouse, having presumed that she'd be back on a plane out of here this afternoon. She supposed that she *had* left that hotel in London a night earlier than planned…

'What time would you have me return?'

'I would have you here ready and waiting,' he said, beckoning for her to keep up with his brusque steps out of the ballroom and into the hallway, where the man who had driven her here was waiting compliantly, head bowed. 'This is Boyet. He will show you to your room and bring you dinner.'

And before she could argue the prince was gone.

CHAPTER FOUR

CALLY picked up her mobile phone from the bedside cabinet and stared at its neon display through the darkness. 2:48 a.m., and still awake. She had tried everything: lying on her back, on her front, and rather awkwardly on her side; shutting the window to block out the sound of the ocean in order to pretend that she was in her bed at home; opening the window in the hope that the ebb and flow of the sea would act as a natural lullaby. Finally she had tried to fool herself into sleep by pretending she didn't care whether she was awake or not. But still the minutes ticked by. And, the more the minutes ticked by, the more questions heaped up in her brain.

Why had she even come here? Life wasn't some fairy tale where princes were valiant men who did noble deeds. She, more than anyone, should know that a man who had been born into privilege was bound to be selfish and dishonest, and, if she'd forgotten, his arrogant email should have acted as a reminder. Perhaps it was because she'd been confident that he was *just* selfish and dishonest, and had thought she could deal with that. What she hadn't known was that the prince would also happen to be *him*. Yet how was that possible when she'd even tried to look him up? Especially as a couple of years ago, she hadn't been able to avoid photos of his late brother and his wife.

Cally took a deep breath and to her chagrin found herself wondering how Girard's death must have affected Leon, how terrible it must have been to lose a brother and to gain such responsibility in the same moment. But that presupposed he had a heart somewhere within his perfectly honed chest, she thought bitterly, and nothing about the way he had treated her suggested that he did. Had he chosen not to reveal who he was in London simply for his own amusement?

Probably. Just like he probably thought that a night in his opulent palace would make her feel like she owed him one. *As if.* The thought of being indebted to him in any way whatsoever made her feel sick. Which was why, despite feeling famished, she had rejected Boyet's offer of dinner last night. Which was why she had got into bed without using a single thing in the pale apricot bedroom, with its beautiful white furniture, including the array of luxurious toiletries laid out for her. Instead she had used the mishmash of bits and pieces she'd thrown in her handbag for freshening up on the flight—even if she hadn't been able to resist removing the lids of the eye-catching bottles and smelling each one in turn…

When Cally's alarm went off four hours later, she felt like an animal who had been disturbed from hibernation three months early. Thankfully with the morning came rational thought: that there was only one question that mattered, and that was whether or not he planned to offer her the job of working on her dream commission.

Which meant she had to treat this breakfast—however unwelcome the concept was to her—like a job interview.

A job interview she wished she could attend in something other than yesterday's crumpled suit, she thought uneasily as she walked towards the veranda where Boyet had told her she would find Leon at eight-twenty. At least she'd had the foresight to pack a change of underwear and a clean top.

Now that it was daylight, she noticed for the first time that this side of the palace had the most fantastic view of the bay below, the ocean so blue it reminded her of a glittering jewel. As she stepped onto the cream tiles of the patio, she was forced to admit that Leon gave the landscape a run for its money. He was sitting on a wrought-iron chair, one leg crossed over the other whilst he leafed through the day's *La Tribune,* looking more like a male model than a prince in his cool white linen shirt which had far less buttons done up than most other men could have got away with. On him, she thought shamefully, it seemed criminal not to be unbuttoned any more.

'You like the view?' he drawled, closing the paper.

Cally turned back to the horizon, all too aware that he had caught her out. 'I suppose it's on a par with the British coastline.' She shrugged, determined to remain indifferent to everything even remotely connected to him.

'Oh yes, this is England—just without rain,' he replied dryly as he motioned to the chair.

Cally sat, resting her portfolio on her knee, her back rigid and eyes lowered. The exact opposite of his languorous pose.

He ran his eyes openly over her face. 'You look terrible. Didn't you sleep?'

The insult cut her to the quick. She ought to be glad that he was through with faking desire where she was concerned, but it only made her feel worse. She could just imagine the kind of woman he was used to having breakfast with—perfectly made-up, top-to-toe designer. Just like Portia had been the morning she'd answered David's door sporting that enormous pink diamond.

'I'm afraid this is the way a woman who isn't plastered in make-up tends to look in the morning, Leon.'

He shook his head irritably. 'You are not the kind of woman who requires any make-up. I simply meant that you look a little—drained.'

The compliment caught her off guard, and she didn't know what to do with it. 'Actually, I could count the number of hours' sleep I've had on one hand. Without the use of my thumb.'

Leon stifled a smile and made a show of furrowing his brow as he poured her a strong black coffee without asking whether she wanted any. 'That suite has just been refurnished. I was assured that particular mattress was the best on the market. I will have to see that it is changed.'

How typical that he thought every problem in life could be solved by material goods, she thought irritably, trying to ignore the delicious scent of the coffee wafting invitingly up her nostrils. 'There was nothing wrong with the bed, save for the fact that it was under your roof.'

'Large houses have a few too many dark corners for you?' he suggested with feigned concern as Boyet appeared with a tray overflowing with food: spiced bread, honey, fruit with natural yogurt, freshly squeezed orange in two different jugs—one with pulp and one without. Cally's mouth watered, and she could feel her ravenous stomach start to rumble, but she cleared her throat to disguise it.

'Whilst you are right that it does have an unnecessarily large number of rooms, it had nothing to do with that. Believe it or not, I simply have no desire to be anywhere near you.'

'Yet you are still here.'

'Like you said, whatever my personal feelings, I would be foolish not to make this important decision in my career without discussing the facts.'

'Over breakfast.' He nodded as if her career was immaterial. 'But you are yet to have a sip of coffee or a morsel of any food. So, eat.'

It was tempting to say she wasn't hungry, but the tantalising aroma of nutmeg and sultanas was too enticing, and she succumbed to a piece of bread.

Leon watched her, thinking it was the most erotic thing he'd ever seen as she bit into it hungrily before twisting her rosebud of a mouth back into a look of disapproval.

'No woman I've ever invited to breakfast has ever tried so hard to look unhappy about it as you.'

Thinking about the different women who might have sat in this self-same seat before her for a second time made Cally fidget uncomfortably, and do up another button on her suit jacket despite the rising heat of the early-morning sunshine.

'Emotions are irrelevant, aren't they?' She slid her portfolio from her side of the table to his, telling herself to ignore his casual attire and the holiday setting and treat this in exactly the same way as she had treated her interview at the London City Gallery. 'This contains photographs of all my major restorations, as well as details of my qualifications. I specialised in Rénard for the theory side of my post-grad.'

He opened it casually, flicking to the first page and briefly reading through her CV as he sipped his coffee.

'You began studying for a fine-art degree in London,' he said thoughtfully, raising his head. 'But you didn't finish?'

Trust him to notice that first. She remembered the owner

of the London City Gallery getting to the same question at her second interview—remembered how, after all the years of hard work, she had finally felt able to answer it with confidence and integrity. So why did she feel so ashamed when *he* asked?

'No, I didn't complete it.' She drew in a deep breath. 'And it was a mistake not to. But for two years afterwards I worked a full-time job, and painted and studied in every spare moment I had. The Cambridge Institute then accepted me on their diploma in conservation based on my aptitude and commitment.'

'So why didn't you finish it?' Leon flicked her portfolio shut without looking at another page. 'Did you fall in love with a university professor and drop out in a fit of unrequited love?'

'I don't think that's relevant, do you?'

Leon saw a flash of something in her eyes which told him he had hit a raw nerve. He was tempted to probe deeper, but at the same time the thought of her having past lovers, let alone hearing about them, irritated him. Which was preposterous, because the women he slept with always matched him in experience.

He looked her straight in the eye. 'Actually, I happen to think the way someone behaves in personal relationships is indicative of the way they are likely to behave as an employee.'

Suddenly, the penny dropped in Cally's mind. So *that* was what London had been about. She felt herself grow even hotter beneath the fabric of her dark jacket as she realised what that meant. It had all been an underhand investigation into whether he considered her fit for the job, and she could only imagine what his conclusion had been!

Wasn't it just typical that the one night she had acted completely out of character was the one night that, unbeknown to her, she'd needed to be herself most of all? But what gave him the right to make such a judgement based on her behaviour, anyway? Just because he was a prince didn't give him permission to play at being some moral magistrate!

She challenged him right back with her gaze. 'Then you don't want to know what your behaviour indicates about you, *Your Highness.*'

'Since you are the one who wants to work on my paintings, my behaviour is irrelevant. Yours, on the other hand…'

'So why bother bringing me here if I've already failed your pathetic little personality test?'

His voice was slow and deliberate, 'Because, *chérie,* although you showed that your word cannot be trusted and that you are only interested in these paintings because you think they will bring you renown…' He paused, as if to revel in her horror. 'After extensive research into your abilities over the past week I happen to believe you are the best person for the job.'

Cally was so taken aback by the damning insult and high praise all delivered in one succinct sentence that she didn't know what to say—but before she had the chance to utter anything Leon continued. 'As a result, I wish to employ you. On one condition. There will be no *renown.* You may detail the commission in your portfolio, but that is it. On this island it is already forbidden for the press to print anything about me and my employees except in reference to the public work I carry out. It is a policy I do my best to ensure is reflected throughout the world, and which I expect all current and former staff to ensure is upheld. Indefinitely.'

Well, that explained the lack of information on the Web, Cally thought, perplexed that he seemed to think that that one condition might be her only bone of contention with his offer of employment, and at the same time wanting to ask if he'd ever heard of three little words known as 'freedom of press'.

She frowned. 'Yesterday you suggested that the Rénards were purchased for the university. Aren't they therefore part of your public work anyway?'

Leon raked a hand through his hair in irritation. Didn't he just know that she would try and twist it any way she could? 'No. The Rénards are for my private collection. I purchased a small Goya at the same auction for the university. Thankfully, it needs no restoration.'

Cally exploded. 'So the Rénards *are* to be treated like some trophy enjoyed by no one but you?'

He took a sip of coffee. 'If that is the way you choose to view my decision, *oui*. How fitting, then, that the two paintings themselves are a celebration of difference.'

Cally felt her temper flare, as much because his crude analysis matched her own studied interpretation of the paintings as at the discovery that he would be keeping them to himself.

'So you lied to me yet again.'

'I didn't lie, I just postponed the truth.' He shrugged nonchalantly. 'Are you going to pretend it makes a difference?'

'Of course it does!'

'Really? As I recall it, you told me that despite your oh-so-ethical principles nothing would stop you working on the paintings. Unless…'

'Unless what?'

'Unless you are going to go back on your word. Again.'

His eyes met hers in smouldering challenge. He was baiting her, she knew he was, and every instinct within her screamed *walk away*. He *had* bought the paintings for no other reason than as an acquisition to boast about. He *was* a damned liar. And she had never felt so humiliated by any other man in her life. *Or so alive.*

But just what would she be walking away to—a blank diary and a pile of bills? Only now it would be worse, because she would know that she had walked away from her dream restoration for the sake of what boiled down to her pride. And, worse, though she hated to admit she gave a damn about what he thought, he would believe that she *was* incapable of sticking to her word, of seeing things through. The very trait that, after that one mistake, she'd spent years proving was not part of her character.

If she turned him down, the only person who would lose out was her. Leon would simply employ someone else to do the work, and a man with more money than morals would have thwarted her dreams for the second time in her life. The thought set free a deep-rooted ball of fury inside her. So what if he and his plans for the paintings were the antithesis of everything she believed in? For once in her life, why the hell shouldn't she turn that to her advantage?

'Do you wish me to begin work straight away?'

'That depends. Will you sign a contract which states that your employment will terminate if you break the condition?'

'I see no reason why not.'

'Then this afternoon suits me.'

Cally smiled a sickly smile, determined to make this difficult. 'In which case, I will require some payment up front in order to rent somewhere to stay, and—'

'Somewhere to *rent?*' he said with unconcealed disgust.
She nodded.

'And why on earth would that be necessary when, as you have already pointed out, the palace has an excess of rooms?'

'Because…because I hardly think living as well as working here is appropriate, under the circumstances.'

His raised his eyebrow. 'Circumstances?'

She felt a whole new level of heat wash over her and wished she had never opened her mouth. 'You know what I mean.'

'If we had slept together I would see your point, *ma belle,* but since you were so vehement that we should not there is no problem, *d'accord?*'

Yes, there is a bloody great problem, Cally thought, *and its despicably handsome face is staring right at me.*

'Fine. So I shall stay here and work here. But I'll need my conservation equipment.' She looked down at her suit and back up at him. 'And, as I thought I was only going to be here for a matter of hours, I'll need my clothes sent from home as well. Surely you can't deny that I shall be needing those for the duration of my stay?' she spat out, before she had time to realise that such a statement was just asking to be twisted.

'Only time will tell, Cally,' he purred. The way the two syllables of her name dropped from his tongue reminded her of hot, liquid chocolate, and she felt a bead of sweat trickle down between her breasts. 'But there will be no need to send for anything,' he drawled, as if her suggestion was utterly ridiculous. 'I will have everything you could possibly need brought over from Paris, a new wardrobe included.'

'I don't need a new wardrobe!'

He ran his eyes over her suit critically. 'Oh, but I think you do.'

Cally's cheeks burned at his insult, her body temperature continuing to rocket. 'Well, then, it's lucky I don't care what you think, isn't it?'

'Lucky? I'd say irrelevant is more accurate,' he said, draining his cup of coffee.

'But…!' Cally glared at him, her whole body teeming with frustration, but he simply ignored her and carried on.

'In the meantime, I presume you will wish to examine the *paintings*.' He emphasised it insultingly, as if she was the one getting sidetracked. 'Make a list of all the materials you will require and pass it on to Boyet by the end of the day. He will see that they are ordered immediately.' He ran his eyes over her figure as he stood up. 'And although it will be tomorrow before the clothes arrive from Paris I'm sure it wouldn't kill you to remove that jacket sometime before then. You look like you're about to pass out.'

Leon got to his feet and Cally stumbled to do the same, determined that this meeting would not end up with him walking away from her. 'You may be used to women fainting in your presence, Leon, but I can assure you that you leave me completely cold.'

'Well, if this is cold, *chérie,* I can't wait to see you fired up,' he mocked, and before she could even attempt to beat him away from the table he was halfway back to the palace, so that to her consternation it simply looked as though she had been standing ceremoniously for his exit.

'Then I hope you're a very patient man,' she yelled back, and, seeing that he had already entered the glass doors, allowed herself to drop back into her chair and tear off the blasted jacket.

'I'm not sure patience will be necessary,' he drawled as he pulled back the inside blind and dropped his eyes to her blouse. 'Are you?'

CHAPTER FIVE

'WOULD you have me carry these to your room now, Mademoiselle Greenway?'

Cally gawped in disbelief as she descended the stairs the following morning to find Boyet surrounded by countless bags and boxes. It reminded her of the sea of gifts that had spilled out from beneath the ten-foot pine at David's house that Christmas eight years ago, and his subsequent withering expression when she'd taken him back to meet her parents and he'd seen their sparse equivalent. It immediately soured her mood.

'I suppose there must be something suitable for work hidden in one of them, Boyet, thank you. Here, let me give you a hand.'

Despite his protests, Cally helped Boyet carry the fifty-four bags and boxes upstairs, but after peeling back enough tissue paper to completely bury the bedroom carpet she discovered that her supposition had been wrong. Yes, in amongst the high-heeled shoes, cocktail dresses and a disturbing amount of lingerie there was the odd pair of fine linen trousers and a single pair of diamanté designer jeans, but there was nothing she would have considered even remotely suitable for getting covered in paint. In fact it was the kind of wardrobe that would better befit a mistress than a woman he'd employed to do a job that could be both mentally and physically exhausting.

Maybe that was because it *was* a mistress's wardrobe, Cally thought cynically as she recalled Leon's comment yesterday which had implied just how frequently women joined him for breakfast. He probably had the whole lot on standby and simply ordered a new batch whenever he chose someone new to warm his bed. Well, she thought bitterly, her purpose here was not to dress for his pleasure. Not that she supposed for one minute that she was in any danger of that; whatever attraction he'd feigned towards her in London had simply been an elaborate plan to test her suitability for this job, hadn't it? She didn't know why that got to her most of all, when the real reason why she was angry was that he obviously had no concept of a woman needing clothes to work in. Well, she thought, grabbing for the designer jeans and rooting around in her handbag, she would soon see to that.

Cally doubted that her nail scissors would ever be fit for their intended purpose again, but twenty minutes later she felt rebelliously gleeful as she redescended the stairs and headed to the studio wearing the freshly cut-off, diamanté-less jeans, which now ended mid-thigh, and a royal blue silk blouse knotted at her waist.

The studio was triple the size of the room she used for restorations back home in Cambridge, but compared to everything she had encountered in the palace so far it was surprisingly understated. Aside from the tall glass doors which faced the sea and let in an ideal abundance of natural light, the room contained very little save for a row of cupboards, a sink, a comfy-looking sofa covered with a red throw and a CD player in the corner.

And of course the Rénards, which now dominated the space. She had been sitting alone on the veranda after breakfast yesterday, her jacket still tossed aside in frustration, when Boyet had approached to inform her that the paintings were being set up on easels in here for her to begin her assessment. Relieved to be able to concentrate on practicalities, her mood had instantly turned to one of resolve. When she had taken Boyet the list of materials she anticipated she would need for the duration of the restoration later that afternoon, she had been even more relieved to hear that Leon had gone out on royal business and would not be back until after dark.

However, though Leon seemed to be leaving her to it this morning as well, Cally was perplexed to find that she was not consumed by the single-mindedness she usually felt when confronted with a new commission, and which she had expected to have in spades when it came to the Rénards.

She pulled up her stool before the masterpieces and drew in a deep breath, forcing herself to block out everything else, but her mind was still running riot. Perhaps it was too quiet. She was used to the buzz of traffic outside her window back home. She went over to the CD player and ran her fingers along the shelf of jewelled cases, surprised to find there was more than one rock album amongst his collection. She hesitated over one of them. Tempting though it was to put it on, she knew it would only serve to remind her of *that* night, and that was bound to skew her thoughts completely. So she put on some contemporary jazz, told herself a prince didn't buy his own CDs anyway, and sat down again.

Being able to focus was her speciality; it always had been. She cast her mind back to her conservation course in Cambridge. There had been plenty of students with more natural talent than she had, but, to quote the words of her tutor, no one who applied themselves in quite the same way that she did. Whilst other students had partied till dawn, and only started thinking about their assignments on the day of a deadline, Cally would be finished with weeks to spare, already working on the next. Maybe it was because she had fought so hard for a second chance. Or maybe it was because since that moment in Mrs McLellan's class all those years before her passion for art had surpassed everything.

Even though her epiphany had initially taken the form of wanting to be an artist in the traditional sense, Cally admitted, unsure why that thought was accompanied by a deep pang of regret today when usually she could view her change of vocation objectively. It was probably because, if she had been able to bring herself to paint any of her paltry compositions after her split with David, even they would have had more chance of appearing in a public gallery than the two most impressive nineteenth-century paintings in existence. Cally balled her hands into fists. How was it possible that a man who was opening a university which encouraged learning about art could keep these incredible paintings for his eyes only? The university was just a princely duty, she supposed, a role which was separate from his own sentiments. Which was exactly how she needed to view this job.

'Before shots, that's where I should start,' Cally said aloud, as if talking to herself might drown out her tumultuous thoughts and help with her focus. She reached into her bag and found her battered camera, then took a step backwards, lining up the lens.

'Thinking of your precious portfolio, *chérie?*'

At the sound of his voice she dropped her hand guiltily. As soon as she did, she realised how ridiculous that was, but by then her hand was too unsteady to continue.

Only because he had made her jump, Cally reasoned. How had he snuck in without her hearing? She was annoyed that she had no way of knowing how long he'd been standing there watching her, and made a mental note to lower the volume on the CD player in future, though the music was far from loud.

'Having a record of their initial appearance for reference is an essential part of the process,' she said defensively, turning to face him. The sight caught her off guard. He was perched on the arm of the sofa in a pair of faded light blue jeans that moulded his thighs, and a white T-shirt that revealed the taut plane of his stomach, the casual attire doing nothing to belittle the power he seemed to exude naturally. She swallowed slowly, her mouth suddenly feeling parched. 'Was there something you wanted?'

'I just came to check you hadn't been attacked by the palace lawnmower,' he drawled, producing two pieces of hacked-off denim. 'Stéphanie was a little concerned to find these whilst cleaning your room.'

Cally's mouth twitched into a smile. 'Well, as you can see, I'm absolutely fine.'

'It's a shame I can't say the same for the jeans.'

'What's a shame is that you didn't allow me to have my own clothes sent from home. How am I supposed to do my job wearing some skintight, dry-clean-only designer outfit?

You're lucky I didn't decide to do a Julie Andrews and take to your curtains instead.'

'Sorry?' Her words shook Leon out of his state of semi-arousal. Ever since he'd entered the room he'd been transfixed by her pert little bottom and her long, shapely legs in her makeshift shorts. Until she'd just revealed that her outing with the scissors had all been a protest because he hadn't let her have her own way.

'You know—Julie Andrews in *The Sound of Music*— where she makes clothes for all the children out of the curtains. Didn't you ever see it?'

'I can't say that I did.'

Cally looked at him with new eyes, truly comprehending for the first time that he wasn't just Mr Drop-dead Gorgeous with whom she'd shared one earth-shattering kiss before he'd humiliated and lied to her. He was royalty, the sole ruler of a Mediterranean island. Whilst she'd spent the school holidays watching old movies with her sister whilst her parents were out at work, what must he have been doing—opening the odd university here, making a state visit there?

Yet, even though he owned this luxurious palace, had the title and the sense of self-importance to match, she still found it somehow difficult to imagine. Maybe it was because he'd described his role here as if it was just a job. But that was ridiculous, because being royal wasn't an occupation, it was who he was. So how was it that he had seemed to fit right into that bar in London when he ought to have stuck out like a Van Gogh in a public toilet?

Cally quickly returned her camera to her bag and moved back to her seat, appalled to realise that she had been inadvertently giving him the once-over. 'Don't you have royal duties this morning?'

Leon had never been so glad that someone had elected to sit on a stool rather than a chair as he watched the waistband of her shorts come tantalisingly close to revealing the top of the perfect globes of her bottom. 'Not until my meeting later with the president of France.'

'Oh.' It took all Cally's powers of concentration to transfer a bottle of distilled water into a small beaker without pouring it all over her lap. 'Then I'm sure you must have a lot to prepare.'

'If it's not distracting, I thought I might watch you quietly.'

It wasn't really even a question, and if it was then he had asked it so airily it was impossible to answer that, actually, she felt seriously in danger of putting the cotton bud through the canvas if he stayed. She'd worked in front of people heaps of times before—students, enthusiastic clients—and, for goodness' sake, the first step of the process was only removing the dirt and grime. All it required was a little focus.

'As you wish.'

Leon witnessed her hesitation and smiled to himself. 'You can begin without the supplies from Paris?'

Cally felt herself marginally relax, glad to talk about work. 'The cleaning, yes. It's more a case of time and patience than apparatus in the early stages.'

'Like so many things,' he said, deliberately slowly.

She told herself she was imagining his suggestive tone. 'I had a tutor who used to say that half the work is in the diagnosis. Each painting is like a patient. The symptoms might be similar, but working out the treatment is unique to every one.'

An image of Cally wearing a nurse's uniform and tending to him in bed popped into Leon's head, and the erection which had begun at the sight of her legs in those shorts grew even harder.

'So, did you always want to restore art?'

As Cally returned to her seat she felt the muscles in her shoulders go taut. 'I started out wanting to be an artist in the traditional sense, but things changed. I don't do my own work anymore.'

She waited for the snide comment, the probing questions, but was surprised to find they didn't come.

'Our lives don't always follow the course we expect, *non?*'

'No,' she said, somehow finding the courage to begin in the top corner of the first painting. 'They don't.'

He must be referring to his brother's death, Cally thought, for it occurred to her that, if Girard had lived, then Leon might never have become prince. She wanted to ask him about it, but at the same time felt bound to show him the same quiet respect.

He broke the momentary silence. 'But providence works in mysterious ways, wouldn't you say?'

'I'd say that view of the world is a little romantic for me.'

She heard him move and saw on the periphery of her vision that he was leaning up against the cupboards to her left, contemplating her profile.

'You mean you do not believe in romance, *ma belle?*'

She dipped the cotton bud back in the distilled water and deflected the question. 'Why, do you?'

'I am a Frenchman, Cally.' He laughed a low, throaty laugh. 'It's in my blood.'

'How curious, when only yesterday you were telling me that you find the idea of marriage intolerable.'

He eyed her sceptically. 'What amazing powers of recollection you have for someone who professed to have no interest in the subject.'

'A good memory is essential for my job,' she replied a little too quickly. 'In order to recall the mixes of different chemicals.'

'Of course.' He stroked a hand across his chin with mock sincerity. 'Your job. That is what we were discussing, after all. So, tell me, is it coincidence that you chose to start with the fully clothed portrait before moving on to the nude, or is the significance intentional?'

Cally's hand was poised in mid-air an inch away from the canvas. 'I'm sorry?'

'Is it deliberate that you have begun on the work which has the least damage first?'

She pursed her lips, knowing that he hadn't been implying anything so innocuous.

'Yes. It allows me to get accustomed to the necessary techniques before moving on to the larger areas of damage.'

'The patient requiring the most intensive treatment.' He nodded seriously, startling her with the evidence that he had been listening thoroughly to her earlier explanation.

He saw her falter a second time and stifled a grin. 'I am sorry. I promised to watch quietly. I will leave you to carry on in peace, if you'll just excuse me whilst I just pick up a couple of things?'

Cally inclined her head, thinking how impeccable his manners could be when he wanted. She did not really take in what he was saying until she saw him move to the cupboard at the front of the room and remove a towel.

'I thought they were all empty, ready for the paint supplies,' she commented.

'They are, except for these few. I've got rid of the majority of my equipment now I have so few chances to use it.'

'Equipment?'

'Diving equipment,' he explained, before catching sight of the intense curiosity on her face which told him that it had not been clarification enough. He supposed no harm could come from telling her. 'Before it became necessary for me to rule the island, I worked as a diver for the Marine Nationale.'

Cally tried to hide the astonishment she felt. 'The French Navy?' As an admiral or a captain she could well imagine, but a diver? She swallowed as he hooked his thumbs under the corner of his T-shirt. It certainly explained his incredible physique—in which she had absolutely no interest, of course. It was just that she'd been trained to admire things that were aesthetically pleasing.

'This room is closest to the sea. I used to train out of here before I signed up full-time.'

Cally watched, her whole body besieged by a frightening and unfamiliar paralysis as he revealed his taut, muscular chest and exceptionally broad shoulders. He had a scar, she noticed, running from just below his belly button to somewhere below the waistband of his jeans. The mark of his fallibility fascinated her. How had he got it? How would it feel to trace its pale crease with her fingertips and find out where it led—and, more to the point, why was she even wondering? Her pulse skittered madly. Good God, now he was unbuttoning his flies! She moved her face closer to the painting, pretending to look at it closely, willing herself to concentrate on Rénard's artistic genius. But the live work of nature before her was suddenly a whole lot more impressive.

When she raised her head to look again he was wearing

pale blue swimming trunks, and she found herself inexplicably frustrated that she had no way of knowing whether he had been wearing them underneath his jeans all along or not.

'We haven't had a day this hot for weeks.' His mouth twitched in amusement as he walked over to the small fridge by the sink and took a long swig from a bottle of water. *Try years,* Cally thought, her mouth growing dry at the sight. They ought to use him to advertise mineral water. Or on second thoughts perhaps not; it would probably cause a drought.

'It's definitely even warmer than yesterday,' she replied weakly.

'So join me.' He nodded at the inviting blue glitter of sea outside the window.

Join him? She followed his gaze and imagined plunging into its cooling depths. Then she turned her attention back to the tanned, muscular profile. Far, far too dangerous.

'Thanks, but it could be detrimental not to complete this part of the process now I've started.'

'Of course,' he said slowly. 'Just don't get too hot in here all by yourself.'

And with that he opened the glass doors, strolled the short distance to the cliff and dived in.

Several minutes passed before Cally realised she was still staring at the empty space where he had been, her cotton bud poised inanely in mid-air. Racked with irritation that the ability to apply herself to her work was now even further from her grasp, she dropped the bud back into the container of water and stood up, hoping that stretching her legs and turning off the CD player would allow her to regroup her thoughts. But before she could stop herself she was stretching her legs back across the room to the wide glass doors.

Cally touched a hand to her hair and looked behind her guiltily as she got closer to the threshold between inside and out. Which was ridiculous, because she was perfectly entitled to get up and look at the view, and it wasn't as though anyone could see her anyway. She peered over the cliff edge and down into the expanse of blue below, then across the bay, out at the horizon and back again. It was so still there was hardly a wave. So where was he? She tried to pretend she didn't care, that she was taking in the amazingly cloudless sky as her eyes frantically skimmed the water. Until—thank goodness—there he was, returning to the surface.

However much she wanted to argue to some invisible jury that she was just admiring the glorious landscape, the sight of him held her transfixed. His muscular shoulders were stretched tight, his strong arms slicing rhythmically through the water; he was so focussed that she was not only mesmerised but envious. He dipped beneath the surface, sometimes for so long that she almost did herself an injury as she strained to see below the water, each reappearance causing a clammy wash of relief across her shoulders and down her back.

Shockingly, half of her—like the woman in the paintings—felt the unprecedented impulse to brazenly remove her clothes and follow him into the sea. Her more sensible half told her that that was not only inexcusable, because she was his employee, but that she had to be deranged if she thought she had anything in common with the siren in Rénard's painting. So why as she watched him was she unable to stop herself running her hands over the silk of her blouse as if to check it hadn't disappeared of its own accord? And why did she feel the urge to close her eyes and explore the unfamiliar ache pooling between her thighs as her hand lingered over her breasts?

Because you're a fool, Cally, a voice inside her screamed at the exact moment that the memory of his kiss on the dark and crowded dance floor flew into her mind, and she suddenly remembered the auction. Remembered that he had lied to her from the moment she had met him, and that even if he hadn't, thinking about him that way could only lead to disappointment. So why was she standing here allowing herself to feel this way—no matter that they were feelings she could never recall ever feeling before—when she was supposed to be working on her dream commission?

It was because the thrill of getting this job had been diminished by the way in which it had come about, she thought pragmatically, knotting her hands behind her and walking back towards the paintings. It was discovering that her employer was not only the epitome of everything she loathed, but that he was also the man who had dented her pride on the first occasion in years when she had actually dared to live a little. If the London City Gallery had won the paintings the night of the auction, everything would have been different; she would have rung her family, euphoria would have hit and single-minded focus would have followed. Yes, Cally thought, what she needed was to be reminded of the enormity of this opportunity, to talk to someone who would know how much it meant to her.

She bent down and rifled through her handbag in search of her paint-smattered mobile, scrolling through the short-list of contacts until she found her sister's number.

Jen answered amidst the usual sea of background noise which seemed to follow her around; if it wasn't the sound of Dylan and Josh using each other as climbing frames, then it was the hustle and bustle of a breaking news story. This time it sounded like the latter.

'Cally? Are you OK?'

'Hi, Jen, I'm fine,' Cally replied, unsure why her sister's voice was loaded with concern. Although she'd wanted to talk about it, she hadn't told Jen anything about Montéz. Last time they'd spoken she'd been ninety per-cent sure that the email was a hoax, and, when the tickets had arrived, she'd decided it would be prudent to wait and see if it actually yielded a job first, rather than have to report back with another story of rejection if it didn't. 'Is it a bad time to talk?'

'No, not at all—I'm outside Number Ten waiting for the prime minister to emerge, but I could be here for hours. It's just that I left a message on your answer phone inviting you to dinner on Sunday and you haven't replied.'

'When was that?'

'Last night.'

Last night? She hadn't replied in less than twenty-four hours and that automatically made her sister think something was up? Cally pulled at a loose thread on her shorts and frowned. She'd always thought her swiftness to reply to people was a positive thing—she was the first one to send out thank-yous after Christmas, always RSVP-ing on time to invitations to weddings and parties, even if it was to decline them. Only now did she realise how much it screamed 'I need to get out more'.

'Thanks, but I'm afraid I can't come. I'm in Montéz.'

'Montéz?' The utter disbelief in her sister's voice bugged her. 'Good for you. It's about time you had a holiday.'

'I'm not on holiday. I'm working on the Rénards.'

'Cally, that's fantastic! How? Tell me everything. You found out who bought them?'

'The buyer found me.'

'That's because you're the best person for the job. Didn't I tell you that was a possibility? So, who is it?'

Cally hesitated, not having foreseen that this discussion would inevitably end up being about the very person she was trying to put out of her mind. 'He's the prince here.'

There was a shocked pause. 'Oh my God—don't tell me you're working for Leon Montallier?'

Cally almost dropped the phone. 'How on earth do *you* know his name?'

Jen whistled through her teeth. 'Everyone who works for a paper knows his name. We're just not allowed to print anything about him. Not that anybody knows anything— he's too much of an enigma.'

'Too much of a bastard,' Cally corrected, turning to pace in the other direction as she realised that during the conversation she'd walked herself dangerously close to the glass doors once more. 'There's nothing else worth knowing.'

'Hang on a minute. Hasn't he just given you your dream job?'

'Yes, he has,' Cally admitted, trying to sound enthused as she recalled that this was the whole purpose for her call. 'And the chance to infill for a master like Rénard is incredible but—'

'But what? Oh, don't tell me that because he's royalty he thought that gave him the right to try it on?'

The frankness Jen had developed from her years reporting on the wealthy and powerful usually amused Cally, but today its accuracy—or rather its inaccuracy—only succeeded in making her feel more wretched.

'But he doesn't plan to display the pictures in a gallery, that's what. They're nothing more than a symbol of his nauseating wealth.'

'Well, I can't say I'm surprised about that, I'm afraid,' Jen said, unaware how close her initial remark had been to the bone. 'But that doesn't mean you can't share your restoration process with the public, does it?'

'Sorry?'

'The paper could run a story. Our arts specialist, Julian, would kill to do a piece on it!'

'I *wish*. But he's so anti-press that it's written into my contract that I can't even— Jen?'

The volume of the background noise suddenly doubled, and Cally could hear the clash of a thousand cameras and the sound of bodies jostling forward.

'Jen, can you hear me?'

'Sorry, sis, gotta go!'

''Course—look, just forget I even mentioned him, OK?'

Leon's mouth curved in amusement as he approached the studio doors to find her concentrating hard on facing the wall as she finished her call. She was making a show of trying to stick to her word, he'd give her that. But, if it was for his benefit, she needn't bother. Didn't she know that he had seen her from the water? And didn't she know that it made no difference whether he witnessed it or not?

Her desire for him was written into every move her delectable body made. It had been from the very first moment she had looked at him with those expressive green eyes. He wondered how much longer she would keep fighting it, pretending that what mattered to her were the paintings. Had she forgotten how clear she had made it in that insalubrious bar in London? Had she forgotten that she had told him she was only interested in this job to gain renown? Since he had made sure *that* wasn't an option, her reason for accepting was obvious—him. But, then, he was well aware that women were experts at pretending to be driven by their careers in order to entice a man. Women who claimed to have moved on from their nineteenth-century counterparts, who learned a handful of accomplishments to try and coerce a man into marrying them, but who really hadn't changed at all. They had simply got more devious.

Not that Cally was claiming to want *marriage,* he thought dryly. But he didn't doubt that those wistful looks into jewellers' windows would inevitably come if he kept her in his bed for too long.

'Someone special?'

Cally jumped and swung round to see him crossing the studio as the deep timbre of his voice reverberated through her body. How the hell hadn't she heard him come in this time? She looked down, convinced he mustn't be wearing shoes. She was right, but for her gaze to have alighted on the bareness of his toes was a mistake. Not only did she notice that even his feet were impossibly sexy, but it only encouraged her to sweep her eyes upwards over the damp hairs clinging to his legs, to the towel slung about his waist and his mouth-watering chest.

'Sorry?'

'The phone call. It must have been someone special, to interrupt what you were doing when you seemed so reluctant to stop.'

'I—I'd finished the section I was on. I'm just about to start on the next.' She sat back down in the chair and made to pick up a fresh cotton bud.

He looked at her with amusement dancing in his eyes. 'I wasn't talking about the paintings.'

Cally froze and felt herself blush redder than her hair as she realised what he meant. Wanting to die of embarrassment, she clutched around in her mind for some feasible excuse as to why she had been looking out to sea with her hands on her body, but it didn't come.

He broke into a wry smile and continued. 'But, much as I would like to watch you continue, I'm afraid I cannot keep the French president waiting.' Cally swallowed as he removed the towel from around his waist and laid it around his shoulders. 'I will be back tomorrow evening, when the Sheikh of Qwasir and his new fiancée will be coming for dinner. I thought perhaps you might like to join us, show them what you're working on.'

Cally stared at him, her embarrassment turning to astonishment. Firstly that he had even asked her, and secondly that, despite his own rebuttal of the press, he socialised with two people who could not have had a higher media profile.

'You mean the couple who are on the front of every newspaper in the world?'

Leon tensed and gave a single nod.

'And you wish me to show them the paintings?' Even though she hated the idea of private buyers wanting famous artwork for no other reason than to impress their friends, she couldn't help feeling both excited and honoured at the prospect of getting to share them with anyone.

'That is what I said,' Leon ground out, only now aware that, whilst he had envisioned a night with her beside him wearing one of those figure-hugging dresses he had selected, she saw it only as an opportunity to get herself known amongst the rich and famous.

'Thank you—then I'm delighted to accept.'

'Of course you are,' he drawled, before walking over to the table and handing her the cotton bud she was still yet to pick up. 'In the meantime, I'm sure you'll want to get on with what you came here to do.'

CHAPTER SIX

GET ON with what you came here to do. Leon's sarcastic words were still reverberating through Cally's mind as she tramped upstairs twenty-four hours later. If only she could. More than anything that was what she wanted, but to her horror another day had passed unproductively. Even though the supplies she needed had arrived that morning, even though she'd had the palace to herself, she hadn't been able to stop herself from gazing up at the glass doors, imagining him rising half-naked from the sea.

Allowing herself to get distracted in any way at all was completely unlike her, she thought as she entered the bedroom, never mind by thoughts of that nature. Everything she ever took on she always committed to one hundred and ten per cent until it was complete. Except her fine-art degree, she admitted ruefully. Was that it then—every time she met a man she found remotely attractive she was reduced to a mess of distraction which robbed her of all her artistic focus?

Cally cast her mind back to the summer she had met David, when she had taken a job as a waitress at the tearoom in the grounds of his father's stately home. Had she been so bowled over by his charms that it had rendered her completely incapable of holding a brush? No, she thought frankly, actually, she hadn't. She'd been flattered by the unexpected attention he'd bestowed upon her, naively impressed by the upper-class world in which he lived, but she certainly hadn't felt this kind of paralysis. That was not what had made her throw in her studies, it was that she'd foolishly believed him when he'd said she would never become a great artist spending all her time working towards a degree. Only later had she discovered that, just like his chauvinistic father, the idea of a woman going to university had appalled him, particularly one whose father was just a postman.

So why the hell was it this way with Leon? Cally wondered as she opened her wardrobe to find it had been miraculously filled with the contents of the fifty-four bags and boxes whilst she had been working—and to her amusement some additional T-shirts and casual cut-offs too. And why was she so tempted to wear one of the glamorous dresses now, when she loathed the excess they represented? Because his guests were an esteemed desert ruler and a model, which meant such an outfit was appropriate for this element of her work in the same way her sister's black dress had been necessary for the auction, Cally justified, feeling both apprehensive and thrilled at the prospect of talking about the paintings. Even if talking about them was all she was able to do at the moment.

In the end she selected a beautiful jade dress with an asymmetric hem that felt so good swishing around her legs as she came down the stairs that, when she reached the grand dining room, it took her a minute to process that the table was completely bare. She looked at the antique clock on the wall, wondering if she had got the time wrong. Noting she hadn't, she decided she must have been mistaken about the place. Heaven knew, the palace was big enough, and Leon could hold the soirée in any number of rooms.

'Boyet!' Cally caught sight of him just as he was about to turn the corner of the inner stairs. 'I was supposed to meet His Highness in the dining room for the royal dinner at eight. Is it to be held elsewhere?'

'I believe there has been a change of plan altogether, mademoiselle.' He looked at the floor, evidently embarrassed that he was in possession of information that she was not. 'The last time I saw His Royal Highness, he was headed outside, as if he intended to go diving.'

'In *this*?' Cally gasped, concern furrowing her brow as she looked out across the hallway and through the high windows towards the inky blue sky, the rising wind beginning to whip against the glass.

'Thank you, Boyet,' she replied with a quick but earnest nod, turning on her three-inch heels in matching jade and hastening to the studio with none of the ladylike elegance with which she had just descended the stairs.

The room was bathed in darkness, and her pace slowed as she approached the glass doors; she was almost afraid of coming upon the view of the sea too quickly for fear of what she might see. Eventually she reached the handle and, finding it locked, began fumbling around in search of a key.

'Looking for something?'

Cally turned sharply to find Leon sitting absolutely still on the sofa, bathed in shadows. The look of accusation in his eyes matched the warning tone of his voice.

'Boyet said you were out in this.' She raised one hand out towards the blackness of the ocean, as if the concept was the most preposterous thing she had ever heard, choosing to overlook his equally sinister mood. As far as she could see, she was the only one who had a reason to be angry.

'I was,' he said abruptly as she turned on the lamp next to the paintings, softly illuminating the room.

He was dressed in jeans and a T-shirt that clung to his body in such a way that she could see his skin beneath was still damp. His hair was dark and heavy with moisture. If she hadn't been so determined not to think it, she would have admitted it was the most alluring thing she had ever seen in her life.

'Are you insane?'

'Insane to risk being late for our high-profile dinner engagement?' he drawled, eyeing her so critically that all the joy she'd felt in wearing the jade dress evaporated.

'To go diving tonight, when the ocean is so restless,' Cally corrected, wondering how he wasn't shivering with cold when just thinking about being in the water had her arms breaking out in goose bumps. 'Isn't one scar enough?'

Leon's mouth twitched into a sardonic smile. 'Though your observational skills are as touching as your concern, I can assure you that swimming in the cove outside my back door is hardly a risk in comparison to defusing a mine one hundred metres below sea level. I'll admit it's been a while, but—'

'Fine.' Cally blushed furiously. 'So, what about dinner? Boyet said there had been a change of plan.'

'There has. Unfortunately Kaliq and Tamara are unable to join us. Exhaustion after their journey here, I believe.'

'And you didn't think it polite to tell me before I went to the trouble of getting dressed up?'

'Given your track record, I had no idea you would go to so much trouble.' He stared at her legs, remembering where her shorts had been. 'But, then, I suppose I should have known, shouldn't I?'

'Known what?' Cally swiped, growing increasingly frustrated at his unaccountably bad mood.

'That everything's different when you're presented with the chance of renown.'

'Renown?' She turned to him blankly.

'God, you really are good, aren't you?' His mouth twisted in disgust.

'Good at what, Leon? At least tell me what the hell I've done so I can *try* and defend myself.'

He had flung it before she'd even finished speaking. It narrowly missed the first painting, hitting the lamp, which crashed to the floor, by luck avoiding the easel of the second painting by less than an inch. It was only after she'd thrown herself in front of both Rénards as if to shield them from further attack that she realised that it was a rolled-up newspaper.

'What the hell do you think you're playing at?'

'I was about to ask you the same question.'

'What?' she cried in exasperation. 'You're the one who just nearly destroyed an eighty-million-pound work of art!'

'*My* eighty-million-pound work of art,' he replied smoothly. 'Which I was nowhere near. It's a shame I can't say the same for you and the press.'

Grasping that there was something she was missing, Cally was already on the floor, unrolling the paper, cringing as she saw the teaser at the top of the page.

* * *

THE WORLD TODAY
Restoring our interest: Rénard's masterpieces since *that* auction.
Art conservator Cally Greenway shares her eighty-million-pound secret!

Cally's eyes widened in horror. She'd told her sister that running an article was out of the question, hadn't she? Cally's cheeks coloured as she fought to remember the details, details which were hazy because at the time she'd been so distracted by the thought of *him*. Yes, she most definitely had, and she knew there was no way that Jen would run a story regardless. Unless…unless in all the commotion on the other end of the line her sister hadn't heard her properly.

'There's been a mistake,' Cally cried helplessly. 'I told her not to print anything.'

'Her?'

'My sister Jen's a journalist.'

'Oh, fantastic.'

Cally's voice became defensive. 'I only called her because I wanted to share the fact that I'd got the job I thought I'd lost.' His expression was utterly remorseless. 'In the same way *she* calls *me* about what's going on in her life. She happened to mention that an article about restoring the Rénards would be a great way of sharing them with the public. I agreed that it *would* be, but I told her there was no way you'd allow it. But…but we got cut off, and she must have misunderstood what I'd said.'

'How convenient for you.'

'Are you calling me a liar?'

Leon looked at her patronisingly. 'I'm saying that, if you

think I have forgotten that night in London, then you are even more foolish than I thought.'

Cally coloured instantly. 'What has this got to do with London?'

'You mean you have forgotten, *chérie?*' he drawled, his eyes lingering on her lips. 'You told me your reason for wanting to work on the Rénards. It was so that your name would be known across the world, was it not? So how can you possibly expect me to believe that this exposure is an accident?'

'I told you! Jen must have misunderstood. Let me call her, get to the bottom of it—'

'I think calling her once has done enough damage, don't you?'

Cally let out a frustrated sigh. 'And for that I'm sorry, but...' She scanned her eyes down the article, and noticed that the 'secret' the headline referred to was nothing more than the fact that she was restoring the paintings for a private collector in France. 'Look.' She pointed to the text. 'You're not even mentioned. Yes, that the article exists is a mistake. But everyone makes mistakes now and again—' she hesitated '—even you.'

'But this isn't about me.' He paused, and then the tone of his voice suddenly turned. 'Unless, of course, what you are really trying to tell me is that I'm *precisely* what this is all about.'

'Please don't talk in riddles, Leon.'

'Well, if I'm to believe that you didn't do this on purpose, that fame wasn't top of your agenda when you agreed to work for me, then what else could possibly have induced you to say yes?' His eyes licked over her.

'I just told you. I'm passionate about the Rénards. I

have been since I was a child.' She avoided his gaze, knowing it was only designed to humiliate her further. 'Is that so hard for you to believe?'

When she looked up he was staring at her with an intensity which told her there was nowhere to hide. 'It is when I know that for every minute you spend working on them you spend thirty thinking about me.'

Cally felt horror tear through every tissue in her body, not only because, to her shame, he was right and he knew it, but because she was terrified that what he implied was true. Had she accepted this job because the feelings he evoked in her obliterated everything else? No, she'd accepted it for the sake of her career, the Rénards.

'You're wrong, Leon.' Her voice was a husky whisper.

'Am I? Then how would *you* explain the symptoms. Dilated pupils, shallow breathing, the way you can't stop yourself from running your tongue over your lower lip every time you look at me? For someone who's supposed to be an expert on diagnosis and protection, I would have thought it was obvious.'

'I don't need protection,' Cally shot out determinedly, not noticing the look that flared in his eyes at her words.

'No, I didn't suppose for one minute that you would.'

But before she had time to process what he meant he slid his hand across her back and drew her to him, until their bodies were pressed so closely together that in the half light it would have been impossible for an onlooker to discern where she ended and where he began.

She froze, wanting to push him away, but unable to muster the strength. 'Leon, don't.'

He held perfectly still, save for his thumb tracing the base of her spine with an affectionate intimacy that made her want to cry out. 'Why not, *chérie,* when we both know it is what you want?'

Cally shook her head wretchedly. 'Be-because you don't want to.'

At her words even his thumb stopped moving and he regarded her with a faint look of surprise. 'Is it not obvious that I want you so much I have lost the ability to think straight?'

'But in London…'

He trailed his hand up her back and rested his fingers on the pulse beating wildly in her neck. 'It seems we were both a little guilty of saying one thing and meaning another in London.'

Her head fell back to look into his eyes, her own eyes widening as she realised that his were completely unflinching. He meant it. Though that ought to have changed nothing, to Cally it changed everything. He *did* desire her. Much as she'd been convinced that was impossible, much as she'd never dreamed she could ever feel such fervent need in return, suddenly it consumed her so overwhelmingly that she didn't even feel like the same Cally she had been two weeks ago. And, although she knew the safest option would be to button down her feelings as if they were nothing but awning caught in a disobedient wind, although she had never felt more terrified in her life, above all she understood that she would never know what it truly was to live unless she let it fly. Now.

'Leon, I—'

'Want me to kiss you again?' he ventured, moving his face so close to hers that his lips were only millimetres away.

The small sound that escaped from her throat said it all. It was unconscious, automatic, and with it he closed the gap between their mouths and gave an equally primal groan.

His kiss was exactly as she'd remembered but completely different at the same time. Not only did it feel like he was slowly turning every cell in her body to liquid with each masterful stroke of his tongue, but now there was no languid music deciding their tempo, his hunger set the pace and dared her to match it. Not only did he smell of that distinctive musk she knew she would never fully be able to drive from her mind, it was now mixed with the smell of the sea—salty, damp and agonisingly erotic. So potent that she had to cling on to him to stop her knees from buckling. As she did, they stumbled forward a little, the heel of her shoe catching something other than floor.

Her eyes flew open to find it was the foot of an easel, and suddenly she remembered where they were and froze. 'The paintings!'

'Forget the damned paintings,' he drawled, steadying the fully clothed *Amour* with unconcerned ease. 'Let's go upstairs.'

The thought of the royal bedroom terrified Cally. Down here she could almost believe that he wasn't the prince, that she hadn't completely taken leave of her senses. She bit her lip for a moment, knowing that suggesting the alternative required a boldness she wasn't sure she possessed. But then she looked at him; his eyes were so hungry for her that it was almost possible to forget that she lacked anything at all. She swallowed down the excess of saliva that had formed in her mouth and imagined her fear disappearing with it. 'Actually, do you…do you mind if we stay here?'

The thought of taking her here and now made Leon harder than he had ever been in his entire life.

'Mind?' he breathed, doing nothing to disguise the

roughness of his voice. 'The only thing I mind is that you are still wearing that dress.'

Cally's moment of relief was replaced by a new army of nerves. 'It does seem a little formal,' she whispered hesitantly as his hand trailed down her neck and swept around the circle of her breast. Instinctively she arched her back to encourage his hand upwards to the unbearable tightness of her nipple, but instead his fingers moved behind her, releasing the zip of her dress with ease and peeling the straps from her shoulders.

It was then that she remembered with horror the jade green basque and panties she was wearing underneath. She had put it on in that insane moment earlier when she'd been filled with delight at the thought of wearing the dress, followed by the girlish longing to try on the beautiful matching lingerie, the likes of which she had never worn in her life. It had felt so good, and, never supposing for a minute that anyone would see it, she'd seen no harm in keeping it on. Suddenly she felt ridiculous. What must he think of her, standing before him in lingerie that made her look like a courtesan at the Moulin Rouge, when she was nothing but an art restorer from Cambridge who hadn't had sex for almost a decade, and had never been good at it even then?

But when he peeled her dress down to her ankles and stepped back the pleasure on his face was so palpable—as if this was exactly how he had expected her to look, how she should look—that he made her feel like a butterfly emerging from a chrysalis. So much so that it was easy to forget how many other more beautiful, more experienced women than her must have stood before him like this. Easy to forget her old insecurities, to think only about how much he seemed to want her, how much she wanted him.

Cally reached forward with new-found boldness to encourage his T-shirt from his jeans.

'Allow me,' Leon interrupted, deftly removing both so that he was standing before her in nothing but his silky dark boxers, every inch of hard muscle illuminated in the refracted light from the lamp still lying on the floor like some piece of modern art.

He pulled her to him with renewed urgency, and she bucked in pleasure as at last his thumb brushed over her nipple through the lace of the bodice, making her whole body tremble.

'I hope you're not cold?' he asked, the corner of his mouth quirking into a smile as he circled the taut peak.

'No.' She shook her head, her breathing ragged. 'Not *cold*.'

'Good,' he rasped, raising his arms and moving behind her to slowly unlace the basque.

'Are you?' Cally whispered.

'Am I what?' he whispered distractedly as he kissed the delicious hollow between her neck and her shoulder.

'Are you cold?'

'What do you think?' he ground out as the basque fell to the floor and he spun her round to face him, revelling in the sight of her.

Slowly, tentatively, she daringly reached out her hand to touch him through the thin, silky fabric. 'You feel pretty warmed up to me.'

Leon closed his eyes and groaned as she gradually tugged down his boxers. When he opened them again her eyes were fixed on him, her whole body momentarily still.

'What are you thinking?' he asked choppily.

Cally forced herself to blink, stunned by her own boldness, by the size of him, by the way his scar led into the mass of thick, dark curls. 'Your ego is big enough as it is,' she breathed, suddenly nervous again.

'So, show me,' he teased in delight.

Cally looked into the depths of his eyes, her mind filling with a host of unfamiliar and erotic images that she was convinced he must somehow be transmitting to her. Images which excited her even more than they surprised her, made her forget that she wasn't the kind of woman who instinctively understood the art of love, made her think quite the opposite. Slowly, slowly, with her breath caught nervously in her throat, she began to feather light kisses from beneath his belly button to the tip of his arousal.

Leon watched. Her breasts grazed the shafts of his thighs as she took him in her mouth. It was almost too much for him to bear. He guided her upwards and towards the sofa.

'I want to be inside you.'

Cally wanted him inside of her too, irrationally, inexplicably. In that instant she understood, however astonishing, that was what she had wanted from the very first moment she'd laid eyes on him. Now he was sitting on the sofa, guiding her legs to either side of him, his middle finger rushing up her inner thigh, finding the most intimate part of her, moist, open, *ready*.

She heard herself gasp in shock as he lowered her down onto him. Not in pain, she thought in amazement, but in pleasure. He was so warm, so thick, and it felt so right that Cally wondered how on earth she'd never known it could be like this before. Before she had time to examine what that meant, her thoughts faded like a watercolour in the rain as he began to rock her slowly back and forward.

'Now you,' he breathed hotly, slowing his pace and encouraging her to set the speed. Cally hesitated and then slowly began to move, heat rising through her. Leon placed his hands on her bottom, watching her.

'Close your eyes.'

Cally felt her breathing grow faster as she increased pace, Leon suckling her breasts. An uncontrollable groan of pleasure broke from her throat. The sound shocked her into opening her eyes, and she slowed the pace fractionally.

'Let go,' he commanded.

'No, I…I don't know… I can't.'

'Yes, you can,' he replied forcefully, and she felt him shift slightly beneath her, reaching even deeper inside her, so deep, she felt her muscles contract around the hard length of him and the beginning of a new sensation that was so frighteningly powerful—like teetering on the edge of an unfamiliar precipice—that she didn't know what to do; she was afraid to let go.

'Now,' he urged, but still her eyes were squeezed tight. 'Damn you, I can't hold on!'

Cally felt his climax rip through him, saw the tendons in his neck go taut, felt his seed spill deep inside her, and…

It was only then, as she had been on the cusp of her very first orgasm, that she realised they hadn't used a condom.

CHAPTER SEVEN

HALF-WRAPPED in the maroon throw that covered the sofa, Cally felt instantly cold. No, cold was an understatement. She felt sub-zero, as though if she went anywhere near a thermometer the mercury would shrink in on itself and disappear altogether.

They hadn't used a condom.

She stared at the black restless sea outside the window, and then across at Leon, who lay by her side in a state of repose, thick-lashed eyes closed. How could they have been so stupid? They weren't a couple of naive teenagers, they were grown adults, for goodness' sake. He was a prince, for whom such basics had to be even more important than they were to the average male, and she was ordinarily so sensible that she never left the house without an umbrella and a packet of plasters. So why on earth hadn't either of them given a second thought to the small matter of protection?

Cally opened her mouth to share the burden of their irresponsibility, but just as she was about to speak a warning siren went off in her brain. *Protection.* She screwed up her eyes, their earlier conversation dropping back into her mind like bad news through a letterbox, her own words echoing back at her: *I don't need protection.*

Oh, dear God, he hadn't actually assumed that she'd meant the contraceptive kind, had he? No, he couldn't have. Perhaps Montéz was a pioneer of the male Pill and he hadn't thought to mention it. Or maybe, since he never intended to get married, he'd had the snip. Oh, who the hell was she trying to kid? She'd inadvertently led the most virile man she'd ever met to believe that she was protected, and it was a lie. And now there was every chance that his seed was already firmly rooted inside her.

Don't be so ridiculous, Cally, she reprimanded herself. *Whatever the movies would have you believe, the chances of getting pregnant after only one night are miniscule. Look at Jen—it took over a year of trying to get both Dylan and Josh. You're just a natural born worrier trying to punish yourself because for once in your life you acted a little recklessly.* Her eyes returned to Leon; his whole body was at ease in the aftermath of their lovemaking. What would be the good in telling him that he'd misinterpreted what she'd said? He'd probably laugh at her for being the faintest bit concerned. Either that, or he'd think she'd done it on purpose because she wanted to have his baby.

Cally untangled her legs and swung them over the edge of the sofa, horrified at the thought. Then she froze again. On some unconscious level, did she want his baby? Suddenly an idyllic image popped into her brain: Leon and her in the water teaching two children how to swim, a boy with dark blond hair like his father's, a girl with little red pigtails. Quickly, she forced herself to snap out of it. She didn't even like the man, and he no doubt took the same view of children as he did of marriage. Which was perfect, because she'd known for years that she was neither wife nor mother material, and that suited her just fine—even if at this precise moment she couldn't for the life of her remember why.

Because it allowed her to focus on her career, she recalled despondently, staring up at the paintings and then down at the rolled-up newspaper below them, remembering she had a whole other set of worries to occupy her mind on that front. Worries that were far more palatable than why she had never known making love could be that good until now, or why she wanted to crawl back into his embrace and stay there for as long as he'd have her.

Worries like whether she even still had a job, she thought, abruptly realising that she was still *sans* clothes, and that if she didn't think fast she was not only in serious danger of being fired but of being fired in the nude. The horrifying thought spurred her into action, and she quickly slipped from the sofa to locate her clothes, not noticing the way Leon's nostrils flared in arousal as he watched her dismiss the complicated hooks and ribbons of her underwear and throw on the dress without it.

Cally tiptoed across to where the newspaper lay pitifully beside the fallen lamp and picked it up. She took one more look at the offending page and then folded it away, trying not to think about how much she still wanted to scream at him for being so unreasonable. She understood now that it would do her no good.

Leon watched through heavy-lidded eyes as she reacquainted the light with its shade. Her hair was mussed from their lovemaking, her expression so misty-eyed that he was reminded of the first time he had seen her at the preauction. It seemed strange that he should be reminded of the moment he had suspected her of being the kind of woman to cloud things with emotion, when she had come to him dressed to seduce. It was perfectly obvious that it had all been an act, that what she really wanted was the kind of no-strings affair she was no doubt accustomed to. After all, why else would she be on the Pill, or have casually got up to retrieve her dress, instead of trying to embrace him afterwards, the way emotional women always did?

It didn't please him as much as it ought to have done. Instead it made him wonder, irrationally, how many men she had gone to like that, straddled and used the sum of her obvious feminine wiles to get her own way with? Yet she hadn't climaxed. For the first time in his life he was struck by a momentary fear of sexual inadequacy, but he dismissed it just as quickly. She had been about to come, and she had fought it on purpose. In some attempt to show him that she was in control? he wondered angrily, irritated that he hadn't been able to hold off his own orgasm.

'I will speak to Jen first thing in the morning, make sure she understands the paintings should never have been mentioned,' Cally said quietly, feeling his eyes upon her. 'And you have my word that I will never find myself in danger of breaking your law again.'

A shadow darkened his face at the note of disapproval in her voice. 'It's not *my* law. The royal family of Montéz has always been forbidden territory to the press. And with good reason. Being followed around like the stars in some hideous reality TV show can only interfere with our work on the island.'

'But your brother—'

'My brother upheld exactly the same law until he met Toria.'

Cally raised her eyebrows and looked directly into his eyes for the first time since she had moved away from the sofa, disturbed as much by the discovery that a reasonable principle lay behind the law as by his glorious nudity. 'She got him to change it?'

'In a word, yes.' It didn't cure the look of curiosity on Cally's face. Leon drew in a short, frustrated breath, not sure why he felt so impelled to explain. 'Toria came to Montéz to star in a low-budget movie one summer when I was serving in the Marine Nationale. She had no talent, but she was desperate for fame and incredibly attractive. When she heard that the Crown Prince favoured a low profile over celebrity status, she thought it was preposterous and decided to seek him out. Girard was fifteen years her senior, lonely and flattered.'

He made a pattern with his fingernail on the arm of the sofa, not looking up. 'By the time of my next visit home, she had convinced him to marry her, and by the time of the wedding she had persuaded him that the media exposure was vital to her career. Which wouldn't have been so detestable if she had accepted even one role after he had given her the exposure she craved. She told him she was waiting for the right part, whilst all the time dragging him to photo shoots for magazines, movie premieres, A-list parties. All the time Montéz was suffering, and Girard was growing more and more exhausted. Eventually it came to a head.' Leon's expression turned as dark and foreboding as the night outside the window. 'They had been invited to a high-profile awards ceremony in New York on the same day as the private memorial service held annually to mark the anniversary of our mother's death. Toria demanded he go with her.' He looked stricken with guilt. 'I told him I would never forgive him if he did.'

'He went with her,' Cally breathed, recalling that the tragedy had taken place in the States.

'No. He decided to try and do both.' Leon gritted his teeth, remembering that, for all his faults, Girard's peace-keeping skills had been second to none. 'Toria went ahead without him. He stayed for the memorial, vowing to meet her at the awards ceremony as soon as he could. And he would have made it—but he fell asleep at the wheel on the stretch between JFK airport and the auditorium.' Leon's eyes glazed with pain. 'When Toria called to give me the news, all she could ask was why he hadn't been using a chauffeur.'

'I'm sorry,' Cally whispered, wanting to tell him not to blame himself, seeing in his eyes that he did. 'I had no idea.'

'Very few people did. Toria adored the press, and the press adored her. After his death everyone wanted to interview the poor, grieving widow.' He gave a bitter, broken laugh. 'It was the best performance of her career.'

Cally could only imagine what it must have been like to deal with that in every newspaper and on every news channel, having just lost his brother and been thrust into the role of prince. 'So you reinstated the law?'

She saw him hesitate, and instantly his expression became shuttered. 'It was around that time, yes.'

'And Toria?'

'Never forgave me for denying her the media circus here in Montéz. So she moved to New York. She still turns up occasionally with a mouthful of idle threats.'

'I'm sorry,' Cally repeated, understanding now why he had automatically assumed that she wanted to use her work here to feed off his fame, that she had planned the article. Somehow, the revelation made her feel even closer to him than she had done when they'd been making love. She looked down at the newspaper she was still holding and clutched it tighter. 'And I meant it when I said that nothing like this will ever happen again.'

She didn't see Leon's gaze drop to her hand, the look of distaste which shaped his mouth, as if he was a soldier who'd just realised he was inadvertently fraternising with the enemy. 'Good,' he replied, reaching for his jeans. 'Because as my mistress I require your absolute discretion.'

Cally's head jerked up in disbelief. 'Your *what?*'

'My mistress,' he said in a clipped tone which suggested he found having to repeat himself an inconvenience.

She stared at him in horror, suddenly feeling like a trapeze artist who thought she'd caught the bar in her hands but was suddenly plummeting towards the ground. 'And when exactly did I agree to be that?'

Leon shook his head. She *had* to be kidding. Surely she didn't expect him to buy the holier-than-thou charade now? 'I rather think your actions did the talking, don't you? Unless you're going to tell me that that little outfit and those moves are all part of some new and innovative conservation technique.' He dropped his head to one side. 'Although, it was certainly revitalizing, I'll give you that.'

The rant she'd been preparing collapsed under the weight of hurt and shame. 'No wonder you insist on never being quoted in the press. You're so crude, your people would question your royal blood.'

For a second an acute sharpness, almost a wince, cut across his face—but then as fast as it had come it was gone.

'I thought you liked your men to tell it like it is. Don't tell me sex has made you sentimental?'

'Hardly.' Cally turned away, fighting the tears that pricked behind her eyes.

'Then I suggest you spare me the lecture and come and have something to eat.'

'I'm not hungry.'

'Really?' he goaded. 'Or is it simply that you can't swallow that I was right all along?'

'Right about what?'

'That you only accepted this job because you wanted to go to bed with me.'

Cally's hurt caught fire, transforming into white-hot fury. 'Is your ego so gigantic that you can't accept that after years studying art restoration, and months of preparing to work on the paintings before we even met, that maybe *they* were the reason?'

'Of course I can accept that, *chérie*. All women who forge a career do so with gusto until they get whatever it is they really want. Fame, sex, whatever. Now you have sex, you may drop the pretence.'

'So, because your brother's wife was a manipulative bitch who wasn't interested in having a career once she'd seduced your brother, in your eyes the entire female population is guilty of the same crime?'

Leon raised one derogatory eyebrow at her hackneyed analysis. 'On the contrary, I've based my assumptions entirely on you. You'd barely touched the paintings before this little—how would you like me to phrase it delicately for you?—episode. And I hardly think touching *them* is your top priority now.'

Cally averted her eyes as he looked down at his body, as if he was remembering where she had trailed her hands, her lips. Why the hell had he still not put on his flaming T-shirt?

'They *are* my only priority, they always have been. Every job takes a while to settle into. You employed me because I am the best person to do it, and I still am. I'm not some virgin priestess who's lost her gift because I've lain with a man!'

'Oh, I think we both know you're not that, Cally, don't you?' he said silkily, his gaze raking over her with renewed desire. 'Just like I think we both know that your being capable of the job is only half the reason I employed you.'

'What?' Cally felt her whole body tense.

With a look of unconcern, Leon reached for his T-shirt. 'Don't sound so surprised, Cally. Do you suppose I employed you, despite the fact that you proved yourself indiscreet in London, purely because of your skills? I employed you for the same reason that you accepted— because we both knew that the sex between us would be *incroyable.*'

Cally wouldn't have thought it possible that her body could wind itself any tighter, but it did, so tight she felt faint. Clamminess broke out at the nape of her neck, between her breasts, behind her knees, heat pouring over her in a wave. It *had* been incredible, and it was incredible that he thought so too. But after everything she had worked for, fought for, clung to... He had only given her the job because he wanted to have sex with her? Cally felt sick. She had supposed there was no greater blow than the gallery losing the paintings that night at the auction, believed there was nothing more mortifying than his subsequent rejection, then discovering that he had lied. But this was even worse.

'I hate you.'

For a second Leon looked slightly taken aback. Only for a second. 'And yet you still desire me.' He shook his head condescendingly. 'Reason is always at such a disadvantage when paired with that.'

'Not any more,' she answered, willing it to be true. 'We shared an attraction, and we saw it through to its natural conclusion, but—'

'So that was the euphemism you were looking for.' He nodded slowly, as if she were one of a new species whose peculiar habits he was coming to learn. 'Attraction, natural conclusion…'

'But now it's over,' she concluded abruptly, catching sight of the Rénards. 'So, if you will just kindly confirm whether I may continue with my work…?'

'Do you really suppose that our shared *attraction* is something that has ceased to exist because we have given into it once?' He stalked across to where she was standing. 'Desire is an animal. We set it free, it cannot be tied up again.'

It can be, Cally thought. *It has to be.* She bit her lip, her mind traitorously filling with the erotic image of Leon tied up.

'Well, I'm sorry to disappoint you, but I think the animal has run off,' she said, so loudly that she gave herself away.

Leon laughed, the sound so deep and low it sent a vibration through her body. 'You still want to pretend you don't feel it, *chérie?* Be my guest, continue with your *work.* I give you a week at most before you're begging me to take you again, because if I don't you'll die of longing.' He stopped at the door, one eyebrow cocked. 'Unless, of course, you want to be done with the whole pretence and join me for dinner right now?'

'Like I said, I'm not hungry.'

'Of course you're not,' he mocked. 'Just like you

weren't thirsty that night in London.' And with that he
turned on his heel and left her once more.

Over the next few days Cally did everything she could to
forget how it had felt to make love to Leon Montallier. She
tried to excuse away that night as a single moment of reck-
lessness she had simply been due for a while, like last
February, when she'd got a sore throat and had conceded
that she couldn't go any longer without succumbing to a
winter cold. She relabelled her desire for him as nothing
more than curiosity about his body which had now been
satisfied. But, no matter how hard she tried, it was impossible not to think about the incredible way he'd made her
feel, about the sensations which she'd never experienced
before in all of her twenty-six years.

   Which ought to have been crazy, because she wasn't a
virgin. Yes, she might have only ever slept with one other
man, but sex was sex, wasn't it? No, Cally thought, apparently it wasn't. What she'd just experienced with Leon had
felt like exactly the kind of lovemaking she'd read about,
whereas with David… Well, from the very first day he had
talked her into it, she'd never really enjoyed their forays
in the bedroom department. They had been rushed, uncomfortable, and had always left her feeling somehow inade-
quate—not least on the night when she had finally plucked
up the courage to ask him if they could try kissing a bit
more first, because she wasn't sure it felt exactly the way
it was supposed to for her. He had told her not to be so
absurd, and that if she didn't like it as it was then she was
obviously just lacking the right gene.

   In her naivety, she had always supposed she did lack
something. Now she understood that she had simply been

lacking the right sexual partner. But 'right' only in *that* sense, she thought grimly; Leon might have altered her perception on sex, but he'd confirmed that Prince Charming only existed in fairy tales. Which was why she had to forget him and get on with the paintings.

It felt a little like trying to push rocks through a sieve— never more so than during the hours in which he insisted on silently watching her work, as if it was an endurance test he was waiting for her to fail—but slowly, slowly, she began to make progress. In fact, after she had completed the cleaning of the first painting and begun work on the infill, she almost felt her old focus return. Almost, because to her surprise she found that, on the few occasions she became completely absorbed in the paint work, she would find herself drifting off into thoughts about two things in particular, neither of which were things she might have expected to find herself thinking about.

The first was that she was repeatedly and inexplicably struck with a burning desire to begin working on a painting of her own, to the extent that one afternoon, when she'd known she had the palace to herself, she had begun sketching the remarkable view from the studio window onto a piece of spare canvas. She didn't have the faintest idea why, because she hadn't painted anything of her own since her split from David, and it seemed incomprehensible that she should do so now when she was finding even her conservation work a struggle, but something impelled her to.

The second distraction was Leon, but not in the sexual way that haunted her whenever she closed her eyes. When she was busy on the paintings what she'd catch herself thinking about most frequently was the conversation they'd had immediately after their lovemaking, when he had told her about his brother. And to Cally that seemed even harder to forget. Aside from Leon revealing that his insistence against media attention wasn't just a dictatorial whim, she couldn't help wondering if it was significant that he, the man who insisted on such confidentiality, had told her something so private about his family. But, just as quickly as such thoughts came, she would dismiss them. After all, he had followed it up with the assumption that she would become his mistress, for goodness' sake, and it didn't come much more meaningless than that. Besides, even if they had been in some parallel universe and his *doppelgänger* had declared it was significant, she'd walk away anyway. Wouldn't she?

Cally's eyelids fluttered down to meet her cheeks in a moment of mortification as she envisioned turning back and walking willingly into his arms. But that was just because in the parallel universe he'd be the complete opposite of who he was, not a heartless prince, not a lying bastard, she told herself at the exact moment he entered the room, sending a shiver of awareness down her spine.

'I'm actually on a really tricky bit. Do you mind not watching today?' she said quickly without turning around.

'You mean I'm in danger of distracting you?' he drawled.

'Not specifically you—anyone,' Cally lied, only hoping he hadn't guessed that when he watched her it felt like every movement she made was being magnified and projected on the wall for his scrutiny.

'If you say so. As it happens, I've only come to tell you that Kaliq and his fiancée will be joining us for dinner this evening, so you'll need to be ready by eight.'

Cally blanched. When they had been unable to make it on Saturday she'd known he planned to reschedule, but it hadn't occurred to her again since… Since he'd made it clear that asking her to join them last time had had nothing to do with her expertise and everything to do with wanting her to become his mistress.

'Actually, I planned to begin work on the nude this evening. I'm almost finished on this one.' They both turned to the first painting, as surprised as each another to see that the restoration work was almost complete, and the difference it made was breathtaking.

'Well, then, it seems the perfect place to stop, does it not?'

'All the same, I'd rather not join you for dinner.'

'Then it's a good job it's not optional, then, isn't it?'

Cally glowered at him. 'Since I declined the generous offer of becoming your mistress, I rather think it is up to me when and with whom I dine.'

'Not if it is a requirement of your job, which, for your information, is the capacity in which I require you to be there.'

'Really? Since my job is only to restore and conserve art, am I to assume that the prince is bringing a painting with him that you'd like me to take a look at between courses, perhaps?'

'Kaliq does not share my passion for art,' he growled.

'Then how can my joining you for dinner possibly be in the capacity of work?'

'The meeting is part business, part pleasure.'

'Well, then, why do you need me when you're the expert on combining the two?'

A cloud settled over his features. 'Kaliq and I have a trading treaty to discuss, but I also wish to toast my acquisition of the paintings.'

'Like a new Ferrari or a penthouse in Dubai,' she said sarcastically. 'So I can't understand why you'd want me there to lower the tone.'

'That's because you have no idea how good you look in that green ensemble,' he ground out beneath his breath. 'But luckily your comprehension isn't a requirement. I am your employer, and I consider your presence tonight a necessary part of your work. And, since I am not asking you to do anything more unpalatable than have a world-class meal in more than amicable company, I cannot comprehend *your* objection. Unless, of course, you are worried that you might not be able to keep your desire tied up when you see me in a dinner suit.'

'God, you're arrogant!'

'So you *do* think you can keep it tied up?'

'Of course I—I have no desire for you!'

'Then we don't have a problem, do we? I will see you at eight. Oh, and wear the green dress, won't you?'

'Over my dead body.'

'Why, does it bring back too many memories?' He raised his eyebrows, daring her to say no.

She stared back, mute, furious.

'Good. Eight it is, then.'

CHAPTER EIGHT

RESISTING the urge to storm into her room and find out why the hell she wasn't ready yet, Leon paced the forecourt of the palace and turned his thoughts to his guests, whom Boyet had gone to collect from Kaliq's villa. After years of failing to convince his oldest friend to bring a female companion to Montéz, he could scarcely believe that tonight Kaliq would be accompanied by his future bride. Leon shook his head. Despite the law of Kaliq's homeland, which stated he had to marry in order to inherit the throne, Leon had never really believed that the cool and cynical sheikh would settle down. In fact, when he had first received word of his engagement, Leon had dismissed it as rumour. Then, when Boyet had confirmed it, he had supposed that in the wake of his father's ill health duty must have forced Kaliq to find a docile Qwasirian bride. So discovering that his choice was in fact a British model had filled Leon with both surprise and concern. A concern which on second thoughts was unnecessary, because Leon knew that Kaliq, unlike Girard, was an astute judge of character and would never marry a woman who wouldn't make a perfect queen and mother to his children.

Leon stopped pacing, wondering if the concern in his

chest might therefore really be for himself, for Montéz. No doubt before long Kaliq would have an heir to his throne. He drew in a deep breath, wondering how long he could go on ignoring his own duty—the duty which should never have been his, he thought grimly. What happened if Toria's body clock started ticking in the meantime? No, he thought, pacing the floor and wishing he had time to tear off his clothes and obliterate those thoughts in the ocean. She didn't have a maternal instinct in her body. It wouldn't happen, and he was only allowing it to bother him because for the past three days he'd been driven wild by her red-haired equivalent.

Cally. Leon's body tightened beneath the tailored fabric of his suit at the thought of her. The rational part of his brain warned him that she was every bit as conniving as his sister-in-law—and ought to be just as unappealing. Except in his mind they couldn't be further apart. Toria had offered herself to him on a plate more times since Girard's death than he cared to remember, but he found the thought of her about as desirable as walking into the web of a black widow spider. Yet Cally…

How many times over the past few days had he gone into that studio and had to leave because if he'd stayed a moment longer he would have ripped the damned paint-brush out of her hand and kissed her until she begged him to make love to her again? So many times he wished he could forget. Was it some kind of elaborate game to ensure his surrender to her was total, helpless? If it was, then it was futile. No matter how many cold showers it took to keep his permanent state of semi-arousal at bay, he would be patient, and he would have her on *his* terms. It was only a matter of time until she came to him again and admitted that he was what she had wanted all along. And, if her resistance to this evening's meal had been anything to go by, it would be soon.

'Sheikh A'zam and Miss Weston are here, Your Highness,' Boyet announced, heading towards him.

'Thank you. Right on time.'

It was a shame he couldn't say the same about Cally, Leon thought, his nostrils flaring.

Cally stared at the jade green dress hanging on her wardrobe door. He had her cornered. If she didn't go to dinner, not only would she miss the opportunity to share her work on the paintings, and be placing her job in jeopardy for a second time, but he would also deduce it was because she thought herself incapable of resisting him. The dilemma with the dress was just as bad. Wear something else, and he'd know it meant something to her. Wear it as he'd demanded, and she might just as well have agreed to become his mistress. But then he'd chosen everything in her wardrobe anyway, she thought sullenly.

Aware that she had been cutting it fine when she'd left the studio at seven-thirty, and that she'd now been staring at the dress for what felt like an age, Cally glanced at her watch. Seven fifty-five. She tried to ignore the usual sense of horror she felt at the prospect of making anyone wait on the rare occasions she was late. So what if she was late for him? He could hardly get annoyed that she had been working late to finish the restoration of the first painting for his guests to see. But it would be mortifying to make *them* wait, Cally thought suddenly, grasping for the dress. After all, they were what this whole evening was about. He wasn't even part of the equation. All she had to do was remember it.

* * *

'Ah, Cally.' Leon turned to watch her descend the stairs with a sardonic expression. 'You decided to join us.'

'I wasn't aware I had a choice,' Cally hissed under her breath, before smiling broadly at his guests, grateful to have an excuse to take her eyes off of the disarming sight of him in his navy dinner suit.

'May I introduce His Royal Highness Sheikh Al-Zahir A'zam, and his fiancée, Miss Tamara Weston. Kaliq, Tamara, this is Cally Greenway.'

'It's a pleasure to meet you,' Cally said genuinely as she shook their hands, grateful that, although the sheikh was just as regal as she had imagined, and Tamara was stunning in an evening gown of mesmerising coral, they weren't the least bit disparaging towards her.

'Do you live here on Montéz?' Tamara asked her amiably as they took their seats at the antique dining table.

'I am just working on the island at the moment—'

'Cally is living here at the palace,' Leon interrupted. 'One of her many talents is restoring fine art. She is working on some paintings I purchased in London.' He looked directly at Kaliq. 'Rénard's *Mon Amour par la Mer.*'

Cally stared at him, so incredulous that he had cut her off that she didn't notice the significant look which Kaliq gave him in return. 'Congratulations, Leon. You must be very pleased.'

'It sounds fascinating. I'd love to see,' Tamara added, too polite to show that she had noticed Leon's rudeness.

'I'd be delighted to show you,' Cally replied, before Leon halted any elaboration on her part by bombarding Tamara with questions about their stay on the island, and cracking open the champagne to celebrate their engagement. And who could blame him? Cally thought as a plethora of palace staff she'd never seen before brought in platters of meats, cheeses, olives and fresh bread. Although Leon spoke to Tamara with appropriate respect, he was no doubt as captivated by her beauty as any man would be.

As captivated as you are by him, Cally thought despondently, unable to stop her eyes from straying to his mouth, or the lance of jealousy which jabbed at her heart.

'You must be used to exploring different countries by yourself?' She made the effort to chip into the conversation as Tamara mentioned that she had visited the university today whilst Kaliq had been working.

She nodded. 'I don't get as much time as I would like to explore when I am on a shoot abroad, but I don't mind travelling alone.'

'It sounds very exciting,' Cally replied with genuine admiration, trying to feel inspired by the possibilities that might await her once she had finished the Rénards. The kind of opportunities she'd spent a lifetime dreaming about but which suddenly seemed to have lost their appeal, she thought bleakly. She wondered how much longer she could go on pretending that was what she wanted when, in spite of all the reasons why she shouldn't, all she really wanted was for Leon to make love to her again more than she had ever wanted anything in her life.

'It can also be very dangerous.' Kaliq cut into the conversation. 'Naturally, once we are married Tamara will give up work, so it shall cease to become a concern.'

Cally registered the triumphant look on Leon's face and hated him for it. She could just imagine him adding Tamara's name to the list in his mind which proved that women only troubled themselves with a career until they

secured themselves a position as a mistress or a wife. But
he was wrong. She might have only just met them both, but
it was obvious that the desert prince had only said that
because he cared for Tamara with such a passion he couldn't
bear the thought of her being at any kind of risk. And she
only had to take one look at Tamara's less-than-impressed
expression to know she would never let her future husband
stop her if she chose to continue with her career.

What would it be like to be here because she mattered
to Leon the way Tamara mattered to Kaliq? Cally thought
hopelessly as the conversation moved on to discussing the
forthcoming wedding. What would it be like to have a man
love you so deeply that he wanted to spend his life with
you, and who actually cared, not just about having you in
his bed, but about your safety and well-being?

She didn't have a clue, and for the first time since David
had quashed her dreams she couldn't think of anything
worse than never finding out. But they were just childish
dreams, she reminded herself as she pushed the main
course of duck around her plate, and that was why she'd
given them up. So why did it seem so difficult to go back
to accepting that she was destined to be alone, the way she
had been before she'd met him?

Because he had made her aware of the gaping hole in
her life, she thought wretchedly as she watched him speak
animatedly about the international trading treaty with
Kaliq, shamefully aware that, though she had spent the
past few days telling herself to forget how it had felt to
make love to him, tonight she was failing more spectacularly than ever.

She drew in a ragged breath. If she gave in now she
may as well toss her self-respect out with the trash. *He*

wants you as a mistress, nothing more, she repeated in her mind. *And you don't even like him.* But as she listened to him chatting about his plans for the university, for cutting taxes, for strengthening the links between Montéz and Qwasir, even disliking him was getting more difficult. She had turned up here believing that, like David and the rest of his moneyed family, the ruler of Montéz was a snob who didn't care about anyone but himself. But there was no denying that Leon had his people's best interests at heart and that, palace and paintings aside, he also seemed remarkably frugal for a billionaire. Apart from one cleaner and the additional staff he had called upon tonight, Boyet seemed to be his only aide, and his pleasures, like diving out at sea, were equally simple. So how was she supposed to focus on hating him when the reasons for doing so were getting fewer by the second?

Because, prince among men or not, the stonking great reason remains: he only wants you to warm his bed. And if you give in to your desire now what does that say about you? That you have no pride, she answered inwardly. *Or you're so delusional that, in spite of all the evidence, you've started to believe in the fairy tale again.*

Either way, Cally knew that to give in to her desire would be to set herself up for a fall, but that didn't make it any easier to step away from the edge. Her whole being seemed attuned only to filling the gaping hole he had opened, she realised as she cracked open the hard layer of caramel on her crème brûlée and stole a glance at him. And she was unable to stop herself from wondering whether, when he looked at Kaliq and Tamara, their evident love for one another made him aware of a missing link in his own future too.

'Thank you, Leon, that was delicious.' Tamara's words made Cally snap out of her lust-induced daze.

Leon turned to Tamara. 'I hope you will persuade Kaliq not to leave it so long between visits in future.'

Tamara nodded.

'So long as you promise to visit Qwasir soon so that we can return the favour,' Kaliq added.

'What an excellent idea,' Leon said, eyeing Cally with increased hunger as he imagined making love to her in the sultry climes of the desert. 'Now, you must forgive us, but I find that tonight *I* am now somewhat exhausted.'

Leon, exhausted? Cally had no idea what he was playing at, but she knew that was impossible. She'd seen him get back from a fourteen-hour day of negotiations on the mainland only to dive straight into the ocean. Not that she had been watching out of her window to see when he got back or anything, she argued inwardly, then wondered who on earth she was trying to kid.

'I thought perhaps Sheikh A'zam and Tamara would like to see the paintings before they leave.'

'Well, that will be an additional incentive for them both to return.' Leon smiled through clenched teeth.

'But—'

He signalled over her shoulder for Boyet to bring the car round and shook his head. 'It won't be necessary, Cally, thank you.'

Cally could barely hide her fury as the two princes embraced and all four of them exchanged farewells, before Leon accompanied Kaliq and Tamara down the steps amidst well wishes for their nuptial plans.

When he returned she was standing at the top of the steps, hands on her hips.

'So you're done with even pretending my presence here tonight had to do with work? The boast that the Rénards were yours might have been enough of an ego boost for you, but surely the least you could do was have me show them to your guests? But, no, you bundle them away before it's even eleven o'clock. I'm not sure I've ever met anyone so rude.'

'There will be another time. I don't consider it rude when two people can't keep their hands off each other and clearly want to be alone.'

Cally smarted, forced to concede his insightfulness. 'They did seem very much in love.'

Leon looked her straight in the eye. 'I wasn't talking about them.'

She flushed crimson and broke his gaze. 'Then you have not only acted without manners but you have also misread this situation.'

'Have I?' he breathed, taking a step so disturbingly close that she had to shut her eyes to block out the sight of him. Except she could still sense him there, smell that unmistakable musk, which tonight was mixed with a citrusy cologne.

'Yes, just like you read everything wrong! That look on your face when Kaliq said that Tamara was giving up work—you think it proves your archaic theory about women using their career until they ensnare a man, then giving it up the second they've succeeded, but you're wrong. Kaliq simply cares about her safety.'

'So now you think you know my oldest friend better than me?'

'Don't you think it's possible for two people with their own careers to meet, fall in love and marry?' Cally cried, wondering whether she was asking the question of him or herself.

Leon gritted his teeth. There was that word again:

marriage. The one she allegedly loathed as much as him. *Allegedly.* 'Do you want me to say yes so that you have something to dream about, *chérie?*'

'I just—' Cally exhaled deeply. 'Aren't you ever worried the endless line of women will come to an end? That you'll end up alone?'

His face turned to thunder. 'Alone suits me fine.'

'I know.' She breathed deeply, trying to focus on one of the regal gold buttons on his jacket, and willing her feet to walk her away from him. But as she raised her eyes to his impossibly handsome face, bathed in the soft lights from the palace, her pride somehow felt like an inevitable sacrifice. Her fight had already gone—left at the bottom of her glass in the Road to Nowhere, lost down the back of the sofa in the studio, gone from the palace with Tamara and Kaliq.

Her voice was a whisper. 'I know, and I thought it suited me too. But I don't want to be alone tonight.'

CHAPTER NINE

IT SEEMED that admitting he couldn't bear to be alone even for one night was too much to ask of Leon Montallier. But, though Cally was well aware that her track record for reading the opposite sex was abysmal, she couldn't shake the feeling that his expression said it for him. In fact, if she hadn't known better, she would have sworn from the grim set of his mouth that she'd just stumbled upon his Achilles' heel. But, as he lightly brushed his hand down her side and resolutely scooped her up into his arms, all she knew was that he wanted her body with the same voracious need that she wanted his, and suddenly that felt like the only thing that mattered.

'This time we're going to do this properly,' he instructed her huskily as he carried her back into the palace and up an unfamiliar spiral staircase.

Unfamiliar, because this was the staircase that led to the master bedroom. Where, unlike in the studio, there could be no more pretending that this was somehow to do with the paintings, no more conveniently imagining that he was just an ordinary man, a diver in the Marine Nationale. He was the sovereign prince, and this was his palace. Perhaps it ought to have felt terrifying, yet somehow, as they entered the room with its stained-glass windows and four-poster bed, it felt utterly liberating. It was as if she'd had an internal pair of scales which she had been trying desperately hard to balance ever since she had arrived and finally she had let them tip. But, rather than the disaster she had felt sure would assail her, she felt a great surge of relief.

'I've been wanting to do this all night,' he breathed, lowering his head and releasing her just enough for her feet to touch the gold-and-aquamarine rug, whilst keeping her so tightly pressed to him she could feel the lines of his suit imprinted on her body through the thin fabric of her dress.

'Just all night?' she whispered against his lips, so provocatively that for a moment she wondered whether she was possessed by the spirit of some other woman, a woman who wasn't convinced that any minute now she'd lose her nerve, a woman who was confident—sexy, even. She realised that, without being wholly conscious of it, every time he touched her she became that woman. A woman she didn't recognise, but who she had always wanted to be.

'What do you think?' he bit out raggedly, answering her with an urgent, drugging kiss and reaching behind her, cupping her bottom, then running his hand down the back of her thigh, balling the dress in his hand.

Cally kissed him back with equal need, snaking her arms behind his back, encouraging the jacket from his shoulders until it fell to the floor.

Leon broke away from her momentarily, his eyebrow quirked at the exact same angle it had been the day he'd walked into the studio brandishing the hacked-off fabric of her jeans. 'You know, I've never met a woman who has so little regard for designer clothes.'

'Is that such a bad thing?' she whispered.

'On the contrary,' he answered roughly, 'right now I find it a very good thing.' And before Cally knew what was happening he reached his hands inside the neck of the jade green dress and pulled, tearing the garment in half and leaving her standing there in nothing but her own plain black bra and knickers.

He eyed them with a puzzled expression. 'That's not the underwear I selected.'

'No,' Cally said, her tone cautious but not without a note of defiance. 'It's not.'

Ever since that night she had steered clear of the tempting drawer full of lingerie and had repeatedly laundered her own set of smalls, not only because they were more comfortable to wear during the day but because she'd decided they were far more likely to prevent her thoughts from wandering than the feel of lace against skin. *Wrong again,* a voice chimed inside her head, but as she caught his gaze sliding over her with lust-filled appreciation it couldn't have felt more right.

'Is it a problem?' she asked, slanting him a daring look as she watched his pupils dilate.

'That depends.' Leon took a step back, drinking her in. 'On what?'

'On how good the show is,' he answered huskily, extending his arm, and she realised that his step backwards had put him in reach of a CD player.

Her legs almost buckled as she heard the slow, familiar beat begin to fill the room.

'Mississippi in the middle of a dry spell...'

It couldn't be a coincidence; it was their song. No, that was far too sentimental. It was the song that had happened to be playing that night. But what was it doing on the CD player in his bedroom if it didn't mean something to him too?

'Don't tell me,' she whispered, trying to make her voice sound light, 'you and Kaliq often meet up in dodgy rock bars, and there's one in the centre of Montéz called *La Route à…*'

'*La Route à Nulle Part,*' he said slowly, sexily, a smile tugging at his lips as she attempted the French for Road To Nowhere. 'Almost. Either that, or for some reason I couldn't get the damned song out of my head and I had to hear it again.'

'And did it work?' Cally asked, trying not to tremble as she slowly began to move in time with the music.

Leon's throat went dry as he watched her. 'Did what work?'

'Did it help you get it out of your head?'

'No.'

Cally felt her heart turn over. She wanted to bottle that feeling—the helplessness in his voice, that one syllable which told her she affected him as deeply as he affected her—but she dared not let him see.

'It is a memorable song,' she whispered.

'Very, very memorable.' He nodded as she daringly slipped down one strap of her bra.

'Has anyone—' he cleared his throat, his voice coming out so low it was almost inaudible '—has anyone ever told you how sexy you are?'

'Once,' she smiled, remembering Leon's warm breath in her ear on the dance floor. Tonight she even believed it. So much so that somehow, she—bookish, bad-at-sex Cally—had the confidence to strip in front of him in his royal chamber.

'Then I think you need telling some more. Because you are the sexiest woman I've ever known.'

And I've known a lot, was the unspoken, implicit end

of that sentence. But she didn't care, because his words were so precious to her that tonight it felt like they were the only two people in the world.

'So would you like it if I did this?' she asked innocently, hooking her thumbs into the sides of her knickers.

'Mmm.'

'Or this?' Cally teased, sliding her hands back up her sides and behind her to the catch of her bra. His eyes were transfixed by the sight of her breasts strained against the thin fabric.

'I've changed my mind,' he said in a clipped voice, and for a minute Cally froze, terrified this was going to be a repeat of that moment in the taxi. But her fears vanished as he quickly closed the gap between them. 'I'm through with waiting.'

Without a moment of hesitation he raised one hand behind her and unclasped her bra, tossing it to the floor to join the tatters of her dress. Her knickers went the same way.

'Perfect,' he breathed, his fingers taking the same path up her body as hers had done until he found her full, heavy breasts.

'Not quite!' she cried breathlessly.

'No?' he murmured against her skin, trailing a line of kisses along the base of her throat, his lips a whisper away from taking her nipple in his mouth.

'No! No. I…I want you naked with me.' Her fingers moved to his shirt, fumbling with the buttons.

'*Now* you decide to be more careful, *chérie?*' he scolded.

Cally pulled back, and, comprehending what he inferred, shook her head with a thrill. But, just as she dropped her eyes to his shirt to ponder how, his hands had covered hers and they were ripping open his shirt, buttons flying in all directions until he was naked from the waist up, every inch of his torso revealed in all its golden glory.

Quickly he pulled her back to him so that her breasts were crushed against the hardness of his bare chest, and with equal speed she reached for the waistband of his trousers. In a second he had discarded them and was standing there in nothing but his dark navy boxers, which did nothing to hide his straining excitement.

But, if Cally had thought their mutual urgency was a sign that their lovemaking was to be as frantic as three nights ago, she was mistaken. As he led her towards the bed and slowly laid her down, she understood that when he'd said they were going to do this properly, he hadn't just meant that this time their lovemaking would take place in bed. Because, although she could see that his body was most certainly ready, his expression told her that he fully intended to explore her as if this was the very first time.

And in a way, as she watched him lick across her nipple with his tongue, the lines of his face taut with desire, it felt like it was. Because it was the only time she had ever truly given in to this kind of pleasure. It was as if until this moment her mind had always been a barren wasteland filled only with fears, but now in its place was a lush and tropical garden with no space for anyone but him. Him, the part of her she'd never known was missing, that she needed to complete her, to fill her.

'Leon!' She threw back her head as his fingers reached lower, dipping inside her. She squeezed her eyes tightly shut, riding the rhythmic sensation of his circling, intimate caress, reaching out to stroke her hand along his silky-smooth length, guiding it towards her. So hard, so virile…

Then suddenly her eyes flew open.

'What is it?' he bit out, afraid that she was going to choose this moment to have an attack of conscience.

'I—we need to use protection.'

Leon frowned. 'I thought you were on the Pill.'

Cally looked up at the ceiling, avoiding his gaze. 'I...I was, but...but, as I didn't expect to be here so long, I've run out.'

Leon shrugged, the momentary tension in his upper body released. 'No problem.'

As he reached across to the drawer of the bedside cabinet, Cally felt a hideous sense of shame wash over her. Not only because she had lied, but because his trust in her was so implicit that he hadn't thought to doubt her explanation for a second.

But as she felt the heat of his thighs parting her own, her mind returned to the tropical paradise, and she let go of her guilt. It was a misunderstanding that would have no consequence, an omission of the truth that he of all people would understand if it ever came to light. Which it wouldn't, she assured herself, as her body parted to welcome him.

Cally slid her fingers up his back and lost them in his hair, loving the feel of his body on top of hers as he entered her. She didn't have a clue how many perfect minutes passed as he moved slowly, assuredly, inside her, determined that they should both savour every second. She could see from the muscle in his jaw that he was fighting to keep his excitement on a leash, and she loved that most of all.

'Do you want to change position?' she asked, pretending she couldn't see that he wanted to up the tempo.

'No.' His voice was throaty. 'This time it's going to happen to you, and I want to watch.'

Once Cally might have blushed, tensed, vowed it was impossible—or possibly all three. Not tonight.

'Then take me a little faster,' she whispered.

Leon's eyes flared in pleasure as he did as she commanded. 'Tell me what else you like.'

'You,' she answered without thinking. 'Everywhere.'

Finding the only part of their bodies that wasn't already interlocked, Leon entwined her fingers with his, and if Cally had been clinging to one remaining sliver of control that was the moment she lost it. For with the tenderness of that gesture she gave in to the mounting sense of longing that felt like an intense pain but without any of the hurt, gave in to every exquisite stroke, each one more insistent than the last, like waves against a breakwater about to give way.

She heard a moan escape from her mouth, low, insistent, infused with pleasure. She felt him grow even harder within her at the sound, and then completely withdraw before deliciously filling her with a thrust that was thick and fast.

'Oh God!'

Cally felt the imaginary breakwater give way as every inch of her body was flooded with an exquisite heat, all-consuming, astonishing. The tide drew back and then washed over her again in a flurry of aftershocks as Leon cried out, reaching the height of his own pleasure just seconds after her own.

He'd been holding off, she realised, had wanted her to come first. It could have been to prove his own prowess, or to demonstrate that any restraint on her part was a thing of the past. But right at that moment as she lay locked in the circle of his arms she believed it was simply because he wanted her to know that pleasure. A pleasure she had never dreamed she was capable of reaching. Whatever happened, she would always be grateful for that.

'Thank you,' she whispered, shifting her body to his side, though her arm remained slung across his chest.

'You're welcome,' he smiled. 'I'm glad I managed to persuade you to give in to it.'

She wasn't sure whether he was talking about her desire for him or her orgasm. Perhaps it didn't matter.

'It was my first.'

Leon blinked in astonishment, observed the slash of colour still high on her cheekbones and the faint surprise in her bewitching green eyes, and felt a surge of triumph accompanied by a slow dawning of something unpleasant he couldn't quite put his finger on. So she hadn't been holding back that first time to prove a point; she simply hadn't recognised the sensation or known how to let go. Which meant nothing, he quickly rationalised, refusing to revisit the thought which had momentarily flashed across his mind when he'd seen her modest underwear. Her usual encounters were probably one-night affairs after a quick fondle on a darkened dance floor, that was all.

'It can take time to get to know a sexual partner,' he said, too patronisingly for Cally's liking.

'If you are implying my sexual history consists of one-night stands, then you're mistaken.' She bristled, moving away from him and tugging the sheet around herself so that there was something more substantial than air between them. He was steering the conversation down a road she didn't want to take, but she couldn't bear the thought of him thinking that way about her.

Leon hesitated, as if unable to decide whether asking the question that hovered on the tip of his tongue was really such a good idea. 'Then perhaps you'd care to fill me in with the correct history.'

'Not really.'

'I am a modern man, Cally. The women with whom I choose to share my bed have inevitably had other lovers. It is not something which concerns me.' At least, usually it wasn't.

'Well, then, I'm afraid my sexual CV is going to be unimpressive in comparison,' she said quietly, not wanting to think about his other lovers, and at the same time wishing he did give a damn whether or not she was a complete whore or not. 'There was only one other man before you.'

Leon's eyes widened in shock, and then the blinding satisfaction of the revelation gave way to something far less palatable: the short stab of his conscience as the truth slotted into place. The day he'd seen her at the pre-auction, the plain underwear... She wasn't some practised seductress who had set out to ensnare him, she was as good as innocent. Suddenly he felt consumed with regret for the assumptions he had made, the wrong he had done her.

And, ashamed though he was to admit it, worst of all he supposed he had always known on some level that she was the sentimental kind. He had simply chosen to believe the opposite rather than stick to his own rule. The rule that, in spite of everything, he wanted to break all over again.

'So who was he?' Leon propped himself up on his arm and looked at her. 'A fiancé?' He paused. 'A husband?'

Cally shook her head. 'No, David was never in any danger of finding himself in either of those categories when it came to me.'

'But you hoped so?'

She nodded reluctantly. 'But I should have known from the start that I lacked the right credentials.'

Leon's mouth was a picture of disdain. 'How do you mean?'

'He was the son of an earl. I was working part-time on his father's estate. I don't know why I persisted in thinking that the difference in class between us was irrelevant. My parents, I suppose.' She gave a brittle laugh. 'They always told Jen and me that there were no barriers.' She shook her head. 'They were wrong. It was nothing more to him than an affair with a scullery maid would have been to one of his ancestors. I let him talk me into sleeping with him because he told me he loved me—and, worse, I let him talk me out of continuing with my degree because he said going it alone would make me a better artist. He lied. One of the other girls working there warned me that David shared his father's misogynistic views on women of a certain class trying to better themselves by getting too much education, but I thought she was just jealous. Until I left uni, turned up on his doorstep and found out that he had got himself engaged to an heiress without bothering to tell me.'

Cally looked up and, seeing from the look in his eyes that she was in danger of being at the receiving end of his pity, she continued quickly. 'So, do you always quiz women about their ex-lovers in bed?'

'Only when they tell me I am the first man to make them reach orgasm,' Leon answered, filled with a new and grim understanding.

'To bolster your ego?'

'Because it's a shame, Cally. Fantastic sex is like…art.'

'You mean everyone should enjoy it, like putting a great painting in a public gallery?'

'*Touché.*' He raised one eyebrow sexily. 'No. I mean the more you learn, the more you enjoy it.'

And the more likely you are to see weaknesses in the work of an inexperienced artist, Cally thought dismally, realising that if her lack of sexual expertise hadn't said it for her then her attack of verbal diarrhoea had just given the impression that she only ever slept with men who she saw as potential husbands.

'I was very young then,' Cally added quickly. 'When I thought I wanted to marry David, I mean. Of course, I was upset by what happened, but I realised very quickly that I was not cut out to be anyone's wife.'

Leon eyed her with a degree of scepticism. 'And yet you say you do not wish to be a mistress either. That makes for a very cold life, Cally.' He ran his hand over her bare arm. 'And, if you are planning on pretending that you are a cold person, don't bother, because we both know different.'

She had resigned herself to the fact that her life was destined to be cold, Cally thought, only now aware of how sad that sounded. But that was because she'd never known this kind of passion, a passion she knew she couldn't fight anymore even if it was destined to go nowhere.

She shook her head. 'No, I'm not going to pretend that. But nor do I want to downgrade my role of art restorer to mistress.'

Cally saw a nerve work at his jaw. 'I shall presume that was a slip of the tongue and you meant *up*grade.'

'Don't. I take great pride in working hard to earn my own living, difficult as that might be for *you* to comprehend. I don't want to toss it in so I can be at your beck and call, have you tell me what to wear and when.'

'So what is it you *do* want?'

Leon wondered if he had heard himself correctly. Since when did he conduct affairs where he invited a woman to lay down the ground rules? Never, he thought, looking at her fiery red hair spilling across his pillow. But then never before had he ever experienced a desire which felt like it would render him permanently debilitated unless it was appeased. Or been so conscious that here was the last woman in the world who needed a man riding roughshod over her a second time, he thought ruefully. Maybe it was breaking his own rule, but so long as she meant what she said about not wanting to be anyone's wife there was no problem, was there?

'I want to carry on working here—under the terms we have already agreed—and I want this…' She scrambled around for a word which described whatever 'this' was, and decided that there wasn't one. 'This sex between us to be something entirely separate. That isn't about anything other than mutual pleasure because the opportunity, whilst I am here, exists.'

'Just like I can dive into the sea because it is outside my back door?' Leon ventured.

'Exactly.' Cally nodded, not knowing why that made her heart sink, when having him agree to treat this as a pleasure they both chose to indulge in was far more preferable to being made to feel like a call girl on extended loan.

'Good,' Leon replied abruptly, having heard exactly the answer he needed. 'Then you shall work during the day and share my bed at night.' He made a show of picking up his watch from the bedside table. 'Which, if I'm not mistaken, still gives us another eight and a half hours.'

And with that he tossed aside the sheet and pulled her to him all over again.

CHAPTER TEN

WHEN Leon had compared fantastic sex to art, Cally hadn't considered it as anything other than a boast about his sexual prowess. But in the weeks that followed she couldn't help thinking that there was more to his statement than even he would have given himself credit for. After the physical abandon of that night, she felt fundamentally altered, as if up until that point her life had been the equivalent of a rather dull and dreary still life, and now he had splashed it with vibrant colour.

As bright and vivid as the underwater paradise beneath them, Cally thought happily as she lay flat on the deck of his boat after an hour just spent snorkelling, breathing in the scent of sun cream and feeling the droplets of seawater evaporate off of her skin. Although she had insisted that she would work during the day, and only share his bed at night, Leon tended to leave the palace early in the morning and return just after lunch, and since it suited her to work to a similar pattern their afternoons were invariably spent together.

Of course, they made love, sometimes in the studio, sometimes in his bedroom if they made it that far, sometimes even out on the terrace. But to her surprise Leon hadn't only wanted to indulge in sex. He had taken her across to the opposite hillside to show her the stunning site where Kaliq had chosen to build his villa, and then for a drive along the coast road with its magnificent cliff-top views. He had taken her down to the harbour with its lively market, to the central square with its endearing medieval church, and of course he had brought her out here to the ocean.

And Montéz had unquestionably captured her heart, Cally admitted, ignoring the nagging voice in her head which said *and that's not the only thing*. But, whilst she could get away with claiming that it was the natural beauty of the island which was responsible for inspiring her to work on her own painting whenever she got a spare moment, she couldn't deny that ceasing to fight her sexual appetite was responsible for the return of her much-missed focus on the restorations. In fact, she had made so much progress that after—how many weeks, three?—it wouldn't be many more days before they were completely finished.

But it wasn't until she'd spotted a missed call on her mobile and listened to the answer-phone message that morning that Cally had really faced facts and realised that she ought to start thinking about what she was going to do next—which went for her relationship with Leon too. The prospect shouldn't have felt like trying to remove a limpet from the bottom of his boat—after all, that night in his bedroom she had been heartened by the thought that their lovemaking would reach an enforced conclusion rather than waiting for his desire for her to wear thin—but it did.

Which was probably because in so many ways it didn't feel just like lovemaking anymore. For, even though she had resigned herself to the knowledge that theirs was a passion that was destined to go nowhere, in these past few weeks Leon had really opened up to her of his own accord.

He'd talked to her about his daily work at the university as they shared their evening meal; he'd told her about his time in the Marine Nationale. In turn she'd told him about her family and her degree, and they'd spent hours conversing about art, a subject upon which he had a knowledge more extensive than she would ever have imagined.

In fact, it felt pretty much like a real relationship in every way—except that their relationship was the one thing they didn't discuss, she thought, looking across at his beautiful body sprawled out beside her, his tanned chest glistening in the sunshine. Was it because, as far as he was concerned, it was already decided that the second she put down her paintbrush she'd be picking up her bags and leaving on the first plane home? He had told her himself that romance was in a Frenchman's blood, so perhaps this sex with added sentiment was just what you got with him, she thought dismally. Or was there a possibility that the reason he hadn't brought it up was because he didn't want her to go?

Not that it would change anything, even if he didn't, Cally quickly rationalised, because her career was what mattered first and foremost. So why did the answer-phone message, which ought to have had her jumping for joy, make her feel like she had been rudely awoken from the perfect dream?

'You know, I reckon it won't be much longer before my restorations are complete,' Cally said, trying to make her voice sound as blithe as possible.

Her words interrupted Leon's unruly thoughts. Thoughts which involved him rolling over and peeling down her black bikini top, which in his opinion had been on for far too long this afternoon, particularly now that the wet Lycra was beginning to dry in the coolness of the breeze and he could see the tight buds of her nipples that cried out for his mouth. Although on second thoughts it wasn't so much her words that had made that image vanish from his mind as her tone, which sounded offhand, as if the actual words were nothing but a code she expected him to crack. It was a tone he had never heard Cally use before, but ever since he had witnessed the starry look in her eyes that night Kaliq and Tamara had mentioned their forthcoming nuptials, ever since she had filled him in on her sparse sexual history, he had always feared she was in danger of adopting it. Had known too, that there was no way he was going to allow it to get to him, any more than he had any intention of allowing their lovemaking to come to an end. Yet.

'It hadn't escaped my notice.'

Cally rolled over, leaning on one elbow. 'So, will you be glad when I'm all done?'

His eyes remained closed. 'Of course. I cannot wait to see them both restored to their original glory.'

Cally hesitated. 'Me too. But I have to admit I shall be a little sad not to be working on them anymore, in that studio and—'

'Are you by any chance trying to induce me to ask you to stay on after you have finished, Cally?' Leon opened his eyes and challenged her with his piercing blue gaze. 'Because if you are may I remind you that *you* were the one who insisted that our lovemaking should only last whilst—how was it you delicately put it?—whilst your work on the Rénards placed us in close proximity to one another.'

Cally flushed, the previously pleasant heat of the sun now making her skin prickle uncomfortably. 'No, I— It just occurred to me this morning that I had finished them a little more quickly than I expected, that's all.'

'It's been a month, as you estimated.'

'A month?' Cally stared at him, dumbfounded. 'No, it can't have been.'

'Time flies when you're having fun,' he drawled, sitting up and drying his legs with a towel.

A month? A month in which they had made love pretty much every day, she thought, suddenly realising she hadn't had a period since before she had arrived. The heightened colour drained from Cally's face as she fished around in her mind for an explanation to quash her fears of the un-thinkable. Her periods were sometimes irregular, weren't they? And if anything was going to change a woman's cycle it was a different diet, a different climate from usual, wasn't it? Yes, that had to be it. In a couple more days, it was bound to arrive.

'Well, anyway, all I'm trying to say is that I hadn't given much thought to any future projects until I received a phone call from the Galerie de Ville in Paris this morning. They have just purchased a collection of pre-Raphaelite pieces and they are looking for an additional restorer to work with their existing team. The London City Gallery recom-mended me, and they want to meet to discuss whether I'd be interested.'

'Congratulations,' Leon replied gruffly. 'You should have said earlier. When's the meeting?'

'I don't know yet. As soon as possible, I think. I missed their call yesterday afternoon and I only picked up their answer-phone message this morning.'

'And you haven't called them back yet?'

'Not yet, no.'

Leon's momentary surprise evaporated. 'And why would that be, *chérie*? Because you wanted to ask me whether I thought it a golden career opportunity first? Surely not, for we both know that it is. Therefore you must be wavering because you wish to see whether I will offer you a more attractive alternative, *oui?*'

Cally flew to her feet. 'As if!' she shot out, terrified that was why she had wavered, that she had been willing to jeopardise her career for the sake of a man who felt nothing for her for the second time in her life. 'I suppose I just hoped you might show a little regret that our *affair* is inevitably reaching its end.'

'Inevitably? Why? Montéz is only ninety minutes away from Paris. You will have weekends, will you not?'

Cally's mouth dropped open. 'You mean... You wish it to continue?'

'Just because I do not ever wish to marry does not mean that I am not interested in extending a mutually pleasurable affair.'

He made it sound like their relationship was a library book he wanted to take out on six-week loan instead of three. Yet, wouldn't he end this now if she meant absolutely nothing to him? *Oh, don't be ridiculous, Cally. He'll end it eventually, so what's the difference?* Agreeing to let it continue could only prolong the hurt until the day he decided that he no longer found her satisfying. Which surely, if they were only to see each other at weekends, would be sooner rather than later for a man with a sexual appetite as insatiable as his. Unless, of course, exclusivity was not part of his offer in the first place, she thought with a start, feeling suddenly nauseous.

'And who will you make love to Monday to Friday, Leon?'

Leon's mouth twisted in disgust. 'You have my word that you will be the only woman sharing my bed.'

She stared at him, wanting to believe him, wanting to believe that it was possible to have a relationship and the career she loved, wondering if she even dared try. 'But why?'

Leon ran his eyes over her face. Her pale skin was flecked with light freckles brought out by the sunshine, the faint mark from her snorkelling mask was still visible on the bridge of her nose and her red hair was matted with seawater. It would have been easy to think to himself that her vulnerability was the reason, that she didn't deserve to be let down for the second time in her life, but the truth was that he had quite simply never seen anything so alluring and he didn't *want* her to go. Was it because she was the first woman who had come out on his boat like this? he wondered, trawling his mind for a logical explanation. No, there had been others, he recalled, surprised to find that his ex-lovers all blended into one faceless, nameless and frankly dull mass. But they had either demanded that he sail them across to St Tropez for lunch at a restaurant followed by an afternoon in the boutiques, or after a few minutes in the water had spent two hours below deck re-trowelling their make-up and ironing their hair. Yes, it had to be because he had never met anyone quite so appealingly *uninhibited* as she was.

'Because I've never wanted anyone as much as I want you,' he breathed, sensing her capitulation as he reached out his arm and dragged her towards him. 'And I'm not ready for this to end.'

Neither was she, she thought, forgetting all the reasons why this was a bad idea when he looked at her like that. And maybe, just maybe, if they both learned to trust, neither one of them ever would be.

'Then I hope you are not prone to dizziness, Leon,' she whispered.

'And why is that?'

'Because the first thing I want you to show me when you come and visit me in Paris is the Eiffel Tower.'

Leon paused. 'Maybe the second thing, *chérie*,' he said with a wicked gleam in his eye, before lowering his head to plunder her mouth.

Cally completed the restoration of the Rénards at lunch-time three days later. Standing back to admire them, she was overcome with a feeling quite unlike any other she'd experienced in her life. It always gave her a thrill to see a work of art restored exactly the way an artist had intended, but this transcended that; it was almost as if a part of her own personal destiny had been fulfilled.

She couldn't wait to show Leon. She looked at her watch. Twelve-thirty. He'd be back at two if not before. Which meant for the first time since that afternoon on the boat she had an hour alone to spare. Since there was still no sign of her period, she decided she really ought to take herself off to the pharmacy she'd spotted in the nearby village just to be sure it was just late and nothing more. That way, when she went to Paris to speak to the gallery tomorrow, at least she could go without any niggling concerns.

Unless of course the niggling concern turned out to be a full-blown worry-fest, she thought. She was still convinced she couldn't be pregnant when she felt absolutely no different from normal, aside from a little tiredness, which was probably due to the amount of time she spent making love to Leon or swimming in the sea. But what if she was? A slow and thoroughly unexpected warmth crept through Cally's body. She didn't know whether it was her buoyant mood or too much sun, but for some reason it didn't feel like something that would be a worry at all; it felt like it would be the most natural thing in the world.

Hearing footsteps approaching the studio door made a wide smile break out on her face. He was back early.

'Finished,' she said triumphantly. 'What *am* I going to do— Oh.'

Cally stopped mid-sentence as she turned round to discover the footsteps were not Leon's. On second thoughts she wasn't surprised, for she so rarely heard him enter, a trait she had come to associate with his natural diver's stealth. The feet belonging to the person who had entered, on the other hand, could not have been less subtle, for they were clad in bright-purple stilettos.

Cally took in the matching purple dress and blue-black hair which reached the woman's waist. A waist which she was sure would have ordinarily been no wider than the span of two hands, if she hadn't looked about five months pregnant.

'Can I help you?' Cally asked, raising her eyes to look at her face for the first time. Suddenly she realised that the woman she was looking at was Toria. Toria, whose face she recognised from the wedding photo that had graced every magazine cover the year she had married Girard. Toria, who, if Leon was to be believed, was nothing but bad news for a list of reasons as long as her hair. But he hadn't mentioned that she was expecting.

'I'm looking for Leo,' she purred, a look of disdain on her wide, painted mouth.

Cally flinched. 'You must be Toria.'

'And you must be his latest conquest.' Toria ran her eyes critically over Cally's paint-splattered outfit. 'How…

charitable of him. Now, where is he, out *there?*' She motioned towards the sea in disgust.

'He's not here at the moment. Actually, I'm alone, and I rather thought all the doors were locked. Do you mind me asking how you got in?'

'Keys,' she said, reaching into her oversized designer handbag and producing a bunch full. 'Don't look so surprised. This *is* my home. Or, should I say, *was.*'

Cally gritted her teeth. 'He's at the university. I have no idea what time he'll be back,' she lied, hoping to make her leave. She had no idea why Toria still had a set of keys, but Leon had said she only ever came back to Montéz to stir up trouble.

'Then I suggest you call him and tell him that I am here with some very important news.'

Cally was tempted to tell her what she could do with her suggestion, but she spotted the opportunity to forewarn Leon that she was here.

'Of course,' Cally replied with artificial sweetness. 'Do take a seat.'

Cally went into his office and dialled his mobile. It rang and rang but there was no answer. Skimming her eyes down a list of numbers on his desk, she found one for the principal's office at the university and tried that instead.

'*Bonjour.*'

Cally hesitated at the sound of the unfamiliar, accented voice. 'Um… *Je voudrais parler à Monsieur Montallier, s'il vous plaît.*'

The man on the other end of the phone clearly recognised her less-than-fluent grasp of French. 'This is Professeur Lefevre. The prince is not here, I am afraid. Can I help?'

'He has already left to return to the palace?' Cally asked hopefully.

'*Non, mademoiselle.* He has not been here today.'

'Oh.' Cally frowned, certain that he had told her he was expected there for the duration of the morning. 'So you haven't seen him at all since yesterday?'

'*Non,* you must be mistaken. I haven't seen him for at least…' Professeur Lefevre gave a considered pause. 'It must be three weeks at least.'

Her breath caught in her throat. 'Then I…I suppose I must have been mistaken. I'm sorry to have disturbed you.'

Cally continued to clutch on to the receiver long after he had hung up, her knuckles white. Leon had told her he had been at the university almost every day for the past month, but he hadn't been. She tried to tell herself it was no big deal. It was probably easier to say he was there than to go into details about his duties. But it grated on her. And now the woman he professed to hate had turned up with her own set of keys to the palace. She took a deep breath, trying to compose herself, remembering that their relationship was never likely to work if she was always so quick to distrust him. Plastering on a smile, she re-entered the studio.

'Men do have a warped idea of beauty,' Toria said, regarding the Rénards with a pinched look as Cally entered.

'Don't they,' Cally replied, looking right at her. 'I'm afraid Leon is otherwise engaged. For all I know, he could be hours.'

'Well,' Toria replied irritably, 'then I suggest, since I cannot be expected to wait around in *my* condition, that you give him a message.'

'Gladly.'

'Tell him I'm pregnant. With the heir to the throne.'

CHAPTER ELEVEN

CALLY stared at Toria aghast, dropping her eyes to the swell of her belly.

Pregnant. *With the heir to the throne.*

Her mind raced as she fought to process the information in some way other than a way which felt like a bullet tearing through her flesh. Toria had to mean that Girard was somehow the father, didn't she? But he had died a year ago, so that was impossible—unless via frozen sperm or IVF? No, she thought, his death had been too unexpected for that.

Cally lifted her eyes to the other woman's face, recalling how Leon had described her as 'incredibly attractive', how she had swung her own set of palace keys from her forefinger, purring his name. Suddenly Cally felt sick.

'Surely you don't mean that Leon…?' Her voice was scratchy, desperate.

Toria hesitated for a moment and then looked at her squarely. 'Yes. Leon is the father.'

Cally blanched and stumbled the short distance to the sofa, her whole body beginning to tremble. 'No. How?'

The other woman gave an acidic laugh. 'How? Surely I do not need to explain that to *you?* Leon Montallier is not an easy man to resist.' She shrugged. 'I made the mistake of believing that because I was his brother's widow he wouldn't set his sights on me unless his intentions were honourable. I was wrong.'

She paused for a moment, and then, seeing that Cally's head was safely buried in her hands, continued unreservedly. 'Afterwards I was so angry that I tried to go to the press, but he got there first. Thanks to his carefully engineered law, his pristine reputation on this island remains intact, just the way he planned it.'

Cally raised her head in horror.

'Oh, don't tell me, he spun *you* that line about reinstating the law to get on with his royal duties without the media circus as well?' Toria clicked her tongue scornfully. 'That was what the last one fell for. If I were you, I'd leave before he knocks you up and throws you out too.'

Cally closed her eyes, missing the malicious smile on the other woman's face.

'I'll bear that in mind,' she choked.

'Good,' Toria said, tossing her dark mane over her shoulder. 'And I trust you'll remember to give him my news. I'll see myself out.'

Cally gazed helplessly at a knot on the wooden floor of the studio. More than anything she had ever wanted in her life, she wanted to believe Toria was lying. She tried to think of her as the witch Leon had made her out to be, of her capacity for deceit. But the more minutes that ticked by the harder that seemed. She recalled the girl she'd worked with at David's father's estate, the one who had warned her about what he was really like, but who she had chosen to ignore. She couldn't help thinking that history was repeating itself—and that she really ought to have learned her lesson.

If Toria and Leon had been living here together after Girard's death, it hardly required a stretch of the imagination to envisage them falling into bed. And if he had romanced Toria the way he had romanced her, particularly under the delicate circumstances, it was no wonder that Toria had mistakenly assumed his intentions were honourable. Most of all it was remarkably easy to imagine his lust turning to disgust the second she'd attempted to sell her story. Cally had witnessed his anger when it came to the press herself.

And, though she knew Toria had taken a warped pleasure in telling her, even that only served to make her story seem all the more plausible. For she had exhibited exactly the kind of behaviour one might expect of a woman returning to an ex-lover with the news that she was carrying his child only to find another woman in her place.

Which could so easily have been her. Cally squeezed her eyes tightly shut, trying not to contemplate the unspeakable possibility that brought to mind.

What if they were both carrying his baby?

She felt the speed of her breathing double, the red of the sofa on which she sat and the blue of the sea outside the window starting to blur before her eyes as though she was spinning around on some garish purple fairground ride. She lay back, curling herself into a ball, threading her fingers through her hair to clutch at her skull, trying to block out everything.

But just as she was about to slip into the oblivion of unconsciousness she heard his voice.

'No wonder you're exhausted.'

It was soft and unbearably tender. Cally blinked and forced her eyes open. He was standing before the paintings, examining the final and most intricate part of her restoration with delight.

'It looks fabulous.'

She didn't move. 'I'm not exhausted.'

'No?' he queried, his eyes never leaving the canvas. 'In that case, how do you feel about celeb—?' He turned round and caught sight of her properly for the first time. 'What on earth's the matter?'

Cally pushed herself up on one arm, the blood rushing to her head. 'Toria was here.'

He visibly stiffened. *'Toria?'*

She nodded.

Leon looked incensed. 'What did she want?'

Cally took a deep breath. She was aware that she should probably tell him to take a seat, do this slowly. Aware, too, that it should never have been her news to tell. But above all, selfish though it was, she just wanted to get it out so that she could see his reaction—because she knew that alone would tell her everything she needed to know.

'She came to tell you that she's pregnant with your child.'

To her disbelief, he laughed. 'She has resorted to lies before to try and scare away any woman she sees as a threat, but this takes it to a whole new level. After everything I told you, I thought you'd know better than to believe a single word that comes out of her mouth.'

'It wasn't her words that convinced me,' Cally whispered brokenly. 'It was her sizeable bump.'

When she saw the look that came over Leon's face then, she would have given anything to have his cynical humour back. The blood shrank from his cheeks and his expression grew so taut that it looked as if his skin had been removed and stretched in order to cover the bones of his face. For the first time since they had met, she witnessed every last glimmer of sardonic amusement vanish from his eyes until there was nothing there but emptiness. It was the look which confirmed that everything she'd feared was true, and which banished Cally's last remaining shred of hope.

And that was the moment Cally knew that, if she had even one ounce of self-respect, she had to leave now. If nothing else, the entire stance of his body told her that the prospect of being a father was on a par to him with being told he had some horrible, degenerative disease. With it she understood that whatever she had started to believe about him opening up to her, human commitment of any form would always be unpalatable to him. She had to make sure *she* was not in danger of carrying his baby, and then she had to get on that plane to Paris and forget she had ever made love with the Prince of Montéz.

Slowly, on legs which felt like their muscles had disintegrated, she found the strength to stand.

'Where are you going?'

So she wasn't completely invisible. 'To Paris.'

'Your flight doesn't leave until tomorrow.'

She stared at him aghast. Surely he didn't actually expect her to stay? 'Under the circumstances, I hardly think—'

'Oh, but of course,' he said, snapping out of his temporary trance. 'Just because *she* says I'm the father, it *must* be true.'

So now that the initial shock had passed he had decided it was in his interests to deny it, Cally thought bitterly. She shook her head. 'Why would she lie?'

'Because she's a bitch, Cally, a cold-hearted, evil bitch.'

'So after Girard's death, when you were both living here, you're telling me you never went near her?'

Leon's mouth soured as if he resented having to explain himself to her. 'No, *I* never went near *her*.'

'What does that mean?'

'It means she lost no time in attempting to seduce me. What she wanted above all else was to be the wife of a prince, regardless of who the prince was. But I made it perfectly clear to her that I would rather stick pins in my eyes than go anywhere near her, and informed her of my intention to reintroduce the law against the press. She left the island almost immediately.'

'You never mentioned that when you told me about her.'

Leon shrugged. 'Compared to the rest of her sins, it's nothing.'

'So how come she still has keys to the palace?'

'Unfortunately for me, as she's Girard's widow there are some rights to which she is still entitled. Access to the palace is one of them.'

Cally closed her eyes, breathing deeply, feeling like she had been presented with the prosecution and defence in a trial for which she would face the punishment however she judged it, wishing she could be handed a simple picture which depicted the truth.

'Toria tells it very differently.'

'So you choose to believe her word over mine?' he bellowed incredulously. 'Why? Because the first time we met I neglected to mention my title? I thought we were past that.'

'We were.' Cally felt tears begin to prick behind her eyes and swallowed hard. 'That's why as soon as she arrived I tried to warn you by calling the university. But you weren't there, were you? You haven't been there for weeks, and yet you've been telling me you have!'

'I—'

'No. Let me finish. I told myself there had to be some logical explanation for that, and then I tried as hard as I could to believe that Toria wasn't telling the truth. That's why I waited to hear your side of the story. But that look of utter horror on your face when I told you she was pregnant told me everything I needed to know.'

Leon paused, and for a moment he actually contemplated telling her, but the thought of saying the words aloud was so agonising that he crossed his arms and turned away. 'I'm just horrified by the prospect of that witch bringing a child into this world.'

'How gallant of you to be so concerned about the life of an unborn baby.'

'It's an insult to the memory of my brother.'

'The merry widow doesn't fit into one of your neat little boxes for characterising women?' she shot out sarcastically.

'Like the giant box labelled "liar" that you have reserved for all men?'

'So, what, you're telling me that you were at the university all along?'

Leon scowled, wondering how the hell the one woman he had broken his rule for wasn't even capable of trusting him in return. 'Yes. Not at the main campus, but at another building off-site.'

'So why did the principal of the university know nothing about it?'

'Because I haven't shown it to him yet.'

Cally looked at him disbelievingly. 'So, show *me*.'

It was then that the room went ominously silent and Leon looked down at her with an expression that was even more crushing than the one she had read there when she had announced Toria's pregnancy. It was a withering look which told her she had just made the unforgivable mistake of assuming that he had to prove anything to her. And with it she saw with agonising lucidity that it really made little difference whether he was telling the truth or not, because she didn't mean anything to him, and she never would.

'And what if I did show you, Cally? Would you demand Toria has a paternity test before we can continue with our affair? Because we could, but something tells me even that wouldn't be enough. You were envious, were you not, when you met Kaliq and Tamara, so newly engaged? And now Toria claims to be having my child and you are practically inconsolable. Are you sure that you aren't so upset because what you *really* want is for me to propose we get married and start making babies of our own?'

Cally tried her best to steady her breathing as the colours of the room threatened to blur before her eyes again. 'No, Leon, what I want is to leave. I want to get on the plane to Paris, and I want to get on with my career.'

'Like hell you do, Cally Greenway.' He raked his eyes mercilessly over her body sending a renewed yearning hurtling through her bloodstream. 'Why cut off your nose to spite your face?'

Because if I don't stem my desire I'll lose my heart, Cally thought. 'Whatever is between us is over.'

'*Over?*' Leon laughed a low, impertinent laugh that seemed to reverberate around the whole room. 'This thing will never be over between us, *chérie*. It's too damned hot.'

She should have been quicker, but Leon was one step ahead, catching the top of her arm with his fingers and spinning her round easily to plant his lips on hers. His kiss was a kiss of possession, hot, furious and undeniably physical; it felt like he had poured his whole body into it, though only their lips were touching. She knew what he was doing as her treacherous body responded with predictable arousal thrumming through her veins, her nipples hard, longing for the press of his chest. Oh yes, he was waiting for her to succumb to him, to draw herself to him and clasp her arms around his back with all the wild abandon which she always did.

Not anymore. Abandoning her senses had got her into this mess, and it certainly wasn't going to get her out of it. She needed to escape now, while she at least had the promise of the career she had worked so hard for. Even if it seemed to have lost all its meaning.

But it had more meaning than his kiss ever would, a voice inside her cried, and somehow it gave her the strength to push herself away from him and she stumbled backwards, desperate to put as much distance between them as possible.

'Like I said,' he breathed, his chest rising and falling in double-quick time, his lips as swollen as hers felt. 'Too damned hot.'

No, she thought desolately as she drank in the sight of him against the backdrop of the ocean for one final time, *too damned cold.*

CHAPTER TWELVE

Four months later

CALLY wanted to like Paris. There were plenty of reasons why she should. For a start, professionally speaking, she could finally say that all the years of hard work and study had been worthwhile. The head of the conservation team at the Galerie de Ville had gladly employed her, and had done so based on her merits alone. The work was stimulating and the paintings prolific; last week they had showcased an early Rossetti that she and the rest of the team had restored, and it had been extremely well-received. The other conservationists were dedicated and friendly, the studio state-of-the-art. And, where once her lunch breaks had consisted of a dash down to the rather lacklustre local shops on the outskirts of Cambridge, now she could take a walk along the Seine, wander through the endless rooms of the Louvre, or, as had been her preference of late, sit in a café in Montmartre and watch the world go by.

When she was not at work, she returned to a small but pleasant apartment near the Eiffel Tower which she was renting from a dear old woman by the name of Marie-Ange who was also giving her French lessons, and with the help of Jen back home she had even arranged to get tenants into her house so that she wasn't out of pocket. What with her earnings from the Rénards, deposited in her account within a day of leaving Montéz, her bank balance looked positively healthy.

Oh yes, Cally thought, on the surface everything looked just dandy, that business with the Prince of Montéz far behind her. All except for a couple of minor details. Like the excruciating pain of finding herself in the most romantic city in the world with a broken heart. And the fact that she was pregnant with his baby.

Cally ran her hand protectively over her stomach as she looked across at the higgledy-piggledy rows of umbrellas and easels of the Place du Tertre and cast her mind back to the day she had left. She'd rushed into the pharmacy at Montéz airport as soon as Boyet had dropped her off, desperate to put her mind at rest before catching her flight. And then she had taken the test. Or rather she'd taken three tests, because each time she'd seen the positive result she had scuttled out of the toilet to buy another, convinced that the previous one had to be faulty. Until the sympathetic look of the pretty girl on the till had said it all, and she'd had to acknowledge that the evidence was irrefutable.

That was also the moment she'd realised that sympathetic looks were categorically not what she wanted. She might initially have been in denial about the possibility of being pregnant because of the less-than-perfect circumstances, but accepting that their lovemaking had created a new life growing inside her brought with it an innate joy that was as profound as it was unexpected. So much so that her first instinct had been to turn around and get a taxi straight back to the palace to share the magic of it with

Leon. But in her heart she had known that he would hate her for it. He'd probably have accused her of having planned it all along in some attempt to trap him into marriage, and then that look of utter horror would have come over his face the way it had when she'd told him about Toria. Toria, who for all Cally knew could be carrying her baby's older half-brother or half-sister.

That thought had had her running back to the airport toilets once more—this time with a violent nausea—and was what had convinced her to get on the first plane off the island. Of course, the most obvious final destination would have been England, and her nice, ordered life in Cambridge where she could have sat down and worked out how to go about this whole thing sensibly. But in a moment of hideous clarity she'd seen what would happen if that was what she did. Yes, she probably would have worked out a way to scrimp and save and continue with the bland restorations she'd survived on to date whilst raising a child. But then what? She would have grown into an old spinster, bitter that all those years of hard work and study had counted for nothing, that her only work of note was the Rénards, and that she'd only got to work on those because they happened to have been bought by a man who had wanted to bed her. And, worst of all, she would have remembered those weeks in Montéz as the highest point in her life because nothing in England was ever likely to eclipse them.

So, although it was the most unsuitable time to take a new job in an unfamiliar city, to Cally the possibility of a temporary contract with the Galerie de Ville offered her the chance to prove to herself that she had felt so alive on the island because of the creative challenge, the change of scene. Living in the French capital was bound to equal her experiences in Montéz, if not exceed them, and she would be placated by the knowledge that in years to come, as well as having achieved her dream of working as a restorer in one of the world's most prestigious galleries, she could look back on that time in her life much more rationally and be better prepared to face the challenges ahead.

But Cally had failed to take into account one very important variable.

Leon Montallier was not in Paris.

And, though she was loath to admit it as she dug into the delicious crêpe that the waiter had just placed in front of her, that was the reason she wasn't even close to the feeling of happiness she'd felt in Montéz. However perfect Paris was on paper, in reality it simply made her realise that everything she had always thought she wanted wasn't what she wanted at all. Even the new restorations which she was supposed to be enjoying were only vaguely satisfying in the sense that she was using her skills, filling her time. Creatively, the only thing she found herself wanting to do was create another composition of her own. But every time she sat down before a blank canvas she just couldn't bring herself to begin; it was as if the vast expanse of emptiness represented the contents of her heart.

It was probably for the best, she thought miserably. Yes, she'd thought that landscape she'd done at the palace had been all right at the time, but she was sure if she ever saw it again without the rose-tinted glasses of back then she'd know it was dire. She should have tossed it into the sea before she'd left, she thought, suddenly hideously embarrassed by the thought that by now Leon had doubtless come across it, vaguely recalled the conversation in which she'd told him she never painted her own stuff and concluded there was a good reason why. He'd probably tossed it into the sea himself.

And, as for supposing that once she was on her own the gaping hole he'd opened would close again, she couldn't have been more wrong. It was irrational, it was hopeless, but the truth was she was in love with him, and there could be no more denying it. Paris had only magnified the very feelings for him which she had come here to try and dispel. Feelings which, as the first few weeks went by, she had hoped would be diminished by the passing of time, but which remained stubbornly unchanged.

Unchanged, all except one thing. Last week she had been practising her French translation by listening to a gossipy radio station when suddenly she'd heard Toria's name. Apparently she was celebrating the birth of her baby boy— a beautiful, mixed-race baby boy—with her partner, a professional footballer, with whom she was now living in Milan.

It was, of course, an enormous relief to Cally to know that she wasn't in the running for some hideous Oprah Winfrey show entitled *I'm pregnant with the prince's baby… Me too!* But in some ways it made coming to terms with her own actions even harder. For whatever reason—maybe purely to stir up trouble for the man who had curbed her fame—Toria had been the one spinning the lies, and Leon had been telling the truth. Except about where he had been all those mornings, she thought in a bid to continue to think ill of him, but now that just seemed petty. That was hardly a crime—unlike not telling someone they were going to become a parent.

Of course, she'd thought about it ever since. The instant she'd heard the news on the radio she'd seriously toyed with the idea of phoning him, or catching a flight out to

Montéz. But every time she imagined his response she lost her nerve. Discovering he was not the father of Toria's baby only changed things from her perspective, she thought as the waiter cleared her plate. Maybe she could trust him, but it didn't alter the fact that Leon did not want a child, and that if it hadn't been for her lust-induced idiocy Leon would not be having a child. So why should he have to feel some burden of responsibility to her and their baby for the rest of his life because of her mistake? She couldn't bear the thought of that. If he had wanted any further part in her life he would have come looking for her, but he hadn't.

'Mind if I join you?'

At the sound of a voice which sounded uncannily like his, Cally's head flew up so fast she saw spots and knocked her cup flying, the dregs of her coffee heading straight for him across the glossy red-and-white-checked tablecloth. She was just about to jump up and catch it, when he reached forward and stopped it with a napkin that he seemed to produce out of thin air and dropped into the chair opposite in one fluid movement.

'Leon.' Her voice came out altogether too breathlessly, part shock at seeing him here, part horror at the realisation that if she had jumped up, he would have seen the evidence of her pregnancy. 'What are you doing here?'

She shifted underneath the table, suddenly grateful for the cover it offered.

'One of your colleagues at the gallery told me I might find you here.'

'Who?' Cally asked, praying he'd spoken to Michel and not Céline, who was bound to have mentioned that Callie had been coming here every day since she'd developed a peculiar craving for spinach-and-gorgonzola crêpes.

'A man. I didn't catch his name.'

'Michel.' Cally smiled and breathed a temporary sigh of relief, not noticing the look of displeasure that flitted across Leon's mouth. 'Anyway, that wasn't what I meant. What are you doing here, in Paris?'

Her mind rewound to what she had been thinking about seconds before he'd appeared out of nowhere. *If he had wanted any further part in your life, he would have come looking for you...* Was it possible? She examined his face, the face that was etched so clearly in her mind that it was there even when she closed her eyes. It was even more devastating than she remembered, but, if it were possible, even more shuttered too.

'Why do you *think* I'm in Paris, *chérie?*' His look was depreciating, and for a second she was terrified he knew. No, he couldn't.

'You're here on business?' she ventured.

He chuckled, running his finger down the menu. 'Partly. What are you having?'

Partly. What the hell did that mean? It meant business and pleasure were always inseparable to him, she supposed, that maybe whenever his princely duties took him within a cab journey of an old flame he looked them up out of curiosity. Yes, Leon was the kind of man who would think it was possible to be friends afterwards, because he was never the one who got hurt. 'Nothing, thank you.'

'Then why don't you let me walk you back to the gallery?'

'Actually,' Cally backtracked, remembering the benefit of the table, 'I ought to have something or I'll be hungry later on.'

Leon gritted his teeth as she pretended to study the menu. The menu from which he had watched her order an enormous lunch less than twenty minutes earlier, and consume with a rapidity that would have made him think she wasn't earning enough money to feed herself properly if he hadn't known the truth. The truth that had stared him in the face from the newspaper article Boyet had left for his attention three days ago—the one about the new Rossetti the Galerie de Ville had on display, returned to its original glory by their team of restorers. With photographs.

At first he had been beside himself with fury. She was pregnant, and he knew the child had to be his—for he could accuse her of many things, but looseness was not one of them. Yet she had kept it from him, after all the accusations she had thrown at him about dishonesty and omitting the truth!

But, alongside his burning rage, he had realised that not only had she neglected to tell him, but she had not gone to the papers or come running back to him either. And that puzzled him. Yes, he had come to believe that maybe she wasn't the kind of woman who would sell her story for her fifteen minutes of fame as he had once believed, but he would have put money on her coming back to try and wangle a marriage proposal out of him. Hell, he had been convinced she would come back for the sex alone, just as soon as her desire for him threatened to consume her the way his desire for her had threatened to consume him so frequently in the weeks since her graceless departure, but to his infinite frustration she hadn't. So why hadn't she, even though she now had the perfect leverage?

The discovery that he did not have an answer to that question was the moment that it had occurred to him that, if he was capable of quelling his anger, then maybe, just maybe, she could be the perfect solution to the unpalatable problem which had been plaguing him ever since he'd heard about Toria. Along with the problem of the unbearable ache in his groin which had only increased at the sight of her newly voluptuous curves, he thought, observing her keenly through narrowed eyes and deciding it was time to find out if she really did suppose he was too stupid to notice.

'I think I'll have an almond *friand*,' Cally said, hoping it was the smallest thing on the menu. 'How about you?'

'I don't know. How about some answers?'

'Sorry?'

She tried to avoid his gaze but she felt his eyes bore into her. 'Some answers,' he repeated. 'Like why you haven't told me that you're having my baby.'

Cally felt a surge of panic knot itself around her heart. 'How—how did you find out?' she asked hopelessly.

'Not the way I deserved to.'

Her eyelids fluttered down to her cheeks and she nodded shamefully. 'I should have told you.'

'So why didn't you?'

She shook her head and fiddled with the menu, unable to look at him. 'Because I knew you didn't want a child, and it's my fault that you're having one.'

Leon frowned, not knowing what she meant, but certain he wasn't going to like what was coming next.

'That first time—when I said I didn't need protection— I thought we were talking figuratively. I didn't realise that… It wasn't until afterwards that I realised that you were talking about contraception.'

'So after that you just lived the lie, whilst accusing *me* of deceit at every opportunity?'

She hung her head.

Leon felt a white-hot anger blaze within him but he forced himself to bite his tongue. If she had come to him with that excuse he never would have believed her, he would have known that it was all part of an elaborate ploy to get him to waltz her down the aisle from the start. But she hadn't. The fact remained that she'd had the perfect reason to throw in her career and get everything he'd thought she wanted but she hadn't used it. Which was why, even though he was livid that she'd lied, it was almost possible that this could work.

'It was an easy mistake to make,' he forced out, biting his lip.

Cally raised her head in utter disbelief. Understanding. From Leon Montallier.

'Yes, it was.'

'And yet you planned to see the consequences through.'

'Just because it was unexpected does not mean I even thought for a moment about not having this baby,' she shot back, a fierce and thoroughly arousing maternal protectiveness glowing in her eyes.

'So what you are saying is since discovering you are to become a mother, your feelings towards the idea of becoming a parent have changed?'

'Yes.'

'Did it not occur to you that if you had told me I was to become a father my feelings might have altered also?'

Cally watched as the lines of his face softened and her eyes widened in disbelief. 'I—I suppose I expected you to react in the same way that you did when I told you that Toria was pregnant,' she said guiltily. 'But I know now that had nothing to do with you.'

Leon nodded gravely, determined not to invite questions

about the real reason for his horrified reaction that day, but Cally was too lost in her own thoughts to notice.

'So, have they changed?' she whispered. 'Your feelings, I mean?'

Leon paused, knowing his answer demanded the utmost consideration, and took a deep breath. 'You are right that I did not expressly want a child, Cally. Not because of any aversion to the prospect, but because I believe that a child is best brought up by a mother and father who are married. Since I have always been disinclined on that front, by default the prospect seemed unlikely. But life is never quite that—neat.' He shook his head and turned away the waiter who had approached the table. 'You *are* carrying my child.' He ran his eyes over her face, surprised to find that the words were ready on the tip of his tongue without any of the resistance he had expected. 'But, even before I knew that, for the past four months I have found myself aching for you in a way that is completely unprecedented—not only to have you back in my bed, but to have you by my side.'

The heavy lashes that shadowed her cheeks lifted in disbelief.

'I therefore find that my inclination has changed. I wish to marry you, Cally. As soon as possible.'

Cally had to pinch her leg under the table to check that she wasn't dreaming. Leon Montallier—*Prince* Leon Montallier, the man who had told her that he found the institution of matrimony categorically intolerable—hadn't *really* just said aloud that he wished to marry her, had he?

Yes, she thought. He had. And, impossible though it seemed, he'd said it in such a way that it sounded like the sincerest thing he'd ever uttered. It hadn't been some overblown, rehearsed proposal that befitted the romantic reputation of his countrymen; it had been a statement, simple and unadorned. It said that, no, this hadn't been the way he had expected things to go, but now that they had he wanted to take this chance because he felt what they had already shared could continue to grow. It said that he trusted her, and he was asking her to place her trust in him right back.

Could she? she wondered. Could she really dare to believe in things that she had spent years, and in particular the last four months, forbidding herself to even dream about? Like sleeping with the man she loved every night and waking up beside him every morning. Taking breakfast at the table on the terrace, a table laid for three, maybe one day even four. Cally closed her eyes to stop the visions overwhelming her. Surely those kinds of dreams were too big? Like he said, life wasn't neat. Even if they could tidy it now, what happened when the swell of unexpected feelings that had hit him with the discovery that he was to be a father diminished, and he remembered that he had never been cut out for family or fidelity after all? Wouldn't she be doing them both a wrong not to be more cautious?

'Don't you think that maybe getting married is a little too *rash?*' she replied hesitantly, focussing on the caricaturist and the small crowd of onlookers on the opposite side of the street, afraid that if she caught his eye he would know that talking him out of this was the last thing she really wanted.

'No,' he replied, his voice gentle but firm. 'And I'm not sure that you do either.'

Cally felt her breath catch in her throat, taken aback to discover that he didn't need to look in her eyes to know exactly what she was thinking. To know that she was looking for a reason to say no because it felt safer, because that was the answer that her nice, ordered life had got her into the habit of. And she understood that even if they'd been in a proper relationship for a year and had already had a conversation about what they'd call their children one day, saying yes would still feel just as scary because it involved her placing her trust in another human being. Rash was just an excuse.

'Perhaps you're right,' she admitted. 'But I just don't want either of us to look back and think this was a mistake.'

'No one can know what the future holds,' he said with all the gravity of a man who had experienced the arbitrariness of fate. 'But surely it could never be a mistake to try and raise our child together?'

He had her there, Cally thought, for how could she ever regret raising their baby with him in Montéz when the alternative was going it alone in her damp two-up two-down in Cambridge? However much she'd once hated the concept of privilege, she couldn't think of any better start in life for their child than growing up at the palace. Besides, she realised with a start, he or she would be first in line to the throne; how could they grow up anywhere else and be prepared for what lay ahead?

Leon hadn't even mentioned that, and suddenly she loved him all the more for it. Of course it would be important to him that his heir be raised on the island, yet he hadn't pushed it, just like he hadn't stressed that her acceptance would mean an official role for her too. But it would, she thought anxiously, wondering whether saying yes would mean kissing everything in her old life goodbye.

'As well as raising our child, I had hoped to continue working, Leon.'

'Of course,' he replied with none of the sarcasm she might once have expected. 'Perhaps you can freelance out of the studio.'

Cally almost couldn't believe her ears. He wasn't asking her to give up the work she loved, he wasn't assuming that that was what she wanted. Yes, there were so many unknowns, so much to overcome, but surely if they were both willing to try…? 'Perhaps I could.' She nodded tentatively.

'Are you by any chance thinking that you wouldn't be averse to the idea of marrying me either, *chérie?*'

'Yes, Leon, I think I am.'

'Good,' he said, leaning across the table and whispering in her ear. 'Because I've already booked the church for this time next week.'

'This time *next week?*'

Leon nodded.

It was arrogant. Maybe it was overly romantic too. But the joy in her heart overtook her exasperation and in an instant she was on her feet and closing the short distance between them. But just as she pressed her body into his and raised her hands to tangle them in his hair he placed one hand on her elbow and stopped her.

'What is it?'

Cally followed his eyes, which had dropped to her pregnant stomach.

'I just—' It was the first time it had really occurred to him that his child was growing inside her womb, and he was shocked by the feelings of both helplessness and strength that swelled within him. 'Can I touch it?'

'Of course you can!' Cally grinned, breathing a sigh of relief and grabbing his hand to place it on her belly. She was equally unprepared for the weight of her own emotions as he stroked her protectively.

'I'm sorry,' she whispered, drawing in a deep breath as the magnitude of what she had denied him truly hit home. As she did, her agitation caused the baby to give a tiny kick. He jumped back and looked at her in awe.

'I'm sorry I didn't tell you,' she repeated.

Leon felt a muscle tighten at his jaw but he forced himself to let it go.

'My twenty-week scan—it's booked in at the hospital here in three days. Come with me?'

He nodded with a conviction that told her he wouldn't miss it for the world. 'And then to Montéz.'

CHAPTER THIRTEEN

'How about Jacques?' Leon grinned as they drove over the hilltop and the palace came into view. It was even more resplendent than she remembered in the low November sunshine.

Cally looked down at her lap. She was holding their marriage licence which they had just collected from the town hall in one hand, and the ultrasound photo of their baby boy in the other. If she had had a third hand she would have pinched herself again.

'Inspired by Jacques Rénard?' she asked, studying the photo as only an expectant mother could, ignoring the fuzzy patches of light and shade and trying to discern whether their son might look like a Jacques. She turned back to Leon and her smile widened in approval. 'I love it.'

They had both wanted to know the sex. Maybe it was because having a baby in the first place had been surprise enough, or maybe it was because they had both wanted to discover one thing about this pregnancy together, but either way they were delighted.

'Remind me again of your nephews' names?'

'Dylan and Josh. Dylan's the eldest.'

It continued to amaze her that Leon had not only insisted

her family be invited to their wedding in four days' time, but that he seemed genuinely interested in them too—even Jen, despite her being a journalist, which she knew deep down he viewed as a heinous crime. However, Cally's amazement couldn't be greater than her sister's had been when she'd called her yesterday.

'Married? To the Prince of Montéz?' Jen had cried when she'd finally stopped apologising for the hundredth time for only hearing 'I wish' and 'Don't mention him' during that telephone conversation when she'd suggested running the article. 'But... I thought you said he was a complete bastard?'

'He has his moments.' Cally had laughed. 'But I've fallen in love with him, Jen, and, well... We're expecting a baby in March.'

Her sister had been even more flabbergasted then. But she decided that no one could be more amazed than she already was herself as she drew up outside the palace and she saw Boyet descending the steps, ready to unload the car of the few bits and pieces she'd brought with her to begin their new life together. Like the beautiful cot that had been a farewell gift from Michel, Céline and the rest of the gallery team, and enough knitted babygrows from Marie-Ange to clothe the entire maternity ward—she had been beside herself to discover that she had been renting a room to a future princess and heir of Montéz.

Yes, she would always recall the friends she had made in Paris with affection, but leaving the capital had been a million times easier than it had ever been to leave here, she thought as they walked through the courtyard and up the creamy white staircase. Montéz felt like home. And, whilst living in a palace was going to take some getting used to, she couldn't help believing her parents had actually been right when they had once told her that wealth and class could be irrelevant. She couldn't help hoping she'd been wrong to stop believing in happy-ever-after too.

Even if there had been a few moments in the past few days when the look in Leon's eyes had been so unfathomable it was like he had momentarily shut her out in the cold. But she told herself it was to be expected, that it was just going to take time for two people who weren't used to sharing their lives to learn to live with one another. She tried to repress the nagging fear that he'd always be closed to her, the realisation that he hadn't once asked how *she* actually felt about *him*. Was it because he didn't want to make her say things that he thought she might not be ready to say? Or because those things would never matter to him?

'*Bonjour, mademoiselle.*'

Cally shook herself and smiled warmly as Boyet opened the car door for her. '*Bonjour, Boyet, ça va?*'

'*Oui, ça va bien, merci.*' He grinned, clearly impressed with her improved accent, and then turned to Leon. 'I alighted upon a newspaper article that may be of some interest, Your Highness. The daily papers are out on the terrace as usual.'

He nodded '*Merci,* Boyet.'

Cally and Leon entered the hallway together, and whilst she popped to the bathroom Leon continued through to the terrace. He was standing above the wrought-iron table when she entered the drawing room, and she observed him as she walked towards the glass doors; his forehead was deeply lined.

'What is it?' she asked anxiously, stepping outside to join him. He raised his eyes casually from the article he was reading, but the second they met with hers he froze. For one long moment he seemed to look at her as if he was seeing her for the first time, and then his frown disappeared altogether and his whole face seemed to lighten.

'It's nothing, *chérie,*' he said, folding up the sheaf of paper and placing it in the top pocket of his shirt. 'Nothing at all. But I'm afraid there are some documents which urgently await my signature at the Treasury.' His eyes dropped to her hand that was still clutching their marriage licence and he smiled. 'I can drop our papers in with Father Maurice on the way. It's been a long day. Why don't you get some rest?'

Why don't you tell me what the article is about, if it's nothing? Cally wanted to retort, but she knew that she was probably just being paranoid, and making him aware of it was hardly going to encourage him to open up. 'You're probably right.'

Leon ran his finger tenderly down her arm and took the papers from her hand. 'I know I am.' He grinned. 'I'll be back in an hour or two, and if you're up to it we can take a stroll along the beach before dinner. It's not quite as warm at this time of year, but the sunset is always spectacular.'

She nodded as he kissed her lightly on the mouth. 'I'd like that.'

Cally tried to nap, but failed. Her mind was too full of all that had happened over the last few days and, if she was honest, too troubled by old insecurities. Which was ridiculous; she was lying on the royal bed, carrying his son, with their wedding just days away.

It was probably just coming back to the palace and trying to get her head around actually living here, she reasoned. For, though she had resided here for that month, it had been as nothing more than his lover and his employee, and as a result she hadn't really ventured beyond his bedroom or the studio. Cally sat up and swung her legs over the edge of the bed, feeling the luxurious rug beneath her toes. If she was to embrace her new life and feel comfortable raising their son here, then it shouldn't feel like the palace was just a sea of closed doors without any idea what lay behind them. *Like Leon,* she thought bleakly, and then scolded herself. It was going to take time. And, since he'd only just been saying that they should choose a room for the nursery, opening a few doors—literally—seemed like the perfect place to start.

Cally exited the master bedroom and turned right. There had to be at least eight other rooms she'd never entered just in this wing, never mind in all the other wings on the other floors. But she couldn't imagine choosing a room for their son's nursery—Jacques' nursery—more than a few steps away from their bedroom.

The first door she entered, opposite the master bedroom, revealed a large room with an oak ceiling and a view of the inner courtyard. It would have fulfilled its function more than adequately, but it didn't feel in any way cosy, and it seemed a shame to Cally for their son's room not to face out to sea when that was the part of Montéz that she most associated with Leon. The second room she entered was to the right of their own, and couldn't have been more different. It was a moderate size with a fabulous view of the bay, a long window seat and lemon walls bathed in late-afternoon sunlight. She could just imagine the cot in here. A rocking horse, piles of play bricks. She smiled, running one hand over her belly, and felt her heart settle. All it needed was some brightly coloured paintings, she thought, catching sight of a large frame propped face down against the wall and wondering if she could make use of it.

Cally walked towards it and wiped the dust from the edge of the frame with her finger. Leaning it back against her body to discern whether or not it was empty, she saw that behind the glass was an enormous royal-family tree. Fascinated, she carefully manoeuvred the frame so that it was propped against the wall face up and sank to her knees to survey it.

Leon so rarely spoke about his family. Not that she could blame him for that, for she had gathered that both his parents were dead and the pain of losing Girard was still very raw. But she couldn't help being curious about the royal dynasty that, incredibly, she found herself about to marry into, that her son was going to be a part of. She ran her eyes along row after row of unfamiliar names, sovereign princes past, their wives, their children. Then she dropped her eyes to the bottom of the picture, desperate to find Leon's name, to trace the branches she knew and to locate the spot where two new ones would soon be added. But the second she saw the swirling typescript of his name she dropped her hand as if she had been burned, shocked to discover that the existing branches around him didn't even begin to lead where she'd expected.

Rapidly, she tried to make sense of what she was seeing. Leon's mother Odette had married Arnaud Montallier, the Sovereign Prince of Montéz, and together they'd had one son—Girard. Seventeen years later, Girard was crowned Prince—the same year, quite logically, that his father had passed away. But it wasn't until the *following* year that Odette had given birth to her second son, Leon. Whose father was not listed as a prince at all, but as a man named Raoul Rénard.

Cally stared in disbelief. No wonder Leon had implied that his title was a fate that should never have befallen him. It was not simply because Girard had died unexpectedly, but because the royal bloodline—if it was like any other she'd ever read about—had technically died out with him. Which meant that Leon had inherited the throne simply because his mother had been the sovereign's widow.

Cally felt an icy fear begin to grip her as all that that meant slowly began to hit home. Her eyes rested on the branch between Girard and Toria. Toria, who was the former sovereign's widow just as Odette had once been. Toria, who had also given birth to a son. A son who—if Leon was an example of what happened in such circumstances—could inherit the throne one day. Unless Leon married and had a child of his own.

Suddenly, Toria's words that afternoon in the studio echoed through her mind with new and devastating clarity: *Tell him I'm pregnant. With the heir to the throne.* That was why the expression on Leon's face had been one of such unmitigated dread. She'd been so convinced she understood it, but she had actually read it as wrongly as she always did. It wasn't because he was the father of her child; oh no, Cally understood now that Toria had simply alighted on that lie as a way of hurting her. It was because the woman he loathed was carrying a child who had the potential to inherit everything.

And, with that realisation, the trust that Cally Greenway had dared to place in Leon Montallier came crashing down around her shoulders, taking her fragile heart with it. He hadn't come to Paris because he had missed her, hadn't proposed because he thought they had a shot at happiness, or even because he thought it was the best thing to do for their child. He had simply discovered that she was pregnant, and that making their child his legitimate heir was preferable to the thought of Toria's child being first in line to the throne. Hell, he'd even waited until he had accompanied her to the scan before they had gone to get their marriage licence. Fit, healthy and a boy; no wonder he'd proceeded with such enthusiasm!

Cally felt a tortured moan escape her lips and sank back on her heels, head raised as if appealing to some invisible god for mercy. Could she have been any more foolish? How easily she had fallen for his honeyed words and feigned understanding! She'd even supposed that he hadn't mentioned the small matter of their child's legitimacy because he didn't consider that to be the most important thing! Why the hell hadn't she learned that with Leon the important thing was always the thing that he *didn't* mention? Like the fact that he was a prince, that he had bought the paintings for himself, that he had only employed her because he wanted to take her to bed. He had lied to her from the day she had met him, and all this time she had been stupid enough to go on believing what she wanted to believe, thinking he simply needed time to open up.

Unable to bear the evidence of his lies in black and white before her, Cally backed away from the family tree and stumbled out into the corridor. Suddenly the whole palace felt like a conspirator in his betrayal. Tearing down the stairs and out into the grounds, she found herself on the grass verge overlooking the magnificent bay. The bay where Leon had planned to take her for a walk before dinner, that had been the subject of the picture he had inspired her to paint after so many years of believing that part of her was dead. Now every part of her felt dead, oblivious to everything except the sobs which began deep inside her chest and took her over. She couldn't remember the last time she had succumbed to such irrepressible tears, but she did know that her practised mechanism of swallowing hard and blinking repeatedly would do her no good, for her eyes were already sore, and her throat was so constricted it was all she could do not to choke on her own sobs.

She didn't even stop as she sensed him come up behind her. Looming. Blurred. She wanted to lunge at him, pound her fists against his chest, but she didn't have the strength.

He swooped down to her level. 'What the hell's the matter, are you in pain? The baby?'

'No, Leon,' she gasped, her words punctuated by sobs. 'The heir to the throne is perfectly safe.'

His brows descended into a dark V, and he ran his eyes over her as if checking all her limbs were intact. 'If not the baby, then what?'

'What else is there?' she swiped.

'Well, clearly there's something the matter with you, and I think I have a right to know.'

'A right to know?' Cally cried hysterically. 'You mean like I had a right to know that the only reason you wanted to marry me was because you couldn't bear a child of Toria's to be first in line to the throne?'

Leon went very still. 'Has she been here again?'

A ridiculous part of her had been waiting for him to deny it all. His response only drove the knife in deeper. 'No, Leon. Toria has not been here. Your pathetic little fiancée worked it all out by herself, from the family tree.'

Leon clenched his teeth. The family tree in his old nursery. The one his mother had given him as a child to try and help him come to terms with the truth, but which had only succeeded in making him feel more different.

'What were you doing, poking around in there?'

'Poking around?' she rasped despairingly. 'I thought this was to be my home, Leon, our son's home?'

'And so it will be.'

'No, Leon.' Cally shook her head. 'How can this ever become my home if there are parts of it I am forbidden to enter? Unless all you want is a wife in name only...' She looked out at the horizon, still trying to come to terms with her discovery. 'Yes. I suppose that *is* all you want.'

'I do not want you as my wife in name only!' he protested—too loudly, she thought, as he raised back up to his full height and began to pace.

'But unless you're prepared to be honest,' she whispered brokenly, 'how could I ever be anything else?'

Leon stilled, and, lowering his eyes, he caught sight of a single tear rolling down her cheek. As it splashed onto her pregnant belly, something unbearable began to invade every organ in his body. Shame? Regret? Fear? No, all three. That afternoon, when she'd left here for Paris, all he had wanted was her trust, to believe that her hysterics weren't some attempt to weasel something out of him. Now he realised that in agreeing to become his wife she had put her trust in him unquestionably, but he'd been so bloody single-minded—so driven by the solution she presented, by his own libido—that he'd trampled all over the one thing he had wanted to protect.

He dropped to the grass beside her, knowing it was too late, but that more than anything she deserved to know the truth, however shameful. 'How I became the prince isn't exactly something I'm proud of.'

Cally read the look of agony on his face. 'Well, you should be,' she said grudgingly. 'Whatever else is true, giving up a career you were passionate about because your country needed you is admirable.'

'It was my duty. It's complicated how that came to be the case, but it was.' He took a deep and ragged breath, his eyes fixed on the horizon. 'My mother's marriage to Arnaud was arranged by her social-climbing parents. It was an entirely loveless match, but she provided him with the son he desired and stayed loyal to him until he passed away. A few months after that, when she was still only in her late thirties, a sailor ran into trouble in the bay and she offered him shelter inside the palace whilst he repaired the engine on his boat. His name was Raoul Rénard.' Leon paused over his name, a tortured expression in his eyes, and suddenly its significance dawned on Cally. 'According to my mother, he was a descendent of the great artist Jacques Rénard. She fell deeply in love with him, and within weeks she was pregnant.'

Cally looked at him in wonder. That was why he had been willing to pay any sum for the paintings, and why he'd done so anonymously too: Jacques Rénard was one of his ancestors! She immediately felt guilty, for all the accusations she'd thrown at him about wanting them purely to boast about, and for how quickly she had jumped to the wrong conclusions about him. But they hadn't been all wrong, she thought, wiping the stream of tears from her eyes with the sleeve of her cardigan. Even if he did have a deep attachment to the paintings, he still had no real attachment to her. If he did, he would have told her sooner, would have understood that her own passion for the Rénards ran just as deep. And he would have proposed because he loved her, she thought, stifling a renewed sob, not just because he needed a son.

'And did he love her?' Cally asked, wondering why, in spite of everything she had always known about true love being the stuff of legend, not history, she wanted to hear that he had.

'Yes.' Leon nodded gravely. 'I believe he did. But my mother's moment of happiness was short-lived. The next time my father returned to sea, the boat's engine caught fire and he was killed.' His eyes clouded as he recalled that the twist of fate which had been responsible for the start of his life had also led to his father's death. 'The shock sent my mother into labour early, and as a result the people of Montéz simply presumed that Arnaud was my father. My mother's closest advisors suggested that was for the best. And, besides, I was the next in line regardless.'

Cally frowned. 'But…how?'

Leon replied in a voice that seemed to come from a long way off, and Cally realised that the guard she had been wanting him to drop ever since that night in London was slowly coming down before her eyes. But only now did she see that she had been wrong to assume that behind that closed door would be the proof that he loved her; the reality was that he felt nothing for her at all. Which probably ought to have fuelled her anger, but all she could think about was how much he'd had to deal with, how much she wanted to hold him.

'The royal bloodline in Montéz differs from that of other countries, or at least it has since the turn of the sixteenth century,' Leon continued, watching the breeze blow wisps of her hair out of her ponytail, wishing he had the right to smooth them away from her face, hating that he didn't.

'At that time, the king of the island, who had subjected

the islanders to a long reign of oppression, was overthrown by a hero amongst the people named Sébastien. He was the tyrannical king's illegitimate half brother—the son of the old king's widow and one of the palace advisors. Sébastien declared that the royal family should be abolished and that Montéz should become a democracy. The people were overjoyed, but they clamoured for him to become the king. He was reluctant, but eventually he agreed, on one condition: that he and his future successors should only ever be known as Sovereign Prince, not King, as a reminder that the greatest power should always remain with the people.'

At what point had he lost sight of what mattered? Leon wondered, and what made him even think that his son would be the worthiest successor to the throne with *him* as a role model? He shook his head and continued. 'But the rest of France was reluctant to accept Sébastien as the new sovereign, because he couldn't prove that he was royal. The citizens of Montéz were outraged, and so, to grant him legitimate status, they voted for a change to the law. It states that any widow of the sovereign retains her royal status after his death, and thus any child she bears afterwards inherits that status and a claim to the throne, so long as she never marries again. Therefore, they argued, Sébastien's mother had passed her royal status on to him.' Leon took a deep breath. 'As my mother did to me.'

Cally stared at him in amazement as all he had said sunk in, and the knock-on effects of the ancient and remarkable law began to crystallise in her mind. No wonder he had always spoken of his title as if it was something that didn't really belong to him, but a job that he had reluctantly taken on. And no wonder he had always found the concept of marriage so intolerable. For when the sovereign of Montéz took a bride, he had to trust her to honour him not only during his lifetime but even after his death.

Which meant he had been willing to place that trust in you, a voice inside her whispered, but she ignored it, for what good was that if she couldn't trust *him?* And what good had it done her to think this was just about feelings like trust or love, when he was a prince for whom marriage and children would always mean something more? Or was it really something less? she wondered sorrowfully.

'So, there you have it,' Leon concluded uneasily. 'I am the prince, but only because of an ancient technicality. In terms of the usual rules of patrilineal descent, I do not have a drop of royal blood.'

Cally's heart filled with empathy. 'Do you really suppose it matters whose blood runs through your veins, Leon?' she answered croakily, conscious that not so long ago she had been guilty of pigeonholing anyone with a title. 'Why should it matter who your father was, whether you inherited the throne because of a technicality or because of biology? What matters is that the prince has the best interests of his country at heart. That was why the people supported Sébastien all those years ago, the same way your people would support you.'

'Perhaps.' Leon turned back to her, his eyes searching her face in wonder, wishing he hadn't allowed the shame he felt for a past over which he had no control jeopardise his future with the only woman he had ever met who hadn't cared who he was, who had cared only whether he was a decent man. Well, he thought grimly, he had proved that he wasn't that all by himself. 'Not long after Girard passed away, the truth began to gnaw at me so badly that I almost made up my mind to find out. But I realised it would not only cause enormous unrest during an already turbulent time, but it would become common knowledge that any man who got Toria pregnant would be the father of the next Prince of Montéz, the consequences of which could have been catastrophic.'

'But Toria herself has always known?' Cally replied, her mind returning to the agonising present.

'Girard explained the intricacies of the law when they married, but it wasn't until after his death that she saw the opportunity to use what she had once seen as some boring old decree to benefit herself. When I resisted her advances, she realised that if she went to the papers with it it would ensure her a permanent following. That was what finally convinced me to reinstate the law against the press.'

'So the only way left for her to take revenge on you was by actually getting pregnant?' Cally stared agog, horrified that any woman could possibly use their potential for motherhood in such a despicable way.

'At the time I thought so, but now I believe that angering me, attempting to drive a wedge between you and me, was a convenient by-product of an accidental pregnancy.'

'Just like the solution to that problem was a convenient by-product of mine,' Cally said despondently, tugging on a piece of grass.

'I can't pretend that isn't partly true.' Leon's eyes were hooded, self-condemning. 'But it isn't that simple. I was always adamant that I never wanted to marry.'

She could understand that now, Cally thought, if not because of the peculiarities of the law then because of the loveless marriage his mother had endured, the union of misplaced trust his brother had fallen into.

He continued. 'I've always been adamant that I didn't

want to marry, but once I met you I had to keep inventing new reasons why that was the case, because you kept proving all the old ones wrong. Like thinking all you wanted was fame or sex. By the time you went to Paris there weren't any reasons left.'

'Even if that is true—' Cally shook her head '—you still didn't do anything about it until you discovered that it was in the interests of your kingdom to act. And maybe I would have understood that too if you'd told me. But you didn't.'

Leon nodded remorsefully. 'I suppose I was still reluctant to admit it to myself, too scared you'd walk away if you knew and... And then it stopped having anything to do with my kingdom anyway.'

'What?' Cally searched his face as he reached into his pocket and unfolded the newspaper article he had put there that morning, the one he had refused to show her, and placed it down on the grass.

At the centre was a wedding photo, Toria's wedding photo, taken yesterday. Cally ran her eyes over the frothy white dress, the groom's garish white suit and their baby son dressed like a cherub as she tried to process what it meant. Leon's words rang through her mind: *Any widow of the sovereign retains her royal status after his death, and thus any child she bears afterwards inherits that status and a claim to the throne,* so long as she never marries again...

What it meant was that the second that Toria had got her figure back marrying a high-profile footballer had appealed to her more than revenge. It meant that Toria's son was no longer in line to the throne. And that meant, as of a few hours ago, Leon had had every reason to call their wedding off.

But he hadn't, because he'd taken their marriage licences to the priest after that. She looked up into his face, her eyes enormous. 'You mean you don't *need* to marry me, but you were going to anyway?'

CHAPTER FOURTEEN

LEON nodded slowly, and part of Cally's heart felt like it was about to explode with unmitigated joy.

He doesn't need to, but he wants to marry you anyway, she repeated to herself.

Yet the other portion of her heart knew that whatever his reasons for wanting her to be his wife now, love couldn't possibly be one of them. If he had loved her, he would have told her the truth about his past months ago, or a week ago, or even this morning. He would have wanted to be open with her and to find out how she felt about him. But he hadn't, and he'd only told her now because she had accidentally stumbled upon his family tree.

'I understand why you were reluctant to tell me,' she said hopelessly. 'I even admire the whole host of practical reasons you had for proposing. But when I agreed to marry *you*...' She shook her head, knowing that now was the time for honesty on her part too, however futile. 'It was because I was in love with you. I think I was from the first moment I laid eyes on you in London, and because of that I thought I could marry you even if you never loved me. But I can't.'

As Leon listened, he felt something deep within him

shift. Once he'd believed that women only used words like 'love' as a means to an end, but Cally meant everything and wanted nothing. And that was the blinding moment when he realised that her love was everything he wanted, but the last thing that he deserved. Which was why, though the three little words hovered on his lips to say right back, he knew they weren't enough.

He took a deep breath, wondering if he was capable of even half her integrity. 'Let me show you something.'

'What?'

'Let me show you something.' Leon rose to his feet, tentatively reaching out his hand to lead her somewhere—to the car parked on the driveway, by the looks of things—but not daring to touch her. He was probably afraid her emotion was contagious. So, the *L* word really did mean nothing to him, she thought. Was he just going to pretend she hadn't mentioned it at all?

'Now?' she asked disbelievingly.

'Yes, now.' His brows creased with concern as he eyed her bump. 'If you can.'

Cally was too emotionally exhausted to argue. So she let him help her into the passenger seat of the car. The plain and perfectly ordinary black car, she noticed dismally as he pulled away, wishing it could have been some ridiculous sports model so that she could loathe its excess. That would have been easier. Easier than thinking about the real reason he had spent a fortune on those paintings, or why he had always been happiest out in the ocean. Things that reminded her that he was not just a billionaire prince with an overly complex family tree, but a man, a man who she admired more than she'd ever thought possible.

Eventually, after what felt like an age of twisting and

turning along the coast road—Cally staring helplessly at her puffy eyes and red cheeks in the wing mirror—he rolled the car to a standstill outside a modern white building just on the outskirts of the main town.

'Where are we?'

Leon unfolded his lithe frame from the seat beside her and walked round to open her door. 'That day when you called the university and I wasn't there—I was here.'

Cally sighed. Four months ago, she had wanted nothing more than for him to show her where he had been all those mornings. Now it just seemed too little, too late. 'You don't need to show me.'

'Yes, I do.'

Reluctantly, Cally followed him round to the front of the elegant building. He swiped a card and led them inside. It smelled of fresh paint, and there were workmen's tools scattered on the floor.

'This part should be finished by the end of the week,' he said. 'The rest is complete.'

Stepping over plastic sheeting, he led her through to an enormous atrium, and that was when she saw them. There, on the wall in front of her, were the Rénards, flanked by enormous windows which looked out over the Mediterranean.

Cally immediately hurried closer, her mind suddenly oblivious to everything except the ingenious way in which they'd been displayed. 'His love by the sea,' she whispered in disbelief, her eyes darting between the paintings and the view, then falling to the beautifully presented accompanying details which gave information on their composition and credited her with the restoration work. 'When, how— What is this place?'

'Ever since my mother told me I was descended from a great painter, it occurred to me that Montéz was lacking its own art gallery.' Leon shrugged, as if it had ceased to matter now. 'Once I started working with Professeur Lefevre, I realised that the students at the university were going to need somewhere to showcase their own work too. So I started to have this place built. I just hadn't planned to tell anyone until it was completely finished.'

'It's perfect,' Cally said slowly, the genius of it running through her mind. 'The big names will draw hundreds of visitors, and the students' work will immediately be in the public eye.' She shook her head in wonder. 'Do you mean to tell me that you planned to display the Rénards here all along?'

Leon ran a hand over his forearm uncomfortably. 'Much as I would like to say yes, that was not my intention initially. I bought that Goya in London, amongst others, to display here. But I bought the Rénards for myself. I suppose I wanted a little of *my* father's history inside the palace.' His eyes lifted to meet hers. 'Until you made me realise that if I kept them there I would have more in common with that tyrannical sixteenth-century king than with my own ancestors.'

'If I had known why you wanted them I would never have been so tactless,' she said regretfully.

'But, like you said, the blood that runs through my veins ought to be irrelevant. They deserve to be enjoyed by everyone. Besides, when it came down to it, they were not as hard to part with as something else.' Leon nodded to the wall behind her and she turned.

'My painting!' Cally cried, utterly overwhelmed, and yet also wholly embarrassed to see her landscape, beautifully framed, hanging just a few feet away from the Rénards. An enormous lump rose in her throat that she had a job to swallow. 'I—I thought if you found it you'd throw it in the sea.'

Leon shook his head. 'It's brilliant, Cally.'

'Hardly.'

Leon raised his eyebrows. She looked at it again, and was forced to concede that it didn't look as dire as she had imagined it might. Not that she had ever expected to see it again.

'I thought you didn't do your own work.'

'I hadn't done.' She shook her head. 'Ever since David. But then I met you.'

She could admit that now—that her inspiration, which had disappeared in Paris, hadn't risen again in Montéz because she'd been in a new and exciting part of the world but because being with the man she loved had been stimulating in every way there was. And constantly surprising, she thought, as seeds of hope dared to take root in her mind.

He nodded and looked up at it. 'I mean it when I say it's brilliant. When I look at it, it's like I can actually feel the passion you felt when you painted it.'

Cally blushed. 'There's probably a reason for that'.

Leon shook his head. 'No, I don't just mean *that*. It's like it's alive with your excitement for the strokes themselves, the colours, the sheer joy of painting.'

Cally drew in a sharp breath and felt the most acutely powerful tears she had ever known prick behind her eyes. He hadn't laughed or tossed it out to sea, wasn't suggesting that her love of painting buried an ulterior motive, nor had he once even implied that a girl like her should never harbour dreams about becoming an artist. He'd framed

it, treasured it and hung it in a gallery beside the paintings which had fired her love of art in the first place.
'Thank you,' she said suddenly, her emotions threatening
to overwhelm her. 'For understanding what it means to
me. I thought—'

'That I'd always presume your career was just something
to fill your time until you married? I know,' he said flinch-
ingly. 'You'd think that with everything you endured in order
to work on the Rénards I ought to have realised earlier.'

Cally drew in a very deep breath, and for a moment it
felt like the world had stopped spinning. All this time she'd
been convinced that he saw no need to let her in because
he had no desire to understand her… And all the while he
had understood her better than anyone she had ever met.
She stared at him in utter amazement. 'It wasn't as hard to
endure as you might think,' she whispered.

Leon didn't seem to hear her. 'I should have brought you
here earlier,' he said hopelessly. 'There are a lot of things
I should have done earlier. But this I had planned to tell
you…at our wedding. I was just waiting for Jen to let me
know whether she could make the date I'd fixed for the
grand opening.'

Cally stared at him, dumbfounded by this new information. 'Jen?' Her *sister* Jen?

'I've invited her to cover the story. I'd planned to invite
Kaliq and Tamara too,' he continued with immense effort.
'Maybe it isn't the only thing I should think about reveal-
ing to the public.'

As she looked up into his face, lined as it was with anguish,
full of strength, that was the moment when she knew that everything was going to be OK. Because she suddenly understood that he hadn't just chosen to keep his guard up when

he was around *her*, but that ever since childhood he had been forced to keep the truth a secret from everyone. But he was trying to change, and it was because of her.

'That's fantastic,' she whispered, her heartbeat beginning to pound in her ears.

Leon shrugged, his whole pose listless. 'I know that displaying the paintings can't undo all the wrong I've done you, but I just… I need you to understand that you have shaped the way I feel about everything. There were a hundred practical reasons that I held responsible for my proposal to you, but the truth is that I would have dismissed them all if you hadn't changed the way I feel about marriage altogether. That month we spent here together— it was the best of my life.'

He took a deep breath. 'I know I can't ask that of you now, but, if you meant it when you said that you loved me, then please let me learn how to love you properly, how to love our son properly.'

Cally felt a warm glow begin to flow through her, like a diver catching sight of the mast of a sunken ship he had given up hope of ever finding. For those were the words which confirmed that unearthing the rest of Leon's heart was going to be the easy part. 'Something tells me that now you've set your mind to it you're going to be a fast learner.' She smiled.

Leon looked at her in awe, feeling the tension in his shoulders begin to seep away, wondering if he dared let it. 'I don't care how long it takes.'

Cally squeezed his hand and fleetingly she thought she saw him blink back a tear. It was a gesture which confirmed that he understood how close they had both come to losing something so precious, that he was happy to take things slowly, and above all that she could trust him. With it, she was struck by the most phenomenal moment of fulfilment she had ever known.

Well, emotionally speaking, Cally thought with a grin, as she ran her eyes over his impossibly handsome face and athletic body, as drop-dead gorgeous today as he had been that night in London…and every night since.

'As long as it takes,' she repeated thoughtfully. 'But, you know, you have taught me the benefits of acting impulsively, giving in to what *feels* right.' Her eyes gleamed wickedly.

Leon took a cautious step towards her, his tone husky. 'What are you saying, *ma belle?*'

'The church is booked for four days from now, is it not?'

He looked at her in amazement and shook his head in joyous disbelief. 'You mean you want to go ahead with the wedding, just as we planned?'

Cally beamed, thinking how far he had come, how far they had both come. 'Unless you think that is a little *too* rash?'

Leon shook his head commandingly and pulled her close. '*Non, mon amour par la mer,*' he whispered. 'I think that would make me the happiest man alive.'

MILLS & BOON
MODERN
Power and Passion

Prepare to be swept off your feet by sophisticated, sexy and seductive heroes, in some of the world's most glamourous and romantic locations, where power and passion collide.

Julia James

Heiress's
PREGNANCY
SCANDAL

MILLS & BOON
MODERN

Jennie Lucas

Chosen as the
SHEIKH'S ROYAL
BRIDE

MILLS & BOON

Kim Lawrence

A WEDDING
at the
ITALIAN'S DEMAND

MILLS & BOON

Sharon Kendrick

The
SHEIKH'S
SECRET BABY

MILLS & BOON
MODERN

JOIN US ON SOCIAL MEDIA!

Stay up to date with our latest releases, author
news and gossip, special offers and discounts, and
all the behind-the-scenes action
from Mills & Boon...

 millsandboon

 millsandboonuk

 millsandboon

It might just be true love...

MILLS & BOON

THE HEART OF ROMANCE

A ROMANCE FOR EVERY KIND OF READER

MODERN

Prepare to be swept off your feet by sophisticated, sexy and seductive heroes, in some of the world's most glamourous and romantic locations, where power and passion collide.
8 stories per month.

HISTORICAL

Escape with historical heroes from time gone by. Whether you passion is for wicked Regency Rakes, muscled Vikings or rugg Highlanders, awaken the romance of the past.
6 stories per month.

MEDICAL

Set your pulse racing with dedicated, delectable doctors in the high-pressure world of medicine, where emotions run high an passion, comfort and love are the best medicine.
6 stories per month.

True Love

Celebrate true love with tender stories of heartfelt romance, f the rush of falling in love to the joy a new baby can bring, and focus on the emotional heart of a relationship.
8 stories per month.

Desire

Indulge in secrets and scandal, intense drama and plenty of si hot action with powerful and passionate heroes who have it all wealth, status, good looks…everything but the right woman.
6 stories per month.

HEROES

Experience all the excitement of a gripping thriller, with an in romance at its heart. Resourceful, true-to-life women and stro fearless men face danger and desire - a killer combination!
8 stories per month.

DARE

Sensual love stories featuring smart, sassy heroines you'd want best friend, and compelling intense heroes who are worthy of
4 stories per month.

To see which titles are coming soon, please visit
millsandboon.co.uk/nextmonth

LET'S TALK
Romance

For exclusive extracts, competitions
and special offers, find us online:

- **f** facebook.com/millsandboon
- 🐦 @MillsandBoon
- 📷 @MillsandBoonUK

Get in touch on 01413 063232

For all the latest titles coming soon, visit
millsandboon.co.uk/nextmonth